THE UNEDITED ST

TÄNKAWORLD

A Novel

By

LEONARDO
STRACCAMORE

TÄNKAWORLD © 2016 All rights reserved

First Edition

ISBN 13: 978-0-9881618-0-1

CONTENTS

BOOK I

MONOCHROMIA

NIRVIA — ... formatted by Lady Crista in the year 2403. Nirvia is the virtual Promised Land as depicted in the Old Age Scriptures of the Eclectic Books of Life and Death. It is also referred to in the EBOLAD as Heaven on Earth, Paradise, or Eden (for full descriptions of the lands of Nirvia see NAT Tech Manual no.4: Lexicon).

2. Nirvia is a virtual world with a finite amount of spatial parameters. It provides fixed communal and flexible personal spaces. Thou may try to add to thy personal spatial allotment in Nirvia before the Ascension through TänkaMatch wagers (see NAT Tech Manual no.2: sec.6 — TänkaMatches). Nirvia's total memory capacity shall be monitored by the TänkaClock (see NAT Tech Manual no.2: sec.5).

3. As on Earth as it is in thy visits to Nirvia thy mind and body experiences shall be registered in thy InsignAnimas. Upon the TänkaClock striking the End of Time thy soul's Ascension shall begin. During which time thy InsignAnima shall release thy personal soul. Thy soul shall then ascend to its awaiting virtual skin in Nirvia wherein it shall continue to live. Thy virtual body shall hereto be referred to as thy Soulful Avatar.

4. In order to accommodate thy soul's continued growth in Nirvia there shall be regular compressions of Nirvia's memory banks. Periodically decisions on which compressed files to be purged shall be made through the predetermined proportional voting system. The voting rights of each Soulful Avatars shall be based on their previously allotted personal spaces.

5. The purging of the selected memory banks shall take place every one hundred virtual years and...

NEW AGE TESTAMENT*

* All noted information is taken from the New Age Testament, 13RD Edition, printed by the Holy W in the year 2676...take note that access to the New Age Testament's Book of Revelations requires the express permission of the Key Keeper.

PART I

THE HOLY WHITES

Chapter One

-1-

A thick mist travels beneath the floor of a faintly lit chamber. Its canvas quietly sparkles with a vast number of stars.

An obscure voice breaks the silence. "It's too late to save them." it says, "They're terminally convinced that they're on their way to a virtual Heaven."

"That's right," says a harder voice, "they unequivocally believe that Eden awaits their personal souls. They remain incapable of seeing that it's exactly such a belief that keeps them away from it."

"I suggest that their fate has become unalterable." says the first voice, "They have found the key to their own inescapable imprisonment. And there's little left that we can do."

"I agree." adds another ethereal voice, "They have been unable to escape their cycle of violence. And now plan to unknowingly export their reality to a virtual one."

"It's obvious that they have reached their inevitable end." says the first voice.

"I concur." says yet another, "They remain glued to their false perceptions and, despite our attempts, remain unmindful of the Truth."

A rattle of agreement echoes throughout the chamber.

"It's a heart-rending outcome." injects a deep disembodied voice, "But they do appear condemned to remain forever trapped in the stagnant pond of their colours."

"It's time for us to leave them to their fate." adds the first voice.

The dark sentiment spreads quickly in the darkness.

Suddenly a door opens and a ray of light slices through the chamber. The chatter suddenly stops as two silhouettes appear at the door's threshold.

The two figures follow their extended shadows inside. The door behind them closes and a spotlight suddenly illuminates the center of the domed chamber. The figures enter the spotlight. Their hooded cloaks hide their faces.

A group of people in white frocks become thinly visible around them. "Why have you asked to address the Council of Elders?" says one of the encircling voices.

The broader of the two hooded figures steps forward. "Ma'am, we are here to argue against what we expect to be your final decision." he says, firmly.

An elder woman steps out of the circle. Her white hair is held tightly in a loose bun. "We have reached our decision. And we have decided not to interfere."

"Ma'am, we already have." rebuts the cloaked man.

"And look at the result!" replies the elder woman.

A chirping sound of agreement quickly filters among her quasi shrouded group.

The hooded man begins to pace side to side in the spotlight. "We cannot just leave them in their purgatorial state."

"I understand, but we've already tried exterior agents and they've all miserably failed." she replies, "They are as lost today as they have always been. So what makes you think that their state of being will ever change?"

The male figure stops his pacing. "Ma'am, we need to help them evolve from within."

"But that's not possible," she replies, "we're not of their collective."

A resonating chatter of agreement spreads around the circle. She nods and steps back in line with her peers.

"My Honourable Council," insists the cloaked man, "without our help they are doomed."

The background chatter suddenly stops as a frail figure of an elderly man steps forward. His long grey hair shines over his white frock. "But they are too long gone." he says, "They no longer fear that which opens the eyes to enlightenment."

"And whose fault is that, sir?" interjects the smaller of the cloaked figures. Her youthful voice is tender and sweet. "We provided the path to their destruction. And now the Truth may permanently disappear from their view."

An uneasy groan filters through the chamber.

"Time is quickly running out, My Honourable Council." adds the young woman, "We must try to free them from their bondage and provide them a way out before it's too late."

"But we've already tried on multiple occasions. And they remain as blocked as ever." interposes another voice from the council.

"But how can we abandon them now? Let me remind my Honourable Council that their predicament is our fault."

Burbling sounds of divergence bubble up around the spotlight.

"We cannot deny them the Truth," adds the young woman, "and then stand by in judgement over their failures."

The elder man approaches the cloaked woman. "What is it that you're asking of us?" he says.

"I would like the Honourable Council's permission to allow us to try one last time."

Twitters of groans sputter around the spotlight.

"We have already looked over your plan. We find it unlikely to succeed." replies the elder cleric, "Have you considered all the ramifications of your proposed intervention."

"I have, my Honourable Council. But I see no other choice but to try."

The robed elder tilts his head at her. "Are you truly ready to make such a sacrifice?"

"Yes." she says, holding firm the arm of her accomplice. "We both are, sir."

There are whispers of discontent from the circle of elders.

"Honourable Council," she adds, her gentle tone is subtle but unyielding. "I understand your concern. But what choice is there but to do what we know to be right."

The elder man edges closer. His long straight hair covers part of his face but not his frazzled brow. His deep voice is suddenly unevenly hoarse. "But what will become of you?" he implores.

The shrouded woman's voice remains touchingly resolute. "Sir, the end is not important when the means are justly guided by that which Truth reveals."

A loud silence spreads quickly with her words.

The elderly man glances at the other elders. He bends his head as if acknowledging their hushed respect. His eyes beam disquietedly at the cloaked woman. He reaches out for her hand. She delightfully takes his hand and accompanies it to her heart.

The old man lets out a heavy sigh. "Do what you know to be right, my dear." he says, struggling to hide the cracks in his voice. He glances at the cloaked male beside her and gives him a supportive nod.

The spotlight shuts off. The door opens once again and the two cloaked figures head towards its light.

The elderly man retraces his steps back to the circle of elders as the chamber returns to its starlit obscurity.

Chapter Two

-1-

A naked man sits quietly beneath a large fig tree. His legs are crossed and his hands lay open upon his thighs. His chest slowly expands and contracts with his deep breaths.

"Ohm..." he hums.

Birds begin to chirp around him as the morning haze evaporates.

The man opens one eye and gazes at a blackbird at his feet. The bird is picking at a freshly fallen fig. The man licks his lips before forcing his eye shut again. His humming sound grows louder.

A murmuring laughter suddenly develops around him.

The meditative man opens both eyes. He scowls at the maundering crowd that has appeared inside the grove. The people pass by him wearing white outfits and laughter on their lips.

The man lets out a discouraged sigh before picking one of the low hanging fruits above him. He bites into the fig and a combination of juice and drool races down his chin. He wipes his mouth with his forearm and leisurely unwinds his legs. He picks himself up from the vividly green grass and playfully kicks at a fallen leaf. A warm breeze pushes his long brown hair back over his shoulders.

The people around him move further down the grove and a small smile returns to his face. He lets his body fall back down to the grass. He leans back and glares up at the clear blue skies. His smile slowly fades as he returns to his contemplative position.

A middle aged woman in a flowery gown materializes near him. Her sunbathed blond hair runs down past her slim shoulders. She glides toward the man as if resistant to gravity. "Lord Set?" she says.

Set's eyes pop open. "My Grace?" he says, scrambling to his feet. "Yes, one moment if you please."

"That's alright." she says, "I'm at your disposal, my lord."

Set closes is eyes for an instant and reopens them wearing a white suit.

"Lord Set, there's no need to be so timid." she replies, gingerly. "I'm after all but a virtually image of Lady Crista. As you know, her soul still rests dormant among all the past Holy Whites in the Key Keeper's Chamber."

"How should I then address you?"

"You may just call me Crista, if it pleases you, my lord."

"Thank-you, Crista."

"Isn't this world a wonder?" says Crista, dancingly.

"This is one of my favourite places to visit in Nirvia." says Set, "I find it a true depiction of the proverbial garden of the EBOLAD."

"It sure is busy today, my lord?"

"Usually it's very quiet."

"If you were looking for solitude why not use your personal space, my lord?"

"I could have, but it's nowhere near as nice as this communal one. I used to have my own grove once." Set points toward the margins of his vision. "But that's long gone now."

"Oh?" says Crista, "I presume that you entered the Key Keeper's Challenge?"

"That's right. I don't know what had gotten into me," replies Set, eyes glazed. "I actually thought that I had a good chance to defeat the king."

"Not an easy task, my lord."

"That's right." says Set, "I see that your program is familiar with King Osiris' exploits in the T-Matches."

"It's part of my function in overseeing the collective mind of the Holy White Order, my lord."

"Of course." replies Set, diffidently. "I've heard that."

"But I'm sure, my lord, that you performed well in the T-Match." adds Crista, "Despite the final outcome."

"Being that I had won a few of the Preliminary T-Matches, I felt pretty confident. I actually thought I noticed a chink in the king's armour of invincibility. But as it turned out I was wrong. And I ended up losing half of my accumulated total spatial allotment to him."

"I understand your gamble, my lord. If you had won you would have become the new Key Keeper. And with that you would not only have gained the Golden Key to the physical Realm, but your soul would have gained a larger share of this one."

Set crosses his arms. "I must admit that it was a real eye opener going against the king."

"The Key Keeper's Challenge is of the highest stakes, and the pressures therein are very high, my lord."

"Pressures?" repeats Set, gazing carefully at Crista.

"I meant that it couldn't have been easy for you, my lord. But never mind, what's really important is that you still retain plenty of space in Nirvia notwithstanding your loss."

Set kicks at the grass with his nimble legs. "I appreciate the reminder." he says, "Your Avatar is a real vision on this of all days."

"You're very welcome, my lord."

"I apologize for my personal ramblings."

"That's alright, my lord."

"My mind should be much clearer at this point in my cycle." Set sits back down on the grass and stares up at Crista with fondness. "What may I ask do I owe the honour of your visit?"

"My lord, it's exactly your perturbed thoughts which have brought me to you."

"Oh? I didn't mean to disturb the collective consciousness of the Holy White Order."

"No need to apologize, my lord. I remind you that I'm but a humble servant here."

"Regardless, you're still a reflection of the Holy Lady. And from what I understand you were programmed by Lady Crista herself. I had heard that you had extraordinary capabilities as a Soulless Avatar. And now I see that it's true."

"Why, thank-you, my lord."

"My own Soulless Avatar shuts down when I'm not transcending, but yet you're able to function independently of your future host. I must admit that it's beyond my faculty to understand how this is possible. But then again I don't have the mind of the woman who programmed you."

"Yes, my lord."

"A mind which was instrumental in the genesis of the world of thought that is TänkaWorld." continues Set, stretching his hands over the velvety grass. "And with TänkaVision we of the Holy White Order can virtually experience her Promised Lands."

"I'm sure that it was an honour for Lady Crista to bring about such a transcendent vision for the Chosen."

"And I would be remiss if I didn't include within her exceptional great accomplishments her TänkaPod innovation." adds Set, "I cannot fully express the numerous exaltations I have felt within the T-Pods during the T-Matches. I could feel my soul's temporary ascendance into my T-Match Avatars. It was truly an impressive glimpse into our coming Ascension. I look forward to making this Soulless Avatar of mine a Soulful one." Set looks around the orchard. "And all this we owe to Our Lady Crista."

"Yes, yes, my lord," says Crista, riding her knuckles along her throat. "And the lady has been highly compensated for her work."

"That's right she has been." replies Set, nodding. "The extensive spatial allotment she was awarded was more than deserved. After all, it was solely her unrivalled mind which was able to decipher the true meaning of the Eden spoken of in the Old Age Scriptures of the EBOLAD. And most importantly we of the Holy White Order owe her our most sincere gratitude for allowing us all to attain what the human race has always fundamentally desired — Virtual Immortality."

-2-

Crista pinches her lips together and slowly walks around the thick roots of the fig tree. "My lord, I too would be very proud of all of her accomplishments."

"Umm..." mumbles Set, raised brow. "Yes, as you say, who would not be proud of her achievements?"

Crista closes in on Set's peculiar expression. "Obviously part of her colourful patterns have been imprinted upon me."

"Of course," replies Set, "There's no need for me to go on about Lady Crista. I'm sure you being her Avatar in waiting are more than sufficiently aware of her accomplishments."

Crista's eyes glisten and her tone heightens. "Yes, Commander, she was an amazing soul."

"Hmm?" moans Set, "She still is."

"Of course, my lord." replies Crista, coldly. "Maybe after the Ascension you can thank the blessed lady yourself."

"I plan to do exactly that."

"Good. Now I will need to return to others who struggle with the Holy White Doctrine. I hope I have helped, my lord."

"Umm—"

"My lord?" interrupts Crista, inquisitively. "Maybe now you can return to a more rewarding state of meditation. Hopefully you will find the peace of mind you search. You may have a diminished status in Nirvia, but you still remain part of a selective few who will survive the physical plane of existence. I hope this shall comfort your thoughts."

"I shall try to find my way again." says Set.

Crista's image slowly begins to fade. Her voice turns mechanical. "You are of the Holy White Order. You are of the Chosen. It is your prerogative to format your personal space to best fulfill your soul's future wishes. And regardless of your more limited personal space you shall forever have available the vast communal space."

"I have appreciated our encounter, Crista."

"Lord Set, has your limited space deprived you of your seraglio?"

"No, it hasn't. That's the one thing that no Holy White can do without."

"I would suggest then that it would be an excellent alternative to your meditation."

"It's definitely a great method for releasing stress."

"Good." replies Crista, her robotic voice dims further as her body slowly continues to disperse. "I hope you will find your release for what ails you there, my lord."

"Thank-you," mutters Set, "But I doubt that any sexual release will put to rest my doubting thoughts about the king."

The dissipating image of Crista suddenly reassembles itself.

-3-

"I did not hear you very well, my lord. What is it that you said?"

Set furrows his brow. "Umm," he says, "nothing really."

"Don't be so flippant, my lord. Do tell me what concerns you about King Osiris?"

Set angles a look at Crista. "I was just thinking that the king never appears startled by the impromptu difficulties involved in the T-Matches. The temporary T-Match Avatars he comes up with have an uncanny unbeatably factor to them. It's as if he's always one step ahead of the game."

Crista moves closer to Set. "What are you trying to say, my lord?"

Set sits back down on the grass. "Oh nothing, it's just that he's never come close to losing his title."

"What do you mean?"

"I just find it suspicious that the king's consciousness is so efficient. I have never seen him even momentarily rattled by the selected T-Planets."

A creeping smile slowly forms on the edge of Crista's lips. "I see." says Crista, pushing her golden hair to one side. "My lord, are you aware that it's my program that randomly selects the T-Planets for the T-Matches?"

"I didn't mean to imply any misgivings about the process."

"Good! Because I am here for the express reason of making sure that the Ascension goes according to plan."

"But why has there been a change in the T-Planet selection process at all?"

"Commander," replies Crista with an escalating tone. "You should know your T-Manuals better by now. My duties are to supervise the collective consciousness of the Holy White Order, and to arbiter the T-Pod's selections of the T-Planets for the remaining Key Keeper's Challenges."

"Hmm, you're probably right — I should be better informed when it concerns the T-Manuals." replies Set, seriously. "Maybe I'm just envious of the king's skills."

"My lord, it's only normal to have reservations about the person who defeated you. So what I would suggest is that you return to the Preliminary T-Matches. They are of course of lesser stakes, but can nevertheless serve to help you recuperate some of your lost personal space in Nirvia."

"I've had enough of these virtual conflicts." replies Set, "I will just make due with the space I have, and hopefully find therein find peace."

"Have it your way, my lord. But you cannot continue to be upset for your loss." says Crista, her face glowing. "After all, the king has an extraordinary mind with just as an outstanding will to win. And that's what the First Holy Whites looked for in their kings."

"Or Queens." adds Set.

"Excuse me, my lord?"

"I just mean that even though we have not had a woman Key Keeper since Our Lady Crista, it's still possible to have a woman rule the Realm once again."

"Indeed." smiles Crista. Her image begins to fade once again.

"Though," adds Set, gazing at Crista's waning image. "I would say that the chances of that are slim since the next ruler shall most probably be male."

Crista's image swiftly regains its full integrity, but absent of its grin.

-4-

"What do you mean by the 'next' king?" asks Crista, firmly.

"It stands to reason that the second in command — Chancellor Horus — shall be our next leader." replies Set, without hesitation. "His Preliminary T-Matches have shown how proficient and focused his mind has become. His skills have placed him in an excellent position for the next Key Keeper's Challenge."

"Is that a fact?"

"The chancellor's followers demand it of him — as is his right as instituted by our Holy White Doctrine."

"Yes, of course." replies Crista, glibly.

"There's an ever growing faction who have become weary of King Osiris. And many of them would like to see a change."

"And are you one of those, my lord?"

"Umm, let's just say that I would feel better about a more rational mind holding the Golden Key. After all that's why T-Matches exist in the first place — they make sure that the key is always held in the most sound of rational leaders?"

Crista places her arms behind her and strolls around Set. "The Key Keeper's primary duty is to use the Golden Key to temporarily halt the countdown to the Ascension if the need would arise. And what you seem to be implying, my lord, is that the current king is unable to perform that duty."

"I'm not sure that that's what I'm saying."

"Then what are you saying, Commander?" replies Crista, hard.

"Crista, my words seem to have upset you."

Crista turns around and her voice quickly softens. "I am not upset, my lord. What you must be detecting is my compassion for your welfare."

"Umm," mutters Set with a wrinkled brow, "I guess what I'm saying must sound heretical to your programming. But fret not, Crista, King Osiris is still well respected by his people despite my misgivings. He has never lost a T-Match and people like winners."

A bright smile emerges on Crista's face. "But yet that does not seem to impress you, my lord."

"I just have a hard time believing how much more advanced the king is in his T-Match Avatar formulations. I find his skills truly uncanny. I've never witnessed such speed and efficiency like his."

"My lord, are you sure that all your conjecture is not just based on your admitted envy?"

"You may be correct." replies Set.

Crista's eyes glisten as Set's gaze sinks.

"I must admit," adds Set, "that my competitive spirit is no longer what it once was and this may be influencing my thoughts on the matter."

"What do you mean, my lord?"

"As you have apparently detected, I've not felt myself lately. The meditative techniques that have been handed down from the EBOLAD have been of some comfort. But yet I still remain troubled," adds Set, breathing deeply in and out. "The moments of silence that I achieve when doing my breathing exercises end quickly as my thoughts inevitably return to the circumstances of my life. I had heard these breathing exercises were meant to quiet the mind with the power of the moment. But it seems that time always finds its way back in, and so do the same thoughts and concerns."

"My lord, why do you remain bothered?" says Crista, pointing to the fig orchard. "This beautiful scenery will also be yours after your body dies. Plus, you will have your own precious space to enjoy. What more would a person want than a virtually eternal life devoid of any concerns?"

"You're probably right." nods Set, "But I can't help but wonder if we're enlightened enough to enter such a paradise."

"My lord, where are all of these thoughts coming from? Why think of such things when Eden is just at your footsteps?"

"I don't know, but there's just something that I've been struggling to reconcile for quite awhile now."

"Oh?"

"Crista, I wonder if I may ask you a question?"

"Lord Set, of course you may. I'm here to listen to all my children."

"Umm?" moans Set, looking around him at the now empty orchard. "I can say that I've been looking forward to all that Nirvia promises for as long as I can remember. But now I find myself questioning whether living forever is the best thing for us. What if the Truth of our existence lies elsewhere?"

Crista scowls and takes a fervent step back. "Truth, what Truth?" says Crista, "Do you prefer the abyss of death, my lord?"

"I don't know."

"You don't know?!"

"I'm just not sure anymore."

Crista wrinkles her face. "My lord, what has brought on these disturbing doubts within you?"

"I've heard the words of a young woman and they've pricked the air out of my undoubting spirit." says Set, rubbing his chin. "Now that I think about it she did say something about doubt being a positive deterrent to ambition."

There is a momentary silence that permeates in the garden.

"Umm..." continues Set, "I think she specifically referred to ambition as one of the symptoms of a sick mind. She also said that ambition is the driver of internal conflict and external violence."

"Is that what all this is about — doubting the attributes of ambition? May I remind you, my lord, that the T-Matches were specifically developed to incite personal ambition and in so doing prevent our civilization from a certain despondent decline. After all, those who say that ambition leads to violence are just frustrated people who use such ideas as a crutch for their own lack of achievements."

Set scowls and looks away.

"But," adds Crista, "if you still believe otherwise then it's your ordained right to challenge the Key Keeper, but alas you've already done so, haven't you, my lord?"

"Yes, I have."

"Yes, you have, my lord. And what happened?"

"I failed."

"You mean that King Osiris' mental acuity won over yours. And isn't that enough proof against your suspicions?"

"I'm not sure."

"My lord, are you questioning the effectiveness of the T-Matches to ascertain the mental clarity of its combatants?"

"I must admit that I still have certain misgivings."

"Oh? And why is that, my lord?"

Set folds his arms tightly. "I hesitate to speak of such things."

"Feel free to speak your mind, my lord," says Crista, reassuringly. "That's why I'm here."

Set tentatively lifts his gaze. "Very well." he says, "King Osiris has over the years become more and more withdrawn. He has shut himself off from his own people and keeps strangely to himself in the Key Keeper's Chamber. All he seems to care about are the T-Matches and..."

"Go on, my lord."

"A Fuchsia." says Set with a heavy whisper.

"A Monochrome you say?"

"Yes, a Fuchsia." replies Set, "He has devoted an uncanny amount of energy in trying to tracking the Fuchsia down. And lately he's even declared her a fugitive."

"And that bothers you, my lord?"

"Yes it does." replies Set, "I believe it's the act an obsessive mind."

"Oh, is it?" says Crista with a twang in her voice, "I don't see any records of you having any particular psychoanalytic aptitudes, Commander. Are you positive of your analyses?"

"No, I'm not." replies Set, gruffly. "How can I be when the king continues to dominate his challengers?"

Crista's appeasing smile disappears. "So, my lord, about this supposed obsession over a Fuchsia. Are you sure that you're not just projecting your own obsessions?"

"I am not—"

"What is the Fuchsia's name, my lord?"

"The fugitive's name is, or was, Sistina."

"And why, my lord, do you think the king could be rendered so unbalanced by a measly Monochrome?"

"I met the young woman at one time."

"Did you?"

"Yes, I did." says Set, staring out at the field. "This young woman had a way of spreading a somewhat disconcerting view of things. Her unrivalled beauty gave her dissenting voice the ability to capture many hearts and minds."

"Maybe yours as well, Commander." replies Crista, "Is this the same young woman you were speaking of earlier — the one who introduced such perilous doubts into your mind?"

"Yes." replies Set, "But how did you determine that it's the same—"

"Woman?" interrupts Crista, "As you've said, my lord, I've been programmed by the best."

"I see."

"What else did the young woman have to say?"

"She raised some peculiarly distressing thoughts about Nirvia."

"What kind of thoughts?"

"Oh, I'm not sure of her words. I don't exactly remember," he says, flinching. "They were abstract metaphysical sounding things."

"Obviously, considering your state of mind, my lord, I would say not so abstract."

"Maybe so." replies Set.

"I ask again, my lord, what is it that the Fuchsia in question actually said?"

"Umm... I've heard her tell the chancellor that deflecting Death was a move away from Truth."

"Huh! It sounds like this woman proposes that she's the bearer of Truth. That usually says more about the person espousing to know the Truth than the Truth itself."

"That's exactly what the chancellor told her."

"Oh, did he?"

"But that's the thing," replies Set, "she doesn't really preach any Truths. She only speaks of negating all that which is false."

"The chancellor spoke to her?"

"Yes, he's tried to put her back in her place many a times."

"Has he, really? Chancellor Horus has crossed paths with this Fuchsia before?"

"Yes, several times." replies Set, "Sometimes my guards and I used to get a big laugh watching them go at it. Their emphatic verbal encounters were livid to say the least."

"Oh, I see." says Crista, nodding. "Is the king aware of this?"

"I don't know, but I'm certain that there's little that escapes King Osiris."

"Well then," stipulates a serenely looking Crista, "there you go."

"You're saying that there's nothing to what she said?"

"You said it yourself, my lord."

"What?"

"You said that the chancellor is of the highest level of rationality. And if he found her words dysfunctional then should that not alleviate any of your concerns?"

"Hmm... And what of the king, you don't think I should worry about his irrational behaviour?"

"My lord, do you know what you're saying?"

"I know, believe me, I know. But what else would you call his obsession with finding this woman? I still don't think his actions are of a stable and clear mind."

"My lord, you're contradicting again the T-Match's ability to test its combatants' mental sharpness."

"That again is what has brought about my conscious dissonance. I cannot understand for the life of me how King Osiris is still king. Especially given that the T-Matches are supposed to weed out troubled minds."

A scowl forms on Crista's face. "You mean like the troubled mind of a doubter?!"

"I see what you mean." says Set, nodding. "Maybe you're right, and it may be just my doubts speaking."

Crista's image begins to flicker different colours.

Set gazes at her distorting image. "I'm sorry, Crista. I'm sure you're not programmed to hear such belligerence towards the sitting Key Keeper."

"Not at all, my lord, I'm glad that you let out your concerns. But did it ever occur to you that maybe the reason the king is looking for this particular Fuchsia is because she promotes such dissonance among the Holy Whites?"

"Umm..."

"Regardless, Commander Set, you do know that your duty towards the Realm is unambiguously clear, do you not?"

"Yes, I know my primary duties — to protect the Golden Key from all foreign or domestic threats."

Crista places her hands on her hips. "Indeed, but—"

"Commander!" snipes suddenly a ghostly baritone voice. "The members of your party are ready." The words ring out in the open grove.

"Yes, I hear you." replies Set, bending his head. "Please forgive my rudeness, Crista. I must go now — duty calls."

"But I've not—"

Suddenly the cornucopian field around Set disappears.

Set sits alone at a table in a decadent apartment. He gets up and adjusts his long flaxen hair as holographic glasses retract into his temples. He picks up a pair of dark shields and limps over to a sun filled window.

"Hmm?" he murmurs as he peers out.

"Commander?" reiterates the voice outside his door.

A Purple crest of an ankh inside of a circle suddenly glows on the chest of Set's white suit. "Tell them that I'll be there presently." he replies, stridently.

"Yes sir."

Set's gaze does not flinch as he continues to stare out. A group of children in grey uniforms are joyfully playing near a coliseum. Among them are several attentive young women in fuchsia dresses.

Set's gaze shifts upward to an imposing dwelling suspended high above the coliseum. "It's now or never." he mutters.

THE EPISTLE OF ZADOK… And on the 13TH Century from the end of the Age of Pisces God spoke unto me.

He said: "Thy forefathers' insatiable external growth has destroyed all that was beautiful and plentiful in thy world. Thou should be the change you want to see, for only the clear mind shall know the true path to Nirvana."

And then I heard His voice again: "Build high atop a singular hill a dome to sustain the life of those worthy. And thy believers shall escape the destructive forces that I shall unleash upon this world."

Then He said: "Make thy dome impenetrable, for the rest shall first deny, fight, and then slowly whither and fall."

Later I heard Him say unto me: "Choose wisely those who shall enter thy dome, for only the purest souls shall find their way to Heaven. And keep out the unfaithful outsiders, for they shall want to force their corrupt souls inside."

Then He told me: "Make thy Holy Order that which humanity has forever aspired to, and use the Old Age Scriptures to help guide thy way."

And then He warned: "But the human condition shall slowly enter thy new home, and thy chosen souls shall begin to degrade. Thou must then ensure the End Times before Evil fully enters the souls of thy Holy Order. But be not afraid for thy key to thy body's entombment shall also open the Pearly Gates for thy chosen souls. And I shall welcome those pure of Original Sin with open arms. And such shall be thy way forth from this time to the End of Time. Such is the word…"

ECLECTIC BOOKS OF LIFE AND DEATH*

* All noted information is taken from the Eclectic Books of Life and Death, 25TH Edition… originally published by the Official Scribers of Doma in the year 2151.

PART II

THE OUTERS

Chapter One

-1-

A candelabrum on an old oval table wobbles from the fidgeting of a young woman's legs.

"Commander?" she whispers.

Set sits next to her blankly staring at the concaved tent above him. "Umm…" he mumbles.

"Commander, you appear distracted."

"I'm just thinking."

"May I ask what about?"

"I'm not sure, Kiya." he replies, pulling up his dark cloak.

"Is it our capes, Commander? I'm sorry, but these were the best I could find."

"Huh?"

"Commander, I was just saying that I know our capes aren't exactly like those of the Outers, but they should keep us from being detected."

Set places his hands firmly on his chair and bangs it hard against a stud directly behind him.

The lieutenant throws back her long auburn hair. Her eyes are fixated on Set's every movement. "Commander," she says, looking around her. "Is the tent not anchored correctly?"

Set persists in forcing his chair over the stud.

"Set, what's going on?" insists Kiya.

"Did you say something, Lieutenant?"

"Yes." she says, softly. "Are you alright?"

Set stops moving his chair around. "I've recently received a visit from Crista and—"

"Oh, is that all?" interjects Kiya, "We've all at one time or another received her visit. We all have thoughts that go awry at times. I mean that with our Ascension growing near I would assume her visits are to be expected."

"Right." says Set, "Nevertheless, I found her Avatar somewhat different from what I imagined. There's something it said that I just cannot shake."

"Like what, Commander?"

"It strongly implied that the T-Manuals would indicate why it has taken over the T-Planet selection process from the automated T-Pods."

"I don't see what you're getting at, Commander."

"Lieutenant, I've checked the T-World Tech Manuals in the NAT."

"And?" says Kiya.

"And I've found no such directive. What's more, the only reference I could find for Crista's Avatar even being active is just an elusive mention of Lady Crista's spirit being with us at the End of Time."

"But, Commander, there's information in the NAT Tech Manuals that we are not privileged to."

"You mean its Book of Revelations?"

"Yes."

"You may be correct, lieutenant."

"So why do you still look worried?"

"There's just something about Crista's Avatar that continues to irk me."

"Oh?"

"I noticed that it acts more dynamic than any static Avatar I've ever encountered."

"Sir?" questions Kiya.

"I just don't understand how Crista's Avatar is awake when Crista's soul is dormant?"

"Didn't you tell me that it's only partially awake?"

"Yes, but—"

"Well then, I don't understand why—"

"But even a partially awake Avatar should not show such highly quantifiable emotional responses."

"Oh? I've never noticed that."

"Neither had I. That is until the conversation began to revolve around King Osiris."

"Maybe Lady Crista's Avatar is malfunctioning." says Kiya, "After all it may have been recently activated, but the Avatar has been detached from its soul for a very long time."

"I did wonder about that," replies Set, "And it made me investigate when Crista's Avatar became the independent overseer of our Holy White consciousness."

"Oh? And when was that?"

"Not long after Osiris became the Key Keeper."

"Commander, are you saying that King Osiris has something untoward going on here?"

"I don't know, but it does add to my worries about how he's still holding the Golden Key despite his obviously unstable mind."

"Commander, I find this reassuring in a way. Because now I'm certain we're doing the right thing."

"I understand, lieutenant, but this also makes me increasingly concerned that the king knows more than he lets out."

"I don't trust him either, but—"

"I've seen him grow more and more suspicious with every passing day." interrupts Set.

"Commander, sometimes we think we know what others are thinking, but many times it's just an outcrop of our own thoughts."

"What do you mean?"

"Commander, are you sure you're not imagining some of this? I mean that we've taken all the possible precautions to keep secret our plan. Not even the chancellor is aware of our attempt to rid ourselves of our irrational king."

"Maybe you're right. Maybe I'm getting as paranoid as the king himself."

"Aww," she smiles, "I don't think you're paranoid at all. Actually I think that it takes a very rational and sane person to become conscious of his king's megalomaniac proclivities."

The lieutenant leans forward on her chair. Her light blue eyes contrast sharply with the dark tenure of her cloak. She places her hands squarely on the table. She reaches over to touch Set's hands. "My dear Set, I think you're a very good and sane man."

Set shuffles uncomfortably in his seat. "Right," he says, clearing his throat. "I just wanted to take this opportunity to mention how much your devotion is appreciated, lieutenant."

"Set, I hope you're aware that I would do anything for you."

Set turns diffidently away from Kiya's receptive eyes. "Thank-you, Kiya. It's very reassuring to have you at my side during these troubling times."

Kiya catches Set's timid gaze. "You're the most honourable man I know, Commander. If you think that what we do is best for the Holy White Order and the future of our Ascension, then I have no doubt that it is."

Set pulls back his hands. "I'm nevertheless concerned as we may be placing the realm in further jeopardy. The Golden Key shall be rendered useless without its Key Keeper. As you know, the Golden Key is only programmed for use by a member of the Holy White Order who has attained the privilege of its use by retrieving the Golden T-Key during the Challenge T-Match."

"Set, we've discussed this already. There's no need to be so concerned. We've already determined that the best solution to the temporary leadership void will be to hold an emergency T-Match Challenge to find our next Key Keeper. There will be little threat to our Ascension then."

"Umm, you're right. I don't know what's wrong with me."

"It seems that your recent encounter with Crista's Avatar has really frazzled you, Commander."

"It's not only that."

"What do you mean?"

"I guess my main concern has to do with the Key Keeper's Challenge itself. Why have these T-Matches allowed the king to continue to retain his title as Key Keeper? Why haven't the T-Matches screened him out? I question if they're still capable of determining the sagacity of its combatants? And, if that's the case, how then will we know if the next Key Keeper will really be of sound mind?"

"I understand your anxiety, Commander. But you're now just hypothesizing. The only fact that we're aware of is that our current king's sanity is highly questionable. And it's our primary duty to protect the Golden Key. In addition, there's little doubt in my mind that Chancellor Horus will make for a better king."

"That would be the best case scenario. Chancellor Horus would make for an excellent Key Keeper."

"Then we should no longer doubt our actions."

"You're absolutely correct, Kiya. Thank-you for helping me with the creeping doubts of my aging brain." Set takes a deep breath. "Sometimes I don't think I'll make it to the Golden T-Hour."

Kiya's eyes sparkle from the light of the candles. "There's only one cycle left to our Ascension, my dearest sir."

"A cycle can feel really long to an aging man."

"I'm sure it'll go by quickly, Commander."

"That's easy for you to say."

"It's really not." replies Kiya, disheartened. "I may be a cycle younger than you, but I promise that my cravings are just as powerful."

Set places his hands over those of Kiya. "Sometimes I too wish I could feel the warmth of your body against mine, for my Soulless Avatar cannot truly express how I feel. But regardless of how we both feel we must wait for our souls to ascend, doing otherwise would deprive us of our eternal happiness."

"My dear Set, I know very well how you feel. Although, I have troubles with what the Holy White Doctrine prohibits us on Earth, I do hold firmly its promises of an eternal connection in the Thereafter." A flaming Red glow appears beneath Kiya's cape. "I nevertheless cannot help but dream of the day that your Soulful Avatar enters mine." she continues, closing firmly her cape. "I just hope that I shall be able to adequately keep up with your imagination."

"Other women in Nirvia are just tools, Kiya. They're not real — they have no soul. Upon our Ascension your Avatar shall carry within its virtual skin all that is you." says Set, caressing Kiya's hand. "And it shall feel as real as your skin does today."

"And so shall yours, my dear Set. But yet I cannot but wonder if you'll grow tired of me one day."

"You're beautiful to me now, Kiya, and you shall forever remain so in Nirvia."

Kiya's lips try to reach for Set's.

"No, Kiya." he says, delicately. "You know how easily one thing would lead to another. It's too dangerous to compromise our souls."

Kiya's face turns dutifully stringent. She quickly recoils away to the back of her seat.

Set tries to reach for her hands, but she drops them off to her side. "My dear Kiya, we cannot risk falling into the physical trappings of the body." says Set, tenuously. "Our solemn duty is the purity of our Holy White Realm. We cannot allow the impurities of our bodies to enter our souls. Our duty is clear — we must make sure that all ascending souls are righteous and without sin — including our own."

"Set, "says Kiya, blushing. "I just wish you knew how much I want to be yours and—"

"Commander!" a voice suddenly interrupts.

"Yes?" replies Set.

"The chief of the Outer West has arrived. His wife and child accompany him."

Set shifts his chair away from Kiya and glowers at a closed slit in the tent. "Guard, what are you waiting for? Show them in."

"Yes, sir!" replies the guard from outside the tent.

-2-

The nondescript tent is among many others in an arid encampment. A large man stands on guard at its side. A sliver of his ultramarine coloured uniform sticks out from his cape.

A squirrelly looking man and a veiled woman approach the guard. The guard pulls open the flap in the tent. "Chief, they're waiting for you and your wife inside." he says.

A young woman walks over to the chief's wife with open hands. "Ma'am, my name is Clarissa." she says, "Please allow me to hold on to your child till you decide otherwise."

The veiled woman groans and tightens her grip on her baby. The baby begins to cry.

"Please ma'am," insists Clarissa, "will you allow me to hold your child?"

The gusting winds briefly expose Clarissa's fuchsia coloured dress.

"Midear," says the chief, "our baby will be fine with the young lady. Can't you see that she's a Fuchsia?"

"Ma'am, I will take good care of your child." says Clarissa, her shoulder length hair waves in the wind.

"It'll be OK, midear." repeats the chief, "Our baby will be in good hands."

The veiled woman hands over her weeping child to Clarissa. The child quickly quiets down in her arms.

"You see?" says the chief.

The tent begins to flutter with the rising winds. The guard struggles to keep its flap open.

"Please, Chief," says the guard, "this way inside."

The Chief and his wife enter the tent. The tent folds shut quickly behind them. They remove their dark nomadic coats and with familiarity hang them on nearby hangers. They try to straighten their worn out clothes before facing the commander and his lieutenant.

"What is your name, ma'am?" asks Kiya.

"Beattie." replies the veiled woman. Her voice is as coarse as is the skin on her hands. She stares back at the closed flap in the tent.

"You don't have to worry about your child, Beattie — honourable wife of the chief of the Outer West." says Kiya, "The young lady shall take good care of your child. Now, please, come and sit with us."

The wary couple shuffles forward.

"Come, please, take a seat." repeats Kiya, "It is after all your home we sit in."

"This tent is a temporary structure that we had set up in response to your meeting request." replies the chief, "It was meant to blend in with the others in the encampment. We may be Outers, but our own sheds are somewhat better built than this raggedy thing."

"Yes, of course," says Kiya, "I didn't mean any offence, Chief of the Outer West."

"None was received, milady." replies the chief, "I was just stating a fact."

"Please sit." injects Set.

The couple sheepishly sit opposite the commander and the lieutenant. The chief's face becomes clearer as the candlelight from the candelabrum touches his skin. His face is lined with several deep scars. The scars are purposely grouted with dirt.

Kiya suddenly snaps back her head as if she was hit by an unprecedented whiff. She instinctively places her hands over her nose and mouth. She sees Set in the corner of her eye remaining stoically unmoved and quickly drops her hands from her face.

"We're sorry, milady." says the Beattie.

"You will need to wash up if you decide to take on this mission." says Kiya, pinching her nose with her nostrils.

"We don't have so much water to do that." replies Beattie.

"We have brought some with us. It's not much, but it will have to do."

"Milady is very kind," says Beattie.

"And you'll also need to apply this cream to your faces. It will hide well your Outer nature."

The chief examines the cream filled container. "And this will work?" he says.

"Yes it will." replies Kiya, "And ma'am, you won't need your veil while you use this cream."

Beattie removes her veil and Kiya's eyes grow large. Beattie's face appears smooth and healthy.

"I don't understand, ma'am. Why do you hide such a beautiful complexion?"

"I don't want other Outer women to feel bad."

"I understand." replies Kiya with a gentle smile.

"We're here to finalize our agreement." interjects Set, "I believe you've already had the details explained to you?"

The chief nods affirmatively.

"Here are all the things that you'll need if you accept the mission." says Set as he swings a full sack on the table. He pours its contents out and divides the junket of items into two piles. "As previously explained, the Mrs shall wear the vest, and carry with her the golden disk." Set places the respective items near Beattie. "And the iris outfit, the backpack, and the blaster are for you, Chief."

Beattie beams over the items on the table. She lowers her gaze and bends her head to her side. "Flint, misweet," she whispers, timidly. "I didn't quite hear what the man said."

"He said that the vest and the disk are for you, midear." Flint pushes the items closer to her.

"And I guess the rest is yours, misweet?"

"Uh-huh." replies the chief as he eyes the commander for confirmation.

"That's correct." says Set, "That should get the job done. And you'll also need communicators."

Kiya pulls out from her cape's pocket a miniature pistol. "Please, give me your left hands." she says with an open hand.

Flint and Beattie glance over at one another.

"Don't worry," says Kiya, "if you decide not to accept the mission the implants will automatically be absorbed by your body and disappear within a week."

The chief and his wife stretch out their fists over the table. Kiya unhinges their gnarled fingers.

"This will only take a few seconds." says Kiya. She injects a tiny chip in each of their palms.

Flint stares down the procedure while Beattie unflinchingly scrutinizes the items near her.

"Are you done, milady?" says Flint.

"Yes, it's all done."

Beattie picks up the iris coloured outfit. "Flint, misweet, you'll look real nice in this." she says, giggling.

"Oh, midear, I'm thinking more of the wings. I'll be like a bird." replies Flint, tapping the backpack.

"Uh, misweet — wings?"

"That's right, midear. Don't you remember how I explained it to you before?"

Beattie looks carefully over at Set, and then turns to Flint. "I'm sorry, misweet. Mi memory is not so good no more." She picks up the thick vest from the items on the table. "Misweet, can you help mi try this on?"

Flint struggles to fit the thick vest around Beattie's ample waste.

A distracted looking Set gets up from his chair and limps to the closed flap in the tent. He spreads it apart and stares out. A microburst of dirt and debris whips through the large encampment. He turns his eyes away from the impediments flying through the air. "I'm sorry about the crudeness of the items that I've brought you, but they're necessary to maintain the ruse."

"Oh that's alright." replies Beattie, "A little extra weight never hurt anyone."

"I've always wondered why you Outers worship trees, animals and such things." says Set, "As I look out at your barren lands, I wonder why you still believe in such gods when there are little of them left for you."

"You're right, milord." replies Beattie, "It's hard to believe in things that are hard to see. But our elders tell us of the things they've seen. And they teach us that we still belong to those things."

The dust outside the tent settles and a monstrously dilapidated building comes into view.

"That Outer building is surely not part of nature." says Set.

"No, it isn't." replies Flint, "It's a remnant of your past decadent society."

"Not my society." groans Set.

"Umm, that's right. It was part of the society that fell while you were building your new one."

"That was a long time ago, Chief."

"Yes it was, wasn't it? We were first on this land and we never forget. We may not have many books and such things, but history is handed down through our stories as it has always been. We still remember the story from the first time the so called civilized people entered our midst. They brought with them many goods and things, and we greeted them warmly with our measly trinkets. We showed them how each child was raised by our whole village, and how we all belonged to the land. That's when the newcomers explained to us the meaning of property, and that a child was also such a thing. They said that that was their lawful ways. The elders had a name for that. What was it that they called it again?" Flint glances over at Beattie. "Midear, do you remember?"

Beattie shakes her head as she finishes wrapping the vest around her waste. She edges closer to Flint. "How does it look?"

"It will hide well." replies Flint.

"There was an old teach that used to scream it out every so often." says Beattie. She suddenly slaps her hand on her head. "Oh yeah, I remember now," she blurts out, "he called it Manifuckdestiny!"

"Beattie!" cries Flint.

Beattie lets out a nervous laugh. Flint places his hand over Beattie's trembling hands. "It's OK, midear."

A whispering wind enters the tent and flickers off half the candles. Set lets go of the open flap and turns sympathetically toward Beattie.

"That's alright," says Set, reassuringly. "That was all a long time ago — a time of rebellious revolutions against the rule of law."

"The law?!" replies Flint, "Things written by those which it served best."

"Without the rule of law societies could not function." argues Kiya.

"You mean that without rules the rule makers could not maintain power?" says Flint.

"No, what I mean is that without the rule of law there would be chaos! Chaos brings about anarchy."

"We wouldn't want that, would we?" replies Beattie, smiling capriciously.

"What's the use of all the fighting that chaos brings about? What has it ever gotten anyone?" says Kiya.

"There has only ever been one fight." says Flint, "Good versus Evil."

"There I agree with you." interjects Set, "The only problem is trying to figure out which is which."

Kiya pulls out a metal flint from the base of the candelabra and reignites the extinguished candles. "Let go of the past and believe in me on this day." says Kiya, "Your sacrifices in this matter shall be rewarded as promised."

"Why should we believe another emissary of the so called Holy Whites?" asks Flint, forcefully.

Kiya opens her cape to unveil her white dress. A crest of a Blue glowing ankh inside a Blue circle glows brightly on her chest.

Beattie and Flint immediately rise up from their seats.

"Oh milady," says Flint, "I apologize for my belligerence. Please don't let the future of our child suffer for my impudence."

"Trust that your child shall be safe for as long as I live." replies Set, showing his own white suit. "I give you my word."

"Thank-you, milord." replies Flint. "But 'trust' is not a word we Outers care much for — all we believe is what we know, and we don't know you."

"My word is my oath, my oath is my life." pronounces Set, sternly. "Unlike you, your child shall have hope. That's the deal that I offer."

"Milord, may we have a moment?" replies Beattie.

"Fine." replies Set.

Beattie removes her vest and sits back down at the table. Her hands restlessly twitch as she sits Flint down beside her. She embraces Flint and mutters something in his ear. Flint warmly nods back.

"Thank-you, milord." says Beattie, softly. "The problem we have is that we don't know what an oath means to Whites."

Set raises his brow at Beattie. He lifts the hood of his cape and briskly exits the tent.

A mortified Beattie quickly cuddles in the arms of her husband.

-3-

Kiya sits quietly watching with her arms crossed.

Beattie and Flint look back at her with peaked brows. Flint whispers into Beattie's ear as a tear drops from her eye. "Midear, isn't being a Monochrome a much better fate for our child. Isn't that worth taking a chance?" says Flint.

"We're talking about mibaby." replies Beattie, "I mean he'll become a believer in their God. Do we want that?"

"Midear, there's less and less out here. And it's getting harder and harder to stop the evil doers. And you know how they can be."

Beattie's eyes fixate on Flint's words. "I'm still afraid for mibaby."

"But, midear, don't you think that our baby will be in bigger danger out here?"

"I don't know, but at least he'd be with us."

"Midear, we've already discussed all this — remember?" says Flint, "We realized that we can't always keep him safe. You know that it's better on the other side of the walls."

"But how do we know if they keep their promises?" Beattie looks cheekily at Kiya. She cups Flint's ear and whispers into it. "Remember what the eldest of our Outer men used to call the Whites?"

"No, midear." says Flint, "I just remember him speaking of betrayal and such things."

"He called them White RATS."

The lieutenant remains coldly unmoved.

"Midear, that's not a nice thing to say."

"I'm sorry, misweet."

"That's alright, midear." Flint caresses Beattie's face. "Just remember that not all rats are bad."

Beattie smiles and nods in agreement.

"What's this about rats?" says Kiya, vehemently. "Are you saying that my commander is a rat?"

"No-no, nobody's a rat," replies Flint, awkwardly smiling. "Midear, tell her about the rat, before she bites me."

"What rat?"

"Milady, I saw you looking carefully at me before." says Beattie, caressing her own face. "I gather you've never seen an Outer with such a pretty face like mine. Would you like to know why?"

Kiya moves her chair closer to the table.

"Midear, I think she does." says Flint.

"Quiet!" replies Kiya.

"You see, midear, she does want to know."

"I said to be quite and let your wife speak."

"It's sort of a bizarre story," says Beattie, "My face was not always like this. As a matter of fact it was pretty in a terribly bad sort of way — it was once all covered with brownish crust."

"Go on." says Kiya, cringing.

"It's a thing that happens more and more often out here to women. I don't know why." says Beattie, "You Whites wouldn't know anything about this, would you?"

"Of course not." replies an irritated Kiya.

"I believe you, milady. Why would you know what goes on out here while you sit nicely atop the hill." adds Beattie, shaking.

Flint reaches over to Beattie and wraps his arm around her. "Forgive her, milady." says Flint, "The crusty times bring back bad feelings for midear."

"I understand." replies Kiya, warmly.

"If you don't want to tell anymore, midear, you don't have to." replies Flint, holding firmly her hand.

"Misweet, you tell it."

"Are you sure, midear?"

Beattie keenly nods.

"Then I will do as you ask." Flint turns to face Kiya and inadvertently blows out a candle. "I remember that very night as if it were last night." he recounts, "We were dead tired from overseeing what our group had rummaged on that long hot day. There isn't much left from the old world, but every once and awhile we get lucky with what we find. That night we found a box full of cans of beans that were just a little dented. We tried one and the beans were still good." Flint turns to Beattie. "Remember, midear, how it made our stew so tasty. It didn't last very long though with all those mouths to feed."

Kiya glances back at the closed flap in the tent.

"Midear, she's not interested any more." says Flint.

Kiya turns her attention quickly back to Flint. "I am interested." says Kiya, "I was just wondering about something. But please continue."

"I think this young woman is in love, misweet." says Beattie, blushing.

"Then I'd better get on with it before her love comes back." says Flint, chuckling.

"Finish your story." says Kiya, hard.

"It was a lovely night." winks Flint, "A night for lovers you might say."

Beattie covers her giggling lips.

"We fell asleep in the dirt that night." continues Flint, "Not clean dirt like over here." He picks up some soil from the ground and breathes it in before allowing it to siphon through his hand. "It was rather the clumpy and smelly type."

Kiya squirms in her chair.

"Milady, dirt is not so bad," intervenes Beattie, "Sometimes a good pile of dirt is better than an old bed, eh misweet?"

"Uh-huh." replies Flint, timidly.

"Go on now, misweet, continue."

Flint straightens his back and stares up at the tent. "It was a strangely murky night." he begins again, "The moon was so big that it seemed to cover half the sky. Even the cold night air felt warm to the heart. It was so peacefully quite. I didn't even snore that night. Remember, midear?"

Beattie nods back with a gleam in her eyes.

"I was the first to wake up the next morning." continues Flint. "And what I saw really did a trick on my sandy eyes." Flint removes his arm around Beattie and stares at Kiya. "I had not seen such a plumb looking rat in quite a long while." He spreads his hands apart. "The rat was this big!"

"C'mon, misweet, don't exaggerate — tell the truth."

"OK, midear." replies Flint, wearing a little smirk. "I had to rub my eyes twice over before they could accept what they saw."

Kiya adjusts her seat and gazes at Flint. "So, what is it that you saw?"

"I saw that the rat had eaten the crust off of the face of mi Beattie."

"Ugh?" says Kiya, wincing.

"Of course I whacked it good. And it made for good eats later."

"You ate it?" replies Kiya, grimacing.

"But misweet felt bad later on." cuts in Beattie, "Tell her why, misweet."

"I will, midear, if you'll let me finish."

"Oops!" says Beattie, tittering. "Sorry, misweet."

"OK then," says Flint, turning his attention back to Kiya. "I did feel sort of bad eating it after I saw what it did for midear's face." Flint gives Beattie's face a soft stroke. "I don't know why, but that rat actually cured mi Beattie. Now look at how pretty she is."

"What do you think, Lieutenant?" says Beattie, "Isn't that a hoot of a story or what?"

"I agree." says Kiya, "That's one bizarre story — if true."

"True, you say?" replies Flint, "We Outers only say what we know. And what I don't know is if we can believe you Whites."

"Our word is our oath, and our oath is our life." replies Kiya, sternly.

"Yeah, we heard that." replies Flint, "But we don't know what that means."

"It means that our word is our bond. Our word means everything to us." replies Kiya, "Commander Set has pledged his life to the Holy White Doctrine."

"But we're not of the Holy Whites." replies Flint, "We don't know how you think."

"Commander Set has undertaken this mission for the betterment of our Holy White destiny. And there's nothing more important to us than our Ascension."

"If you were us," asks Flint, running his hands through his thick dirty hair. "Would YOU trust a commander who betrays his own King?"

"If Commander Set thinks it necessary to do so, I would trust him unquestioningly."

"Would you really?" groans Flint.

"With my life!" replies Kiya.

"There you go again with more nice sounding words."

"They are NOT just words."

"Oh?" smiles Flint, poking at the items on the table. "Your life you say, hmm?"

Flint looks over at Beattie and gives her a wolfish wink. He picks the blaster from the pile and tauntingly spins it over to Kiya. "Show us." he says, smiling.

Kiya unexpectedly picks up the weapon. Beattie and Flint pull back from the table.

"What are you doing?" says Flint.

"I ask you to trust my commander." says Kiya, eyes glaring. She points the weapon to her head and discharges it. She falls from her chair. The blood gushes out from her head wound and runs into the ground.

"NO!" screams Beattie. A look of incredulity stares back at her from the glistening spatter of blood on the table.

-4-

Set rushes back inside the tent followed by his guard. Set's woeful stare at Kiya's body sends Beattie and Flint stooping down. "What's happened here?!" he hollers.

The guard quickly unsheathes his weapon from his holster. He lifts his weapon and points it at both Flint and Beattie.

"Milord, we never thought..." cries Beattie, weeping.

"Please, please, forgive us milord!" implores Flint, with a wild eyed gaze. "We didn't think her words serious."

Set draws closer to Kiya's body and kneels down next to her. "Get out!" he exclaims, "Before I do something that I—" he stops himself and points at the exit.

Beattie and Flint appear unable to move.

"I said out!"

"Yes, milord," replies Flint, solemnly. "And you have a deal
— we will make the exchange."

The commander remains unresponsive on his knees.

Beattie walks gently over to Set and remorsefully kneels
down next to Kiya's body. She affectionately caresses Kiya's
unmoving face. "We're so sorry, milord."

Set gazes at Beattie and points her away. "Go then — do as
you have promised."

Beattie is tearfully pulled away by Flint. The guard bags the
selected items from the table and escorts Flint and Beattie out.

The winds have stopped and a dead silence has entered the
tent.

Set parts Kiya's cape from her body. He pulls out a curved
dagger from his coat and cuts through the cleavage of her white
dress.

A small translucent sphere lies embedded in her chest.

Set takes his knife and gently carves the sphere out. "I shall
make sure that your soul is readied for the Ascension." he
whispers, wiping clean the sphere. "Just one more cycle and
our souls shall be together again. And if you'll have me I will
forever be your soul-mate."

Set rises to his feet and places the colourless sphere in his
pocket as he leaves the lifeless tent.

MONOCHROMIA — ... ergo thus shall be the name of the hillside of Mountdome. Monochromia shall shelter the servants of thy Holy White Order till the End of Time.

2. Hereto the people inhabiting Monochromia shall be referred to as Monochromes. Their genetic aptitudes shall determine their hierarchical colours.

3. The housing provisions in Monochromia shall be allocated by the prescribed echelon of colours (see NAT Tech Manual: no.1: sec.5).
Nota Bene: Only the Imperial Guards, the Doma Scientists and the Fuchsias (keepers of our children) shall have the privilege of a Doman Citizenry.

4. All other Monochromes shall be sheltered in the original subterranean bunkers of the builders of Doma (see EBOLAD Tech Manual no.2: sec.1). The upper echelon of colours shall reside closest to Doma while the rest shall be located in descending order in Monochromia.

5. The Monochromian lodgings are designed to accommodate each level of coloured servants. They shall house and protect Monochromes from Outer threats and the ever-growing perilous weather conditions.

6. The Monochromian ecosystem shall be managed by Doma's Hydroponics Laboratories which shall feed the necessary nutrients to the Monochromian greenhouses which will in turn disperse its food supplies according to the ordained hierarchy of colours. Monochrome men shall be subjected to...

NEW AGE TESTAMENT

PART III

THE MONOCHROMES

Chapter One

-1-

A translucent monolithic dome sits high atop a solitary hill. The rear of the dome securely rests on an overhanging cliff. The front of the dome has a large arched entrance.

A train slowly descends down the hill's gentle sloping face. The train slows and stops near an embedded hillside door. The door opens and from inside its cavernous quarters a line of men in iris outfits exit. The men board the train as it moves on to the next subterranean lodgings. The train stops and women in rose dresses debark. Some of the women stay outside caring for their gardens while others go inside. The train continues to wind its way down the hill toward two paralleled walls.

"So, Pete, you really don't think that I could blast that Outer's head from here?" says a man in a teal uniform. He stands high atop the first wall. His long gun angled outward toward the top of a disembowelled building outside the second wall. "Look at him over there," he adds, pointing to a vagrant rummaging through the towering building. "Doesn't he know that we can see him — what a fool!"

"No!" replies Pete.

"What no? You don't think that I can get him from here?" reiterates the other. "Watch this then—"

"Paul!" interrupts Pete, "I don't think it's a good idea."

"Why not?" replies Paul, continuing to refine his aim. "They know they shouldn't be up there anyway."

"Don't be an idiot." says Pete, pointing down at the parched land separating the two walls. "Just look at all those bony tumbleweeds in the Dead Zone. Don't you think that we've got enough skeletons running around us?"

"Yeah but it's not my fault that the Outers keep trying to cross over. Monochromia is only for the Faithful — it's not for them. They're lucky the Whites still allow their children to join us. If it were up to me—"

"Put your bloody rifle away." interrupts Pete, "And leave the poor guy up there alone. Anyway, he's like 2 klicks away."

"So?"

"So forget about it."

"Let's see now," says Paul, looking across. "From here to the Outer Wall it's a quarter klick. And from the Outer Wall to that miserable building it's about a full klick. Let's add another quarter klick for the height differential and—"

"Ooh... height differential." interrupts Pete.

"Anyways," says Paul, sticking out his tongue. "I'd say that idiot up there is about 1.5 klicks away."

"Whatever you say." says Pete, casually wiping his gun.

Paul sticks out his rifle and a laser carefully refines his aim. A miniature screen on the rifle registers 1.55 klicks. "You see — look!" he says, tilting the screen over to Pete. "Am I good or what?!"

"Yeah, yeah, you're a fucking genius." replies Pete, yawning. "Now, can you drop that stupid rifle before you get us in deep shit again?"

"Oh c'mon, how much T-Coin do you wanna bet that I can pick him off?"

"Zero!" replies Pete, "I'm short enough this month."

"Just admit it," says Paul, "you're scared that I'm a better shot than you."

"I don't know about that." replies Pete, turning his back.

"Oh c'mon, you're not going to admit it?" says Paul, "don't you remember that last guy I took out?"

"What guy?"

"The guy that I got right through the eye." says Paul, keeping his aim at the man atop the dilapidated building.

"Anyway, the guy up there looks like he's got a wicked hunched back. Maybe I'd be doing him a favour."

"Forget about it. I'm not playing your stupid game this time. Plus remember what the commander said?"

"Yeah, something about our job is to protect our hill solely from those stupid enough to try to cross our border walls — blab, blab, blab."

"Keep talking like that and you'll never make an Azure. You'll probably remain a Teal forever, or worse."

"Worse?"

"Yeah, you could end up in maintenance." says Pete, turning his back.

"Hey, don't even joke about that." replies Paul, sneering. "I don't want to be demoted to an Iris — I'm still too young."

"So stop fucking around. Anyway — look!" says Pete pointing up the hill, "The train is on its way."

Paul turns to face the hill. "I always enjoy the train rides." he says, "The best part is when it makes its turns — those steep curves — oh man!" He feints a loss of balance. "I just love that feeling of being suspended — it's like falling without falling."

"As always, you say the stupidest things." replies Pete, "Nobody likes the idea of ending up in the ravine. That's probably why Zadok chose to built Doma on this hill. The cliff on the other side makes for a perfect natural defence."

"Eh?"

"It's for defence purposes, stupid. There's only one possible way up to Doma. And it's by going through Monochromia."

"Yeah-yeah," replies Paul, "no possible flank attacks — blab-blab-blab."

"Keep talking like that and you'll see."

"See what?"

"That you're stupid." replies Pete, grinning.

"Hey, that Zadok guy must have been a pretty smart fellow." says Paul, pointing to the lands beyond the walls. "I mean the way he found the only hill in sight. The Outer Lands look more and more like deserts. Too bad Lake Alba dried out too, I'm sure it made for a great moat at one time."

"Zadok was definitely smarter than you."

"Oh yeah, and probably not as ugly as you." replies Paul, giving Pete a push.

Pete pushes him back with a grin.

"C'mon, will you look at that guy up there," insists Paul, "Please let me take him down."

"Listen, I said NO!"

"Hey Pete, you think that it might actually rain today?"

"My bones ache." says Pete, "It's been awhile since I felt like this. And the last time I did we had a real downpour."

"I remember that. Wasn't that like 5 months ago?"

"I don't remember, but whenever it was I think it's on its way again. And that'll probably knock your target down all by itself. And if that doesn't do it, the next dust storm surely will."

"Yeah, those dust storms are getting worse every passing day."

"That's why we live in underground bunkers, stupid."

"So, you don't think he's a threat?"

"That guy up there? Yeah sure, what's he going to do from up there — jump off? These Outers have no real weapons. Plus, we can blow him to smithereens anytime we want." replies Pete, "Anyways, I don't want to get in trouble again. I told you that I'd like to be an Ultramarine one day. I'm tired of having to live in a hole. So don't do anything stupid — you hear?!"

Paul changes the direction of his weapon and aims it at Pete. "Are you calling me stupid?!"

"I told you — stop fucking around and put the rifle down."

"Bang!" cries Paul, "Ha-ha! Almost made you blink."

"Idiot!" says Pete, dismissingly pushing Paul's long gun to the side.

"Oh c'mon, where's your sense of humour."

"Look, we've got lots of work to do today."

"Fine." mumbles Paul.

"The good news is that this is the last time we have to go through this shit. So let's get it over with, OK?"

"Good stuff!" replies Paul, "I really can't stand these exchanges. First the babies start crying and then the mothers. I tell you, if I hear much more of these blabbering cries I'm going to throw myself off this Inner Wall."

"Now that I'd like to see." replies Pete, grinning.

Paul fakes throwing himself over the wall. The other guards along the wall gaze over at Paul. Paul smiles and waves back at them.

"Sometimes you really are stupid." says Pete.

"Look!" says Paul, holding out his hand. "The first warning drops of dusty rain. I have a feeling you're right and it's going to come down hard. By the way, did you know that there was a time when rain used to last a whole season? Nowadays all the rain seems to do is burn the ground. We should thank God that our Monochromia remains somewhat fertile. I mean look at those dry flatlands out there."

"Monochromia is good for now, but living in Doma is my dream." replies Pete, "That's why I'd like to be promoted to an Imperial Guard before the Ascension. Once the Holy Whites depart the Ultramarines will get first choice in their living quarters."

"Yeah, but it's almost impossible to become one of them." says Paul, "That's why I'm aiming lower. The Azure's may not live in Doma, but they're the closest to the entrance and will be choosing their residences way before us."

"Whatever, but if you don't get things moving out here you'll never make an Azure."

"Don't say that."

"So stop wasting time and get the drawbridge going. You never know with this freaking weather what to expect."

"OK-OK, relax. What's your hurry anyway? Look, the train has only just made it past the Pinks." replies Paul, licking the spittle from the corner of his mouth. "Boy-oh-boy, too bad the Pinks have to rear kids in their bunker, because I'd love to live in that hole."

"Hmm," replies Pete, "maybe you're not so stupid after all."

-2-

In the light rain the train chugs its way to the bottom of the hill. It comes to a full stop near the first border wall. It makes a loud clunk as the tracks switch direction.

"You hear that noise out there?" says Pete, pointing over the second border wall. "The Outers are already getting riled up."

Paul unfolds a short ladder and mounts it. He leans precariously over the wall. The ladder begins to jangle with the gusts of wind.

"Get down from there you idiot!" warns Pete. A multicoloured flag flaps rigidly on a pole above Paul. "Paul, can't you see how the wind has picked up?"

"Yeah, yeah, I'll just be a minute." says Paul, "Now if I could only see over the Outer Wall."

Further away the decrepit building begins to perilously sway back and forth.

"Look at your scavenger up there." says Pete, "I'll bet you that he's going to fall off!"

"Good!" replies Paul.

"You will too if don't come back down."

"You know, that shitty building really looks like it's going to come crashing down along with that hunchback." says Paul, "Hey Pete, do you think it'll hit our Walls?"

"Will you come down from there?! It won't hit us, but it might take out some of the Outers waiting out there."

"Good! Maybe the exchanges will end faster." says Paul. "By the way do you think we'll get enough rain to have a moat again?"

"Lake Alba hasn't risen in generations. It's a wonder that it gets wet at all. It's usually as dry as a Rose."

"Hey, that's funny!" chuckles Paul as he makes his way back down the ladder, "I guess that's why aged Pinks become dried up Roses."

"So, what did you see up there?"

"Yup, they're out there alright. I could see the end of the long line. It's going to be another long day of whimpering women and weeping babies — I hate it."

"You said that already."

"Hey Pete, how do they know that we're about to push out the drawbridge?"

"They can hear the train, stupid."

"Oh, that's right." replies Paul, "I keep forgetting."

"That's because you don't ever listen." replies Pete, sighing.

"Hey Pete, do you think we're going to see some more of those crusty women?"

"Probably — why?"

"They give me the willies."

"I guess everything's relative." replies Pete, brushing his short hair back. "Considering that they still make babies, I guess some Outer men don't mind their looks."

"Hey, what's that old expression? Oh yeah, beggars can't be choosers!" says Paul, laughing hard.

"You're hilarious." replies Pete, "Now get your ass in gear and prepare for the exchanges."

-3-

Behind the first wall the train passengers disembark. Young women in fuchsia dresses exit the train first. Older men in iris coloured outfits exit right after them. Each male accompanies one of the females into a large greenhouse.

A middle aged woman wearing a rose dress steps out last from the train. Her auburn hair holds firmly in a small tight bun. She places a long pink scarf over her shoulders and waves at the guards on the wall. Some of the guards place their hands over their chests as she walks by their posts.

The woman reaches a single story building with a metallic fish spinning on its steeple. She bows and the doors open.

"I feel rain my worthy flock." she says as she enters, "The water to wash out our sins has come once again."

There is a rousing applause that emanates from inside the structure as the doors slowly close behind her. A sign above the door reads:

'TEMPLE MONOCHROMIA: We welcome all colours.'

"Hey Pete!" says Paul.

"What do you want now?"

"I think High Priestess Anora waved at me."

"Sure, sure, she waved just at you."

"That reminds me — did you donate?"

"I told you that I'm short of T-Coins this month — look!" says Pete, opening his hand. A small hologram of a gold coin pops up. The gold coin has a number 13 on it. "You see, I barely have enough to buy one magenta fantasy pill."

"God's not going to be happy with you, you know?!"

"Right!" replies Pete.

"Hey, I wouldn't take it too lightly if I were you. Remember what the high priestess said last time?"

"You mean about God's temperament when people don't give?"

"Yeah, like that thing about our prayers not being answered if we're not willing to suffer some inner cost."

"Isn't it strange how my inner costs end up in their inner pockets." replies Pete.

"Did you ever think that the reason you don't have money is because you don't give enough of it to the Temple? The high priestess said last week that T-Coins won't make you happy if God can't hear you."

"You mean God needs to hear the virtual chimes of my T-Coins in order to pay attention?"

"Oh c'mon, I'm being serious here. You've got to give. It's embarrassing standing next to you in the temple when you don't."

"That's enough, Paul. I don't need another sermon this week."

A sudden flash of lightning hits the flag pole. It sends both sentries scurrying under the wall's extension.

"Jeez that was close." says Pete.

Paul couches next to Pete. "You see? Maybe if you had given—"

"Shut-up!" blurts Pete, "If I here another word from you about giving to the Temple, I'm going to smack you with your own rifle!"

"You better be careful what you say," says Paul, raising his head upward. "God's up there looking down on us, you know."

"Well, unless he's looking down through the lens of a rifle, I don't give a shit!"

"Maybe the lighting strikes are his bullets. Ever think of that?" replies Paul, pouting.

"Right." replies Pete, shaking his head.

-4-

The lightning flashes have dwindled. The fuchsia dressed women exit the greenhouse. The young women carry with them empty wicker baskets. The men in their iris outfits exit the greenhouse carrying bulky brown boxes. The men follow the young women toward the first wall.

"OK. I think God has emptied his rifle." says Pete, grinning. "Let's get the exchanges going."

Paul pulls down a handle on the wall. A siren loudly whistles as a metallic plank spawns out. The plank slowly extends from the first border wall to the second. There is a big thump as the conveyer reaches the other side.

"It's fastened."

"Good!" replies Pete, "Let's do this!"

An escalator opens down the outside wall. It extends out over the dried lakebed.

A woman in a tattered coat suddenly appears on the ledge of the outside wall. She holds tightly a baby in her arms. Other women begin to line up behind her.

The first fuchsia and iris dressed pairings make their way up the inside wall to the bridge.

Pete takes the lead and accompanies the first pairing to the center of the drawbridge. He signals the first itinerant woman to approach. The woman walks over to them and hands over her child to the fuchsia dressed woman. The man in his iris outfit gives her his brown box in return. The distraught homely woman returns to the outside wall and disappears down its stairs. The fuchsia dressed woman gently places the child in her wicker basket. She and her companion make their way back down the inside wall. Another fuchsia and iris pairing come up.

Pete suddenly stops the new pair as he spots three cloaked figures standing on the outside wall.

Paul turns to Pete. "Pete, what's the matter?"

"Hey there!" yells Pete, "Only women with babies up here!"

One of the cloaked figures lifts his hands and approaches.

"Stop right there!" commands Pete.

"Soldier, may I have your permission to lower one of my hands." says the cloaked man.

"Why?!" jumps in Paul with his cocked rifle.

"So that you won't make a fatal mistake." replies the man.

Pete squints through the thin rain at the man. "Yes, but I suggest you do so very slowly." says Pete.

The man nods as he carefully spreads open his cape. A Blue crest glows from the chest of his white suit.

"Commander?" cries Pete, "Is that you?"

"Yes, soldier." replies Set.

"What did you say?" says Paul, confused.

"That's our commander!" replies Pete, dropping to his knee. "Lower your weapon, stupid."

Paul hesitates for a second before following Pete to his knee. Other sentries behind the first border wall quickly lower their weapons.

Set waves over the rest of his party. He bends down and whispers in Pete's ear. Pete stands up and waves the rest of the commander's entourage through. The commander and his party make their way down the steps to the hillside.

Paul raises his shoulders and approaches Pete. "What was that about?"

"Who knows?" replies Pete, "Let's get moving with the rest of the exchanges. This way we can get out of here."

"But what did the commander say to you?"

"Nothing!" reiterates Pete.

"What do you mean — nothing?"

"I mean he said to say nothing."

"Nothing about what?" asks Paul.

"Who the fuck knows." replies Pete, "So let's get this over with, OK?"

"But what was Commander Set doing in the Outer Lands?"

"Shut the fuck-up, and maybe we'll live long enough to never find out."

"Oh, I see." replies Paul.

Pete waves up the next iris and fuchsia dressed pairing.

THY HOLY WHITE DOCTRINE

I.   Thy Holy Costume shall be as White as thy untainted Soul

II.   Thy Holy Bodies shall remain as Pure and Virtuous as thy Sacred Birth

III.   Thy TänkaWorld Crest shall bear at all times the Colours of thy Soul

IV.   Thy Ascension shall bring forth thy Resurrection

V.   Thy Holy White Soul shall be Reborn into thy Avatar in Nirvia

VI.   Thy Avatar shall personify thy spirit in Death as thy body did in Life

VII.   Thy Keeper of the Golden Key shall be the Ruler of thy physical Realm

VIII.   Thou shall have the right to Challenge thy Key Keeper through the glory of thy TänkaMatches

IX.   Thy TänkaPods shall randomly select thy TänkaPlanets for thy TänkaMatches

X.   Thou shall obey thy Holy White Doctrine or be eternally Excommunicated

NEW AGE TESTAMENT

Chapter Two

-1-

The temple is filled with people dressed in a multitude of singular colours. There is an inviting applause as the high priestess steps up to the podium.

Her tight dress rises with her voice. "We have waited a long time, but I promise that the words of the EBOLAD are true!" she cries out, "Believe me!"

A heartfelt applause spreads quickly through the temple.

"Thank-you!" says the high priestess, "I love you all."

The applause grows louder.

"People of Monochromia," she says, gripping tightly the podium. "Let me end this evening with a reminder of that which has been long promised to us. It is we, the meek, who shall inherit the Earth." Her bosom bobbles up and down with the voraciousness of her words. "We shall soon be free of the subservient colours we wear, because Doma will be ours!"

The worshippers rise from their pews clapping relentlessly.

"Thank-you!" repeats the high priestess, "Thank-you!"

"We want more! We want more!" chant the parishioners.

The high priestess straightens her dress. She waves her admirers back down to their seats. "Alright, alright, I will share with you one last story. This is a story of redemption."

The gathered crowd quiets back down.

"There was once an obedient Pink who had lost her way. She found herself one day in a deep dark place. She thought she had found love, but instead found herself suffering like only a young innocent girl could understand. The hole she found herself in grew darker and deeper everyday. She was convinced that she had been left for dead, for she felt dead. But she still believed in her Faith. And that's when she saw a long white tunnel."

Oodles of gentle murmurs rise from the attentive crowd.

The high priestess stops and takes a sip of water. She sets the glass back down, and continues, "And that distraught Pink could feel herself being pulled towards the light. And she smiled as she saw her loved ones waiting for her on the other side."

A whispering murmur rises from the crowd.

"The distraught Pink knew then that the Heaven of the EBOLAD was there waiting to receive her." continues the high priestess, softly. "She was ready and willing to let go of the misery of her life. But in that very last moment a colourful light came unto her and said, 'You shall no longer be harmed. You are free to return to your people.'"

The murmurs grow louder.

The high priestess wipes a tear from her eyes. She takes another sip from her glass. "And the Pink knew then and there that that was the God of the EBOLAD working His magic." she says, devotedly. "And that little fragile Pink found within her the power that only Faith could bring. It is that strength that lifted her scraped soul out of its depths of despair and allowed her to flourish and grow till she could stand strong — as she does in front of you on this day — for I AM her!" She raises her hands toward the ceiling. "And YOU are my people! Halleluiah, I say, Halleluiah!"

The crowd responds with a thunderous chorus of applause. Many of the rose dressed women sit sobbing in their pews.

"God never abandons his worshippers, for I can still hear his words in my mind." The high priestess stretches out her arms in opposite directions. "And He has told me NOT to be like the Outers, for they are Faithless. And to forgive the Whites for they have placed their Faith in the devious hands of their science."

A disparate murmur trickles through the crowded temple.

"No-no, my friends." she intervenes, "We shall need to forgive the Whites for only then shall we be able to fully enjoy their home upon their Ascension."

Murky murmurs resonate in the crowd.

The high priestess raises her hands. "I understand your anger, my friends, for we all carry their scars. But it's only God who will judge the Whites. He has told me that those who create their own Heaven shall never truly know Him." Her voice hardens. "Let the Whites believe in their NAT. For the true meanings of the EBOLAD can only be seen through Faith in God, and not in a scientific extrapolation of His words."

Some in the fold turn and suspiciously look around the Temple.

"I know, I know..." she interjects, "You may think that I may be precariously besmirching the Whites. But fear not, my people, for God is with us. Only He holds the real key to the Kingdom of Heaven. It is only He who can truly release us from the shackles of servitude." She points to her temples. "We Monochromes have no need of T-Vision to see the Promised Land, for our God is in our hearts and not in our brains."

A mumbling echo of satisfaction gathers smugly among the spectators. The high priestess humbly lowers her head in prayer.

"God made us all with an empty space in our hearts," she says, "But He gave us the Free Will to choose what we fill it with." The high priestess lifts her head and points to the crowd to rise. "Fill thy void with thy Faith in thy Lord and thy true Heaven shall be yours one day — Amen!"

"Amen!" reply in unison the parishioners.

The high priestess picks up her neatly folded scarf from her pulpit and steps off the stage. A boisterous applause follows her down. She is quickly surrounded and congratulated by her doting followers while the rest of the congregation mingle about in discourse.

From the back of the temple a man hollers out, "Thank-you, High Priestess!" He turns to those around him with a wide smile. "Wasn't that just one incredible sermon, or what?"

"Yes." responds a soft voice, "Incredible is the correct interpretation."

-2-

The man turns his head toward the origins of the comment. "I know what I—" he says, open-mouthed. His blue eyes melt into his azure uniform. "I-I," he stammers. His mouth remains breathlessly open.

A young woman stands unassumingly serene and upright behind him. Her soaked fuchsia dress has attached itself to her voluptuous curves. She bends backwards to strain the rain out of her glistening black hair. "Before getting attached to another's story," she says, "one should understand their own."

"Huh?" replies the young man, slack-jawed. He gets up from his pew and combs back his short hair. "I've never seen a Fuchsia in here before," he finally mumbles out, "Especially one like you." His eyes roll up and down her body. "Wow! Where have you been all my life?"

"In the soaking clouds." she replies. The young woman continues to squeeze the rain water out of her shoulder length hair.

"I guess you're not a big fan of the high priestess." he says, "But I think she's great. She's done an amazing job in unifying our beliefs, you know. We Monochromes used to fight over who had the right to worship in the Temple. But the high priestess showed us that we're all children of the same God. And that we all share the same fundamental belief."

"That makes sense. But that doesn't make her bolstering beliefs any more meaningful." replies the young woman as she gazes out the temple window, "I think the rain has ended."

"Eh?" replies the young man, edging closer to her. "So, if those are just words why then are they so inspiring?"

"All that means is that you've been successfully indoctrinated into her beliefs."

The man scratches his head.

"Let me ask you something," she adds, "Do you lose your inspiration if you don't attend her weekly sermons?"

"Yeah." he replies, "So what?"

"The good feeling of being motivated by another is therefore a temporary thing. And like fantasy pills you feel the need to come back for more. Isn't that right?"

"Listen, Fuchsia. The high priestess shared with us her afterlife experience. And she has sworn that when she died she saw a light at the end of the dark tunnel of death." He folds his arms with glaring condescension. "Who are you to question her, eh?"

The young woman stares back at him with her glittering black eyes. The man's estranged leer thaws.

"Questions towards Faith can be provocative indeed." she replies, "Especially when Faith is ingrained in one's way of thinking. But the fact is that the finite self can create all sorts of ideas to appease its own limitations."

"What?"

"In other words, if the high priestess had truly experienced death how then could she have been present to witness it?"

"I don't know?" the man replies, his eyes swishing from side to side.

"The only thing one can bring back from having had such an existential experience as death is its residual feelings, but not the thing itself. That is unless you continuously die each moment of every day."

"Wait, are you saying that the high priestess is lying?!" he replies, grumpily loud. "Does that mean you think she's corrupt?"

Other worshippers turn their attention toward them.

The young woman points to him to lower his voice. "Being corrupt is part of the human condition. It's just the degree that's different."

"Are you saying that I'm also corrupt?"

"Where the self exits so does corruption."

"I'm not corrupt."

"Oh? What if I asked you if you've ever put your own interests ahead of another's, how would you respond?"

"Alright, alright, but the high priestess does her sermons out of unselfishness — so there!"

"Does she?"

"What do you mean? She brings uplifting feelings to all her followers."

"Yes, I've noticed that. She appears to like that very much."

"So you do think she's lying."

"That's not what I'm saying."

"What are you saying then?"

"I'm saying that she probably does believe what she's saying, but that doesn't make it true."

"Hey! You know what? Maybe she believes it, because it is true."

"In the Virtual Library there's an ancient replica of a CRT that shows—"

"A what?" the man interrupts.

"A Cathode Ray Tube." she whispers back, "It was the basis of the first virtual reality technology. Its brain was made up of electrically stimulated vacuum tubes. It was called a television."

"Oh, you mean like the Holy White's T-Vision thing?"

"Sort of like that, except more of an external rudimentary machine."

The man gives a half hazard nod. "So?"

"When the CRT was turned off, the screen would go black. But in the middle of the screen a white dot would remain lit for a few extra seconds. This was due to the lingering electrical discharges still present in the device."

Deep ridges form on the man's forehead. "Miss, I don't understand what you're saying?"

"Think of the CRT device as the brain. Normally, when the body dies the brain will not cease to function immediately. It will have its own electrical stimuli still flickering inside it till it shuts down completely."

"Do you mean to say that the light the high priestess saw is like the dot in the machine?"

"Uh-huh."

"But," he says, intensely. "The high priestess said she saw people she knew on the other side of the light."

"Those images are part of her personal memory banks, are they not? And even if she didn't recognize the people waiting for her, they'd still be but figments or extrapolations of past visions."

"I still don't see what you're getting at."

"Alright then," replies the young woman, "let me put it another way: There's absolutely NO ONE on the other side waiting for you."

-3-

"Are you crazy, Fuchsia? What kind of a Monochrome are you?"

"One that does not think much of fairy tales." she replies.

"Fairy tales?!" he says, fanatically. "I believe in what the high priestess shared with us."

"There are no two more redundant words that actualize the ego more than 'I believe'."

"Oh yeah, and what would you have without beliefs, eh?"

"Clarity!" she replies, stalwartly.

"My beautiful Fuchsia," he chuckles, you've been hanging around the Whites for too long — they've brainwashed you."

"First of all, I'm NOT your Fuchsia! Secondly, I do agree with the high priestess about one thing — the Holy Whites have been misdirected — just like she has been."

"Are you ridiculing our beliefs? This is a very dangerous thing you're doing, you know."

"I don't mean to sound glib about your beliefs. All that I'm trying to explain is that there are different paths to the Truth, and none of them include the self-delusions that come with Faith."

"This just sounds to me like you're reproaching the high priestess of being a liar again."

"No. That's not what I'm saying. Like I've already said, I'm sure that in her mind she believes her story."

"Oh, story you say. And how about you — what's your story?"

"What difference does my story make to you?"

"Well, obviously it would make me understand what you're all about."

"Oh?"

"You disagree?"

"I think the curiosity about wanting to learn someone else's story is really about trying to understand your own."

"Uh?" he mutters.

"Never mind." she replies.

"Miss, what did you mean that there's no one waiting for me on the other side — how do you know?"

"Look at the facts. You are your brain, and when your brain dies so do you — period!"

"But my soul doesn't die."

"What do you mean by 'my soul'?"

"I mean the spirit inside me that makes me, me."

"I'm sorry to inform you, but there's no such thing."

"Woman, you're killing me."

"Sure, that would work." she replies, her face glowing. "Mister, have you ever sat back on your bed and considered what happens when you die?"

"Not really."

"Close your eyes one night and think on what it would mean if all your thoughts and beliefs died along with you. Then ask yourself what would truly remain of you?"

"I-I-I?" he replies.

"Yes, you-you-you, would no longer exist after death." She pauses as she peeks over his shoulder at the window. "You still look confused," she says, casually. "You are after all your thoughts and memories which form your beliefs, no? Without which you would not be you."

"I wouldn't? Then who would I be?" he quietly asks.

"You would be no one."

"But how could I survive without being somebody?"

"Now that's a really good question. How does a world survive when everyone wants to be somebody?"

"I don't want to be somebody — I just want to be me."

"If you want to find the answer to the question you first asked, then you must die."

"I don't want to die."

"That's a normal response. And I'm not proposing that you physically die either."

"Eh?" he replies, "You want me to die without dying?"

"The real question is if it's possible to find out what death is without physically dying?"

"I have no idea what the hell you're talking about, girl?"

"Alright!" she says, slowly moving closer to him.

He suddenly perks up with a popped gaze.

"To be psychologically free is to be free of psychological baggage." she says.

"What do you mean free of baggage?"

"Imagine if you carried memories that were formed by a distorted view. Would you be able to see things clearly, or would your vision be obstructed?"

"Why would I have a distorted view?"

"To be human is to have distorted views. You see things differently than another because no two minds are wired exactly the same. So your view is subjectively based on your own brain's wiring. Is that not why you wear different colours?"

"That's only because we have different aptitudes." he boldly replies.

"And those aptitudes make you feel different, do they not?"

"Yes. That's because we are."

"Are you?"

"Aren't we?"

"I truly doubt it."

"What do you mean?"

"Do you feel afraid at times?"

"Sometimes, yes." he admits.

"Do you sometimes feel lonely?"

"Uh-huh."

"Do you sometimes feel anxious?"

"Uh-huh."

"Do you sometimes feel envious?"

"Yup." he says, eyeing her closely.

"Do you feel a sense of desire at times?"

"That's a definite yes."

"Do you sometimes feel insecure?"

"Umm, sometimes." he replies.

"I can go on and on, but I think you get the point."

"So, what you're saying is that we're maybe not so different after all?"

"Mister, if you understand your own story you don't need the story of another."

"What do you mean?"

"I mean that there's actually just one fundamental story. And that's the story of the human condition."

"But what does this have to do anything?"

"This has actually to do with everything. To know what it means to be human is to know what it means to live and die."

"But, miss, we already know that death is only the beginning for us all."

"The beginning of what?" she asks, softly.

"The beginning of me in Heaven." he replies.

"Sorry, but as I've mentioned before — all your memories, all your thoughts, all your beliefs, and all else that makes you, you — remain buried here."

"Shit! You're scaring me, girl."

"Good. Now think about why I'm scaring you and you may find your own light."

"I feel so confused." he says, as he notices others around him puzzling over the young woman.

"You're confused?" she replies, smiling. "That's a good start."

A line of young women in fuchsia dresses are passing outside. The young woman inside the Temple hurriedly picks up a wicker basket next to her feet.

"Hey! Where did that come from?" the man asks, pointing at the basket.

"Just don't be fooled into finding solace in another's light," she tells him, "Unless you can be a light unto yourself you'll always be destined to follow your shadow."

"What?"

"Find inspiration from within."

"How would I do that?"

"Just don't let the fog of irrational beliefs deter you from searching for the clarity of thought that Truth brings."

"What irrational beliefs? What Truth?"

The young woman hastily pushes herself through the thickening crowd toward the exit.

"Hey wait!" yells out the young man, "What's your name?"

The woman is no longer visible inside the temple.

The man smiles uneasily at the bewildered eavesdroppers. "Yeah, I know!" he says, biting nervously his fingernails. "That girl must be totally crazy. She must have some kind of death wish or something. I mean looking like that and talking like that."

Chapter Three

The white clouds have begun to disperse in the night sky. Beattie is next in line outside the wall. She struggles to shift her roundly coat into place.

A bright holographic sign above the escalator reads:

'MONOCHROMIA: Last Day of the Last Cycle.'

The woman in front of Beattie nervously shuffles her baby from one arm to the other. The woman turns and gives Beattie a smirk of derision. "Where's your baby?" says the woman, "Did you eat it?"

An unresponsive Beattie looks shyly down at her bulky coat. She tries to streamline it with her hands.

A middle aged woman comes down the outer escalator. She tears open a brown box and starts to furiously munch on a piece of its content. "How, how is it possible?" says the woman with tears rolling down her dirty face, "How have we gotten to this point?"

A loud sound of an engine igniting suddenly permeates through the walls. The holographic sign suddenly begins to flicker.

"Let's go! Move it!" says Beattie, nudging the woman in front of her. "They'll soon stop the exchange."

The woman quickly mounts with Beattie right behind her. They both reach the outer edge of the drawbridge as the holographic sign goes dark.

Beattie closes her eyes for an instant and expels a big sigh. "Phew. I made it, misweet." she whispers in her hand.

The air atop the drawbridge is silent and still. The moon pops in and out of the clouds.

The sentries wave the first woman forward. The woman ahead of Beattie moves to the center of the drawbridge. She trades in her child and returns with her brown box.

Beattie nods at the tattered woman as the woman heads back down the outer steps with the box quivering in her hands.

Beattie is now alone on the drawbridge. She turns her sight on the grumbling sentries across from her. She glances back at the high feeble building behind her. The building has stopped its precarious swaying. Beattie takes a deep breath and with her head down begins to cross the bridge.

Paul scowls at an empty handed Beattie walking toward him. He puts his hand up. "Halt there!" he cries, "Go back down — the last cycle has ended. Plus, we don't accept babies still in the womb," he adds, laughingly. "Or is that just fat under that ugly coat?"

The train bells ring out as its engines roar.

Beattie quickens her pace across the bridge.

"Hey!" cries Paul, "I didn't give you permission to come across!"

Beattie disregards Paul and edges closer.

"Stop right there!" repeats Paul, raising his rifle.

Beattie takes out the golden disk from her pocket and waves it at him. "But I have an entry pass." she says.

Pete jumps on the drawbridge with two other sentries behind him. "At this time of day?" he says, "Where do you come from?"

Beattie unflinchingly stares down the sentries. "I'm on a Magisterial Walkabout." she says.

"What Magisterial Walkabout? We know nothing of this." says Pete.

Beattie looks above her with an air of concern. "My permit allows for mi entry into Doma at any time of day or night."

Pete pops a look at Paul.

"Oh? And why would an Outer have such a pass?" says Pete, "Leave the pass there and step back."

Beattie places the disk down but does not move away. She squints up at the dark skies.

"I said to move back!" repeats Pete, arrestingly.

"OK-OK." replies Beattie, taking one step back.

"That's not enough." says Pete, raising his weapon.

"Move further back or we'll shoot." adds Paul, as he edges closer to the disk.

"Paul, be careful." says Pete.

-2-

The heated encounter on the drawbridge becomes clearly visible as the moon fully escapes the clouds. The train is slowly making its way back up the hill.

"At a girl!" says Flint, precariously leaning over the edge of the tall building decaying outside the walls. He opens his backpack and two black metallic wings partially flap open. He momentarily loses his balance before forcefully holding them down. He pulls the wings to his side and aims his eye at the upwardly mobile train. He watches the train make its first turn before jumping off the building. The wings immediately expand as he takes flight. He fights hard to steady them as he swerves up and down. Flint quickly manages to smooth out his glide as he nears the border walls.

Beattie glances up from the drawbridge and heaves a big sigh. A relaxed gaze overtakes her.

"What is this?" says Paul, busily scanning the gold disk. "There's nothing on this."

"I'm sorry, sir." replies Beattie, "I gave you the wrong disk. I have the right one right here." Beattie reaches inside her coat.

"PAUL!" yells Pete, "Get out of there!"

Paul turns to Pete, and says, "What did you—"

The rest of Paul's response is immediately torn apart by a loud screeching sound.

Beattie's body is the first to be macerated. The rippling wave of the explosion spreads quickly from her to the others atop the bridge. Paul is the first sentry to be eviscerated. The other two guards are blown off the bridge and land impaled on the protruding skeletons below.

Minuscule particles from the explosion form a white dust cloud around the bridge. Pete walks out of the cloud and gazes with stunned disappointment at the large hole on the bridge. He then slowly collapses to his knees as he becomes conscious of the shrapnel running through his head.

Confusion spans throughout the hillside as running screams spread from both sides of the walls.

Many on the hill rush inside their respective subterranean bunkers while teal uniformed soldiers rush out of theirs. The soldiers quickly run to reinforce their defensive positions atop the inner wall. The drawbridge begins to retract but blocks midway.

The foragers outside the outer wall scatter quickly. Some run to take refuge in the derelict structures nearby.

In the confusion the black glider manages to land on the snaking train. As the train makes its last turn Flint detaches his black wings and allows them to fly off and tumble quietly into the ravine below. He lays himself flat on the top of the train and holds on tightly.

The train slows down as it nears the dome. Fully armed soldiers in azure uniforms race out of their subterranean bunkers. They swiftly take positions all around the dome's entrance.

The train comes to a full stop.

A sign over the dome's entrance reads:

'GATEWAY TO DOMA'

The doors of the train slide open and a multitude of monochromatically dressed passengers descend from the train.

The station platform fills quickly with the chattering voices of the newly arrived. Flint slides down unnoticed from the top of the train and with his iris outfit effectively blends in with the new arrivals.

"Freaking Outers!" a woman cries out, "Why can't they just leave us be?!"

"They should be thankful that the Whites give them anything at all." says a balding man in a cerulean coloured outfit, "But NO, it's never enough for them. What do they want from us?"

"Maybe they just want what we want." says Flint, smoothly infiltrating his reply.

There is a little pregnant pause as the group notices the new voice.

The balding man examines Flint. "That's right!" he says, "They want to take over. The Outers are so green with envy that it makes crazy! I can't wait till the blessed Whites ascend." he adds, "Doma will be ours and we'll no longer have to hear their cries."

"We are the Monochromes, and only we shall inherit Doma." says Flint. "So it was promised to us, and so it shall be — blessed are the Whites."

A woman in a rose dress extends her arm around Flint. "Blessed are the Whites," she repeats, supportively. She winks at Flint as she pats down her short brownish hair.

"For only the Faithful shall inherit the Earth." says another.

The discussion widens within the group. Flint shyly slips from the woman's affectionate embrace. And with a nervous grin dovetails his way back into anonymity.

The corridor ends and the new arrivals are funnelled inside a large gated area. The fuchsia dressed women with their closed wicker baskets are grouped together while the rest wait nearby.

Flint stumbles forward as his eyes grow big at the sight of the domed city.

The city is a pristine looking mausoleum of marble and granite. A series of white terraced houses form three circular walls around a coliseum. On the sides of each of the residences are colourful hieroglyphics.

Flint shakes his head and his eyes return to normal. He checks his palm and a hieroglyphic image pops up from the embedded chip. He inspects the area and spots a wall with the matching image.

"So that's the way through to the Palace." he whispers.

A greenish beam suddenly scans over Flint.

"Hey you!" calls out a guard.

Flint jerks to a stop and shuts his hand. He cringes at the sight of the approaching sentinel. And as Flint begins to raise his arms the guard stops.

The guard cups his ear and says, "Yes sir!"

The guard moves past Flint and heads farther down to the fuchsia dressed women.

Flint quickly puts his partially raised arms down. He discreetly reinserts himself into his group and quietly accompanies them through the gate.

The group around him disperses and Flint is left gazing up at an imposing chamber above the coliseum.

Flint suddenly capitulates to one knee. "C'mon, courage!" he whispers, "Beattie, please help me. This is for our little boy." He grips his shaking hands and with a less shaken determination continues forward.

Chapter Four

-1-

The fuchsia dressed women still wait in their reserved area. The sentinels guardedly screen their wicker baskets.

"Tim!" exclaims a stocky sentry, "Look at that one."

"Where?" replies Tim, "You mean the Fuchsia with the deep black hair?"

"That's the one."

"Wow! She's quite something, Sergeant."

"How'd you like for her to be your first?"

"Eh?" grunts the young sentry, "My first what, Sergeant?"

"Don't you want to try out your pecker?"

"Sergeant, she's a Doman Citizen." replies Tim, "I don't want to get in trouble."

The sergeant places his arm around Tim. "Kid, call me Bill."

Tim lowers his head bashfully.

The sergeant laughs out loud. "Hey, don't worry, kid." cries the sergeant, waving in another sentry. "I'll fix that shyness of yours."

The other sentry comes over. "What is it, Sarge?"

"Hey, Rod," replies the sergeant, "I'm thinking of helping this young Azure have a little taste of honey?"

"Oh yeah?" replies Rod, smiling. "Like with who?"

"See that Fuchsia over there."

"You mean the gorgeous tall one with those nice—"

"Don't point!" replies the sergeant, "But yeah, that one!"

"You sure, Sarge — that's a Fuchsia."

"Yeah, I'm sure."

"Then count me in, Sarge." answers Rod, smiling. "What about her basket?"

"Don't worry about it."

Set suddenly appears from behind the conspiring sentries. No longer wearing his dark cape his white suit is fully in view. The sentries swiftly stand at attention.

"Commander!" says Sergeant Bill, pop-eyed.

Set points to the sergeant to approach. Bill immediately moves closer to the commander. Set says something unintelligible while pointing at the fuchsia dressed women.

The sergeant walks by his two armed colleagues with raised shoulders. Tim and Rod look over at the glowering commander and quickly straighten their pose.

The sergeant reaches the young woman from the Temple. He turns to the commander. The commander shakes his head. The sergeant furrows his brow and points to another young woman. He looks back over at the commander. The commander this time replies with a nod.

"Is your name, Clarissa?" asks the sergeant.

"Yes."

"The commander has asked for you to follow me."

"Of course." replies Clarissa. She picks up her basket and follows the sergeant back to the commander.

"You can go back to your post, Sergeant." says Set, "And I would suggest that you and your little entourage stop harassing the Fuchsias."

"Yes, Commander." says Bill, smiling back at his buddies.

"What are your guys up to, sergeant?" says Set.

The sergeant immediately stands at attention. "Nothing." replies Bill, "Nothing at all, Commander."

"Fine." says Set, "Then you won't mind if I let the rest of the Fuchsia enter as well."

"Yes sir — I mean no, sir." replies Bill, moping.

-2-

The young woman from the Temple reaches the outskirts of the city. She stops near a building with people in sapphire outfits going in and out. She gently puts her wicker basket down and waits.

The baby inside her basket begins to stir. She bends down and rocks the basket side to side. "It's alright, sweetie." she says, soothingly. She gets on her toes and peeks about. She spots a man in a sapphire uniform waving at her. She smiles at him as he makes his way toward her.

The young woman suddenly feels a hand on her shoulder. She turns to see Tim standing firmly behind her. His eyes are wide open and his face is demonstratively red.

"Umm, what is your name, miss?"

"My name?" she replies, bemused.

"Yes, your name?"

Boisterous laughter can be heard from a distance.

"Who cares what her name is," cries out Bill, "Just ask her!"

"OK-OK!" replies Tim, loudly. "Mademoiselle, we just wanted to know if you'd like to join us later."

"No thanks, I'm not interested."

"She's not interested guys." shouts Tim.

"So?" replies the sergeant.

The man in the sapphire uniform arrives at the woman's side. He is a tall man with sculpted facial features and short black hair. A white patch on his sleeve shows a symbol of an "S' inside of a 'D'. His dark black eyes glower at Tim. Tim instinctively takes a step back. The other sentries quickly abandon the immediate area.

"I'm sorry, sir." says Tim, guiltily.

"Fine." replies the man, "Now get lost!"

The sentry promptly heads back to the gated entryway.

The man in sapphire takes the young woman's hand. "Sistina, are you alright?" he says.

She places her hand on his chest. "Yes." she says with a heavy smile, "Thank-you, Logos."

"I'm glad you made it through." says Logos, touching the wicker basket. "The child is inside?"

"Yes, she's sleeping."

"This will not be easy for you, Sistina. But I must ask you to leave immediately."

"But—"

"No buts! You need to leave before someone recognizes you. The glitch I have installed in the T-Ports is not fully reliable."

Sistina opens her basket and watches as the baby comfortably sleeps. Her eyes begin to water as she tenderly seals the basket.

"Please Sistina."

"But maybe I can help if—"

"It's too dangerous for you here." interjects Logos, "Please, get out while you still can. The rest is up to me now."

Sistina reluctantly lets go of her basket. Logos kisses her on her cheek. "Quickly now — go!"

"I have a strange feeling that I'll never see either of you again."

"That is why you need to leave straight away."

Sistina stares down at the basket.

"Please, Sistina, you've done your part."

Tears roll down Sistina's face as she walks back toward the dome's gateway. Logos follows behind her watching her make it past the sentinels and into the corridor leading out the dome.

He turns and starts to walk in the direction of the coliseum. "Now then," he sighs, looking down at the basket. "It is all up to you little girl."

-3-

Sistina exits the dome with an aimless gaze. The train revs up and its clunky sound rattles her. She moves over to the train and distractedly joins the boarding line.

"I'm so tired." says a middle aged woman in a rose dress, "I hope to get some REM tonight."

Suddenly two sentinels grab hold of Sistina.

"We've got her, Sarge." says Rod to his open hand. A tiny microchip flickers beneath the skin of his palm.

"You've got her. Good! Hold on to her." replies the sergeant as he emerges from the corridor. He moves in on the captive. "So, where do think you're going?"

"I have another job to do in Monochromia." replies Sistina.

"Do you? I don't think so. But there's a job I'd like for you to do for my friend here." replies the sergeant, winking at Tim.

Sistina stares desperately at those who boarded the train.

"C'mon guys." says the rose dressed woman on the train, "Leave her be."

"Mind your own business, Rose." says the sergeant, "If you have any complaints you can come along with us."

The woman does not reply.

The sergeant pulls out a pad from his pocket. "Fuchsia," he says, rigidly. "Place your hand here."

Sistina obeys.

"Well, well." says the sergeant, "Look at what we have here."

Tim approaches the sergeant. "What is it, Sergeant?"

"This is really your lucky day, my young Azure," replies the sergeant, "this Fuchsia is an actual living fugitive."

"She is? Really?" replies Tim.

The sergeant pulls Sistina close to him. He runs his nose along her neck and breathes her in. "Yummy!" he says, swallowing his drool. "Nothing smells like a nubile fugitive."

"Is she really on the wanted list?" says Rod.

"She's wanted for questioning." replies the sergeant, "It's by order of the Ultramarines."

"You've been a naughty girl, haven't you?" says Rod, winking. "Sarge, I think we should take her to the interrogation room. What do you think?"

"Shouldn't we report her to the Imperial Guards?" injects Tim, "We can get in big trouble if we don't."

"Fuck'em! It's enough that they give those Ultramarines more T-Coin than us." replies the sergeant, ardently. "Why should they get better pussy too?"

Tim notices the people on the train staring at him. "Sergeant, if any of the T-Ports detect what we're doing we'll be in big trouble."

"Don't worry about it. Where we're going there aren't any." replies Bill, "Plus we have an unwritten agreement with the Ultramarines about our extra carnivorous activities."

"That's a good one, Sarge." says Rod, loudly laughing. "Carnivorous activities — I like that."

"But we're talking about a Fuchsia here." says Tim.

"Shut-up!" says the sergeant, "I just want to find out if she's different from the Pinks."

The middle aged woman in her rose outfit steps off the train. She opens her mouth to speak but is abruptly pulled away by two men in periwinkle outfits.

"It's none of our business." says the short man. The other tall and slinky man nods in agreement. They both push her back on the outgoing train.

She struggles to push back at them. "You Periwinkle men disgust me." she says.

"You shouldn't talk like that to us." says the tall thin man, "We saved your wrinkled hide, you know. Can't you see that it's too late for that Fuchsia?"

"Anyway, it's late for us too. And we've got to get some sleep before our next shift." says the short stocky man.

The woman glares angrily around her at the other passengers. "What's wrong with y'all?"

The passengers look passively away.

"Your colour fits you both perfectly." she says, peering at the two men in their periwinkle outfits.

-4-

The sentries drag a rebellious Sistina back into the gateway corridor. A holographic sign flashes on a side door:

'PRIVATE: Interrogation Area.'

Bill pushes down a lever on the wall and a door opens.
"There you go, Tim. I give you the pleasure of being first." says the sergeant.
Tim peeks inside the room. "C'mon guys, it stinks in here."
"Your nose won't notice it." replies the sergeant, "Especially since it's going to be up her—"
"Stop it guys," interrupts Tim, "this doesn't feel right."
"I knew it, Sarge." says Rod, "The boy is just a scared little mouse."
"He's just young and stupid." replies Sergeant Bill, "He doesn't know what's what yet. C'mon kid, we'll show you."
Tim's face turns red.
"Aww, look Sarge."
"Yup, he's still just a shy young lad."
"Sarge, he probably doesn't even know if his rod still works."
"I think he knows, Sarge." replies Rod, "He just doesn't have the balls to use it."
"That's a good one." replies the sergeant, laughing. "I don't know what's wrong with these kids nowadays."

"That's what happens when the youngsters get hooked on fantasy pills." says Rod, "They don't realise how good the real thing tastes."

"Is that true, Tim?" says the sergeant.

"I don't know, Sergeant."

The sergeant opens the door wide.

"So kid, are you coming in or what?" replies Rod, smiling at a terrified looking Sistina.

"Last chance." says the sergeant, slowly closing the door.

Tim takes a step back. "I thought you guys were just joking around." he says, stiffly.

"Hey Sarge, I think the kid is a little slow." says Rod.

Tim remains unresponsive.

"Fine, stay outside." says Rod, "But warn us if you see any Imperial Guards coming."

"Yeah," adds the sergeant, "this is one piece of ass that they're not getting before us."

The sergeant shuts the door on Tim's crumpled face.

DOMA — ... and thus Zadok named his sacred city under the dome. Doma's Citizens will hereto be addressed as Domans. Doma shall permanently remain fully translucent and impermeable.

Doma provides a homeostatic environment for its Citizens as its source of geothermal energy in combination with the dome's translucent photosynthetic membrane permits its perpetual sustainability (see EBOLAD Tech Manual: no.1: sec.1: Self Sustaining Structure).

Doma has a subterranean aqueduct system which collects and conserves water. The water is also used to filter the air inside the dome. The water is then treated and conserved for daily usage.

The dome's internal waste residue is also systematically processed in the hydroponics laboratories (see EBOLAD Tech Manual: no.1: sec.3: Hydroponics Sub Center) before it is redistributed into externally connected hydroponics greenhouses. The greenhouse shall be housed on the hillside of Mountdome.

...

Nota Bene: Information on Doma's End of Time locking mechanism may only be accessible with the specific authorization of the Key Keeper.

ECLECTIC BOOKS OF LIFE AND DEATH

PART IV

THE DOMANS

Chapter One

An infant in a grey costume sits on the steps of a headless statue. The statue is among many other items on display in an open area near the coliseum.

The boy sits up and caresses the statue's marbled stola. He waves his hand over the statue's plaque and a holographic image of the head of the statue appears. Its features are that of a round faced woman with a greenish hue.

The boy stares at the holographic head with a barely audible curiosity.

"The reason why my head is missing is because of the pilfering and pillaging that occurred during the Dark Ages." says the holographic head.

The young boy tilts his head to his side.

"Barbarians took my head instead of my entire body because it was less heavy and burdensome to steal away."

A lightning flash suddenly skids over the diaphanous dome.

The young boy looks up and quickly covers his face. A crest of a Yellow ankh within a Yellow circle suddenly appears on his grey costume. He scurries inside a model dome behind him. The small dome seals its door and its internal structure lights up.

"Doma is a marvel of human technological ingenuity." says an incorporeal voice, "It has a diameter of just over 8 klicks with a peak height of 5 klicks. The city of Doma was built by Zarak Zadok the discoverer of the impermeable translucent material that makes up the membrane of the dome."

The little boy shakes his hand.

"Zadok is the man who brought his sacred vision to life as expressed in his Epistle in the EBOLAD — your sacred Eclectic Books of Life and Death."

The boy curls his long hair.

"The city of Doma protects its citizens from all dangerous externalities."

"The scary skies too?" says the boy, pinching his lips.

"That is correct, young lord. Nothing can get in from outside."

The boy sits down with legs crossed and head in hands.

"The center piece of Doma is the Imperial Palace. The Imperial Palace is encircled by three rings of Holy White residences. In addition, a subterranean train allows rapid transit around the circular city."

The little boy points to the coliseum.

"Yes, the coliseum is part of the Imperial Palace. The Imperial Palace includes the Holy White Arena and the Key Keeper's Chamber. The Key Keeper's Chamber became the Sanctum Sanctorum Animarum or the Chamber of Souls after the Holy Wee rose to power. But the Key Keeper's Chamber is the name still used to describe the residence of the Ruler."

"What's the Holy Wee?" whispers the boy.

"The Holy Wee is the governing body of the Holy White Order. The head of the Holy Wee is the Key Keeper."

The boy blinks intermittently at the chamber as a greenish hue suddenly highlights its four connecting columns. The arching columns rise up from the four cardinal sides of the coliseum.

"As shown here the four pillars arching over the Holy White Arena support the Key Keeper's Chamber. The pillars also hold the main entrances to the Imperial Palace."

The boy points at the abode high atop the model coliseum.

"Yes, the Key Keeper's Chamber is the structure high above the Holy White Arena."

The boy remains fixated at the holographic diagram.

"The Key Keeper's Chamber sits above all because the Ruler of the Realm is responsible for all."

The child's eyes beam at the miniaturized chamber.

"The only way up to the Key Keeper's Chamber is through the guarded lifts inside the supporting pillars."

The boy points to the four pillars emerging from the sides of the coliseum.

"Yes, the pillars form the four entry points into the Imperial Palace. And hold the lifts that lead up to the circular hallway of the Key Keeper's Chamber."

"How do you know what I'm thinking?"

"The Virtual Library allows its interactive programs the ability to answer questions based on the analytics of facial recognition."

"Umm..." mumbles the little boy. "Can you guess what I'm thinking now?"

"The Holy Whites are the descendants of the First Whites. The First Whites provided Eternal Salvation to all Holy Whites who worship the Holy White Doctrine."

The boy giggles.

"Salvation is the moment when the Golden TänkaHour ends and the Chosen souls ascend to Nirvia."

"Hmm?" bubbles the child.

"The Golden TänkaHour is the last Conclave to the Ascension. A last Challenge shall take place at that time that will unite all the Chosen for their final journey."

"Conclave?" says the boy.

"Any member of the Holy White Order may be part of the TänkaMatch Conclaves."

A smile rises from the little boy.

"In order to be a combatant in the TänkaMatches you must be part of the Holy White Order."

"Uh?" the boy mumbles.

"To be part of the Holy White Order you must first attain the Age of Ascension."

The boy's brows wrinkle.

"The Age of Ascension is attained when the Chosen enter their second cycle of their lives."

"Am I a Chosen?" says the little boy.

"Yes, but you are still a Grey. When you reach your Age of Ascension you shall become a White."

The boy squishes his face.

"That is because your InsignAnima must first be allowed to record enough data in order to provide a fully distinct persona with a certain level of rational thought."

The little boy pouts.

"It is important to have a minimum age requirement as the responsibilities of the Key Keeper are gravely important."

The boy flickers his fingers on his lips.

"The Key Keeper is the one and only soul responsible for opening the Pearly Gates to Nirvia — the Holy White Order's place of Rebirth."

"The second cycle?" says the boy.

"The first cycle begins after the Chosen's anointed birth. The anointment periods lasts 5 years. The second cycle begins at the age of 16, the third at age 32, and the last cycle begins at age 48."

"And me?"

"Young lord, you are 5 years old today. This means that you are among the oldest in your first cycle."

The boy gives a broad smile as the crest on his grey costume glows Blue.

"The oldest of the last cycle is 48 plus 16 plus 5."

"Uh?" says the little boy.

"The end of age 69 is the limit before being redistributed."

"Redistributed?"

"It is when the bodies end their usefulness and hence are redistributed by Doma's automated Hydroponics Sub-Center."

The little boy's smile turns upside down.

"This is nothing to be feared. Your InsignAnima will join the other dormant souls to be resurrected in Nirvia at the End of Time."

The boy peeks inside his grey costume. The tiny sphere embedded in his chest turns Yellow. His crest now reflects the same colour.

"The colours that emerge from your InsignAnima are a manifestation of the bearer's mind and body."

"Huh?" mutters the boy.

"The InsignAnima is that which represents the anima of the Chosen. It absorbs all thoughts and feelings that make up the soul of each individual."

The boy touches his crest.

"Correct. The spherical implant is the InsignAnima beneath your crest."

The boy puckers his lips.

"It is not a bad thing." replies the disembodied voice, "It is a very good thing."

The boy looks at the glowing sphere underneath is uniform.

"The InsignAnima allows all those in the Holy White Order to ascend to Nirvia."

The boy fidgets around.

"Nirvia holds the Promised Lands as depicted in the Old Age Scriptures of the EBOLAD."

The little boy pulls at his ears.

"Nirvia was designed by Lady Crista. It is the virtual Heaven that awaits the Holy Whites after their Ascension."

The boy gazes at the hologram.

"Nirvia is a place that has almost anything imaginable."

A little smile rises from the little boy.

"When in Nirvia you can live near a beach, a garden, a mountain, a river, or in a modern or ancient city, or many other destinations or livelihoods."

The boy's smile broadens.

"Nirvia waits for all the Holy Whites. That is unless the Key Keeper decides to use the Golden Key."

The boy sourly scrunches his face.

"The Golden Key is the one and only emergency key. It was specifically designed to override the countdown to the End Times in accordance with the Epistle of Zadok. But when the First Whites came into being they usurped the timeline."

"Huh?"

"The First Holy Whites created TänkaWorld thus the New Age Testament was written and the Holy White Order was founded. Doma became the home of the Holy Whites and new timeline was determined for the End Times by the new Order."

"Timeline?" says the boy.

"The new timeline to the End Times was pushed forward from what had been scheduled by Zarak Zadok. This new timeline was technically determined by measuring the vast memory storage of new world of Tänka and its rate of consumption reflected by its TänkaClock."

"Where is the key?" whispers the boy, quizzically.

"The Golden Key is held by the Key Keeper and is partly shaped like an Ankh."

"Ankh?" says the boy.

"The Ankh symbol represents the soul. It is the symbol inside the circle of your TänkaCrest."

The boy looks at his crest.

"The TänkaCrest represents the circle of life and death."

"Can I have a Golden Key too?" says the boy.

"There is only one Golden Key. It is held by the Ruler of the Realm."

The boy squints hard.

"The Ruler achieves his status by winning the yearly Key Keeper's Challenge. The winner of a TänkaMatch is the first combatant whose Avatar captures the Golden TänkaKey."

The boy's eyes widen.

"The Golden TänkaKey is the virtual representation of its physical counterpart that is borne by the Ruler."

The boy gets up and excitedly points at a residence near the coliseum.

"Yes, that is the Fuchsia and Grey residence. The Primary schools and the University are also situated near the Imperial Palace."

"Thank-you." says the little boy.

"You are welcome, young lord." says the disembodied voice.

The boy exits the model dome. The model dome returns to its original translucency.

A silent lightning flash scrapes the cloudy skies above the dome. The boy nervously runs around.

"Hey, what are you doing over there?" bawls out a woman's voice.

A young woman in a fuchsia coloured dress walks over to the boy. The little boy keeps running around the model dome holding his hands over his ears.

The woman catches the boy's arm. "Did you not hear the bell?" she says.

The young boy turns in confusion at the empty exhibits around him.

A virtual banner overhangs the open display area:

'WELCOME TO THE VIRTUAL LIBRARY'

"Is it the storm, Teacher?" says the boy.

The teacher notices the boy's Yellow crest. She softens her grip on the little boy's arm. "Of course not, young lord," she says, "It's the bell signalling your mealtime."

The little boy gazes down at his crest and pouts.

"Why are you sad?"

The little boy pouts.

"I know you like the Virtual Library, but you can't stay here all day."

"I just don't want others to see my colour."

"I see that you're afraid." says the teacher, "What is it that's scaring you, my young lord?"

"I'm afraid of the flashes."

"There's nothing to be afraid of."

"But they are so bright and—"

"My young lord, the lightning will never hurt you in Doma."

The little boy covers his Yellow crest and shyly lowers his head. The teacher bends down to her knee and tenderly caresses his face. "You should never be ashamed of the colours of your TänkaCrest. You should be proud of your colours, because you are one of the Chosen. Your colours honour the sacred Testament of the Holy White Order." She raises his little chin. "Look at your classmates over there."

The little lad raises his head. His classmates stand waiting outside the entrance of the library staring up at the sky. Their crests display different intensity of colours.

"You see," she says. "Everyone feels something different, but yet you're all full of the same primary colours."

"Uh-huh." replies the boy.

"Just don't let fear guide you."

"Uh?" mumbles the boy.

"When something frightens you, you frighten it back."

The boy begins to sneer at the fulminating skies above. His Yellow crest slowly changes to Purple. The teacher smiles and pats him gently on the head.

"That's very good, young lord."

The boy smiles proudly at the teacher and his crest changes to Blue.

The bell rings one more time.

"Would you like to go now, Lord Ramsey?" she says, holding out her hand.

The schoolboy nods and grabs her hand. His Blue crest is reabsorbed into his grey costume and disappears. The teacher gets back up to her feet and accompanies the boy to his classmates.

"Finally!" says Flint, stepping out from behind one of the nearby statues. "Jeez! I thought that kid would never leave. I should have found a better place to spend the night."

He carefully zigzags through the shadows of the library methodically dodging the greenish hues streaming from the varied portholes.

He reaches the base of the palace. A tiny figurine pops up from the palm of his hand. It points him away from the south pillar's entrance. Fling finds himself near a manhole cover. The figurine nods its head. Flint pries open the cover and drops down inside it. He opens his hand again and the minute hologram lights his way forward. A soft droning sound hums around him as he slowly crawls through a vent. He reaches a forked passageway. The little hologram points right. Flint turns right and begins to spiral down another vent where he ends his slide by crashing into a closed hatch.

"Ouch!" he mumbles, rubbing his head.

He places his ear on the hatch and listens closely. The hatch suddenly opens and he continues to spiral down. He stops as he hits the ground.

Ugh!" he mumbles, massaging his shoulders. "What is that smell?" he whispers.

He quickly covers his mouth as his whisper resonates through the cavernous pathways. He glances at his palm and continues to move toward the figurine's indicated direction. He moves quietly through several cavernous pathways.

Suddenly he comes to a halt. His eyes grow big as two large guards in ultramarine uniforms appear a short distance away. Flint quickly ducks under the cover of a large container. He sneaks a peek and sees the guards have not moved from their posts.

"Phew." he murmurs, wiping sweat from his forehead.

A commanding voice emerges from the guards' position.

Flint carefully raises his head again above the container.

"I need you in the Arena." says set. The guards follow Set into the elevator. The elevator door closes leaving a dead silence behind.

Flint checks to confirm that his path is clear before moving toward the elevator. He takes a deep breath and flashes his lit palm over the elevator's door. He pulls a blaster from a hidden slot in his outfit and sets it to its highest level of penetration.

Suddenly a noise from another passageway sends Flint scurrying back behind the container. Two more guards approach. In between them is a young woman in chains. The elevator door opens and they half drag her inside. The elevator door closes.

Flint leans back on the trunk with a furrowed brow. "What was that about?" he murmurs, "My path is supposed to be clear."

TÄNKAVISION (T-Vision*) — … an internal projection technology of TänkaWorld that provides those of the Holy White Order the ability to visualize eorum future life in Nirvia.

2. Thy T-Vision of TänkaWorld shall be activated when thou have attained thy Age of Ascension and thy soul registered in the collective consciousness of the Holy White Order.

3. T-Vision shall enable thy respective physical representation, thy persona, thy Avatar, to manifest itself in Nirvia (see NAT Tech Manual: no.2: sec.1: TänkaVision — Temple Implants).

4. Thy T-Vision shall make possible thy thoughts to select and format thy available spatial allotment in Nirvia wherein…

NEW AGE TESTAMENT

---

* Abbreviations taken from the New Age Testament Tech Manual no.4: Lexicon — Definitions and Abbreviations.

Chapter Two

A middle aged woman in a sapphire dress sits on a stool in front of a long laboratory table. She meticulously rubs a dry cloth inside a wet beaker.

"Logos," she says, "I am relieved to say that we are finally done with anointments. The last day of the last cycle has ended and this laboratory is officially closed."

"It does seem that way," replies Logos, with a roguish smile. "But it nevertheless appears that we have one last baby ready for its anointment."

The woman looks up with a quickly dissolving glower. "We do? I was not made aware of this."

"Yes we do." says Logos, "The baby was delayed up the line."

"Oh? That just will not do. I have closed up shop here and I refuse to test the DNA of another child."

Logos pulls out an empty stool next to her and sits down.

"Sennia, my good friend," he says, softly. "How are you doing?"

Sennia stares at her polished beaker. Her reflection shows dark bags under her eyes. "Oh Logos, I am tired." she says, setting down the beaker. "I just want to finish with these test tubes."

"I understand, my friend."

"I know that hair turns white at some point in one's life, but have you noticed that D-Scientists appear to age faster than the norm?" says Sennia, carefully aligning the clean beaker with other clean ones. "I remember noticing in the middle of my second cycle the first signs of my premature aging. I have noticed that among other Sapphires as well. I have not yet had a chance to test my hypothesis, but I think that it must have something to do with our ECCD implants."

"Oh?"

"I think that as our implants redirect our emotions for an increased analytical rate, we also incur a physical deterioration of our metabolic rate. Hence, I theorize that our premature aging is symptomatic of the ECCD induced suppression."

"Sounds interesting." replies Logos.

She turns and picks at Logos' black hair. "Though, you are something of a black sheep when it comes to my theory." she says, "You are at the beginning of your third cycle and yet you appear asymptomatic of any aging. How do you explain that?"

"Better genes?" replies Logos, smiling.

Sennia remains frigidly impassive. "Logos, are you making a joke?"

"Apparently not." replies Logos.

"Logos, you are a strange Sapphire. Your ability to emulate emotions puzzles me." Sennia squints at Logos' deep black hair. "Maybe we should check your implant."

Logos hesitates for a moment. "My head is fine, my dear. I have done much of the programming on the Virtual Library's facial recognition system, and I guess that I have managed to retain some of its abilities."

"But—"

"In addition, my increased exposure at the University to the student population has allowed me to further study the correlations between their abundant facial expressions and their moods. I find that there is always a certain pattern that develops."

"Your assumption does have some logical merit to it, but—"

"I have found that mimicking emotions is not so difficult when one discovers their patterns. But what I find much more complicated is the formulaic nature of comedy."

"Well." says Sennia, patting Logos on his shoulder. "Whatever is the case, my friend, your brain appears to have retained its fluidity. Mine, on the other hand, feels like it is drying out very quickly." she says, dryly. "I speculate that even mimicking emotions must provide a similar lubricating effect for the brain as real emotions do."

"So, my dear Sennia, what do you think?"

"What are you referring to?"

"I am talking about the last of the White babies."

"I think we should inform the Holy Wee. I think one of their own commissioners could then explain to the embryonic unit of the time lapse problem."

"I am not certain it is a good idea to inform the Holy Whites that the last of their own genetic descendents is to be rejected."

"Hmm…" murmurs Sennia, shoulders drooping. "These Whites can be quite unpredictable at times. I am still capable of remembering this one time when King Osiris—"

"You have better watch yourself, my dear." interrupts Logos, "There are ears everywhere."

Sienna examines the lab. "There is no need to worry here." she replies, "There are no T-Ports in my lab. Unless it is your ears I should be worried about."

"No need to worry about that."

"Does that mean that you no longer have access to the king?"

"I have not had the king's ear in quite awhile now."

"Good!" replies Sienna, "That is a man with a mission. And I am not sure it is a good one."

"I appreciate your warning."

"Do not take my words lightly, Logos. You may have heard his stories but not mine."

Logos moves closer to Sienna. "What stories?"

"I am not sure I should venture in that direction." replies Sienna.

"It is you who opened the path, my friend." Logos tilts his stool closer. "Go on, please."

"Fine, but this must stay between us."

"I would never betray a friend."

"Well, alright then." replies Sienna, quietly. "A cycle or so ago three Sapphires disappeared."

"Oh?"

"These three also thought they had King Osiris' ear."

"Now that you mention it I do remember seeing them on occasion."

"What did you see?"

"Not much." replies Logos, "I just noticed that they seemed to spend an inordinate amount of time in the Key Keeper's Chamber."

"That's right, these scientists worked diligently for the king."

"So, who were they?"

"They were experts in T-Pod technology."

"Interesting." replies Logos, "Did you ever get a chance to speak to them?"

"No, I did not."

"Why not?" asks Logos.

"They were for all intense and purposes incommunicado."

"So, what it is that you think they were up to?"

"I do not know. I just know that the day after the king's first defence of his title they vanished."

"What do you mean vanished?"

"The Imperial Guards said that they had betrayed the king and were supposedly expelled to the Outer Lands."

"What do you mean, 'supposedly'?"

"I found no evidence of such an action. In addition, no one had seen the D-Scientists leave Doma. There were no reports of them passing through Monochromia either. Now how could that be?"

"So what do you think happened to them?"

Sennia picks up a dirty beaker and tries to peer through its obscurity. "There are different stories about that, but I cannot prove any of them. Therefore, I do not know. But it is not difficult to surmise that it is not safe to be in the king's entourage. His intentions are not always clear."

"Sienna, I shall take careful note of your warning."

"Good!" she replies, as she wipes the beaker clean.

"And what of the last White child?" asks Logos.

"Oh." she sighs, "Do as you wish." She opens a small safe beneath the table and hands Logos a small translucent sphere. "I guess there is no reason to go through its genetic verification if this InsignAnima has little chance of becoming part of the Holy White Order."

"We never know." replies Logos, "It will be close, but it may still manage to reach its Age of Ascension in time."

"But if she is left behind because there is no spatial allotment left for her in Nirvia, I would not want to be the one to have to deal with her dejected mind."

"That is a good point, my friend." replies Logos, "But maybe I can observe the child and help to defuse her potential disillusionment when the End of Time comes."

"That does sound like a responsible measure to take as an instructor. Our studies of the quantum leap phenomenon have shown that that which is being observed does have the tendency to have a symbiotic relationship with that that is doing the observing. I would say a sort of shared existential blink. This is of course just an extrapolation from our studies on the potential positive effects of the observer on that which it is observing."

"Sienna, are you trying to tell me that I am a good teacher?"

"Now it is you, Logos, who are doing the extrapolating."

KEY KEEPER — ... in the footsteps of Doma's Key Keepers the bearer of the Golden Key shall hereto Rule the Realm with regards to the new ruling class. The new Key Keepers shall have an uncompromising devotion to the Holy White Order and its Ascension to Nirvia.

2. From this day forth the new Key Keeper must first become the reigning champion of the Key Keeper's Challenge. This T-Match selection process shall continue to provide Key Keepers with highly evolved intellectual capabilities. This shall protect the path to the Ascension (see NAT Tech Manual: no.1: sec.4 — Key Keeper — Intellectual Superiority).

3. The Key Keeper must accept all challenges throughout his or her reign. This will allow the normal evolution of consciousness within the Holy White Order.

4. Thy Key Keeper shall preside and protect thy Holy Whites till all thy dormant and active souls are ready to ascend. They shall also be rewarded an added compensatory spatial allotment in Nirvia for their added responsibilities.

5. Thy Key Keeper shall in addition have the solemn responsibility to oversee and safeguard any and all disseminated information from the Book of Revelations*. This necessary duty is for the successful completion of...

NEW AGE TESTAMENT

* Restricted: Key Keeper's authorization is mandatory

Chapter Three

-1-

A man in a white suit stands motionless in the middle of a shady chamber. The moonlight glowers over him as he stares down through a translucent pane in the marbled floor.

"Your Majesty," says a voice outside the chamber's high door, "we have the Fuchsia prisoner."

"Enter." says the king.

Two guards in ultramarine uniforms enter with a chained Sistina in tow. Her chains grind and rattle along the chamber's marbled floor. The guards deposit Sistina in front of a decadent desk near the front of the chamber. The guards take their posts near the door.

The king continues to gaze down at the arena far beneath the translucent pane. He slowly turns his head toward Sistina. He raises his brow as he walks toward her. His long blond hair falls neatly over the shoulder pads of his white suit.

"Now is that really necessary?" he says, "Are my infamous Imperial Guards afraid of a young woman?"

"Sire?" says the heftier of the two guards.

The king waves his hand and the guards immediately unshackle Sistina. "That's much better." he says, "Sistina, please take a seat."

Sistina looks at the empty space around her.

"Well." he says, eyeing his guards. "What are waiting for? Can't you see she needs somewhere to sit?!"

A guard immediately pushes a chair behind Sistina. Sistina grabs hold of the chair and unsteadily sits down.

"Thank-you, Sire." she moans.

"How is it that a young woman in pain can still look and sound so tempting?" he says, rubbing his chin. "Hmm, I guess it must be most men's fantasy to see a beautiful girl groan under them."

The moonlight brightens behind the king. He scans the floor and finds his podgy shadow. He sticks out his stomach and the shadow fattens. "I, on the other hand, only see my chubby shadow under me."

Sistina remains quietly still as a tear drops from her cheek and lands on her inner thigh. The droplet turns pink as it merges with her bruises.

"My, my, you do appear distressed." says the king, "Guards, get her some water."

The second guard immediately brings Sistina a glass filled with water.

"Thank...you...Sire." she says, her tender voice cracking intermittently.

She eloquently crosses her long streaming legs. The move displaces the king's attention from his own shadow. She quickly tries to pull her torn dress over her exposed legs.

"Guards, leave us!" commands the king.

The guards clack their feet together and step out into the hallway. They forcefully close the chamber door behind them. The lights in the chamber automatically turn on and dim.

The chamber is decadently decorated with a variety of hovering artefacts. The walls of the chamber hold thousands of small translucent spheres.

The king walks over to the see through pane again and peers down. "I love watching the little ants working hard in the arena." he says, chuckling. "I'm the king of the ants!"

Sistina grimaces as she shifts her sitting position.

A Blue crest suddenly glows on the crest of the king's white suit. "How do you like what I've done with the Key Keeper's Lair?" he asks, dancingly. "I know, I know, it's normally called the Key Keeper's Chamber, but I like the sound of Lair much more. I find that it gives my home a sort of dramatic obscurity, don't you think?" He ambles over to the chamber's wall and caresses it. "Touching some of the dormant Holy White souls makes me wonder how the different generations will adapt in Nirvia."

Sistina looks at the ancient artefacts around her. Her hands shake as she takes a sip from the glass.

The king walks over to an encased mummy. He glowers over it for a moment before moving to the golden sarcophagus beside it. He rubs a gold key that is fastened on the sleeve of his immobile arm. "But what I love most of all are my ancient relics." he says, slowly making his way back. He grabs a regal chair behind a flamboyant desk and drags it to Sistina's side.

Sistina straightens her posture.

"Hard to believe that these walls hold most of the memory storage of Nirvia." he says, "And to think, this marvellous Lair was actually designed by a woman." A vein throbs on his forehead. "No matter," he smirks, "everything has its time."

Sistina glances up at the king's Purple crest. Her legs begin to involuntarily shake.

The king lets go of his chair and moves over to his flamboyant desk. He sits on its edge and warmly runs his hand through his hair.

Sistina groans as she struggles to stay upright.

The king's crest dissolves as his fierce gaze turns soft and comforting. "I'm sorry, Sistina. But it appears that some sentinels are obviously still afflicted by sexual desires."

Sistina shakes her head silently as she holds tightly the arms of her chair.

The king quietly looks her over once again. He presses a button on the side of his desk. "But rest assured," he says, "that those who have committed such an unwarranted atrocity shall be dealt with."

The guards walk back inside.

"Did you hear?"

"Yes, Sire."

The king flicks his hand at his guards.

The guards slowly back out of the chamber.

"Good." he says, jollily. "And that's that." He turns his attention back to Sistina. "Now, what I would really like to know is why you've been hiding all this time?" he says with an unbridled ogle, "how silly you've been."

Sistina leans forward as if trying to force out a response. Her mangled dress accidentally reveals her deep cleavage. She leans back on her chair as the king's crest turns Red.

"So, you've managed to disappear for over a year. I've had my best guards trying to find you, but with no explainable luck. Regardless, I'm happy that you're back in my life."

"I'm not here for you, Sire."

"Oh? Who then are you here for?"

Sistina looks away.

"You have nothing to say?" says the king, "Women like you are hard to figure at times." He gets up from his desk simpering. "Our Holy T-Crests shows exactly how we feel — unlike you Monochromes we always show our true colours. And can you not see how much I've missed you?"

"I was unaware of this, Sire."

"You must be clueless then. Oh that's right, a woman like you must drive all Holy Whites to their knees with just a wink and a smile." he says, fingering a pair of shaded glasses on his desk. "Just because our Holy White Doctrine prohibits me from having you that doesn't mean that I don't feel the pains of rejection." The king's Red crest changes to a bright Purple.

"You frighten me, Sire."

"Oh, do I? I see, you think I'm the predator here. But instead it's you who preys on our immaculate souls."

"I don't know what you mean, Sire."

"Don't give me that innocent look. You know very well that it's an eternal Sin for the Holy Whites to have sexual intercourse in our terrestrial existence."

"But why—"

"It's not for you to ponder why," interrupts the king, "But I will nevertheless explain as there's little that shall escape here tonight."

Sistina's face suddenly pales.

"Some of the first inhabitants of the dome became obsessed by the technological possibilities of actually recording one's soul before the End Times. And about one and half centuries later they did. Lady Crista became the first successful child to have survived the anointment. Her spherical implant that we know today as our InsignAnima was successful in recording her soul. This new generation became known as the First Whites. This was at a time when the first signs of degradation forewarned in the Epistle of Zadok began to take hold in the Doman Citizenry. This coincided with the predetermined End Times scheduled by Zadok and his Dome. But that's when Lady Crista usurped the scheduled apocalyptic event by introducing her New Age Testament. The Holy White Order was then born and a new countdown to the End Times had begun."

"Sire, why are telling me all this?"

"Thereafter", continues unabatedly the king, "no new babies were to be reproduced naturally in order to lessen the corrosion in the original genetic pool. Those who refused to follow the New Age Testament were expelled outside Mountdome's protective walls to join the rest of the drifters. And those who were deemed less problematic were kept within the walls. They were also provided hierarchical positions based on their colourful aptitudes. We call them the Monochromes from Monochromia — that's you, my dear." An eerie smile rises from the king's lips. "And after that one thing led to another and here we find ourselves on this beautiful night. Interesting, no?"

Sistina shrugs her shoulders. "Sire, I do not—"

"You may not think them wise," interjects the king, "but the Domans were descendants of the cream of the crop of the human race." adds the king, "A crop of believers who dedicated their lives toward the fulfillment of Zadok's vision. They committed their abundant resources to provide the means for Zadok to build his dome."

Sistina winces as she shifts in her seat.

"These well to do people drafted the best scientists as well," continues the king, dispassionately. "And as time would have it someone finally realized that virtual immortality was possible and the End would be a much different matter. It took the birth of the First Holy White to show the believers in the EBOLAD that its words were purely biblical in nature, and that their abstract Heaven was meant to be one of a virtual kind." The king rubs his hand against a small sphere embedded in the wall. "And the essence of her soul lies dormant here waiting to rise and lead in the next plane of existence. And so it would seem."

"Seem, Sire?"

"Imagine, we're just one cycle away from a place in Eden."

"Hmm..." mutters Sistina.

The king gets up from his desk and pours himself a drink. "And such is the genius of our First Whites and their faithful descendants." His crest turns Blue as he gulps down his short drink. "I have held my post as Key Keeper for longer than any other before me, and I shall continue to do so till the T-Clock strikes Zero. No one will stop us from cheating death."

"But Sire, death has its purpose and—"

"Right, death does have its purpose. And I find it comforting that it can be controlled." he adds, grinning. "For instance, I control not only mine but yours as well."

Sistina grabs on to her shaking legs. "Sire, you don't understand—"

"Yes, yes," interrupts the king, "But I do understand. And yet I don't blame all your missteps solely on you. After all, you're but a Fuchsia. I admit a stunningly captivating one, but nevertheless still just a Fuchsia." he adds, with a sour smile. "It's hard to believe that some combination of Outers created such perfection. But yet here you are."

Sistina shuffles uncomfortably in her seat.

The king gawks for a few long seconds at her. "So, as I was saying, I don't really blame you for your natural disruptive nature. It's not your fault that you were born a woman."

Sistina sadly shakes her head.

"You may disagree, but that's the reality of it. Unlike us men, you women have a vacancy that needs to be continuously replenished. Instead we males are external creatures. You can say that what pleasures us is filling holes, but what truly drives us is a hole that's uneasily breached."

The moonlight disappears into the clouds. The lights in the chamber brighten.

The king slowly pulls back his long hair. His blue eyes stare back at the little spheres incorporated in the walls. "After all," he continues, "women are but a jumble of irrational emotions. That's probably why women are such terrible T-Matches combatants."

"Sire, I don't think—"

"We men instead know exactly what we want." interrupts the king, "Yet your own jumbled thoughts can confusingly feel both attracted and repelled by the male genital appendage." The king struts around the room chuckling. "I declare that most women have no idea what they really want."

"I don't think—"

"But despite my reservations," the king interrupts again, "I should still thank-you, Sistina. Because my inability to breach your attention has helped my ambition to flourish and grow into the untouchable king you see in front of you this night."

"Huh." mumbles Sistina.

The king glowers at the dormant spheres. His crest glows vividly Green. "And to think that a woman could have the most influence in Nirvia upon our Ascension is something that disgusts every part of my soul. Nevertheless, I would never have made it this far without the unfulfilled cravings you've placed in me."

"I don't know what to say, Sire. But I'm truly sorry."

The king fists his hand. "Sorry you say. Why are you sorry?"

"Sire, I'm sorry for being part of that which has enticed such rampant ambition within you."

"How sorry are you?"

"Sire?" replies Sistina, fretfully.

The king's crest turns Red as he moves in behind Sistina. "Yes, I know." he says, placing his hand on her shoulder. "We Whites are prohibited by the Holy White Doctrine to have carnal relationships, but I doubt you'll have time to bear my fruit."

Sistina jolts her chair away from the king. "No Sire!"

The king softly slaps her atop the head. "No, Sire?" he says, "Where was this pureness when you seduced another?!"

Sistina's eyes widen.

"What? You didn't think I knew? Why do you think you've been registered as a fugitive?"

"Sire, I didn't think it a crime."

"You know very well that it was a crime." he says, his Red crest changes to Green. "You just preferred to commit it with another."

"I didn't commit a crime, Sire."

"You seduced and hence perverted a Holy White."

"I didn't pervert anyone, Sire."

"But you do admit having seduced a Holy White."

Sistina does not move or say a word.

"And in so doing," continues the king, "you allowed him to break our Doctrine's most sacred of laws!"

"Sire, I will not confess to something that's not a sin."

The king's crest changes to a solid Purple. "It may not be a sin for you Monochromes, but it is for us — the Chosen. So stop your blasphemous commentary."

Sistina holds her head high. "Physical love is part of a normal expression. You must know this, Sire — don't you?"

"What do you know of what I know?" he replies, lowering his brow.

"Sire, I know of the real Truth spoken in your scriptures."

"You can't know that?!" he replies, glowering at the sarcophagus behind him. "The Book of Revelations is solely for the eyes of the Key Keeper — ME!"

"You can keep your little worldly secrets, Sire. I speak of something much more vital. I speak of a love that is beyond our petty selves. And that's something you sadly know little about."

The king slams his fist down on his desk. "That's enough! How dare you speak to me like this?! Have you lost your senses woman?!"

"Sire, I speak of love that only Truth can bring."

"Oh, I see." gurgles the king, his crest slowly returns to its neutral translucency. "Then I take it you speak of the silliness of an existential Truth."

"There's nothing silly about the Truth, Sire. For it's the way into the light of enlightenment."

The king waves his hand over his desk and a time clock momentarily appears. "Look at us," he says, nonchalantly. "We're behaving like two old lovers. How stereotypical we must sound — the story of a bad man wanting the love of a good woman, etcetera."

"Osiris, you've changed." says Sistina, softly. "There was a time that your mind—"

"I've changed?" interjects the king, "Life has a tendency to that. Sometimes life trips us up and we stumble and fall. Then sometimes when you get back up you're not the same anymore. Because you realize that you're all alone in this miserable world."

"That's a very dark sentiment, Sire."

"I think there's great power in embracing that sentiment."

"What do you mean, Sire?"

"I've accepted that I am that darkness."

"That's a sad thing to hear, Sire."

"Is it?"

"Yes."

"But I don't feel sad at all."

"That's what scares me."

"Hmm...do I really scare you?"

"Yes, Sire."

"Maybe I wouldn't be so scary if you had filled my heart with your love." he adds, tauntingly. "Did you ever consider that you made me the repulsive man you think I am?"

"Sire, I never—"

The king rubs his immobile arm. "Or is your love not a fate reserved for a cripple?"

"Sire, your physical condition is not the question here. It's the belief that your heart needed to be filled by another's love that is. It's this quintessential narcissistic narrative that the human consciousness continues to erroneously espouse."

"Be careful what you say, woman."

"Sire, you think love is something someone gives you. But the love I speak of is something much more ineffable than that. This is something difficult for your mind to grasp as it would mean that you would have to let go of your ingrained colours."

The king begins to pace back and forth. "It's been a long time since I've heard such didactic spiritual meanderings. I've always found them wonderfully insignificant, unlike the package they came in. But I'd like to thank-you for refreshing my mind of that. I've just realized how much I've moved past all that jargon."

"You're sadly mistaken, Sire."

"I'm warning you..."

"Sire, just because you know not of what I speak, that does not mean there's no Truth in what I say."

"Alright, I'll play." he says, pacing around Sistina. "Love... what is love? Love, my lovely, is just another detrimental by-product of a deluded mind — that's what it is. Sistina, you speak of love as if it were a beautiful dream. But even an insomniac like me knows that dreams are but illusions of the mind. One image deluding itself with that of another's because it feels a certain reflective resonance — it's all rubbish!"

Sistina tries to move her chair but the king pushes his leg against her.

"Some talk about the act of falling in love." He continues, placing his hand on her face. "Interesting expression it is 'to fall in love', don't you think? It's like an angelic thought which 'falls' from the heavens above. And since you seem to care so much about the Truth, I'll tell you the Truth of Love." he says, flippantly. "Love is but a biochemical reaction between two lonely souls looking to escape their mundane lives."

Sistina shakes his hand off her face.

"But I'm sure you know little of this as beauty such as yours is rarely left alone."

Sistina grimaces as she straightens herself on the chair. "Sire, being alone and being lonely are not at all the same thing. You speak of the illusion of romance from the point of view of a disgruntled man. What I speak of is a love that is not part of consciousness and—"

The king presses his finger over Sistina's lips. "Shush-shush, my lovely," he interposes, his crest glows Green. "I remember the first time I saw you. You were in the company of one of my top D-Scientists. I remember that moment because I found it curious that a beautiful young Fuchsia could take such an interest in an emotionally dry Sapphire. Although, I admit that he was quite an attractive fellow, wasn't he?"

"He was just a friend, Sire."

"Oh, was he? Well then, maybe I shouldn't have dismissed him so readily from my personal entourage." continues the king, "Maybe I should have asked him how to be your so called friend as well. Maybe then I could stop thinking of you. Even my T-Vision could not help me escape the fire of my thoughts. And no amount of self flagellation could stop the tortuously delightful dreams I had of you. Just the right look from you could have—" the king interrupts himself, "But your eyes were obviously aimed elsewhere, weren't they? I thought at first it was that fetching Sapphire, but I slowly realized that your eyes aimed much higher."

"With all due respect, Sire" says Sistina, placing her shaking hand on her leg. "My aim is not at all what you may think."

"You know not what I think, my lovely girl. But I do know what other Whites think. And I've had to council quite a few because of you."

"Council, Sire? What do you mean?"

"Umm, that is none of your business." he replies, grabbing hard her leg.

"Sire, you're hurting me."

"Oh, I'm sorry." he says, loosening his grip. "I realized long ago that this life was empty for me. That's why all my efforts have gone toward my afterlife. The Ascension draws ever closer and that world of infinite happiness shall provide all the satisfaction I shall ever need. I will soon have accumulated so much space in Nirvia that I shall have all that one would ever desire in any eternal life." His lubricious hand begins to slowly drift up Sistina's leg.

"Sire, what are you doing?"

"Though," he adds, his crest glows solidly Red. "There's one thing that I would like to taste in this life before moving on to the next."

Sistina stumbles out of her chair and falls to the floor. She stares back up at the king. "I see, Sire." she says, pulling the chair closer to her. "For you happiness is all about fulfilling your desires. Not having it in this life, you believe that it waits for you in another. Right, Sire? But your Nirvia was founded on the conceited colours of your T-Crest. And where you may find a sense of eternal self-fulfillment you shall nevertheless remain prisoner to that which you are fulfilling."

"There you go again with your exhaustive gibberish."

Sistina gazes up through the chamber's skylight. The moon has been joined by a twinkling star. She staggers back up to her chair. "Sire," she says, softly. "What I speak of is neither part of a perceived deterministic view of life, nor one that is part of a perceived choice. Both are parts of the duality of our limited perceptions. And neither is part of that which is limitless."

The king strolls around Sistina while gazing impassively at his fingernails. "My dear, I see that you haven't lost any of your illusory skills. You can still make even the most meaningless tautologies sound profound."

Sistina strains to straighten herself on the chair. "Sadly, Sire, the only illusion here is that built on your dogmatic beliefs. And all organized beliefs are cults that deter from the Truth."

"You mean like you Monochromes," replies the king, "You yourselves believe in the literal meaning of the EBOLAD, and not their true interpretations as defined in our New Age Testament. You Monochromes actually believe that Heaven is an imaginary place that God has created for you among the stars. But yet are unwilling to believe that Nirvia is the true Heaven of which the EBOLAD spoke of?!"

The king walks toward his desk and waves his hand. A small virtual image appears and just as quickly disappears.

"Zadok, our Patron Saint," he continues, "foretold of the decline of the human race in his Epistle. And he was first ridiculed as being a modern day Noah. But with time his predictions of the planet's inability to further sustain human life began to swing the opinions of those that really mattered. And those who heard his calling came down from their ivory towers to profess their devotion to him. They proceeded in expropriating the hill and its surrounding lands and help raise the funds that necessitated the construction of our great city under the dome. Zadok brought us the tools to survive the physical world. But it was the First Whites who brought us the way to immortality. What have your stagnated beliefs gotten you — a temple filled with candles and foolish dreams."

"You think you know me, Sire. But you don't! All you have ever known was the false image that you created of me."

The king mulls around his desk. His crest glows Orange as he greedily grins at Sistina.

"I hate to disappoint you, my lovely girl, but I really don't care anymore about who you think you are, or what you think." he replies, his tone turns venomously dark. "The only truth I care about now is my own, and that is that Nirvia will help me cheat death."

"Ah! That's it, isn't it?" inserts Sistina, "It's always been about you and your own fear of death."

"What's wrong with that?"

"Sire, facing death allows for the necessary questions to arise about life. Understanding the profound meaning of death is the intervention that irrational beliefs need. Don't let fear—"

"Don't underestimate fear," interrupts the king, "it's a great motivator."

"Yes it can be, Sire, but the right action rarely comes from fear. But it always does come from the love I speak of."

"You make it sound illogical to avoid death, but believe me when I say that you too will fear death when it calls."

Sistina returns a tearful stare. "Sire, what I speak to you about is the dire state of the human condition. The Truth is that without confronting the significance of death there can be no true understanding of love. And without this understanding life is meaningless."

"You and that love thing." says the king, spreading his arms. "What's wrong with you? Your verbiage reminds me of that Sapphire friend of yours. No wonder you two got along so well." The king stares blankly into space while caressing his chin. "Logos used to be as provocatively erudite about existential matters as you are. And just as much of a pain in the ass as well."

The king sits leisurely back down on his desk. He callously watches Sistina wavering in her chair. "Or maybe the real reason you were friends with Logos was to get closer to power."

"Sire?" replies Sistina.

"Now that makes lots of sense," states the king, "that would certainly make it easier for you to manoeuvre yourself closer to your ultimate goal."

"I don't understand, Sire?"

"Yes, that would explain how you were able to hook yourself such a predominant White."

"How do you mean, Sire?"

"Who knows what capricious ways run in and out of a woman's mind, but the fact is that you attained you objective."

"I don't understand, Sire."

"You wanted to have easier access around Doma, and you did. You wanted to get yourself a Holy White, and you did."

"But—"

"Don't get me wrong, because I think it was a surprisingly enterprising of you to first acquire a Sapphire friend."

"I did not acquire anyone."

"That must have been it." injects the king, shaking his head. "But I can't blame a man, even one with reduced emotional capacities, to for fall prey to your charm. But I will blame the Holy White who should have known better." The king's tone turns oddly compliant as he gazes at one of his encased relics. "Though, I wonder what Holy White could resist your sensuality trap. Sistina, you're like a modern day Cleopatra. I have a feeling that Cleopatra also used words like Love and Truth to hypnotize and enslave her lovers."

"Sire, I don't think you've listened to anything I've said."

The king runs his hand over his desk again. A small virtual image reappears. He glowers impatiently at it before slapping it away. He turns toward a distressed looking Sistina. "Sorry, busy day." he says, "Anyway, if I remember correctly, it didn't end particularly well for Cleopatra either. I believe she killed herself with the aid of a venomous snake. I don't know about you, but that sounds to me rather like a biblical end? I wonder if that snake spoke to her as well."

"Sire, what are you saying?"

The king appears to stall his thoughts for a moment. "Umm, I was just thinking about how Cleopatra died. I mean that as a Pharaoh she must have really believed that she was just moving on to her next life. But unless she had a space reserved in Nirvia she was sadly mistaken."

The king moves over to a mummified body hovering near a sarcophagus. "Her actual body is right there." he says, proudly. His crest turns a vivid Blue. "But I still prefer her marbled bust. It's less gruesome of a depiction I think. As for her soul, it's certainly gone into the empty void. But I'm glad she left me her sarcophagus. And you, my lovely, what do you think of entering the abyss of death?"

Sistina gets up from her chair and instinctively backs away. "Death, Sire?"

"Yes."

"Physical death is something I fear, but not the Truth that it carries within it's meaning."

"Oh?"

"Sire, I have looked into the void."

"Oh, and what did you see?"

"Salvation." replies Sistina.

"Salvation coming from death's void is the most ridiculous thing I've heard this night." he smirks, "And that's saying a lot."

"Sire, you believe that by not facing death you shall save yourself. But I put it to you that all you're doing is saving your colourful self from the profound Truth that the question of finality brings." says Sistina, her voice grows softer. "Without which, Sire, you shall never know that which is truly eternal."

"And here I was before you came along thinking that avoiding death was a good way to be saved."

"You can ridicule what I say, Sire, but the fact is that the true key to enlightenment lies in death's hand."

The king furrows his brow and caresses his gold key. "Are you calling me the Grim Reaper?"

"Sire, please, for just one moment try to listen without judgement." Sistina's tone turns into a heavy whisper. "Sire, in all that which is sacred there's one profound Truth that cannot be denied when confronting death."

A deadly silence fills the chamber.

"Funny thing about Truths," replies the king, "Everyone's got one — just like secrets, right?" he snarls, his crest turns a bright Purple.

Sistina cautiously backs up to the chamber's door. Her deep penetrating eyes fill with dread. She clutches her hands tightly. "Sire, the Truth I speak of is NOT a secret." she argues, "A simple glimpse of it would free your vision from the fiend that blocks its view."

The king takes a quick unemotional glance at the sarcophagus behind him. He turns and gazes back at Sistina. "What do you know about what I see? I carry the greatest honour and the heaviest burden that has ever been bestowed upon any human." he says, moving behind his desk. "We, the Chosen, are all that stand in the way of humanity's preordained extinction. And I alone hold the key to the survival of our consciousness." He softly pats the gold key on his sleeve. "I and I alone have the final responsibility to protect the Ascension for all the Holy White souls — those of today and those who came before. So what do you really know of my faithful responsibilities?"

"Sire, you and the rest of the Whites can escape death all you want, but without having to face the colourless eventuality of death you shall forever be inescapably trapped in the static mind of your primitive colours."

"What are you trying to tell me?"

"Oh what's the use, Sire? You may be hearing me, but your beliefs are preventing you from listening."

An image pops up on the king's desk. "No-No, go on." he insists as he rummages through his desk drawer, "You're saying that my beliefs cloud my judgement and—"

"No!" interjects Sistina, "What I'm saying is that you ARE your beliefs!"

The king stops his movements and stares back at Sistina. "Hold on a second." he says, "So, let me see if I've got this straight. If you would succeed in convincing me to change my beliefs you'd also change who I am. That would mean that if you want to destroy me you just have to destroy my beliefs — pretty smart. I guess that's why you're introducing all these doubts in our collective. Wow! You're more dangerous than I thought. Maybe I should just take my own life, right here, right now. Would that fulfill your objective?" he adds, laughingly. "Because I must admit that after listening to all your existentialist crap I'm tempted to do just that."

"Oh, Sire, you've become so hopelessly blinded by that which you hold so dear."

"Oh how much longer do I have to listen to this?"

"Sire, I feel my time is short — please listen to me. The voice inside you has become so largely dominant that it's now too big to pass through the eye of the needle of enlightenment. You need to find the neutrality of investigative thought so that you may see the path to the profound significance of the finality of death. It's this Truth that shall free you."

"The truth, my dear, is that you have used up all your time. And nothing will save you here tonight."

"Osiris, you have me all wrong. I'm not here to be saved," replies Sistina, "I'm here to try to save you!"

"Save me?" says the king, mockingly.

"Yes, Sire. I'm trying to save you all from yourselves."

There are loud ricocheting shots emerging in the hallway. Sistina pulls back away from the door. A short silence follows. The door is pushed open. Flint rushes in and comes face to face with Sistina.

"It's about time!" says the king.

-3-

"What took you so long?" asks the king, dourly. "I was really getting fed up of this inanely frustrating conversation."

Flint pushes Sistina aside and glares all around the relics in the chamber. "Umm, what the fuck!?" he says.

"What are you looking for dummy — I'm right here." says the king.

Flint shakes his head and targets the king. He raises his weapon and a flash suddenly blinds his view. Flint's arm drops to his side and his weapon falls to the floor. He looks down at the large hole in his chest and his eyes crack open. He lifts his head and sees the king holding a smile on his face and a smouldering blaster in his hand. Flint's eyes droop as his legs bend beneath him. He glances at Sistina before his face smashes hard against the floor.

Sistina runs over and kneels next to Flint's body. "Sire, what have you done?"

The king points his blaster toward Sistina. "Move away from the intruder."

Sistina slowly backs away. The king closes in and gives a swift kick to Flint's head. "Idiot!" he says. He puts his weapon down and picks up Flint's blaster. "You expected that I wouldn't be ready for such a foolish attempt on my life?!"

"Sire, what's going on?"

"Umm," mumbles the king, turning his attention to Sistina. "And now, my lovely girl, it's your turn." He points Flint's weapon at her. "When I heard that you were found I knew that that was destiny whispering to me. And it said that death wants a word with you."

"No, Sire."

"It's become obvious to me that you're dangerous." he says, calmly. "You're a hedonistic vixen that has been put here to test our Faith in the Holy White Doctrine. And although I've passed, you've nevertheless succeeded in using your virginal condition to seduce another of my kind."

"Please hear me out Sire."

"Enough!" he replies, "There's only one truth I'm interested in now. I have no intentions of having a Brutus in my midst. I want you to confirm for me the name of the White you have seduced. Only then may I change my mind and set you free."

The king watches a suddenly quieted Sistina.

"Answer me!" he cries.

"Sire, I'm already free." replies Sistina, assertively. "As for you, Sire, there may come a day when you will not be able to escape Truth's grasp."

The king's crest glows vividly Green. "The penalty for a Monochrome corrupting a White is uncompromisingly severe. I suggest you tell me his name."

A large tear drips down to Sistina's closed lips.

"Oh well, it's probably best you don't answer. I can't have you remain in our midst anyhow. We have an old saying that warns of women like you. It says that if you cannot trust yourself with another, then you cannot trust the other."

Sistina's gaze remains focused on Flint's dead body. "I have a thought for you as well, Sire." she retorts, vehemently. "Without the Truth there is no axiom that shall save you."

The king turns Flint's weapon toward a resigned looking Sistina. "Please stand over there." he says.

Sistina moves a few steps to her right. A blast suddenly tears a hole through her chest. She stumbles to the floor. Blood gushes out of her.

Sistina turns to stare pitifully back at the king. "You're such a lost child." she moans, blood spews from her mouth. Her convulsing gulps sent blood all around her.

The king pulls back from Sistina's body in disgust. "Yuck!" he says. His eyes wonder vacantly for a moment and his Green crest slowly dissipates into his suit.

-4-

The king roams around the chamber stopping near Flint's body. "I wonder why I feel nothing at all when something ugly dies." he says as he fires another shot. This time the laser travels over Sistina's prone body and hits the wall behind her. The king replaces the blaster back in Flint's hand and picks up his own. "But yet why do it feel sad when something beautiful dies." he adds as he steps around Sistina's body. He nears the wall and examines the broken sphere in it. His crest turns a vibrant Blue. A pedantic smirk rises from his lips. "Hmm... that's not a bad shot." he says, twirling around. "Not bad at all."

He smugly walks back to his desk. He places his own blaster down and then calls out for his guards. He listens carefully for a response. There is no sign of any movement coming from the hallway. He grabs a small globe on his desk and an alarm bell rings out. He opens the bottom drawer of and a multitude of coloured holographic buttons appear. He groans and presses down twice on the ultramarine coloured button and once on that of a fuchsia colour. He retrieves his regal chair and flops down on it. He puts his feet up on his desk and waits.

He lowers his brow at Sistina. "What is that blood drenched fuchsia colour — auburn? I should check out if that colour is available for my girls in Nirvia." he says, dispassionately scratching his head. "Oh, my dear departed, you should have been a White. I think you would have been the most enticing of all the Soulful Avatars. My girls are obedient little programs, but are somewhat stilted. When I look into their eyes I know there's no one inside. Don't get me wrong, it's not their fault." he continues, "Their limited programming can never match the recorded intricacies of a human mind and body. I sometimes wonder what I myself will be like after thousands of years of living in Nirvia without my physical frailties and without the constant persecution of death." he adds with a smirk, "Maybe it'll make me the type of man that would finally be worthy of a woman like you."

The alarm bell keeps ringing throughout the palace.

The king looks over the spheres on the walls. "But hopefully in one of these dormant InsignAnimas there's a soul that will have your looks and spunky spirit, because I think I'll miss the drive of an unquenched hunger."

There are noises coming from the arena beneath his feet.

"But I'm disappointed in you. Did you actually think that you would be safe in the arms of the chancellor?"

Dark clouds slowly block the moonlight.

"And thanks to the misconceived plans of my doubters I've managed to make available even more space for me to conquer in Nirvia." he says as he inspects his fingernails, "Eventually I will reign in Heaven as I have done on Earth."

At that very moment a huge flash of lightning arcs over the entire dome.

The king gazes up at the light show. "Oh, what a glorious day tomorrow will be. I know that this fortuitous night is one of those little gifts that only Fate can give the Faithful. The dominos have begun to fall as expected, thank-you."

Sistina's eyelids quietly open. She pulls one of her hands over the other. She etches a sanguine sign on her left palm before expulsing a long exhaustive breath.

The lightning strikes dwindle. The king returns his gape to the motionless body of Sistina. "Wow! I knew women bled, but look at what you've done to my floor. What dummy, couldn't they have given that idiotic assassin a more modern blaster?" he grumbles. "The old ones had no cauterizing technology."

Scrambling sounds suddenly rise in the hallway. "What the Hell!" a voice rings out, "Quickly! Check on the king!"

The sounds of scurrying boots approach the king's chamber. The king puts his feet down. He slaps himself and quietly crows, "And here shall fall the rest of the dumminos."

Chapter Four

A broad shouldered man with long brown hair and deep brown eyes steps out of an elevator. He circles the hallway amid a flurry of incoming and outgoing guards. He reaches the door to the Key Keeper's Chamber where two guards lay dead. He carefully assesses the carnage and enters. Two guards stand at attention inside. The king sits with his head down on his desk with the commander at his side.

The brawny man scans the room. He spots the peculiarly silent king. "Sire, are you alright?"

The king rubs his watery eyes and looks up. "Oh, Chancellor, it was just horrible!"

The chancellor glares at the two dead bodies lying on the floor. One has coagulated blood puddles around it, while the other is bone dry. "Sire, what happened here?" he says, his voice is as deep as is his gaze.

The king begins to breathe erratically. He fights to pick himself up from his chair. "Chancellor Horus, I just don't know. That man over there appeared out of nowhere, and then tried to shoot me. But..."

"Yes Sire, but what?"

The king places his hand over his mouth and points to Sistina's body. The chancellor kneels next to her body and turns her face toward his. His facial features suddenly harden at the vision. The crest on his white suit turns a deep Purple. His protruding forehead deepens with the darkness of his gaze.

"I was having a deeply interesting conversation with this lost Fuchsia." says the king, "Then I heard a rumbling noise outside. And without warning this vial intruder entered my Lair and pointed his weapon at me. But," he says, trembling. "This beautiful Fuchsia jumped in the way, and, and..." finally exclaims the king, snivelling. "He murdered her!"

The chancellor stares deeply at the king. The king's crest turns a tepid Yellow.

"This woman was brought to me as a fugitive, but leaves here as a real heroine." says the king, wiping his nose. "She spoke to me about her Truth and Love. She even confessed to me the errors of her ways. And I was ready to forgive her indiscretions towards our own vows. Because she showed me how she was so full of...lovely thoughts."

"Was she, Sire?"

"Yes, Chancellor, she was. She told me about how her love was unconditional and, in an uncanny foreboding moment, she also said that her fate was to save me... and then... she actually did." The king wipes the slick tears away from his eyes. "Forgive me, Chancellor, I am not myself."

"Take a deep breath, Sire." says the chancellor.

The king takes a deep breath, and continues, "If it were not for her selfless act I would not have had the time to take out my blaster and..." He chokes up and points to Flint's body. "And expedite that horrid soul to oblivion."

The chamber is uncomfortably silent as the king faintly sits back down on his regal chair.

The chancellor turns a befuddled gaze at the passively looking commander. "Commander Set!" blurts the chancellor.

Set is shaken by the chancellor's call. "Yes, Chancellor." he replies.

"What are you doing just standing there?"

"Excuse me?" replies Set.

"Who is that Iris?"

Set limps over to Flint's body. "Umm?" he mumbles.

The chancellor springs from Sistina's side and walks over to Set. He glowers over Flint's body while ferociously rubbing Sistina's blood off his hands.

Set makes a concerted effort to tilt his Yellow glowing crest away from the chancellor's line of sight. He bends over Flint's body and pats him down.

"I'm not sure, Chancellor." replies Set, "There's nothing on his person that identifies him."

"Commander Set, maybe you should turn the intruder around first and look at his face before you complete your answer."

Set nervously turns over Flint's body.

"Do you see?" asks the chancellor.

Set stares blankly down at Flint's face. "Umm, I'm not sure what you mean, Chancellor?"

"Look closely at him." says the chancellor, "He's obviously not a Monochrome."

Set feints an intense look at Flint's body.

The facial expression of the chancellor turns grave as he vehemently stares at the obtuse looking Set. "Commander, you're being deliberately dense — why?"

Set's brow fills with perspiration. He glances over at the king. "I'm sorry Chancellor, but I don't know what to say."

"Commander, where's Lieutenant Kiya?" asks the chancellor.

"She's on the wall behind you, Chancellor." replies Set, sadly.

"Hmm," interjects the king, "so that's the InsignAnima that was unceremoniously immortalized here today?"

"Yes, Sire." replies Set.

"How did she die?"

"She died in the line of duty, Chancellor."

"And what happened to the Fuchsia woman over here?" asks the chancellor, his teeth visibly grinding. "Her thighs are deeply bruised. That certainly did not come from the blaster."

"I don't know, Chancellor. I—"

"It appears the practice of sexual abuse is still occurring among some of the sentries." interrupts the king.

"Is that true, Commander?" says the chancellor, hard.

"I'm sorry, Chancellor, I was not aware of this." replies Set, nervously. "After what I witnessed I had thought that you had put an end to this dishonourable practise within our military."

"I had thought so as well." says the chancellor.

"What did you witness, Commander?" inquires the king.

Set turns to the chancellor. The chancellor permissively nods back.

"Sire," explains Set, "it happened about a cycle ago. A Pink was being held in a dungeon for some of the guards' amusement."

The king bends his ear. "Go on."

"Yes, Sire," replies Set, dutifully. "Chancellor Horus, who was our commander at the time, found out. And after personally helping the young woman out of her dark hole, he took the three guards into the dungeon and subjected them one by one to the Black Box." Set's crest turns Yellow as his voice begins to crack. "Sire, I'll never forget the empty stares those guards had after coming out of the Black Box — like semiconscious vegetables."

"Oh?" says the king, rubbing his chin.

"What is authority without accountability?" injects the chancellor, with an alarming calmness.

Perspiration begins to leak down from Set's sideburns. His Yellow crest glows brighter. "Sir, I don't know what you mean." says Set, glancing over at the steely eyed chancellor.

"It was a rhetorical question, Commander." says the chancellor, "You're obviously afraid, why?"

"It's just the thought of the Black Box, Chancellor."

The chancellor gives Sistina another protracted look before his gaze fixates at the perturbed commander. He signals the two guards at the door to approach. "Commander, I want you to follow the guards to the dungeon for further questioning."

"The dungeon?!" replies Set, disbelievingly. "No! Please! I implore you, Chancellor — Not the Black Box!"

The two guards approach Set.

"Do what the chancellor commands, Commander Set." interjects the king.

Set precipitously whisks out a shiny ampoule from his garment. He breaks it open and quickly swallows its liquid content. "My word is my oath, my oath is my life." he sobs, "I claim Ascension!"

Set immediately begins to gasp for air. He strains feebly to whisper, "Kiya, my love, we'll be together soon." His face whitens as he slowly falls to his knees and then to his back. His pupils dilate and roll up and out of sight. His empty gaze stares mortally outward.

The king points to the stunned guards. "You — come here!" he says, pointing to the more agile looking of the two.

The guard moves weightily over to the king. He removes his ultramarine helmet and places it to his side. His short brown hair sits flat and wet on his head. He tries hard to disregard the body of his fallen commander.

"Sire?" he says, fretfully.

"Do YOU fear the Black Box?"

The guard shivers as if the question crawled over his skin. "Uh-huh." he admits, with a steady composure. "Yes, Sire."

The king slaps his hand on his desk with a skulking laugh. "I like it!" he says, "A good honest answer. What's your name, soldier?"

"My name is Noa, Your Majesty."

"I like the name too." replies the king, "Noa, I appoint you the new lieutenant."

The guard bows his head. "Forgive me, Sire, but I'm just a simple Ultramarine." he says, "I'm not a Holy White."

"That's alright." replies the king, "The way Holy Whites have failed me lately I would prefer having a Monochrome as a Lieutenant. After all, a simple unquestioning mind makes for the best of soldiers."

"Lieutenant Noa," interjects the chancellor, coldly. "Take the body of what was your commander out of here."

"Yes, my lord chancellor — right away!"

"And destroy his InsignAnima." inserts the king.

"Your Majesty?" replies the guard, baffled.

The chancellor stares back at the king. "Sire, that's not our way." he says.

"But it is my way!"

"Sire, the former commander claimed his last right as a member of the Holy White Order."

The king points to the contorted body of Set. "This Holy White has, in not so many words, intimated his betrayal to the Realm. There's no place in my Nirvia for a traitor's soul."

"You mean OUR Nirvia, Sire?!" replies the chancellor.

The king plays with his fingernails. "Do as I command."

The chancellor nods reluctantly at the new lieutenant. Lieutenant Noa waves in his cohort and they both proceed to drag Set's body out of the chamber. Two other guards come in and take their vacated posts.

"Look!" says the king, alarmingly. He gets up from his chair and points behind the chancellor.

The chancellor glances behind him. "What is it, Sire?"

The king points more specifically at a cracked sphere in the wall. "Chancellor, this foul intruder has accidentally hit one of our dormant InsignAnimas."

The chancellor walks over to the shattered sphere. He picks up the broken pieces from the floor and examines them. The pieces of the sphere have turned completely Black.

"I'm afraid you're right, Sire. The persona that this InsignAnima held dormant within is no longer with us."

"That's terrible." says the king, broodingly. "Whose is it?"

The chancellor presses a button underneath the destroyed sphere. A lodged piece of the sphere crumbles to the floor as a holographic image of Crista appears.

"NO!" shouts the chancellor.

"What is it, Chancellor?"

"It's Our Lady Crista, Sire."

"Oh no, that can't be." says the king, placing his mobile hand over his head.

The chancellor examines the fallen pieces of the sphere. "How could this happen?" says the chancellor.

"Yes, who could imagine such a destructively errand shot." says the king as his crest turns Blue.

"I promise, Your Majesty, that I shall not rest till I find the truth of all this."

"Good!" replies the king, "Lady Crista will be sorely missed in Nirvia."

"Yes, Sire, she will."

"This is probably a poor time to bring it up, but there's also the question of her spatial allotment in Nirvia." notes the king, coldly.

"Umm...what of it, Sire?"

"I believe her New Age Testament is clear on that matter. In case of any dysfunctional or destroyed InsignAnima its spatial allotment shall be added back to the general pool."

"But, Sire, we have just completed the birthing procedures for our last cycle. Adding back her spatial allotment would result in the T-Clock rewinding and this will create havoc within our final preparations."

"Good point." says the king, "But Crista's spatial allotment in Nirvia shall not be added back to Nirvia, it shall be part of the final Key Keeper's Challenge."

"But, Sire, Crista held the largest amount of space in Nirvia. This will make the last T-Match one of epic proportions."

"Yes, it would — wouldn't it? But nevertheless the rules as set in the New Age Testament are clear on the matter." replies the king with a sly grin.

"Sire, this large increase in the unclaimed pool could have the effects of providing an uncontested amount of voting rights for one soul in Nirvia."

"That seems to be the case, Chancellor."

"And it might not be you, Sire."

"That does seem like a possibility." replies the king, dryly. "But it was Our Lady Crista herself who established the rules for the last cycle. It was for the exact reason you alluded to, that is to keep the T-Clock countdown on schedule. So, for the sake of her memory, we must do as she instructed."

"Yes, Sire." replies the chancellor, glumly returning to Sistina's side. He kneels back down next to her and gently untangles her arms. Her clenched hands slowly unravel. One hand holds a fragment of the shattered sphere while the other a scratched etching. The chancellor gently examines both her hands.

The king gets up from behind his desk and approaches the distracted chancellor. His brows lift at the sight of the engraved symbol in Sistina's palm. "Is that a vertical line splitting a circle?" he says, curiously.

"It appears so, Sire."

"What does it mean?"

"I don't know, Sire."

"If I had to guess, Chancellor, I would say it must be a symbol of her Faith."

"Umm?" mumbles the chancellor.

"Don't you think so?"

"I said that I don't know, Sire."

"Fine, you don't have to get upset about it."

"I'm sorry, Sire."

"That's alright, Chancellor. It's been a devastating day for us all."

"That's true, Sire."

"It appears that we've lost three women today that despite their differences were of the highest quality."

"Yes, Sire."

"And to think this Fuchsia gave her life for her king is quite inspiring."

"She was that, Sire."

"I think it's sweet," says the king, "to think that with her final gesture she tried to honour her renewed Faith."

"Honouring her Faith?"

"Yes, Chancellor." replies the king, "She may not have believed in ours, but she did believe very much in hers."

"Belief in Faith?" mutters the chancellor, shaking his head. "Not Sistina."

-2-

The king captures the chancellor's inward remark. "Lord Horus, why do you think that she would mangle herself like that, if not for her Faith?"

The chancellor remains quietly fixated over Sistina's body.

"Maybe she meant nothing at all." continues the king, "Or it could have been a last ditch effort to send her love a message."

The chancellor abruptly scowls at the king. The king quickly steps back.

"But where I had my doubts, I no longer do." declares the king. He waves his hand around in a truthfully dishonest manner. "I did not mention her name. Yet, you affectionately pronounced her name, Chancellor."

The chancellor's crest turns Purple as he snarls at the king.

The king's own crest turns a bright Yellow as he quickly waves in his guards. The guards immediately position themselves in front of the king. They unhinge their holsters and gaze at the chancellor.

"What are you implying, Sire?" says the chancellor.

"Chancellor Horus," says the king, his crest glows Green. "I believe that you've had carnal relations with this woman. And in so doing you have broken your sacred vow of celibacy."

The two guards look in astonishment at one another. They quickly draw their blasters and point them at the chancellor.

"Lord Horus, I accuse you of breaking our most sacred of laws as dictated by our Holy White Doctrine." says the king, "Lord Horus, how do you plea?"

The chancellor glances blankly at the king. He bends a heartfelt look at Sistina and aberrantly gives up a deep sigh.

"Lord Horus, I will take your acquiescent response as an affirmation of your guilt."

The chancellor remains motionless.

"And in so doing you have forfeited your status in the Holy White Order." adds the king, pompously. "You know what you must now do. Do you not?"

The chancellor nods lightly over and over again before jadedly turning towards the king. He rips open his Purple glowing crest and exposes a small Purple sphere embedded in his muscular chest.

"Yes, Chancellor, that IS the price of Excommunication." says the king, moving farther back behind his guards.

The chancellor bends a look at Sistina's body. Then without any further hesitation he pulls out a dagger from its sheath and dutifully slices the small spherical implant out of his chest. The detached sphere immediately turns translucent. Blood edges out and curdles around his chest.

"Guards," says the king, "give him this."

The chancellor dejectedly takes his ripped suit off and puts on the new white one. The blood slowly permeates through his new suit and forms a peculiar bloody blotch on his chest. The crestfallen commander stretches out his hand and offers his blood soaked sphere to the king. The king signals his guards to retrieve it. The largest of the guards carefully approaches the chancellor's outstretched hand. He quickly grabs the sphere and warily backs away.

The guard wipes the translucent sphere clean and hands it over to the king. The king precipitously drops it to the floor and stamps his foot right next to the sphere. The wide-eyed guards snap back a look at a defeated looking chancellor.

The king smiles as he picks up the unharmed sphere. He backs away to the shadowy corners of his relics, and says, "Lord Horus, your penance shall be to retain the bloody mark on your crestless White suit. The carmine blotch upon your chest shall serve as a reminder of your defrocked state of being."

The chancellor remains uncaringly silent as his engrossed gaze unblinkingly examines Sistina's torn dress.

"But let it not be said that the Key Keeper is without compassion. I therefore offer you the opportunity for a rebirth as a Holy White in Nirvia. I shall hold onto your soul, as it was before its removal, till the End of Time." The king fondles the small sphere in his hand. "If you dedicate the rest of your life to my service I shall allow the persona within it to ascend."

The king places the translucent sphere in the top drawer of his desk. "And with that," he furthers, "what I offer you is a return to your former position as Commander." says the king, hiding a smirk. "It appears we're currently in need of one."

The two guards glance nervously back at the king.

"There's no need to be concerned." says the king, gazing at his troubled guards. "I know this man, and Lord Horus may have fallen from grace, but his word is still his oath. And no one is better suited to execute the full darkness of our Black Box than your renewed Commander. He shall be the perfect deterrent to those who may wish to try and harm the Key Keeper again. Isn't that right, Lord Horus?"

Horus unfeelingly nods his accord.

"I need to here it, Horus. Do I have your word of honour?" insists the king.

"Yes, Sire, I will be your henchman."

"I see we understand one another." says the king, stirringly. "But we must address one last thing. While your past soul retains its NAT name, you may not. Thus, we must choose a name that best befits your current status from the EBOLAD." The king pauses as he examines his relics. "Yes, I have just the name for you." he suddenly says, "From this day forth you shall wear the name of LAZARUS. You will be known henceforth as Commander Lazarus — The Truth Seeker." says the king, giving a hidden wink at Sistina's body. "Your name shall be feared by all those wishing harm to the Holy White Order."

"As you wish, Sire." shrugs the commander.

"Don't be so disappointed, Commander Lazarus. You will have the best of both worlds. Your past soul may rise with me, and your current soul can have as many Fuchsias as you desire."

"I will not have another."

The king's crest fumes Purple. "You dare reply to me in such a disrespectful manner?!"

The commander bends his head. "I didn't mean to be insubordinate, Your Majesty." he says, "It will not happen again."

"Good! And don't forget Commander that I could just as easily destroy your InsignAnima and demote you to the status of a miserable Periwinkle. So, from this day forth, I expect and demand your unconditional devotion. Is that clear, Commander?"

The commander gazes despondently at the king. "Yes, Sire."

The king turns away with a malevolent sneer. "Exactly!" he says, "And thus your first duty is to bring to justice those who have schemed to try to murder your king."

"Yes, Sire." replies Commander Lazarus, signalling the closest guard to approach.

The guard sheaths his blaster and walks over. "Sir?" he says, with a heavy gulp.

"Take a platoon of Teals to the Outer lands. Find one hundred Outers." says Lazarus, "And decorate Lake Alba with their crucified bodies."

The shadowed king grimaces as he wipes away the vindictive slaver from his mouth.

The commander continues, "If by the midnight hour they have not relinquished any information concerning this most heinous of crimes — light them up for the rest of them to see."

"Yes sir."

The commander's head tilts heavily toward the ceiling. "I hope you will forgive me, Sistina, for I shall not rest till I have found the truth." he says, shaking. "I've never understood your love, but those responsible shall understand my hate."

"Commander, take the body of Sistina to the temple in Monochromia and I'm sure they'll cleanse her body for her rise to their abstract Heaven." says the king, "I don't think it necessary to punish further such a young woman for your sin, for she has shown great courage in protecting her king."

The commander remains silently fixated over the body of Sistina.

"Yes, Sire." replies the guard in his stead.

"Now, take her body away and leave me alone in my Lair." commands the king, gawkily.

The guard places his hand gently on the commander's shoulder. The commander bends a look at the guard and stoically nods back. Commander Lazarus gently picks up Sistina's body and proceeds out of the chamber.

The king watches impatiently as his chamber empties. He secures the chamber door shut before releasing a mischievous smile. His crest turns Orange as he walks over to the standing sarcophagus nestled within his relics. He taps it in sequence and the sarcophagus opens. The king backs his way inside it.

"This turned out even better than I thought." he whispers. His smile broadens as the sarcophagus slowly closes in on him. "Now then," he concludes, "let's see if there are any other Whites who dare think of plotting against me."

INSIGNANIMA —... ('I') shall represent the spherical Insignia of thy Anointed Anima. Thy Sanctified InsignAnima shall possess the data accumulation of thy mind and body.

2. The "I" shall be born within the Chosen upon its selected Immaculate birth (see NAT Tech Manual: no.2: sec.8: InsignAnima — Genetic Selection) and upon the Age of Ascension thy InsignAnima shall become part of the collective consciousness of the Holy White Order.

3. Thy InsignAnima shall also reflect and record thy blessed colours throughout thy physical life (see NAT Tech Manual: no.2: sec.8: InsignAnima — Translucent Spherical Module Implantation)

4. Thy sacred 'I' shall also formulate the initial personification of thy corresponding Soulless Avatar in Nirvia (see NAT Tech Manual: no.2: sec.8: InsignAnima — The Anointed)

5. Thy sanctified InsignAnima shall transmit and update during the T-Matches thy evolving persona in Nirvia (see NAT Tech Manual: no.2: sec.6: T-Matches — Avatar)

6. Upon thy Ascension thy soul shall upload to thy awaiting Soulless Avatar in Nirvia wherein it shall be Reborn and become thy Soulful Avatar. Thus it was written on this day of...

NEW AGE TESTAMENT

Chapter Five

-1-

Inside a split laboratory two men sit facing a sealed screen. On the other side of the screen is a crying baby in a wicker basket. The sound it is making fails to pierce the partition.

"You know, Verme, I had a dream about that woman last night."

"What woman?"

"That really hot Fuchsia at the train station."

"You mean the one that got arrested?"

"Who else do you think I mean?"

"Yeah, Meno, she was a real spreader. She made me wish I was still a White. Even without my stuff I could still feel my juices boiling."

Meno lowers the top of his periwinkle outfit to show a small cavity in his chest. "Look at this!" he says, "First they take our InsignAnimas and then our genitals. You'd think they'd at least leave us our pricks. But NO! Now we're even worse off than the rest of the Monochrome men. And as if that wasn't enough punishment we have to wear these despicable Periwinkle outfits. It's really freaking embarrassing to be the lowest of the lowest of colours — I hate it!"

"Yeah, and don't forget our shitty bunkers. There last down the hill and we always end up getting the last bits from the Hydroponics Lab."

"Yeah, so we sinned and broke the sacred law?!" says Meno, nodding. "Do they have to treat us like shit too?!"

"I still think that a pussy in hand is better than two in the Thereafter."

"That's right," says Verme, "as if the other holier than thou Whites haven't thought the same thing at one time or another."

"Yeah, I know." says Meno, "I mean first they defrocked us and took away our InsignAnimas, but then to convict us for being pedophiles was just too much — it's not our fault we like them young."

"Yeah!" says Verme.

"But what really gets me is their hypocrisy."

"What do you mean?"

"I mean they're all puritanical about what we did, but then the King's guards give us this job?!"

"It's true," replies Verme, "I never thought about it that way."

"I mean what we do now is much worse than what we were put down here for in the first place."

"Yeah, it's true!" replies Verme, "Maybe that's why we have to keep what we do a secret?"

"Yeah, and they threatened to kill us if we don't."

"Yeah, what's up with that?"

"Anyways," adds Meno, "the hell with the Holy White Order and their two-facedness ways."

"Yeah, the Holy Whites can have their Nirvia. But once they're gone we'll be back on top again."

"Yeah, that's right!" says Meno, pompously gesturing his plump fists upwards. "We'll show them what real men are like."

"Hey, you know what? After the Ascension let's make sure that we erase what we've been doing down here in the Hydroponics Sub Center. I don't think the other Monochromes would appreciate the job we do for the Whites. You know how squeamish people can get when it comes to babies and stuff."

"I don't think we have to worry about that." replies Meno.

Verme stops taking notes and looks up at Meno. "And why's that?"

"First of all," explains Meno, "most people don't want to know things that will bug them. So I doubt that they would care to find out. The other thing is that none of this will matter once the Ascension begins."

"Oh, what's that supposed to mean?"

"You never pay attention, do you? I told you this last year."

"OK-OK, I just don't remember."

"The Ascension is supposed to permanently clear all of Doma's subterranean systems."

"What? No more labs? No more dungeons?"

"That's right."

"How's that possible?"

"I have no clue. But I heard through a Cerulean that it's got something to do with the restricted sections of the NAT."

"You mean the Book of Revelations?"

"Oh, and that of course you'd know. Verme, you're so peculiar."

"Thanks, man."

"It wasn't a compliment."

"Anyways, who cares what happens down here after we leave. We'll be back in our nice and comfy Doman homes by then." says Verme, kicking at a box under the table. "And we'll definitely be well armed if anyone thinks otherwise. You know, I got really scared when that Fuchsia was getting arrested. I thought they were looking for us. I thought they had found our illegal stash of weapons."

"You were worried for nothing." says Meno. "Nobody ever comes down here anymore. Who'd want to anyway?"

"You're right. I mean just the smell takes a year to get used to down here. And it gets in the skin too. I can't really tell anymore, but I know others can smell on us. Did you notice how every time we take the train the rest of the Monochromes always hold up their noses at us?"

"Oh, how I miss being a White." says Meno, pensively. "I can still taste the Doman food. It may come from the same source, but it's always the freshest."

"Yeah well, it'll taste even better after the putrid shit we've had to endure eating."

"Speaking of which," says Meno, "remind me to sneak out some of these leftovers. They're not great, but I like the texture of the hard protein sticks. Plus I already ate yesterday's food rations at home."

"You mean there's nothing left in our Periwinkle bunker?"

"Nope — there's nothing left, my slinky friend."

"Great!" says Verme, "Can you at least sneak out some of my leftovers too?"

"No problem," replies Meno, giddily. "Anyways, it should be easy to sneak things out nowadays. I got the feeling that the Azures are busy prowling for Fuchsias."

Verme returns to jotting down information in his note book.

"Yo!" exclaims Meno.

"What do you want now? Can't you see that I'm busy over here?"

"What I want is for you to stop that!" says Meno, gripping still Verme's leg. "Man-oh-man, how many times do I have to tell you to stop shaking the desk when you write?!"

"Stop bugging me," replies Verme, "And close your mouth when you eat."

"Why is it that when you take notes you shake your legs like that?" asks Meno, loudly chewing. "I'm really interested, because it really drives me nuts."

"Stop bugging me. Or else we'll be here all night."

Meno gobbles up the remainder of his brown stick of food. "Fine!" he says, "You're no fun." He taps his dirty hands on a towel and then presses a button near the sound proof screen.

The crying baby on the other side of the screen is twisting and turning inside its wicker basket.

Two virtual arms suddenly appear in front of Meno. He places his own arms inside them. Two mechanical arms suddenly drop down from the ceiling behind the screen. They follow perfectly Meno's arm movements. The robotic arms reach into the basket and lift the baby up to the screen. A greenish hue scans the baby and a series of notations scroll across the screen:

'DNA analysis: One critical error detected: lead level 93 — unable to delete. 10 non-critical errors have been detected and deleted...'

The long thin legs of Verme continue to nervously tap underneath the workbench.

"OK. Are you about finished or what?" says Meno.

"Wait just a sec." says Verme as he finishes his last scribble, "OK, you can put him down now?"

Meno places the baby back in his basket. He drops his arms to his side and the virtual arms disappear. The robotic arms quickly retract to the ceiling above the child.

"Good." says Verme, "One down."

Meno moves over to a nearby sink and as he rinses his hands smiles at Verme's leftover platter. He picks up a crunchy piece from it and gnaws at it loudly. He dips it into a side sauce and clumsily lets it drip on his periwinkle outfit. He tries to wipe away the dirty blotch but creates a bigger smudge. "I hate this freaking outfit." he grumbles, as his teeth continue to tear away at the stringy morsel.

The complaint goes unanswered.

"Did you hear me or what?"

"Yeah-yeah, I see what you did. Do you want a bib?"

"That's not nice. Why are you making fun of me?"

"Why do you keep eating my food?"

"You know that I can't help myself."

"Yeah, I know you're a glutton. Your T-Crest was always the same colour when we were Whites. I remember some people used to call you Lord Orange."

"That wasn't funny then, and it's not funny now." replies Meno.

A holographic black bulb suddenly flashes on their control panel. A number '1' in a fuchsia colour appears in it. It is replaced by a teal coloured number '4'. Then an ultramarine colour '2' appears, and lastly a number '3' in white.

Meno suddenly stops his languid munching. He elbows Verme on the head. "Look Verme, we'll never fill this new quota in time."

"Uh?" mutters Verme.

"The only good thing is that we don't have to worry about doing anymore anointments." says Meno, "I'm pretty sure the Whites have closed shop up there."

"Good!" replies Verme, "No more boring rituals to deal with. By the way, do you think that all these replacements have something to do with what went on yesterday?"

"I don't know, but I heard this morning that Commander Set and his lieutenant died yesterday." says Meno, "Which explains at least two of the new White requests."

"Shit! But it was Commander Set who told us to approve this baby boy over here." says Verme, pointing to the silently crying child. "So what do we do with it now? It barely qualifies as a Monochrome."

"Yeah, but which one of the Outer children does nowadays?"

"That's a good point." says Verme, "The quality of these Outer babies has declined sharply over the last couple of generations. It's probably the lack of food and the increased cases of cannibalism."

"Yeah, it's a proven fact that eating one's own leads to more madness."

"Regardless, an order is an order."

"Is it, Verme? Is it really?" says Meno with a spiteful sneer.

"What do you mean?" replies Verme, excitedly squirming.

"This is what I mean." Meno pushes down a pedal next to his chair and a chute opens that swallows up the child and its wicker basket.

"No!" cries Verme, mouth agape. "I can't believe you just did that!"

Meno playfully slaps at Verme's head while another wicker basket rolls in the other's vacated place.

"Stop that!" cries Verme.

"Hey don't worry about it, man." says Meno, "There are no T-Ports down here. So who cares? Anyway, we don't have to obey the instructions of a dead man."

"You're absolutely insane!" says Verme.

Meno tries to finger out food lodged between his teeth. "Yeah, tell me something I don't know."

"I don't think you should have done that."

"Why not?" replies Meno.

"Have some respect, man. Some say that Outers used to be just like us at one time."

"What are you talking about? They're animals! What's their motto again — 'Eat or be eaten'?"

"Yeah, but—"

"C'mon man, just look at your log. All they're really good for now is for their protein." Meno uses the robotic arms to pick up the new baby from its wicker basket. He presses it against the screen. "Look!" he says, spreading the baby boy's legs apart. "At least that last boy doesn't have to go through what this next one might."

"Yeah, I guess the procedure hurts at any age." says Verme, looking down at his vacant crotch.

"There you go then." says Meno, dropping the boy back into the basket.

"You know what?" says Verme, yawning. "I really can't wait till the Whites ascend. I'll show you then how to grow good food, and not like the shit we get from the Hydroponics Lab."

"Well, some of it isn't so bad." replies Meno, licking Verme's empty leftover platter. "I mean considering what we're feeding it."

Verme suddenly grabs the plate from Meno's hands and throws it behind him. "I can't believe you finished all my leftovers too." says Verme, "Now what are we going to bring back home, eh?"

The plate continues to rattle on the floor. The jangle suddenly stops. The two technicians look behind them. A tall man has his foot pressed over the still plate.

-2-

"What's going on here?" says Logos, stepping forward with a commanding presence.

Verme and Meno stumble over each other to address him. Meno ineptly steps on Verme's foot. Verme's face squirms in pain as he kicks at Meno.

"Stop that!" says Logos, holding a naked baby in his arms. The baby playfully pulls at Logos' short black hair. Logos walks over to the dividing screen and sees the crying baby behind it. He lingers pensively as he probes at the technical reports on the workbench. He gazes at the two technicians with disdain. "This is a disgusting mess." he says.

"We're sorry, sir." says Verme.

Meno gulps down the food fermenting in his mouth. "We didn't expect any visitors, sir." he says, "Especially a Sapphire."

"This child is to be immediately anointed." says Logos, holding out the baby from his arms.

"That's not part of our protocol, sir. We need to receive the InsignAnima first." replies Verme.

Logos pulls out from his pocket a small translucent sphere. "Here is her InsignAnima."

"But sir, I thought the genetics lab had stopped ordaining any new Whites. This child may not reach her Age of Ascension in time and may remain a Grey." Verme says, timorously.

"Are you questioning me, Periwinkle?" replies Logos, prominently displaying his badge.

The two technicians gawk at each other.

"No, sir!" says Verme, the words gallop out of his mouth. "It will not be a problem whatsoever, sir!"

"Good!" says Logos, "Now do what I have asked and I will forget your reprehensible behaviour. But keep in mind that I am known to have the ear of the king. And if any part of this argumentative encounter reaches him, he will not be so forgiving."

Meno stares with his mouth open at Verme. They both swiftly fall to their knees. "Please, please, sir." says Meno.

"Fine, now stop your grovelling. Get up from your knees and follow the assigned ritual of anointment."

Meno and Verme simultaneously reply, "Vestri mos est meus to order."

Verme carefully places the baby girl on a plinth next to the control panel. The baby tries to grab his ears but flips over to her stomach. Verme pulls back his hands and backs away from the child. "Look!" says Verme, "She's got a birthmark. I've never seen a White with a birthmark."

"Neither have I." replies Meno, "It looks like the capital letter Phi."

"What do you know what it looks like?" replies Verme.

"Hey! I was a pretty good student once, you know. If I remember correctly I think this symbol has something to do with the design of the dome, or something like that anyways."

"Uh?" groans Verme.

"I don't exactly remember, but I think it was referred to as a golden something. I think that it—"

"That's why you remember." interrupts Verme, chuckling. "You probably thought it held the secret to making gold out of food."

"You shut your mouth!"

"No, you shut your mouth!"

"Are you both finished!" interjects Logos.

Verme and Meno are frozenly startled.

"Continue your work." says Logos.

The technicians silently nod back.

Meno places the child in a mechanical capsule. Verme enters an alphanumeric sequence on its screen. The machine presses firmly down till the child is unable to move. Two tubular extensions emerge from the machine and connect themselves to the child's temples.

"Sir, what name has been chosen for this child?" asks Verme.

"Istina." replies Logos.

"Uh?" mumbles Verme.

"I-S-T-I-N-A." spells out Logos.

"I've never heard of this name." says Verme as he inputs the name on the screen. "She must be the first of her name. Where in the New Age Testament was the name found?"

Logos pays little attention to Verme's question.

Verme stares at the more receptive Meno. "Meno, do you know?"

"Nope!" replies Meno, "But it could be from the Book of Revelations." Meno looks over at Logos with a smile. Logos returns to him a pernicious gaze. "But I may be wrong." adds Meno.

"Stop talking and finish your job." says Logos.

"Sir, yes sir!" blubbers Meno.

"Her name means Truth." states Logos, suddenly.

"Oh?" mutters Meno, looking curiously at the child.

Meno picks up an archaic jue and tilts it over the child's head. A few drops of thick red liquid trickles down on the child's forehead.

Verme holds up his notepad to Meno's eyes.

"Beatus niveus civis," reads Meno. He places his index finger on the baby's forehead and ceremoniously draws a sign of an ankh inside of a circle.

The child's face squirms uncomfortably and objectionably puckers its lips.

Meno continues to read, "Futurus unus cum pesterus mundus sententia vestri Tänka Mundus Crista vadum incendia sursum iam."

An incandescent beam begins to flicker from the machine. A hue of Red, Blue, Green, Orange, Purple and Yellow exudes out of the apparatus. The capsule slowly decompresses and its protracted tubular extensions retract. Verme takes the child out of the capsule and gently places her in a golden cradle.

A small translucent sphere is now embedded in the child's chest. And two tiny implants are lodged in her temples.

"It's done!" says Verme, "Her temple implants will immediately begin to transmit her thoughts and emotions to her InsignAnima. And upon her Confirmation her T-Vision will become operational and she will join the Holy White Order."

"Hey Verme, do you remember ever seeing a White with such deep black eyes?"

Verme squints hard at the baby. "Nope." he answers, glibly. Then turns to Logos and says, "We're finished, sir."

At that very moment the baby's newly implanted sphere momentarily turns Black. Meno gazes at the transformation as the baby twists and turns with a beaming smile. The gold cradle is cordially lifted toward the ceiling by an automated arm.

Meno nudges at Verme's arm. "Did you see that?"

"Umm?" replies Verme, "See what?"

"Over there — the baby girl." says Meno.

Verme turns his eyes toward the ascending cradle. The baby's sphere appears translucent as its cradle makes its way up and out of the lab.

"Uh?" grunts Verme, disinterestedly. "What are you going on about?"

"You didn't see that?" says Meno with a contorted face.

"See what?"

"Never mind." says Meno.

"You know what, Meno? I think you've been down here too long."

"Hey!" exclaims Meno, looking around the lab. "Where did that Doman Scientist go?"

Verme shrugs his shoulders. "Boh?" he mumbles.

They both gawk blankly at one another.

"Hey Verme, did you ever get the feeling that there's something going on that we don't know about?"

"Umm, like what?"

"I don't know — that's my point!"

Φ

End of Book I

BOOK II

DOMA

TÄNKAMATCHES (T-Matches*) — ... shall form a temporary interface between the qualified combatants and their T-Match Avatars (see NAT Tech Manual no.3: Book of Revelations* — Conclave).

2. T-Matches shall enable combatants to contest their strength of intellect on a randomly selected T-Planet.

3. Each T-Match Avatar shall originate from the consciousness of each participating combatant. The Avatars shall then fight to be the first to capture the Golden T-Key.

4. Only the winner of the yearly Key Keeper's Challenge T-Match shall be declared thy Ruler and bearer of the Golden Key (hetero referred to as thy Key Keeper).

5. Thy Key Keeper shall be the bearer of the physical Golden Key till otherwise deposed in a subsequent match.

6. All Holy Whites shall assemble during the Key Keeper's Challenge in order to ascertain the remaining time on thy Ascension's T-Clock (see NAT Tech Manual no.2: sec.8 — uploading data from InsignAnimas).

7. Upon thy Conclave Insignification wagers may be placed on the overall results (Nota Bene: thy wager shall not be accepted if thou minimum spatial requirement necessary to maintain thy place in Nirvia has been exceeded).

8. The Golden T-Key is the virtual representation of its physical counterpart. The physical Golden Key is worn at all times by the Key Keeper. The T-Ports shall only accept the Golden Key from the officially recognized Key Keeper. This is in accordance with the rules set out in...

NEW AGE TESTAMENT

PART I

THE CONCLAVE

Chapter One

-1-

In an early morning haze a young woman stands alone facing a high dwelling. Her white dress accentuates her long black hair and deep black eyes.

The address on the building's façade is designated with the number '1'.

The girl parts her hair from her face and gradually counts the floors of the low-rise.

She suddenly finds herself inside an elevator speedily moving up the building. The elevator comes to a stop and pings its arrival. The girl steps out and swaggers diffidently down a narrow hallway. She slides her hand along the wall as her high heels threaten her balance. She momentarily stumbles but with the aid of the supporting wall manages to quickly regain her stride. She looks around her bashfully before knocking on a door with the number '618'. The door slowly opens and a tall virulent man in a sapphire coloured outfit stands opposite her. A black mask covers his eyes but not his inviting smile. The girl steps on the threshold of his apartment and stops. She tilts her head up and a viscous chocolate shower sprinkles down on her. She spreads her lips slightly apart and lets run the creamy liquid along her mouth. She licks her lips and sensuously moves closer to the strapping man. She lifts her heels and stretches her puckered lips up toward his. The man hesitates to touch her advances. She instead moves tight against his body and gently cups her hands around his face.

"Professor," she whispers, "I understand you have a sweet tooth. Do you think I can help you with that?"

The professor opens his mouth and a loud ringing sound emerges from it.

The young woman takes a step back in surprise. "Huh?!" she mutters. She puts her hands over her ears and shuts her eyes.

Suddenly her eyes pop open and she finds herself sitting up on a bed. She unblinkingly looks around.

The ringing sound reverberates around the room.

"Oh no!" she says. She tries to get up but finds herself tightly wound around the bed sheets.

The sound of a bell pierces inside the room once again.

"Yikes!" she says, bouncing off of the bed. She untangles herself from the twined linen and flips the bedcover over her half naked body like a shawl. She scrambles over to the window and watches a myriad of young adults parading by.

She nervously scours the messy room. "Where's my dress?" she says, "Why can't I ever find anything in my room?!" she says, hurriedly. "I'm really not in the mood to deal with that idiot today."

She looks around her room hysterically. She finally locates her dress. She drops her bedcover and tries to quickly slip her grey dress on. A small birthmark of a vertical line through a circle rests on her shoulder blade.

The bell rings once again.

"C'mon girl, let's go!" she says with her head stuck in her dress. The motion lifts her cleavage and reveals a small Orange glowing sphere embedded inside her chest. She twists and turns until the dress finally falls into place. An Orange crest of an ankh inside of a circle suddenly appears on her dress. The Orange glow quickly dissipates and the crest disappears. Her dress has returned to its singular grey colour.

The young woman puffs and blows as she gives a glance out the window again.

A large holographic sign adjacent to a coliseum reads:

'UNIVERITAS DE DOMA'

She glances up at the translucent dome in despair as the last group of students pass by her residence. "Oh for Nirvia's sake, I'm late again." she says, rushing.

There are running footsteps coming from outside her room.

The young woman quickly grabs an oversized book from her dresser and runs out the door.

Young adults in white outfits dash past her down the corridor. The girl rushes after them down the staircase. Once outside she swerves apprehensively through the trailers until she catches up to the last grouping. She slows down and slips into the all white dressed group. She breathes a sigh of relief.

A gang of students sit idly ahead of her group. They sit on a picnic table like a murder of white crows. Most of them appear enthralled by the virtual glasses encircling their heads.

The girl grimaces as her concealing group approaches the gang. She tries to inconspicuously tighten her rank, but those around her notice her attachment and slowly move away. The girl sulks as her cover wanes.

"Hey, Ramsey." says a young woman sitting at the picnic table.

A young burly man sitting next to her opens his eyes. His virtual glasses retract inside his temples. "What's up, Titi?" he says.

"Look over there." says Titi, nodding toward the passing group.

Ramsey laughs out loud. "I see you!" he yells out. His loud brooding voice scatters the rest of the students around the grey dressed girl.

The gang around Ramsey awakens from their virtual distractions.

The girl tries to disregard the far reaching cry, but Ramsey's voice continuous to hound her.

"Hey guys!" says Ramsey, waving over an iris dressed worker. "Here comes the last of the Greys."

A middle aged man in an iris outfit arrives at Ramsey's side. "Yes, my lord?" he says.

"Blue — large!" replies Ramsey.

The man nods and quickly makes his way to a rainbow coloured machine nearby.

The young girl continues to move nakedly worried past the picnic table. She holds close to her chest her wide book.

"Hey little Grey, I thought you were an expired species." cries Ramsey.

The girl puts her head down and keeps moving forward toward the school.

"Tia!" cries Ramsey, unabashed. "Where are you going in such a hurry?"

Tia keeps her eyes down and does not reply.

"I'm speaking to you, Grey!" says the boisterous Ramsey.

Tia again does not respond.

"I just want to know," he says as she passes by, "how does it feel to be such an alien?"

A large chuckle gurgles up from his gang.

"I don't know," replies Tia, "maybe less incestuous?!" Tia lifts her hand over her mouth. "Oops!" she winces.

The click around Ramsey look momentarily stunned before letting out an encompassing cackle.

Ramsey sneers at his gang's snickering disloyalty.

The gang immediately stops laughing.

Ramsey readdresses his attention towards Tia. "What did you say?"

Tia does not reply.

The grimace on Ramsey's face sends his entourage a twitter. With a heavy scowl he stands up on the picnic table. His blond hair flashing about as his crest glows angrily Purple.

"Hey Grey, do you think you're funny?!"

"Maybe I am," replies Tia, moodily. "But I'm sure you are."

The man in the iris outfit returns and serves a large blue beverage to Ramsey.

"What's this!?" exclaims Ramsey, throwing the drink to the floor.

The subservient man gets down on his knees and with a rag quickly proceeds to clean the liquid mess.

Ramsey makes a threatening move toward Tia, but Titi grabs his arm and pulls him back. "Forget her," she says, "she's not worth the trouble."

"You're right," he replies, loudly. "She'll probably be left behind anyway."

"Who cares!" replies Tia, "At least I won't have to see your ugly face anymore."

Ramsey's face turns red. "I'm going to kill that girl."

"Ramsey," says Titi, "why do you let her get under your skin like this?"

"She's not under my skin." replies Ramsey, hard. "She's just a know it all."

"She does say the strangest things in class." replies Titi, "Maybe there's something wrong with her."

"Yeah, she's a little ALIEN!" hollers Ramsey, "That's what's wrong with her."

Tia picks up her pace and makes it past the gawking gang.

"We'll see who gets the last laugh!" cries Ramsey.

Tia continues walking straight ahead till she reaches the main building. She notices that all of students are instead heading in the direction of the coliseum.

A holographic banner ahead of them reads:

'KEY KEEPER'S CHALLENGE'

"Shit!" she inauspiciously exclaims, exhaling a deep heavy sigh. "And the day just keeps getting better."

She turns herself around and without raising suspicion heads in the opposite direction of the banner.

She reaches the school's confines and flings her book on top of its defining wall. She lifts herself over it and tries to slowly descend to the other side. But she slips and unconventionally tumbles straight down. She unceremoniously finds herself on the unsuspecting lap of the man of her dream.

-2-

Logos lays flat on a collapsed chair. His dark sunshades lie twisted on his nose. He shrugs his head and looks up. "Hello, young lady." he says with a disarming smile.

Tia sits accidentally straddled over his waist. "I'm so sorry, Professor." she says, her Red crest momentarily matching her cheeky colour.

"You certainly have a way of making an impression. I think part of it has left an imprint on my body." replies Logos.

Tia apologetically lifts her body off of his. "I'm really sorry, Professor." she says, with a surreptitious smile. "Did I hurt you?"

"I am fine, young lady. But please, I know that you are relatively new to my class, but I prefer that you address me without my title." he adds, smiling. "I think 'Professor' sounds too smart for my own good."

"I'll try to remember that, Professor." she smiles, shyly. "I mean Logos."

"Thank-you, young lady." he replies.

"Please return the favour and call me, Tia."

"As you wish, Tia." he replies.

"Not to be a bother, but it's just that I don't need a reminder that I'm still a Grey. Plus, I'd like to hear my name coming from a source that I actually like for once." she says, smiling. "And I'd like to think that I could have at least one friend in the school."

"I do not know if that is prudent, Tia. I am after all just a Monochrome, and one who is much older than you."

"Oh?" she replies, "How much older?"

"I am at the beginning of my fourth cycle."

"No way!" she exclaims, blinking rapidly. "I would have never guessed that. You barely have any grey hair. You look really good, Logos. I mean for your age that is."

"Thank-you...I think." replies Logos, smiling.

"Aren't you afraid of getting old?"

"No, I am not." replies Logos, "Getting old is quite natural. Aging allows us to learn how to let go."

"Let go of what?"

"Our attachments." replies Logos.

"Oh." says Tia, "Well then, I'm glad that the Ascension is drawing near and this way you'll be able to live out a full life once the Whites are gone. I remember the Virtual Library explaining a time when people were allowed to live way past the end of their fourth cycle."

"That does seem like a more natural way of things." replies Logos.

"You know something," says Tia, "today just happens to be the first day of my second cycle."

"I know, Tia."

"What do you mean, 'you know'?"

"You are the only Grey student left. It is my job to know when you achieve the Age of Ascension."

"Oh, OK." she says, twirling her long black hair. "That makes sense."

Logos gets up from the floor and dusts himself off. He removes his warped shades and tries to straighten them back into a functional shape.

"Professor, I mean Logos. I'm sorry about your sunshields."

"My sunshields will be fine." he replies, grinning. "I am just happy they helped break your fall."

Tia stands in front of him sulking.

"There is no reason to pout, Tia." he adds, "There are a lot worse things in life than a pretty lady running into an aging man." he says, smiling reassuringly. "Though you do seem to have the reputation of running into things — mostly trouble."

"Yeah, I don't get it?" she says, giggling. "I try so hard to avoid people altogether."

"Speaking of avoiding people, what are you doing outside the school grounds?"

"I just don't want to be in there." says Tia, pointing glibly at the coliseum.

"Why not?" says logos, "Most Holy Whites look forward to the yearly Key Keeper's Challenge. I hear King Osiris is an impressive and exciting combatant to watch. Are you not interested in seeing if he'll retain his Golden Key, and hence his title?"

"Yeah, no — I don't know. First of all, he never loses. And secondly, I don't care." she says, scowling.

"You don't care who will lead your Resurrection?"

"I've given some thought to this—"

"Oh-Oh?!" cuts in Logos.

Tia disregards Logos' reaction. "I don't know, but there's just something that feels strange about ascending to a virtual Heaven."

"What do you mean?"

"I don't know exactly." says Tia, brooding. "It's just a feeling that makes me wonder about stuff."

"What kind of stuff?"

"I'm not sure. I mean the thought of living virtually forever sounds like pretty interesting, but it also sounds like a very long time. What if I don't like it?"

"Do you not wish to be Reborn?"

Tia leans against the marbled wall. "I guess so."

"Don't you want to go to Nirvia? It is after all comprised of the Promised Lands promised to the Holy Whites."

"Yeah, that's what I've been told ever since I was a child."

"Umm..."

"Don't say it!" interjects Tia, "Please don't say it. I know I still look very young."

"Umm..."

"It's my Grey uniform, right?" interrupts Tia, "Until I become a White I'll always have the title of Young Lady. Some of the students treat me like an alien, just because I'm the last Grey. The thing is that I don't feel as little as they think I am."

"I can attest to that." says Logos, straightening his sapphire suit.

"Sorry about that." smiles Tia.

"Actually, I think that some of the things you've said in class are highly intuitive and insightfully quite mature."

"Thanks." she says, smiling brightly. Her crest shines briefly Blue.

"Do you think that maybe the reason you have doubts about ascending to Nirvia is in part because you will be in similar company as you are here."

"I wish."

"You wish?"

"Oh, you're referring to the students." she says, "Yeah-no, that's not what bothers me, although that's another good reason."

"So what is it about living forever after in Nirvia that concerns you?"

Tia steps away from the shadow of the wall and into the sunlight. "Like all mortals I too am afraid of the unknown that death brings." she says, "But ascending to an eternally blissful existence has just a strange feel to it. I don't know exactly why. I just feel like I'm missing something."

"What do you mean?"

"I sometimes wonder what if death holds a more important purpose in our existence than we think. I mean Nirvia sounds like a great place to visit, but I'm not sure I'd want to spend eternity there — I'm not sure I like myself that much." she says, a hint of a smile emerges from her puffy lips.

"It sounds to me that you are questioning whether your transcendence will lead to a somewhat redundantly perpetual afterlife."

"Right." replies Tia, rolling her eyes.

"In other words," adds Logos, "you may be wondering if virtual immortality can actually resolve the true mystery of existence. And that the answer may rest outside of that."

"Yeah, that's pretty much it. But then again, what do I know?" says Tia with a sardonic smirk, "I mean, we came from the unknown, became part of the known, and are terrified to return to whence we came — the unknown. What's up with that?"

"That sounds like a confusingly good question." replies Logos, smiling. "Though it does sound like you are asking if one's consciousness, or what the Whites refer to as their personal souls, can actually know the unknown?"

"Yeah, that's much clearer." giggles Tia, "All I was saying is that it just seems weird to become like immortal without understanding what that really means. I mean things aren't so great on this plane, so why would they be different in another. We are after all the same people here as we would be there. And what happens if I do change and then realize that I'm stuck in a place that I don't want to be?"

"Tia, you are definitely wiser than your years."

"Do you really think so?" she asks, graciously.

"Yes, of course I do."

"You know, there are times when I feel…"

"When you feel what?" asks Logos, taking an inquisitive step toward her.

"Never mind, it's probably just my fall talking." she snickers, "Or maybe it's just the effects of having reached the Age of Ascension. I wonder what it'll feel like to finally be connected to the collective consciousness of the Holy White Order."

"Is that why you are so apprehensive about attending today's T-Match? Are you reluctant to be part of TänkaWorld?"

"I don't know, maybe. I sometimes wish I wasn't one of the Chosen at all." she replies, looking down at her grey dress. "Not that I feel like one anyway."

"Be careful what you say." replies Logos, seriously.

"Be careful?" Tia walks up to Logos. "Why?" she says, wild-eyed. "Is it because I question the idea of a private little Heaven that bars others to enter? I don't know about you, but I think that if I lived in Heaven while knowing that others were being left behind, that would feel more like Hell to me." Tia's crest momentarily glows Purple as her tone flares up. "It seems to me that if those who were not Chosen were bestowed an InsignAnima like mine, their colours would be no different."

"I do not think it a good ideas that you—"

"And what of the Outers?" she interrupts, "Sure they're wild and vicious, but so are their conditions. Why do they deserve the brunt of the wrath for what our forefathers did to this planet?"

"I suggest you lower your voice."

Tia catches her breath and slowly expels it. "Anyhow," she adds, "even if Nirvia turns out to be all that's been promised, at what point does a beautiful dream that I know will never end begin to feel like a nightmare? I mean how much pleasure is enough?"

Logos edges closer to Tia. "Be careful, young lady. What you are saying may be considered heretical."

"No need to be concerned, Professor. I'm just venting." she says, gazing into Logos' eyes. Her crest briefly turns Red. "What was I saying?" she blushes, "Oh yeah, even the most delightful of dreams can turn stale after a few thousand years or so. Don't you think?"

"That does seem logical."

"Professor Logos, I'm afraid that my Grey dress fails to make me the little angel that I'm supposed to be." Tia's crest turns Black.

Logos wipes his smudged sunshields and peeks through them at Tia. "Hmm?" he murmurs, "All I can say is that from my point of view your observations appear quite angelic."

Tia's Black crest disappears.

"Thank-you." she says. Her crest turns momentarily Red again as she shyly gazes at Logos' effervescent smile. "Alrighty then," she says, walking away. "I think I better go now."

"What do you mean? Where do think you are going, young lady?"

"I don't know, maybe I'll take the Tube and hide in the Virtual Library for the day."

"I am sorry, but you cannot escape your fate today. As you know, you have attained the Age of Ascension and you must enrol yourself in the Holy White Order."

"Do I really have to?"

"I am afraid you must."

"And where do I do that?"

"You will need to go to the Holy White Arena. They will need to process your Confirmation before assigning you a seat in TänkaWorld."

"A seat?" replies Tia, eyes wondering.

"First of all, you will be provided a seat for the Conclave. Secondly, your Grey dress will be transformed into that of a Holy White. And lastly, your T-Vision will become operative."

"My temple implants will light up and I'll have the virtual glasses like the others?"

"Yes, and then you will be able to visit Nirvia."

"I have to admit that I'm somewhat curious about what my Avatar will be like."

"The Avatars in Nirvia are specifically designed to be a direct reflection of your persona here, except without any apparent faults."

"Oh, is that all?" says Tia, "That sounds boring."

"I thought you no longer wanted to be picked on as a Grey. Don't you want to be like all the other Holy White students?"

"I know some of the so called Holy Whites, and I'm not sure I'd describe them as Holy."

"Nevertheless, you must go." says Logos, firmly. "Time is running out for your Confirmation."

"Do I really have to go today?"

"You must." Logos replies.

His laconism seems to pull Tia closer. "Why must I?"

"You pointed out that you are not happy with some aspects of this world. Would you not like to see those things change?"

"I do."

"How do you intend to do that?"

"I don't know."

"Do you not think that maybe if you were part of the collective mind of those who govern that that could provide you a way?"

"You mean that I can make changes inside the Holy White Order — little me?"

"You may be little, but your ideas are not."

"But, how can I effect such change? What do I know of such things?"

"Tia, you are a free spirit that sees things beyond what can be measured by colours..." Logos is suddenly disquieted by a dark cloud passing over the dome.

Tia curls her hair around her finger. "Hello?" she says, quizzically.

"And maybe you have an insight into that which cannot be measured. And with that you may be able to share it with the collective."

"Huh?" mutters Tia, "What insight?"

"Tia, think of your consciousness as the known Universe."

"Okay?"

"Now imagine if you had the ability to go beyond the limits of your consciousness?"

"Wait. Are you saying that I can find out what exists outside of the Universe by going outside of my own consciousness?"

"To be able to extend our perceived limits beyond the known Universe is an interesting question." says Logos, smiling. "Why there appears to be a Universe rather than nothing at all has puzzled mankind for millennia."

"Huh?"

"Tia, imagine space as being your brain. And time as being your thoughts."

"OK?"

"Space cannot exist without time and vice versa." says Logos, "So, what would happen if thought could be halted?"

"I guess time would stop."

"And with that space could not exist, right?"

"OK?" replies Tia, "Now I forgot my question."

"The question I think you hinted at was whether that which may exist beyond the known Universe can be found out by looking inward?"

"Is that what I said?"

"I think so."

"Now I can see why people think I'm weird."

"Weird or different is not necessarily a bad thing."

Tia bends a look over the wall as if it were a parapet to another world. "Maybe in your world, Professor." she replies, her crest glows momentarily Green. "But not in mine."

"Is that why you lack Faith in Nirvia?"

"No, I just find it strange that we created Nirvia and then we turn around and worship that which we created."

"How is that different from what the many Monochromes believe? They created God in their own image and then worship that which they created."

"I guess it's not so different." replies Tia, "I just find it peculiar how we divide ourselves with our thoughts on what we believe, but yet we all believe in our thoughts."

"As always, Tia, you have an interesting way of looking at things."

"I don't know why, but I feel lots of energy when trying to figure out why I think the way I do. It's like the answers are hiding somewhere inside me."

"What answers?"

"The Truth about why we exist and do what we do." says Tia, "I think we'd all like to know that, no?"

"Why would you assume that?"

"Why in Nirvia would we not?!"

"Do not underestimate the power of evasion." says Logos, loudly whispering. "Collective beliefs exist to skirt the Truth. Unlike the internal struggle of enlightenment, organized beliefs provide appeasing pre-packaged explanations for what people believe ails them."

"But that's stupid."

"Not at all, it's more of an answer to the despair that most people feel. Organized Faiths present a deep sense of significance, acceptance, and belonging. Sometimes people's need for hope is much greater than their need for rational thinking."

Tia looks beside herself. "I don't think we're all slaves to irrational thinking." she replies, pacing back and forth.

"But that's what the human condition is founded on — the intransigence of thought. Whether one is a believer, or a nonbeliever, the static mindset inhibits an open investigation into the Truth."

"Sorry, Professor, but that sounds like you're saying that we can't help ourselves but have divisive beliefs."

"That does sound like a logical conclusion."

"Yeah but that's like saying that the problem is in our genes, and that we're like hell-bent on destroying ourselves with one belief or another. I don't know, but that just sounds really bad."

Logos reconstitutes his flattened chair to its original condition. He places it against the thick wall of the school grounds. He sits back down on it.

Tia scowls at him with her arms crossed. "Professor Logos, in case you haven't noticed I'm not very happy, and I feel like I need to do something about it."

"That is exactly why you should go and get Confirmed." says Logos, edging forward on his chair. "But just be careful what you say to others."

"What do you mean?"

"People do not like to be shaken out of their comfortable beliefs." he whispers, "If you threaten what they believe, you threaten who they are. Just keep in mind that the pedestal of Truth is a slick place to be standing on when speaking to the power of Faith — especially if you offer no replacement."

"I'm not afraid to speak the Truth." replies Tia.

Logos prays his hands together with an imploring concern. "You should be!" he whispers, hard. "The closer you get to tearing apart delusions, the closer you yourself may come to be torn apart."

"But how can I change anything if I can't confront what others believe?"

"Throughout the ages," says Logos, "many different religious and secular leaders tried to change the human condition, and it never ended well."

"I don't like the sound of that."

"Whenever a secular society loses its way it turns to Faith for the answer." continues Logos, "When an answer is purportedly found, it gets organized and institutionalized back into a hierarchical paradigm that constructs a new society using the same old roots."

"You mean like we did?" says Tia.

Logos quietly nods back. "Your forefathers realized that their economic archetype would no longer be able to sustain the insatiable human appetite for unsustainable external growth. So they found their prophet in Zadok and built themselves a posh self-sustaining dome. They understood that this would shield them and their descendents from the cannibalizing currents that would eventually sweep the world. And then came the Holy Whites—"

"I don't understand," interrupts Tia, "why do we keep creating the same sort of societies and then expecting different results?"

Logos takes a deep breath. "That is a really good question." says Logos, "Maybe it is because the human condition has never really changed."

"So how do we change it?" she asks, palatably biting her nails.

"I think that—" says Logos, interrupting himself. A dust cloud spreads over the dome. "I think there is a dust storm brewing out there." he continues, "I hope the people outside are safe."

The dome's internal lights slowly turn on as the skies darken.

"Professor, you didn't answer my question."

"What question?"

"What do you mean what question — how do we change?"

"I think that..."

"You think that what?"

"That you should rejoin your classmates." says Logos.

"What?!" snarls Tia.

"You must go now." says Logos, firmly cemented in his seat. "The T-Match is about to begin."

Tia dejectedly ladders the school wall. Her crest flickers briefly a fiery Purple. "This is just unreal!" she complains.

"By the way," says Logos, pointing to the large book Tia left on the wall. "Why do you carry that book around?"

"It helps me to hide." she solemnly replies, "Plus IT at least answers my questions!"

"I guess there is no better world than that formed by the dreams of the written word." he says, smiling warmly.

"Who doesn't like to escape into dreamy worlds." she replies, huffing. "But no matter how dreamy a world may feel I still wouldn't want to spend eternity in it."

"Most people would die to do just that." replies Logos.

"I don't know, but that sounds rather suspiciously ironic to me." She turns and notices Logos beneath her with his arms outstretched. She pauses at the edge of the wall as if reconciling her thoughts. "Don't worry, Professor, I won't fall."

"I am sure that even at your youthful age you are more than capable of handling yourself. But be careful, anyway."

"No!" she suddenly exclaims.

"No?"

Tia sits down on the wall. Her legs swing over Logos' head. "The more I think about it, Professor, the less I like the idea of ending up in Nirvia. Maybe it's the eternal happiness that's been promised, but without sadness what would such happiness feel like? I guess that sounds like the duality trap you were referring to before, right?"

"You are quite a young lady, Tia."

Tia's crest turns Blue for an instant. "Plus, what if life holds part of the answer, and death holds the other part?"

"What answer?"

"I have no idea. But it seems to me that the ultimate duality thing is that of life and death, no?"

"That does sound logical."

"I mean the two do seem intertwined. What meaning would life have without death, and what meaning would death have without life?"

"That is another good question."

"Yeah and what if one must experience the two in order to figure out the answer."

"Do you not think that you would need a question first?"

"Yeah, that makes more sense." giggles Tia, "Maybe that's what I'm missing — the question."

"Well, if death may have the answer that life does not, then maybe the question may be to find out what happens at death."

"Is that possible?"

"Maybe questioning what it truly means to die could be a good starting point."

"Hmm?" mutters Tia, "Why do I get the feeling that you're sort of guiding me through this?"

"Speaking of guiding," says Logos, "you need to get to the Holy White Arena."

"Oh," grumbles Tia, "I'm really not looking forward to this Confirmation thing."

"Yes, I've noticed."

"Do you think that they'll even notice me in there?"

"I would."

Tia's crest briefly turns Red. "Alright, I'll go." she says with a quaint smile.

"Do you promise?"

"Umm?" mumbles Tia.

"I must remind you that you are the last to attain the Age of Ascension and your attendance today is mandatory. Your seat must be readied for your Insignification." says Logos, "Nirvia cannot construct the parameters of your Avatar without your encoded InsignAnima."

"But Logos—"

"I am sorry, Tia, but you must attend." interrupts Logos, "You may feel like you have a choice, but I think fate has other plans for you."

Tia stands tall on the wall. "Sure," she gripes, "that's if fate's name is Logos that is."

"Go on now." says Logos, smiling. "Plus I need someone to keep me informed on the goings on in there. And who better than my favourite little alien?"

Tia rolls her eyes. "Fine!" she says.

She rumbles down the other side of the wall to the school grounds. "Wait just a sec!" she says, "Logos, you're not coming?"

"My attendance is not required. Plus, my main job here today is to keep the student inmates from going AWOL."

Tia scowls as she tightly grabs on to her book. She walks grudgingly toward the south pillar of the Imperial Palace.

"Lady Tia?" cries Logos, "Just try to stay out of trouble, alright?"

Tia sneers capriciously back at the distant voice. "What's he intimating — me — trouble?" she murmurs. Her mumblings continue as she inattentively passes through the pillar's door.

"I feel so duped." she says, walking distractedly past the imperial guards and up the stairs. "Maybe he really is too smart for his own good." she giggles, "And definitely too cute for mine."

Her mutterings evaporate as she enters a bustling stadium.

TÄNKACLOCK (T-Clock) — ... it has never been halted from its countdown. Since the beginning, when the Holy White Order took over the Realm, thy T-Clock has continued to tick down the time left to thy Ascension.

2. The Challenge T-Matches allow the T-Clock to record the amount of total memory that remains in Nirvia through the Insignification updates (see NAT Tech Manual no.2 sec.5 — TänkaClock).

3. The T-Clock shall signal the arrival of the Golden T-Hour wherein the remaining memory shall be filled by the last Key Keeper's Challenge. This will take place in the final Conclave of the Holy White Order (see NAT Tech Manual no.2: sec.10 — Golden T-Hour).

4. The Golden T-Hour shall signal the T-Clock's Final Countdown.

5. When the T-Clock strikes Zero thy Resurrection shall begin and thou shall shed thy body on Earth and thy Holy White soul shall be transmuted to thy awaiting Avatar in Nirvia (see NAT Tech Manual no.3: Book of Revelations — Ascension).

6. Thy soul shall fill thy Soulless Avatar and thy Soulful Avatar shall continue to live in thy heavenly Nirvia. Thus shall begin...

NEW AGE TESTAMENT

Chapter Two

The palace arena is filled with people dressed in white. The crests on their chests form a kaleidoscope of glowing colours. Inside the isles are scantly dressed holographic cheerleaders performing sensually provocative routines.

"Wow!" says Tia, screening her eyes from the dazzling show. She walks up an empty isle to a waiting area. "This is crazy. What am I doing in here?" Her voice is easily muffled by loud chants of:

'TÄN-KA-WORLD, TÄN-KA-WORLD, TÄN-KA-WORLD...'

Tia slowly retreats to the obscurity of the back wall. Her eyes remain engrossed by the arena's rambunctious scene.

A bald man in a cerulean suit stands on center stage. He invites four people seated in the front row to come up. The hexagonal stage has six circular pods at its edges. Each translucent pod has a guard in an ultramarine uniform at its side.

The contestants step up to the stage. The colours of their crests change as they ponder and wait. One by one a different colour remains statically unchanged on each of their crests.

The bald man takes hold of a virtual microphone. "I would also like to announce that it is time for those of you who would like to place a wager on this T-Match to do so."

There is a moment of shuffling in the arena's seats.

The announcer raises his hands and the arena's lights slowly dim. "Please combatants," he instructs, "select your T-Pods!"

The first combatant walks over to one of the pods. She undresses and walks inside. The sphere inside her chest has remained fixed on Blue.

The pod suddenly forms a Blue hue around it. The rest of the combatants do the same as they enter their own reflective pods.

"Holy White Order — Insignify!" yells out the announcer.

The seats in the arena slowly recline. Beams of light spawn out of the crests of those seated. The lights flow up and through the translucent floor pane of the suspended chamber. The beam suddenly stops and a virtual vortex forms beneath the chamber. The vortex explodes to form an inverted holographic parabola which domes the arena. Inside the hologram appears a dry sandy planet. A beacon flashes in the middle of a singular oasis. The holographic image zooms out and the beacon becomes a tiny dot on a beige planet. The planet is the second of five in its planetary system. Appearing at the edge of the holographic solar system are four different coloured spaceships.

The announcer abruptly yells: "Go!"

The spacecrafts quickly take off in the direction of the beige planet. A Red spaceship takes the lead, just behind it is a Green one, a Blue spaceship is running third, and trailing farther behind is an Orange spaceship.

The Orange spacecraft bursts forward and bumps into the back of the Blue spaceship. The Blue ship picks up its speed. The Orange craft continues its pursuit. It starts to fire lasers at the Blue craft. The Blue craft swerves and ducks away. The Orange spacecraft shoots again and this time makes a direct hit. The Blue spacecraft splits in half.

There are groans of disappointment in the arena.

The host of the Blue pod exits. She is handed a towel by her corner guard. She angrily throws it to the floor. She puts on her dress and bows to the audience. Her Blue crest loses its fixed glow as she leaves the stage. Her pod returns to its original translucent state.

The Orange spacecraft continues unobstructed toward the beige planet. Meanwhile the other two spacecrafts are violently crashing into one another. The Green craft makes a hard turn and comes around Red spaceship. It blasts its Green lasers and obliterates the Red ship.

The man inside the Red pod walks out. He is handed a towel by another guard. The combatant hastily dries his perspiration before putting back on his white suit. He bows to the audience and sadly returns to his seat. His Red glowing crest disappears into his white suit. His Red glowing pod becomes translucent.

On the top right hand corner of the hologram is a time clock ticking down:

'0000:000:02:07:36, 0000:000:02:07:35...'

A loud roar rises from the arena as the Green spaceship catches up with the other. They both take turns dodging each other's lasers until the Orange craft manages to extend its lead.

The Orange spacecraft is the first to orbit the beige planet. It hovers for a few moments before dashing down toward the planet's southern hemisphere. The ship lands hard on the planet's sandy surface.

There is a small pause before its door slides open. A humongous head of a snake peers out. Its Orange eyes gaze outward till it locates the not too distant oasis. It slowly slithers the rest of its gargantuan body out of the spacecraft.

"EWW, Gross!" a woman's voice yells out from the audience.

The snake submerges itself beneath the sandy surface and slithers towards the flashing beacon nestled in the oasis.

The stadium fills with sounds of nervous laughter.

The holographic time clock continues to tick down:

'0000:000:01:53:02, 0000:000:01:53:01...'

The Green spaceship lands a short distance away. Its door opens and a Green eyed dragon edges out. It dexterously widens its fiery wings as it sends out a shrilling cry.

The arena is momentarily quieted by the dragon's screech. A burst of excited applause quickly follows.

The sandy planet's atmosphere turns suddenly violent as it fills with electrifying lightning bolts.

The mammoth dragon inspects its surroundings before taking flight in the direction of the beacon. It swerves left and right trying to pass through the relentless barrage of fulgurating lightning strikes. It spots low sinusoidal waves of sand moving in the direction of the beacon. The dragon plunges toward the undulating sand dunes. It inflames the area with its flaming breath. The firestorm bounces off the hard sand. The waves in the sand continue to move unhampered toward the beacon. The dragon tries to fly past the fast moving sand wave, but its tail is suddenly struck by a bolt lightning.

There is a simmer of worry rising in the audience.

The dragon is hit once again and loses its balance. It stumbles and falls to the surface. It tries to quickly take flight but is unable to as it slips and slides on the surface's fulgurites. Unable to gain traction it desperately flaps its large wings.

Out of the depths of the sand the ominous head of the snake reappears. Its speed sends half of its body high above the surface. And as it comes down it strikes the skull of the dragon with its heavy weight. The stunned dragon tries to breathe out its fire, but the snake rapidly unhinges its jaw and clamps it down over the dragon's mouth. The muzzle successfully smothers the dragon's aspiration as the dragon's breath turns into harmless fumes.

The dragon flaps its wings frantically as the snake tries to wind its long body around it. The disoriented dragon staggers further and the snake successfully wraps its long body around the dragon's wings.

There are squeamish sounds from the audience as the crushing sounds of the dragon's bones fill the arena.

The snake unwinds its body and slithers toward the beacon. The crushed dragon lies motionless on the sand with smoke seeping from its mouth.

The snake slithers around the oasis and stops at the beacon. Just beneath the flashing beacon is a gold key. The snake draws out its bloodied fangs and captures it. The holographic image freezes. The clock inside it reads:

'0000:000:01:36:66.'

The hologram enveloping the arena disappears. The vortex momentarily returns before collapsing unto itself.

The stadium's lights turn back on. The seats in the arena reset to their original horizontal position. Congratulatory cries suddenly invade the arena as bells and whistles ring all about.

The last two heavily perspiring participants step out of their respective pods. They are handed towels and proceed to dry themselves off. They put their white suits back on and walk over to the announcer.

The stage announcer raises the hand of King Osiris. "Winner — Orange!" he loudly declares.

A loud cheer rises in the audience.

The king waves to the crowd as he continues to pat down his lightly wet and whitely blond hair.

"Let's also give a warm applause to our third and fourth placed combatants." says the announcer, pointing to the front row seats. The defeated combatants reply with a short wave to the audience.

A light applause ensues.

The announcer points the audience to the man from the Green pod. The man steps forward and bows to the audience.

"And let's give a warmer applause to the courageous second place finisher — the Tenth of his name — Lord Sheshi — The Master."

A more vigorous applause rises from the crowd.

The announcer raises his hands. The crowd quiets down. He points to the commander standing near the stage.

"To reassert our present Key Keeper as the Ruler of the Realm we have the privilege to have with us today our illustrious Commander: Lazarus — The Truth Seeker!"

The commander is welcomed on stage by a loud thundering applause. He places his large hand over the carmine stains of his white suit and bows.

"I see that your past exploits in the T-Matches have not yet been forgotten." says the announcer.

The king shoots the announcer a glancing command. The announcer raises his arms and the audience quiets down.

The announcer invites the king to come forth. "Here again is our winner." declares the announcer, "The Pharaoh of Pharaohs — The King of Kings — The Keeper of the Golden Key — Our Glorious Ruler — the Thirteenth of his name — Lord Osiris!"

The king steps in front of the commander. His crest still glows Orange as he waves to the invigorated audience. He glances at his opponents with a congratulatory nod. And lastly he acknowledges the presence of his commander.

Celebratory virtual fireworks light up the coliseum. The audience fills the arena with vigorous cheers of:

'OSIRIS, OSIRIS, OSIRIS...'

The king steps off the stage and the stage guards follow him. His fixed Orange crest dissolves and the Orange pod becomes translucent.

The applause grows louder still as the king walks up the isle. His crest is now a bright Blue. The guards escort him to the north pillar where an elevator waits open. Two of the six guards remain behind while the others enter the elevator with the king. The elevator door closes.

The applause slowly dampens.

High in the back shadows of the arena a woman's voice suddenly rings out, "Hey! What are you doing over there?"

"Huh?" answers a confused looking Tia.

-2-

A tall elegant woman in a sapphire coloured dress quickly approaches Tia. "What are you doing back here?" she says.

Tia gazes blankly back at the attendant. A Yellow crest momentarily appears on her grey dress.

The attendant slows down her pace. "I am sorry for my aggressive tone, young lady." The woman takes out a small circular instrument and scans it over Tia's crest. "Oh?" she says, "I see that you have just today attained your Age of Ascension."

Tia nods up and down silently.

"Congratulations." replies the woman, sincerely. "All that is left now is your Confirmation."

Tia remains silent.

The attendant flashes another instrument over Tia. Tia's grey dress slowly transforms into a pristine white dress.

"There you go, young lady. You are now part of the Holy White Order. You have been registered and are henceforth permitted to enter TänkaWorld."

Tia places her hands on her suddenly flickering temple implants. "Ouch!" she says, "They hurt!"

"My lady, your ocular synapses are coming in line with your T-Vision. The pain will stop in just a few moments."

"Are you sure?"

"Yes, my lady."

"Hey, you're right." says Tia, smiling.

"Good." says the attendant, scrutinizing her scanner. "Your seat in the Holy White Order has just been assigned. It is the alphanumeric designation: C-7."

"C-7?" repeats Tia.

"Yes, my lady. Please go now to your seat."

Suddenly the amplified voice of the announcer rings out: "Ladies and lords, we have a surprise for you today."

Tia stands confused at the top of the isle. The attendant tugs at Tia's white dress. "My lady, your seat is down there."

she whispers, "Third row from the stage and seven seats to your right." Tia heads down the stairs towards the stage.

The announcer continues, "Since the T-Clock has spatial time to spare before reaching the Golden T-Hour, we have the permission of our majesty the king to hold a second T-Match. It shall be a Preliminary T-Match that will not accept any spatial wagers."

The bells and whistles start up again with the announcement. "Holy Whites, this shall be the last Preliminary T-Match before the Final Conclave."

The audience begins to chant:

'TÄN-KA-WORLD, TÄN-KA-WORLD, TÄN-KA-WORLD...'

Tia stoops down as she walks down the stairs. She reaches the third row from the stage. Her presence on the isle is lost in the midst of the revitalized crowd. She carefully tries to slip past those seated to her right.

"Watch it!" cries out a young woman.

"I'm sorry." replies Tia, "I didn't mean to step on your foot."

Tia unwarily nudges herself along while continuously repeating, "Excuse me... excuse me..."

"Please give a warm welcome to one of our best. The Seventh of his name, Lord Narmer — The Conqueror!" says the announcer, loudly.

A youthful Lord Narmer bows to the audience.

The audience reacts with a loud cheer.

"We need a volunteer from the audience. Which one of you would like to stand up and take up the Challenge?"

The crowd suddenly turns quiet. Many Yellow crests suddenly appear in the audience.

"Do not be alarmed my ladies and lords. I'm sure that Lord Narmer shall be relatively kind to whoever is hearty enough to step forth and face him."

Tia finally reaches her seat, but the leg of a young man is straddled over it. The young man is unaware of her presence as he is conversing with others behind him. Tia taps his leg and gets his attention. He stirs his head and Tia's face turns pale.

"Well, well, look who we have here!" says Ramsey, winking to his gang. "What a nice surprise."

His sarcasm weighs heavily on Tia's depressed lips. "Oh, great!" she says. She tries to sit, but Ramsey kicks at her and dislodges the book from her chest.

"What are you doing masquerading yourself as a White." he says.

"I am NOT masquerading myself." replies Tia.

"Oh, so you're now a full fledged White? That's just great!" he says with a sneer.

Tia tries to pick her book up from the floor, but Titi kicks it farther down the isle.

Tia puts her hands on her hips and waits as her book continues to be kicked around. "That's really mature of you guys." she says. She remains firmly waiting while others around her chirp with laughter. "What are you all laughing at?"

People sitting above are laughingly pointing behind her.

Tia looks around her and embarrassingly realizes that she is the only one standing. She notices the announcer pointing at her.

His voice finally penetrates Tia's consciousness. "My lady, I am speaking to you."

Tia's disgruntled face wrinkles at the announcer.

"My lady, did you not hear me?"

"I'm sorry?" says Tia.

"My lady, I said that you can come on up now."

"Are you speaking to me?"

"Yes, my lady." says the announcer, pointing to another man in a cerulean outfit. "The steward will escort you up."

"Huh?"

The arena is filled to its capacity. Starting from the youngest in its lower rows and ending with the eldest in the upper rows.

The steward waits just outside Tia's row. Tia looks helplessly around.

"Yes, my lady." the announcer reiterates, "I am addressing you."

"But—"

Her objection is quickly drowned out by loud disruptive noises from Ramsey and his gang.

"It takes courage to stand up to such a challenge." says the announcer, "What's your name, my lady?"

"Tia." she timidly replies, looking bemused.

"Welcome to the last Preliminary T-Match of our Age."

A coordinated series of physical nudges from Ramsey's crew push Tia out into the isle. A bombastic chant follows her:

'TIA, TIA, TIA...'

"This way, my lady." says the steward.

The steward accompanies Tia up to the stage.

"Lady Tia?" says the announcer, waving his hand over her dazed stupor. "Lady Tia, are you ready?"

Tia nods back at him as her eyes flutter. The chant turns into laughter as Tia's crest freezes at Yellow.

"Holy Whites — select your T-Pods!" the announcer says, signalling Tia and Narmer to the pods.

Cheers burst out throughout the arena as Lord Narmer removes his white suit and enters his selected pod. The pod immediately forms a Blue hue that matches his Blue glowing spherical implant.

Tia is snapped out of her daze by an encouraging push from the announcer. "My lady, choose a T-Pod." he says.

Tia looks paralysed. "My lady," whispers loudly the announcer, "you must enter one of the T-Pods."

Tia robotically moves near one of the pods. "My lady, please remove your clothing before entering."

Tia shakes her head.

"No?" says the announcer, "My lady, it's going to get hot in the T-Pod."

Tia disregards the announcer and steps inside the pod fully dressed. Her feet and hands are quickly sucked into the pod's malleable gyroscopic frame. She stands inside the round pod with outstretched hands and feet locked in place. The pod forms a Yellow hue around it.

"Haven't seen that colour in a T-Pod in a long time," chuckles loudly the announcer.

There is a loud gaggle that follows from the audience.

"Holy White Order, if you please," he loudly declares, "Insignify!"

The audience simultaneously place their forearms on their arm rests. Their seats recline and beams of light immediately emanate from their crests once again. The beams streak up to the chamber and after the vortex momentarily forms a holographic image envelopes the top of the open arena. An intermittent beacon suddenly appears deep beneath a watery planet. The holographic picture zooms out and shows that the planet is the sixth in its large solar system.

The announcer calls out: "Combatants — are you ready?!"

Narmer nods at the announcer from his Blue tinted pod.

The announcer turns to Tia. Tia looks confused within her Yellow tinted pod. The announcer walks over to her. "Are you ready, my lady?" he softly repeats.

"Ready? What do you mean?"

"My lady, are you ready for your T-Match?" the announcer specifies.

"I'm sorry, sir, but I've never participated in TänkaWorld."

"You've never partaken in any Conclave?" he says, stunned.

"I have not, sir."

"Well, well!" he loudly declares, "Audience, we have here an uninitiated Holy White."

The audience starts to boo laughingly.

"Well then, this will be a very public baptism." he says, taking the liberty to wink mischievously to the gawking audience. "So, my lady, I guess you're unfamiliar with the rules?"

Tia's eyes glaze over. "Rules? What rules?"

The announcer lets out a haphazard chuckle. "My lady, here is a quick synopsis of how T-World Matches function. Something that I confess I haven't had to describe in quite awhile." he says, regaining his professional formality. "It's actually not as difficult as it may appear. T-World Matches are about being the first to reach the beacon on a randomly selected planet and obtaining the Golden T-Key within."

"Oh, that doesn't sound so hard." replies Tia, grinning.

"In order to arrive at the beacon first you must formulate a T-Match Avatar that will maximize your best chance in retrieving the prize before your opponent's Avatar does."

"And how do I do that?"

"My lady, if you make it to the planet with the beacon your consciousness will be prompted to create an Avatar based on the nomenclature displayed inside your spacecraft."

The crowd's chatter quickly turns into a chorus of impatient mutterings.

"Does that clear things up for you, Lady Tia?"

"Nuh-huh?" mumbles Tia.

The announcer lets out a visceral laugh. "I know it must sound complicated for a first timer, but don't worry, my lady." he says, "The T-Pod will do most of the work for you."

"But I don't understand—"

"My lady, you really don't know, do you?" The announcer raises his hands and quiets the crowd.

"My lady, this is not just about the conscious world, but also that of your subconscious. The process is similar to that of a lucid dream, where your semi-conscious state takes part within. Your mind will assess the given parameters and create the best corresponding Avatar within a given time limit. At that point, your anthropomorphized virtual concept will appear as your Avatar and the T-Match will be afoot. The victor shall be the first Avatar to capture the Golden T-Key."

"Oh?!" utters Tia.

The announcer tries to hurry as he sees Narmer uncomfortably fidgeting in his Blue tinted pod.

"There's one more thing, my lady. We have placed a time limit on this T-Match of 36 minutes and 66 seconds in order to have the T-Clock descend to exactly one hour — the Golden T-Hour. If neither of you succeeds within the time allowed to capture the Golden T-Key the T-Match will end in a draw. Just remember that time in T-World does not necessarily reflect our own time. I hope this is clear?"

Tia remains beckoning inside her Yellow pod.

"Good luck, my lady." says the announcer. He raises his hands toward the raucous crowd.

Without any time lapse two spaceships appear within the hologram. Tia finds herself sitting in a Yellow spacecraft. A Blue spacecraft waits next to her.

"Ready — set — Go!" yells the announcer.

The Blue spacecraft quickly takes off. The Yellow craft remains still.

Tia looks curiously inside her spaceship. "Wow!" she says. She looks out her cockpit and sees the Blue craft way ahead of her in space. "Hey, how do I follow him?"

Suddenly her spacecraft takes off. Her body begins to turn inside the pod. The Yellow spaceship moves as she does. "This is so cool!" she murmurs.

There is a slight reflection of Tia's avatar in the spaceship.

"Hey, I look like me. I guess this is my future self." Her avatar touches its nose with the curiosity of a child learning to become aware of its own image. "This is really cool. I can sort of feel my Avatar's nose. And my Avatar sounds just like me."

The Blue spaceship stops before reaching the navy blue planet. It turns back and swirls around the approaching Yellow craft. It fires a series of Blue lasers which graze the Yellow ship.

"Hey!" says Tia, "Stop that!"

A loud gaggle rises in the audience.

The Blue craft stops firing and moves to orbit the planet first. It dashes down towards its northern hemisphere.

Tia's Yellow spacecraft finally reaches the planet. A virtual screen pops-up in front of her. A light flickers on it with the specific location of the beacon.

"Oh, I get it." she says, "That's where the Golden T-Key is."

As soon as she finishes her sentence her spacecraft plunges toward the beacon. It swerves and ducks through the planet's heavy clouds.

"There!" she says.

Her spaceship crash lands in the Ocean near the flickering beacon. The spacecraft bubbles back up to the surface.

In her pod Tia wobbles from side to side along with her virtual ship.

Her avatar scratches its head as the virtual screen lists the planet's nomenclature. "What does this all mean?"

The only response she hears is laughter from the audience.

Tia's avatar traces her finger over the information on the screen. "Now let's see," she says, "The planet surface is made of H2O — it's like a lake. Well that seems simple enough."

The holographic clock continues to tick down:

'0000:000:01:25:66, 0000:000:01:25:65...'

The exit door of the Yellow spacecraft gradually slides open. Tia's personal avatar moves to the exit. It starts to transform itself as it steps out.

An anxious sound vibrates in the audience as a flipper like foot edges out first. Then the rest of her game avatar emerges.

A loud scuffed laughter suddenly rises from the audience.

The avatar is Tia wearing a wet suit. She carries with it a long Yellow spear-gun. She places the cumbersome spear-gun into the buoyant water and flops in next to it. She puts on a pair of goggles over her Yellow glowing eyes and places a snorkel in her mouth.

The voice of Ramsey can be overheard yelling, "Look everyone — it's FROG-GIRL!"

Frog-Girl sinks her head into the ocean as if to drown out the ridiculing comment. "Now," she gurgles, "where's that freaking beacon?"

She scans the deep waters and locates the direction of the flickering signal. She starts to swim down toward it. She suddenly stops. "Hey!" she mumbles through her snorkel, "What happened to the other guy?" She restarts her downward course with a little more speed. "Alright, it's not that far."

A gold key glows beneath the beacon.

"This is easier than I thought." she muffles.

But something suddenly whizzes by her.

The audience's mocks ominously change.

Frog-Girl turns abruptly as something swishes by her again. "Huh?" she bubbles.

Again something whisks by her. She turns quickly and sees a creature disappearing in the waters behind her.

"What the hell was that?!" she says, panting. Her heavy breathing fogs up her goggles. She closes her eyes and slows down her breathing. "C'mon girl, it's just a game." she mumbles. She regains her composure and continues her dive with her Yellow spear-gun pointing the way.

Out of the deep the creature suddenly slaps her spear-gun out of her hand.

"Shit!" she says, breaking her dive. The spear-gun slowly drops away from her. She spots it and starts to flap her fins towards it. She stretches her arm out but the spear-gun's gravitational descent keeps it just out of her reach.

Out of the dark waters a reptilian creature lunges straight at her.

A loud cry surfaces from the audience.

Frog-girl manages to swerve away from the creature's attack. "Yikes!" she grumbles.

She sees her spear-gun slowly fading out of view. She scrambles to pick up her pace in its direction.

Griping sounds suddenly reverberate in the audience.

The creature reappears and playfully tugs at frog-girl's feet. Frog-girl kicks and twists as hard as possible. She accidentally smacks the creature on its long toothed face. The creature appears stunned for a moment as it watches frog-girl swim away. Its encrusted Blue eyes glow wild. It violently snaps its serrated teeth and shoots down after her.

A rousing applause rises from the audience.

"Go get her!" screams out Ramsey, "She's dead now!"

The creature moves with deadly force toward frog-girl. The creature captures frog girl's leg. It flings her back and frog-girl comes face to face with the reptilian creature. The creature stares directly into her Yellow eyes. It snaps out its teeth and edges closer to frog-girl's throat.

The audience's demeanour turns deadly silent.

The creature's face suddenly turns flaccid. The reptilian creature looks down and finds the Yellow spear lodged through its chest. The creature gazes intensely at a shocked looking frog-girl. Frog-girl in turn glares at her discharged gun. The creature relinquishes its hold on frog-girl as it begins to sink.

There is absolute silence in the arena as the heavy body of the reptilian creature is being slowly swallowed up by the dark ocean.

Tia profoundly stares at the reptilian's fading Blue eyes. "Oh No!" she says, sadly. "I didn't mean..."

The Yellow spear sticking out of the creature's body turns Black and so do frog-girl's eyes. Frog-girl speedily swims down toward the creature, but its lifeless body has already disappeared into the abyss. She turns worriedly around and sobs. The bright light of the gold key is by her side. She edges closer to it but does not grab it.

The virtual clock continues to tick down before automatically stopping at:

'0000:00:00:01:00:00'

The holographic vortex above center stage closes in on itself and disappears.

Tia is crying in her pod. "I hate this game!" she cries, "Can I leave now?"

The two pods open and both Tia and Narmer step out. Tia picks up a towel and wipes away the glow of perspiration from her face. She looks over at the naked Narmer and gazes at the Black sphere in his chest. She gawks at the Black hue around her pod. She lowers her head in dismay and her eyes suddenly pop at the sight of the Black crest on her dress. She turns to the perplexed looking audience. Their crests are a myriad of colours, but with one glaring exception. Sitting in the fourth row is a disquieted Ramsey staring at his own Black crest.

Over on center stage Tia watches as the perplexed Narmer puts his white suit back on. A Black crest momentarily forms on his chest before disappearing. His suit is again a pristine white.

Tia gazes in shock at the audience and sees Ramsey's Black crest also disappear. She glances back down at her own crest and confusingly watches her crest remain Black.

The shocking silence in the audience slowly breaks and a vigorous grumbling takes over.

"Look at that black sheep!" hollers Ramsey, "Baaaah!"

The audience's silent mystification turns loudly aggressive.

Tia jumps off the stage and quickly starts climbing the stairs. A hand suddenly grabs her arm. "Let go of me!" she says. She turns her head and sees Ramsey holding her.

"What did you do to me?" he whispers, his grip tightening.

"You're hurting me!" says Tia, staring deeply into his eyes.

Ramsey gently loosens his grip. Tia shakes her arm away and swiftly runs up the isle. She looks behind her and sees the audience gawking up at her. She quickly runs down the pillar's staircase and out of the palace.

Chapter Three

A man in a sapphire uniform sits at laboratory table. His face is reflected by the glassy panel opposite him. A brawny man in a white suit stands behind him.

"Sir, how can this be?" says the scientist.

A holographic image of two intertwined helical strands hover over the laboratory table. The strands coil together like two subatomic snakes in a mating ritual. A flickering diode appears in the place of a missing particle in one of the strands.

The man behind him moves closer. His carmine stained outfit becomes clearly identifiable.

"Commander, how is this possible?" reiterates the scientist.

Commander Lazarus places his large hand on the scientist's shoulder.

The lab engineer turns squeamish at the touch. "I am sorry, Commander." he says, watching carefully the commander's cold reflection. "I-I lost my place."

"Sapphire, are you sure about this test result?" asks the commander.

"Yes sir!"

"What steps have you taken to make sure?"

"Commander, I have performed the test several times with the exact same results."

"And what do you make of it?"

"I am completely baffled, Commander." replies the perturbed looking scientist, "I have never seen such a mutation before."

"And you still haven't." corrects the commander.

The scientist gulps at the commander's intimidating tone. "Yes sir." he stutters, "This-this will not leave the room, sir."

"Make sure that it never does."

The scientist nods in continuity. "Yes, Commander Lazarus, I understand."

Lazarus leaves the laboratory.

The technician lets out a deep sigh. He stares at the holographic strands and scratches his head. "I do not like incongruent results. No, I do not like them at all."

Resting beneath the hologram of the helix is the notation:

'D.N.A. Test results for subject number A809: Discrepancy found: INERT GOD GENE.'

DOMA SCIENTISTS (D-Scientists) — ... D-Scientists are specially selected Monochromes whose exceptional aptitudes for science has made them the ideal receptacles for the Endo-Chromatic Cybernetic Diffusion implants (ECCD).

2. The Endo-Chromatic Cybernetic Diffusion technology shall increase the intellectual capacity of the selected brains through the reallocation of their emotive synaptic energies (see NAT Tech Manual: no.1: sec.6).

3. The primary duty of a D-Scientist is to serve as medical and technical support to Domans. Subsequently, they shall also instruct at thy Holy White Schools.

4. The D-Scientist's Sapphire outfits shall be of the highest level in the monochromatic colour ranking. Along with the Ultramarines and Fuchsias the Sapphires shall be the only other Monochromes to reside in Doma.

5. The Sapphires shall also serve during the Conclaves. They, along with the rest of the Doman Citizenry, shall also have the honour to accompany the Holy Whites to the End of Time in the Final Conclave (see NAT Tech Manual no.2: sec.3 — Book of Revelations).

6. The D-Scientists may also be addressed as Sapphires as this shall be in keeping with the hierarchical system of colours of the Realm and...

NEW AGE TESTAMENT

PART II

THE GOD GENE

Chapter One

A light rain drips over the dome and disappears down its geodesic sides. The lights inside the dome brighten as the moody skies darken.

Tia sits at the back of a rising lecture hall scribbling. Her classmates are all gathered together gesticulating in her direction.

"Alright class." says Logos, "Break is over."

The students continue to whisper loudly among themselves.

"That's enough!" says Logos, "Please pay attention."

Suddenly the focus of the class returns to their teacher as a life size hologram appears behind him. The hologram holds within it a heavenly looking garden with a beautiful fig filled tree at its center. A man and a woman stand naked under the tree. Partially hidden in one of the branches is a long snake. The snake slithers down and hisses to the woman. The woman detaches a fig from the tree and bites into it. Leafs fall from the shaken tree as she shares the fig with the man. Suddenly the naked man and woman look at each other with reddened cheeks. They each pick up the fallen leafs and use them to cover their genitalia. The hologram freezes still.

"Class, what do you make of this ancient EBOLAD story as recounted here?"

There is no response as belittling murmurs continue in the direction of Tia.

"Lady Tia," says Logos, "please come and join me."

Tia looks up from her desk. "Huh?" she mumbles.

"Please, my lady." says Logos, politely. "Will you come to the front of the class?"

Tia timidly picks up her notebook and holds it tightly against her chest. She walks down through the sneering sounds of her classmates.

"Thank-you, my lady." says Logos, "If you would not mind I would like to know if you have any thoughts on this matter."

"I'm sorry, Logos — Professor. I don't understand what you're asking."

There is a collective titter of laughter in the classroom.

"Alright class, calm your puerile snigger down." says Logos.

The classroom slowly quiets down.

Logos places his hand on Tia's shoulder. "My lady," he says, "are you alright?"

"I'm fine, Professor."

"Good." he says, staring down the class. "As I was saying, the story that the hologram has just recounted for us comes from one of the retrieved scripts that make up the amalgamated scriptures of the EBOLAD. It describes a garden where a man named 'Adam' and a woman named 'Eve' coexisted peacefully till a snake convinced them to betray their God's confidence — A God who forbade his creations to consume the fruits from the Tree of Knowledge."

Logos glances over at a glumly looking Tia. "Are you sure you are alright, my lady?" he whispers.

"Please go on, Professor." she says, pleading the attention away.

Logos enters the stationary hologram behind him.

"As we can see here," he says, pointing to the bitten fig. "It is at this point that both Adam and Eve were expelled from Eden. I am sure you are all familiar with this story, as it was the inspiration for the virtual world you know as Nirvia. The name Nirvia by the way was derived from an ancient word that referred to a spiritual place of great peace and love."

Logos walks out of the hologram and sits on his desk.

"So, Lady Tia," he says, "What do you think this story is about?"

"I...don't really know."

The class glees with her lack of response.

Logos stands up and glares at the students. "Lady Tia, do not let others dictate what, if anything, you would like to say. This is a Doman approved Philohistory class, and NO logical ideas will be curtailed or suppressed by stupidity or ignorance."

The smirking smiles in the class disperse. The ridiculing guffaws swiftly halt.

"Please, my lady." says Logos, drawing Tia's notebook out of her arms. He invites Tia to enter the historical hologram.

Tia takes a deep contemplative breath and steps inside. "I think that this story is not a literal one. I think this garden was like a place of peace," says Tia, "where time did not seem to exist till it slithered its way in."

"Slithered like you?" says Titi, goggling. She glances behind her at a distant Ramsey.

"I would say that that is a very interesting interpretation, my lady?" says Logos, his gaze continuing to control the class. "You see, class," he continues, "the warning associated with the eating from the fruit of the Tree of Knowledge was to prevent the corruption of one's conscience from the duality associated with self-consciousness. It appears that here human beings coexisted peacefully among all life forms, but once human beings consumed the fruit from the Tree of Knowledge, they became dividedly self-aware."

"Umm?" mumbles Tia.

The professor winks encouragingly at her, and continues, "You see class, when the circumstances for the early humanoid species improved so did the size of their brain. The brain was then able to memorize more and more data. This increased ability allowed the brain to capture and store ever more complex experiences. These learned experiences were then accessed by the brain to compare and judge in order to enhance the probability of its survival. This psychological time differential between one memory and another is what formulated the early developments of subjective thought. It is the rise of this conscious ability that provoked the human species to evolve beyond that of other primates. Hence when the fruit of knowledge was consumed, subjective knowledge became part of their being. And so biting into the Tree of Knowledge was the actual advent of the self."

"And your eyes shall be opened upon the eating of the fruit..." says Tia, softly. "At least that's what I think the Old Age Scriptures say."

Logos places his hand pensively on his chin. "That is correct," he says, "this story is but an allegorical interpretation of when human beings became self-conscious. That's why Adam and Eve suddenly felt the need to cover up their shame."

There are murmurs in the class.

"The self then developed a moral compass based on what it did not want others to do to it. Then it used this compass to differentiate itself from others of its kind. This differentiation brought about the divineness that has plagued mankind from its beginnings. The self became judge and jury of its peers, as it now saw itself different from another. This individuality separated it from the holistic garden you see here."

"And you will know both Good and Evil." whispers Tia.

"Exactly, Tia." says Logos, "It is the development of the self that is the Original Sin depicted in this story."

There is an immediate increase in the classroom chatter.

Logos stops and addresses his agitated students. "But I am afraid, Holy Whites," he incites, "that Nirvia is but a continuation of this story."

A student jumps up out of his chair. "That's blasphemy!" he shouts, "Sapphire, you dare mock our heavenly Nirvia."

"You are wrong, Professor." stridently adds another student, "Because we, the Chosen, shall return to Eden."

"Alright, alright, calm down." says Logs, "But how does retaining the essence of your personal souls and transcending that same divisive essence to another reality help you evolve?"

Suddenly there is an eerie silence that overtakes the class. Their crests flicker through different colours. Tia's white dress remains untouched.

"You will be reported, Professor." says one of the students displaying a Purple crest.

Inconspicuously Tia's crest flashes briefly Black. "Back off the Professor!" she says.

The lecture hall suddenly dims. The students quietly stare up at a dark cloud travelling over the dome.

"All the professor is saying is that without a ME there would not be a YOU!" adds Tia.

Titi jumps up from her seat. "What do you know!" she loudly chortles, pulling back her long slick hair. "I'd rather be ME than YOU anytime. My name is Nefertiti — Tenth of her name! And who are you — First of your name?"

"No one!" says another student, "She's No One!"

The mockery provokes a cackling condemnation.

"Before thinking you're something," replies Tia, bolting through her classmates. "You should first realize you're nothing."

"Ramsey was right about you," says Titi, pointing to the hologram. "You belong here as much as that talking snake belonged there."

"Oh c'mon, now I'm a snake?!" replies Tia, "You guys should make up your minds — am I an alien or a snake?"

"You're a talking snake, which makes you an alien!" cries Titi.

Tia exits the University mumbling. "Sure, it's always the alien's fault."

TÄNKAPORTS (T-Ports) — ... are small modular casings embedded throughout the dome. They transmit and receive data through the synaptic interchange of the dome's translucent membrane.

2. T-Ports may, at any and at all times, be available to receive the Key Keeper's Golden Key and stop the TänkaClock Countdown.

3. T-Ports monitor all thy sanctified InsignAnimas throughout Doma (see NAT Tech Manual no.2: sec.7).

4. T-Ports use a laser scanning technology to detect any unauthorized personnel in Doma.

5. T-Ports are also the primary disseminators of Imperial Holocasts throughout Doma as ordered by the Key Keeper for...

NEW AGE TESTAMENT

Chapter Two

The king stands eerily fixated near his desk. His shadow waxes along the marbled floor to a tile with an engraved blood stain.

A sudden knock on the door does little to disrupt his haunted gaze. A louder knock echoes further inside the chamber.

He slowly moves over to the shadows of his relics. "Come in." he says.

The commander walks in and clacks his heels together. "Sire?" he says, looking around the shadowy chamber.

"Commander Lazarus," replies the king, "I'm right here."

The commander finally spots the king lurking near the sarcophagus. "I'm sorry to disturb you, Sire. But I have the test results you ordered."

The king skulks his way out of the shadows. "You may stand at ease, Commander."

The commander immediately takes an akimbo pose. "You were correct, Sire. There seems to be a correlation between the recently reported sightings of the malfunctioning T-Crests and the Preliminary T-Match."

"What have you found out?"

"The results are quite bizarre, Sire."

"Bizarre?"

"One of the combatants appears to have a genetic abnormality."

"What do you mean?"

"Sire, the combatant has an inert God-Gene."

"That's not possible." replies the king, hard. His crest turns Purple.

"I too am angered by this turn of events, Sire."

"What's this Holy White's name?"

"The lady's name is Tia, Sire. But we've learned that this isn't her anointed name. Her true name is Istina."

"Istina?" replies the king, "That doesn't sound like an official name from the NAT."

"You're correct, Sire. But her name is nevertheless referenced in both the New Age Testament and the EBOLAD."

"How can an obscure name like Istina be of such notoriety? I've never heard of it."

"Sire, the origins of her name translates as Truth."

The king tightens his lips. "The woman's name is Truth?" he says, moving his hand roughly through his long hair. His crest flashes to Yellow and then back to Purple.

The commander gazes at the king's peculiar reaction. "Sire, is there something wrong?"

The king scowls back. "I don't need to explain myself to you, Commander."

"Of course not, Sire."

"That's right!"

"Sire, about the lady..."

"Yes, yes, go on."

"Sire, we've also determined that there's a high probability that she had something to do with the reported glitches in the TänkaCrests."

"How's that possible?"

"Sire, it seems that the first reported sighting of the malfunction occurred after she tied her T-Match. It was at that point that her T-Pod became devoid of colour."

"Did you say she tied her T-Match?"

"Yes, Sire."

"She succeeded in obtaining a draw with Lord Narmer?"

"Yes she did, Sire." replies the commander, "As a matter of fact she was in a position to win, but for some reason did not pick up her prize."

The king walks back to his desk. "You're telling me that she actually won?!" he says, glancing back at his sarcophagus.

"Sire, if I may continue."

"There's more?"

"Sire, the D-Scientists appear completely baffled by the malfunction."

"What's this all about, Commander?"

"That's just it, Sire, we don't know. This is the first case reported of any living T-Crest devoid of colour," says the commander, he closes his stance. "That is since..."

"Yes, since what, Commander?"

"Since the first recorded trials of the InsignAnimas, Sire."

"I don't remember this."

"It's our D-Scientists who, with your previously given permission, have studied parts of the Book of Revelations that concerned the original InsignAnimas."

"And what did these documents show, Commander?"

"Sire, these documents also contain records of the first failed trials. The ability to retain the living experience of our body and mind was still a work in progress at that time."

"That does not answer my original question, Commander."

"I will try to be more succinct, Sire."

"Good."

"Basically, Sire, the reports show that in the first trials showed that the spherical implants failed to record the essential body and mind patterns of their hosts. Therefore, their souls, or what they used to call their personas, were not fully retained by their InsignAnimas."

"And?" replies the king, fidgeting.

"The original InsignAnimas ended up killing their hosts. But, just before their death was declared, their translucent InsignAnimas turned dark."

"Did you say that this occurred before they died?"

"Yes Sire."

"What does it mean?"

"We're not exactly sure, Sire. The D-Scientists think that the only time an InsignAnima can turn dark while operational is if it somehow loses all recordings of the soul within."

The king shrugs his shoulders.

"It has left us perplexed as well, Sire. So we decided to run a myriad of tests on the other combatant, Lord Narmer — he was observed to have been afflicted with the faulty T-Crest."

"And what have you found out?"

"Sire, we've found that his God-Gene has somehow become dormant."

"What in Nirvia is going on here?" says the King, loudly.

The commander remains stoically rigid. "All we know, Sire, is that the only unexplainable constant in this equation is the young girl."

"How young is she?" says the king, his crest glows Red. "What does she look like?"

"Sire, we don't really have much information on the girl. She's a neophyte to T-World and her Avatar has just begun to take shape in Nirvia. All we know for now is that she appears strangely out of place among her peers."

"Apparently just like her genes." the king adds, broodingly. "Oh, young women..." he mutters, glancing at the speckle of dried blood in his marbled floor.

"Sire?" says the commander.

The king's Red crest is slowly reabsorbed back into his insalubrious white suit. "Commander, I want you to find out who this Sistina character really is?" he says, "Umm..." he mumbles, unable to retract his misspeak.

The commander sharpens his attention. "Sistina, Sire?"

The king's crest twitches Red, Blue, Purple, Green, Orange, and Yellow.

"I mean — what's this girl's name again?"

"Lady Istina, or Tia, Sire." replies the commander with a highly raised brow.

The king turns momentarily away. "That's what I meant." he replies, waving his hand. He takes a deep breath and the flickering colours of his crest are recaptured by his white suit.

"Of course, Sire."

The king glowers at the attentively puzzled commander. "Lazarus, I would like to share with you something highly private." says the king. The inflection of the king's voice is calmingly soft. "Eugenics is one of the forbidden acts in the Book of Revelations. So, my loyal Lazarus, I would like to know who broke such a fundamental law."

"I don't think this was a case of genetic manipulation, Sire."

"What do you mean?"

"All we know for now, Sire, is that the young woman in question was born with an inert God Gene."

"How's that possible?"

"We don't know, Sire."

The king scowls at the sarcophagus behind him. "This is unheard of!" he says, "Commander Lazarus, I will not allow any interference toward the coming Ascension. This young girl must be amputated from the Holy White Order. See that it's done without raising any undue suspicions."

"But Sire, she has not broken any laws."

"Commander Lazarus, do you not realize how grave a threat she is to the stability of the Realm?"

"Sire, she may not be aware of her mutation."

"That is an assumption that the Realm cannot afford to wager one. Commander, can you imagine if this were to happen again? What do you think would happen if the Holy White Order began to doubt the functionality of their InsignAnimas?"

"I see, Sire."

"Good, now do what you've sworn to do and protect the Realm."

"Yes, Sire."

The king walks back behind his desk and breathes a restorative sigh. "As for Lord Narmer, I will deal with him personally."

"Yes, Sire."

"Now leave me to my thoughts." says the king, his crest glows Purple.

The commander makes an about face and promptly leaves the king's chamber.

Chapter Three

Two men in iris outfits busily mop the stairs leading to a train platform. A gust of wind blows past them as a slick train departs from the opposite side. The train quickly vanishes through a tubular subterranean passageway.

The older of the two workers stops mopping and points his cohort to the waiting passengers. "Look at them with those virtual glasses." he says, "They look like they have halos around their heads."

"It's true, Jacob." replies his co-worker, smiling. "It's funny how the Whites just close their eyes and those things pop up out of their temples. I wonder what they're looking at?"

Jacob rests his arms over his mop. "They're all busy exploring what Nirvia has in store for them."

"That's their lands in Heaven, right? How does that work anyway?"

"Nathan, you know when they have those T-Matches?"

"Yeah," replies Nathan, "what about them?"

"Well, during those T-Matches their respective profiles are uploaded to Nirvia and that data is used to create an updated version of their persona, or what they call their Avatars. Then, using their Avatars, they roam around experiencing the different things that Nirvia has to offer in its communal spaces."

"What's a communal space?"

"They're large areas in Nirvia which they can all share."

"What kind of areas?"

"They've got all sorts of them."

"Like what?"

"Like anything you can imagine."

"Uh?" mumbles Nathan.

"There are places that existed at one time or another as depicted in the EBOLAD and even some that didn't."

"That sounds amazing."

"I hear that the places are so beautiful that they can't wait to go there. Plus, they can have their own personalized areas."

"What do you mean?"

"They each have a certain allotted space in Nirvia. They're allowed to fill those spaces with whatever fancies them."

"Things like what?"

"All sorts of things." says Jacob, "Even other Avatars — that is as long as they choose Soulless ones."

"Uh?" replies Nathan, "What's a Soulless Avatar?"

"You really don't know anything, do you?"

"I've never really cared." replies Nathan, "But this Soulless Avatar sounds interesting — what is it?"

"It means that they can choose from a wide selection of subservient Avatars for their own private usage."

"What kind of usage?"

"What do you think?"

"You mean like for sex?"

"Yeah, and pretty much anything else they want to do with them."

"Is that it?"

"No, there's much more."

"Oh?"

"You see, the Avatars that the Whites will ascend to will look similar to the Soulless ones, but only their own will contain their souls."

"I don't get it."

"Of course you don't — I haven't finished explaining it yet."

"Oh, OK."

"The Soulless Avatars are simple automatons, while their own Soulful Avatars are highly dynamic and complex. Their own Avatars will actually contain all that makes up their human soul. And from what I hear they can even compress and purge some of their past memories to make room for their souls to grow."

"Wow! How do they know which memories to purge?"

"I think they have some kind of voting system for that."

"That's incredible!" replies Nathan, "Nirvia must be some place."

"The system is so advanced that it actually knows what the Soulful Avatars want even before they do themselves."

"No way!" replies Nathan, mouth open. "How's that even possible?"

"Well, if I knew that do you think I'd be washing their floors?"

"Good one!" replies Nathan, leaning hard on his broom. "Though, if I had all the stuff they've got here, I wouldn't be spending so much time up there."

"Me too." replies Jacob, "But I hear that they can experience things in Nirvia that they're not allowed to down here."

"You mean that they have sex with their Avatars?"

"It's more like virtual sex right now."

"What a waste." says Nathan, "Too bad we can't help them with that — if you know what I mean?"

"Yeah, that's the only thing that we've got over them. They may have transformed us into part eunuchs, but we can still manage to get some action down here."

Nathan lets out a hearty laugh. "That's right." he says.

One of the white suited men suddenly opens his eyes and his virtual glasses recede into his temples.

"Shush!" whispers Jacob, "I think we'd better be quiet now. That is unless you want to end up like a Periwinkle."

"OK-OK!" replies Nathan.

One after another the virtual glasses of the waiting passengers begin to retract.

"We'd better get back to work." says Jacob, throwing his mop around the steps. "I think the West Tube is on its way into the station."

"OK." replies Nathan.

Suddenly Tia walks right through the two men. She slips on the wet steps and lands on her bum. A Blue crest momentarily appears on her chest.

The two coworkers frantically try to pick her back up. "We're so sorry, my lady." pleads Jacob.

Tia gets up and wipes her behind. "I needed that — thanks!" she says, shaking her head. "Where in Nirvia am I?"

"You're in Station 33, my lady." replies Nathan, "But on Earth."

Tia grins at Jacob.

"These Tube Stations all look alike." she says. She walks down the rest of the steps to the platform.

The waiting passengers curiously watch her.

"Wow! Quadrant 33?!" she says, "I must have been walking around in circles for hours."

She rubs her legs and looks around. Her face blushes as she notices that she is still being stared at. She glares back at those near her and they dispassionately close their eyes and their virtual glasses envelope their visions once again.

"I should try my T-Vision." she says.

"Be quiet!" a voice rings out.

"Or maybe later." she adds, noticing the scolding stares around her. "Whites are so touchy."

"Shush!" says another waiting passenger.

"I've got to stop talking to myself." murmurs Tia, quickly covering her mouth. She discreetly makes her way in front of the waiting passengers and looks nonchalantly around.

Suddenly her crest flashes a bright Yellow. Standing on the opposite side of the tracks is Ramsey.

"Yikes!" she whimpers, "Now what does he want?"

Ramsey looks firm and serious as he returns her gaze. The lights around the platform begin to flash green.

"Good." she sighs, "The Tube is almost here." She moves closer to the edge of the platform. Ramsey does the same on the other side. A blast of air blows Tia's hair around her face. She peeks through her hair and pouts at the sight of Ramsey still glowering at her. "Why is he looking at me like that?"

The lights around the platform suddenly dim.

Tia looks around and then back over to Ramsey. Ramsey starts to frenetically wave at her. His yells are muffled by an incoming burst of wind.

"What's that nut doing?" she grumbles.

Suddenly a cloaked man pushes Tia from behind. She precipitously falls onto the tracks. She tries to get up, but stumbles back down.

Screeching screams reverberate around the platform.

Tia manages to stand back up, but becomes transfixed by a light speeding towards her. "Train!" she says.

Suddenly the strong arms of a young man lift her and throw her back onto the platform. The force rolls Tia safely away from the edge. A stunned Tia foggily watches as the incoming train brightens Ramsey's Black crest before wiping him away. Tia flops down and smacks her head unconscious.

Chapter Four

In a kitchenette Logos is restlessly cooking. The steam from the pots and pans partially hide his rigid frown. He repeatedly glances toward the other end of the loft.

Suddenly a cry rings out, "No! No! Not the train!"

Logos hastily gathers a glass of water and brings it to Tia's bedside. Tia is uncomfortably twisting and turning beneath the bedcovers.

Logos carefully checks a small bump on the back of her head. "You will be alright." he whispers, delicately stroking her hand.

Tia strains to open her eyes. "Logos...is that you?"

"Yes sweetie."

Tia struggles to lift her head from the pillow. "Where am I?"

Logos sits down at the edge of the bed. "You are in my apartment." he replies.

"What happened?"

"We can talk about that later. You need your rest now."

"No-No!" she exclaims, trying hard to raise her torso.

"Please, do not try to get up."

"No, I want to know what happened." says Tia, her head giving way to the pull of her pillow.

Logos draws out a pink pill from the bed drawer. "You have suffered a concussion." says Logos, lending support to her head. "Please take this." He offers Tia the pink pill. Tia takes the pill from his hand and drinks it down.

"Logos, I need to know what happened." she asks with heavy eyelids.

"Lady Tia, do you promise to rest afterwards?"

"Yes, I promise." she replies, her words softly fading.

Logos holds her hand firmly in his. "Alright then — someone tried to hurt you."

"What?!" she replies, trying to spur herself awake.

"But you are safe now," insists Logos, caressing her hand. "And what you need now most of all is rest."

Tia groggily checks her hand. "Where did the pink key go?" she says, softly. "Wow...this is nice...thank-you so much for the massage...it feels so good...I feel...hmm...your hands are so warm...and so strong," she mutters, breathing deeply. "That feels so good...Oh please...hmm..." she says, inhaling heavily. "Oh my...no...yes...I mean...oh my...that's good...please don't stop...deeper...yes that's it..."

Tia slowly opens her eyes. Logos sits beside her on the bed holding a damp cloth over her perspiring forehead.

"Are you alright, my lady?" he says while handing her another glass of water.

"I'm all wet." she says, feeling her face.

"It sounded like you were having quite an intense dream — were you frightened?"

Tia twists herself up from the bed covers. "Umm...yeah-no, not really." she says, bashfully sinking her body beneath the covers. "But yeah — definitely intense."

"I have to admit that you had me going there." says Logos, "You dozed off as soon as you took the pill."

"The pink pill?" she asks, scratching her head.

"Yes."

"Oh."

"What did you dream?"

"I don't remember exactly," says Tia, shyly. "But it felt like I had already died and ascended to Nirvia."

"I was afraid of that."

"Huh?" mutters Tia.

"The pink pill is a derivative of a fantasy pill."

"You mean like you Monochromes take?"

"Not all Monochromes take it. But yes, you are correct."

"Will it do me any harm?"

"Not the pink pill I gave you. It sometimes has minor adverse effects, but it does effectively cure concussions. So, to answer your original concern," he says with a tender wink, "you are still on Earth among the mortals."

"Right." says Tia with a little smile.

"Though, you did sound pretty out of it." he says, placing his hand on Tia's forehead. "You still feel hot. I hope the effects of the pill were not too mischievous."

"Umm," mumbles Tia, batting her eyes. "I'd say they were just naughty enough."

"I see." says Logos.

Tia nervously gulps down the rest of the water and bashfully retreats beneath her Red glowing covers. Bit by bit her weighty eyelids succumb to their weight.

Chapter Five

A solitary light bulb hangs on a wire in the center of a stuffy dungeon. A dark metallic box glitters beneath it.

A door squeaks open and the light bulb begins to swing back and forth. The intermittent light touches the sides of the life size box. One side shows an engraving of a man hanging upside down and a saw carving him in half. The other side shows a machine stretching a man into two pieces.

The king nods to his lieutenant. The lieutenant slides open the door of the box. A naked man stands heavily perspiring inside it. His legs and arms are outstretched and locked in place.

"So, Lord Narmer, have you had enough or do you want more?"

"But, Your Majesty, I've told you all I know. I don't understand — I didn't do anything — why are you—"

"Lord Narmer!" interrupts the king, forcefully. The king pats Narmer on his sweaty back. "This isn't about you, but more about what was done to you." The king grimaces at his wet hand. "Sadly for you," he continues as he wipes his hand on the box, "I see no distinguishing differentiation."

Tears roll down Narmer's quivering chin. "What can I say or do, Sire? Please believe me — I'm innocent!"

"I'm sure you are." says the king, half nodding to the lieutenant. "Yet, there's one unanswered question that I need answered."

The lieutenant unnervingly pushes down a lever. The gyroscope attached to Narmer's limbs begins to wobble. The sphere inside Narmer's chest suddenly turns a bright Yellow.

"I'm sorry, Lord Narmer." says the king with an empty tone, "But you need to understand that I cannot allow this genetic contamination to spread."

"No! Please Sire — Please!"

"Lieutenant Noa, shut the door."

The lieutenant follows the king's command.

The king peruses the dungeon. He takes his time before returning to the side of the flickering box. "This is quite a dreary place. I've never liked the dungeon. Actually, I don't like being down here at all."

The king nods again and Noa immediately reopens the door of the dark box.

"Sire, please." cries Narmer.

"Lord Narmer, you have to understand that what I do here is for the safety of the Holy White Order."

"But Sire, please, I can feel the abyss drawing near — help me!"

The king eyes his lieutenant. The lieutenant slides the door shut again and presses the lever all the way down.

The dark box begins to spark a variety of colours. The king backs away from it as the iridescent lights spread out into the dungeon. Suddenly the lights stop.

"I think that it's all over." says the king, "Lieutenant, open the door!"

Noa opens the box's door and looks inside.

"Well," says the king, "has his mind left him?"

The guard returns a befuddled gaze to the king. The king apprehensively approaches the open box. He looks inside and quickly backs away. "Why is his face like that?!" he scowls, "What is this? His face should have signs of pure agony. Instead he looks like..."

"At peace, Sire." says Noa.

"What the hell is going?!" says the king, angrily. His crest glows Purple.

"Your Majesty," points out the lieutenant, "Lord Narmer's InsignAnima."

"What about it?" The king nears the box. His eyes grow big. "No, how can he be dead? The Black Box takes the mind not the body."

The lieutenant places his fingers on Narmer's throat. "He's not dead, Sire."

"What do you mean?"

"Sire, Lord Narmer is still breathing."

The king ferociously bangs his hand on the pod. "This doesn't make any sense," he says, "How can his soul be gone if he's still alive?!"

"I don't know, Sire." says Noa, raising his shoulders. "Maybe we should summon the Commander."

"No. That won't be necessary." The king suddenly takes a slow looping turn. "Lieutenant, just get rid of him!" he says, snapping his fingers.

"Sire?" says Noa, befuddled.

"Lieutenant, I want you to quietly dispose of Narmer's body."

"But Sire what about the unwritten White rule?"

"What about it?"

"Sire, Whites don't kill Whites."

"Well Lieutenant, then it's a fortunate thing that you're not a White, isn't it?"

"Yes, Sire." replies Noa, head down.

"Then do as I command."

"Yes Sire."

"And don't forget to incinerate his InsignAnima."

"But Sire, Commander Lazarus will question such an action."

"Lieutenant, why are you so concerned about what the commander may or may not think?"

"Umm..."

"You may speak freely, lieutenant."

"Sire, Commander Lazarus is a feared man."

The king's crest glows Green. "Feared?"

"Yes, Sire."

"Why?"

"It's not my place to say, Sire."

"But it's my place to know, lieutenant."

The lieutenant stays undecidedly still. "Sire..."

"Yes, yes — feel free to speak your mind, lieutenant."

"I'm not sure I should speak of—"

"Lieutenant," interrupts the king, "I think you're making a terrible mistake thinking that it's the commander you should be worried about. Do you understand?"

The lieutenant swallows hard. "Yes, Sire."

"Then answer me."

"Sire, many years have come and gone since the night of the attempt on your life. And the commander finds himself no closer to finding the truth of that night. It has become a sort of obsession for him. I think that it's made him a very hard and unforgiving man."

"That's good." replies the king, "I want my commander to be tough."

"Yes, Sire." adds Noa, "He is certainly that."

"And that scares you?"

"Sire, he can be quite vicious with anyone who he deems untrustworthy."

"I see."

"Sire, what will be my explanation for the destruction of Lord Narmer's InsignAnima?"

"Tell the commander that it was rendered dysfunctional by that young troublemaker."

"Young troublemaker, Sire?" replies a discombobulated Noa.

"He'll know who I mean."

"Yes Sire."

Chapter Six

The king sits alone in his chamber. His hand waves back and forth over a small globe on his desk. A miniature holographic image of Sistina appears and disappears in front of him.

A hard knock on his door suddenly awakens him from his contemplative state. "Yes, what?" he says.

"Your Majesty, it's your Commander. May he come in?"

"Wait!" the king replies, swiping away the holographic image. "Come."

The guards open the door and the commander walks in. The king looks pensively obtuse.

"Sire, am I interrupting something?"

The king pushes away from his desk. "No, not at all." he says, squirming. "Why do you ask?"

"You appeared troubled, Sire."

"I was not troubled! I-I had just fallen asleep and you surprised me — that's all. What are you doing up here at this time anyway?"

"Sire, as you have warned your subordinates before, you require that all relevant news, whether good or bad, be delivered to you as soon as possible."

"You have news for me?"

"Sire, I have failed — the girl got away."

"What do you mean the girl got away?!"

"Something happened that I didn't account for, Sire."

"What kind of something?"

"A young man jumped in out of nowhere to save the girl."

"What?" says the king, his crest turns Purple. "Who was it? I want to speak to him immediately."

"I'm sorry, Sire, but that won't be possible."

"Not possible — why?"

"He's dead, Sire."

"Dead?" replies the king, "What do you mean he's dead?!"

"Sire, the White Lord's name is, or I should say was, Ramsey. He was her schoolmate."

The king slaps his hand on his desk "And he gave his life to save hers? I'm disappointed in you, Commander. How could you miss profiling her friends?

"But that's the strange thing about this, Sire — the girl doesn't have any friends." The commander edges closer to the king's desk. "And there's something else, Sire."

The king's brow piques. "Well, spit it out?"

"Sire, before this young man jumped in to save the girl his T-Crest became as dark as the void."

The king runs his hand hard through his hair. "What in the Hell is going on here?!"

"Sire, I think the young White must have also been afflicted during the Preliminary T-Match."

"Afflicted?!"

"Sire, we have retrieved some of his tissues and the tests show that his God-Gene had also been neutralized."

The king crosses his arms. "Commander, why is this happening?"

"Sire, the D-Scientists don't exactly know. They can only speculate that there must be a correlation between this young man's gallant action and his God-Gene being dormant."

The king's crest turns Green. "My-my, Lazarus, it sounds like you admired the young man."

Without responding the commander places a small electronic chip on the king's desk.

"Is this your full report, Commander?"

The commander returns a confirming nod.

The vein on the king's forehead begins to twitch. He picks up the chip and inspects it closely. "Fine." he says, waving the commander away. "Leave me to it."

The commander does an about face and immediately leaves the chamber.

The king watches the door close before angrily tossing the chip away.

Chapter Seven

Two plates sit empty on a dinette table. Logos skilfully whisks and stirs food inside a steaming pan. He suddenly stops and thoughtfully listens at the groans emanating from the other end of the loft.

Inside the bed Tia is twisting and turning. "No!" she mumbles, loudly. Suddenly she sits up and looks around in a daze. Her body is tightly wrapped in the sheets. "How do I get out of this?!" she says, "Freaking sheets!" She kicks and pushes her way out. "Where am I?"

"You are safe in my apartment."

"Is that you, Logos?" says Tia, trudging over to the kitchenette.

"I think not, therefore I am not." he replies, smiling away the lines on his forehead.

"That's definitely you." she replies, yawning.

"Have a seat, my lady."

Tia sits down at a small dining table. Logos brings over the pan and proceeds to fill the dinner plates.

"Logos, is this your place?" she says, cosily shivering.

"Do you like it?"

"It's nice. It's certainly better than my dorm room. You know, I've never actually been in a Sapphire residence before. Though, it does feel familiar somehow."

"As you can see," replies Logos, "they treat D-Scientists relatively well...considering."

"You mean considering that you're a Monochrome with an ECCD implant in your head?"

"My lady, dinner is served."

"It sounds amusing!"

"What does?"

"My lady." she denotes, "I suddenly feel much older."

"Lady Tia, you are no longer a Grey. But you are still your youthful self."

"Brrr," she mutters, "I think your place needs to have its temperature adjusted — it's quite chilly." She palms down her smooth skin to her unobstructed spherical implant. "Oops!" she exclaims, feeling herself topless. Her sphere glows momentarily Blue as she scurries back under the protective covers of the bed.

"My lady, your White dress is on the stand next to you." says Logos, unperturbed.

Tia's face turns red as she dresses. Her crest momentarily appears Red. She makes her way back to the dining table. "Sorry about that."

Logos politely holds out her chair. "No need to apologize, my lady."

"OK. First of all, please stop calling me my lady." She takes a deep whiff as she takes her seat. "Secondly, this smells really good. What is it?"

"Just a little something I made."

"You made this?"

"I hope you like it. But just in case you do not I have also prepared a dessert platter."

"That sounds like a lot of work. Why not just order from the FPU?" she says, pointing to a wall unit behind Logos. The entrenched box has a sign above it that reads:

'Food Preparation Unit'

"I am not sure we want people to know that there is anyone up here right now." says Logos with a disarming smile, "Plus, the food from the FPU tastes just like it sounds."

"Professor, do you realize that you're comments are sometimes quite humorous?"

"Are they?"

"Now that I think about it — sometimes they are. How is—"

"Tia, have you ever done any cooking?" says Logos, "It is not so complicated. And it helps with meditation."

"Meditation?" replies Tia, "I've actually tried that. I was in a Meditative Technique seminar, but I didn't get it. All that breathing in and out just made me dizzy."

"They were probably just trying to show you how to silence your background noises."

"What background noises?"

"They are the noises that rise between the judgemental thinker and the thought."

"Oh, you mean like you spoke about in class?"

"That is correct." replies Logos, "Most so called meditations are used to try and silence the splintered thoughts of the participants."

"So called?"

"The problem is that meditative techniques have always been a sham. Because all techniques do is atrophy the brain."

"I don't understand?"

"People are generally convinced that in order to find pure peace they would need to silence their noisy thoughts through some-kind of repetitive mental exercise." says Logos, "Apparently unaware of the contradiction of such a methodology."

"Huh?" mumbles Tia, digging into her platter.

"The thinker setting out to silence thought is like a tongue deciding not to taste the food passing over it. In a similar manner how can the thinker ever create a technique to silence itself?"

Tia stops chewing. "Huh?"

"The fact is that the thinker can only delude itself into thinking that it has managed to turn itself off, just because it has managed to block its thoughts. But in actuality the thinker has only managed a temporary escape from what truly ails them. Because as soon as their obstructive focus has gone the undesired thoughts rush back in." says Logos, "At the end all this ends up doing is provide a temporary transcended feeling that diverts the confused mind from searching for true clarity."

"What do you mean?"

"It was also referred to as enlightenment at one time."

"Oh?" says Tia, "So how does one reach this enlightenment thing?"

"Now that is a question that has been around a very long time."

"And what's the answer?" replies Tia, smiling.

"There is no one way, because there are no two minds that are conditioned alike." replies Logos, "So each way lies in what it would take for each mind to fully grasp its conditioning."

"How does one do that?"

"First of all, one would need to investigate the origins of their noisy thoughts."

"Oh, I see." says Tia, "You mean that instead of trying to shut off the background noises one should figure out where they're coming from?"

"That is correct."

"So once the origins of the thoughts in question are found, what do we find?"

"Nothing really," replies Logos, "just an amalgamation of predetermined electrochemical impulses."

"Yum," hums Tia, her lips seemingly kissing every bite. "I've never tasted anything like this."

Logos places a few more pieces of the dish in her plate. "I am happy you like it."

"So," she says, "I don't understand why people continue to meditate, or do whatever they do, if they're getting just a temporary solution to what they're looking for?"

"Many do feel their getting results." replies Logos, "There is a sense of empowerment that comes from being able to focus on a present moment."

"But as you said that's only a temporary thing, right? So why continue down that same road and expect a different result?

"Hope."

"Hope?"

"There is always the hope that one day they will find enlightenment through their repetitive ways."

"Huh." mumbles Tia, "And you really don't think they're going about it the right way?"

"Unless they clear the clutter that forms their background noises all they will unwittingly find is just another type of irrational belief."

"Did you say, 'clutter'?"

"Yes, I did. The clutter of the mind is all the things that create the noises that block it from thinking clearly."

"Like what?"

"Like any type of conflicting or divisive thought." replies Logos, "Especially those which end up creating irrational beliefs."

"Huh? What irrational beliefs?"

"The kinds that manage to suppress or evade the Truth."

"But how does one decide how to deal with all this stuff?"

"What makes you think that one decides anything at all?"

"What do you mean? It's our Free Will that does, no?"

"Tia, what if Free Will was just another irrational belief?"

"What are you saying?" says Tia, purposely choosing a green vegetable from her platter. "I don't make my own choices?"

"Yes, each being does make its own choices. But those choices are NOT free. They are determined choices that are made from an ever changing synaptic wiring of that being's brain."

"Huh?"

"Every step we take in life is predetermined by our previous step."

"So we don't really choose?"

"Think about it," continues Logos, "the illusion of choice itself comes from a state of confusion."

"Huh?"

"Tia, when a mind is clear there is NO choice."

"But what did you mean when you said that one step leads to another?"

"Maybe an example may shed some light on the concept of Free Will." says Logos, "Let's say that a brain has been unknowingly wired to be attracted to a certain type of person, and upon meeting such a person that attraction raises certain urges. One such urge may be to be with that person, and in so doing that creates a drive to fulfill that urge."

Tia's crest flickers momentarily Red. "Yes, go on."

Logos serenely continues, "At this point, one would normally want to try to appease this internal friction derived from the original stimulant. And one may feel like it is willing itself to do so. And such a drive leads to an ambitious yearning to achieve the desired goal."

Tia holds up her chin with a little contented smile.

"So," continues Logos, "although one may believe that they are freely choosing to follow their desire, one is actually just reacting to the emergence of a conscious feeling of an unconscious attraction which already existed subconsciously."

"What?"

"In other words, the reaction to the stimulus in question was already determined even before the person in question ever even made its appearance."

"Huh." mutters Tia, squinting hard at Logos.

"This is not to say that people are not responsible for their programmed actions or reactions. But it is to say that it is vitally important to first become cognitive of the steps we take and then allow the next step to come from a mind that has broken away from its programming."

"How does one do that?"

"Definitely not by replacing one sort of programming with another, like changing romantic feelings with those of hate or indifference, but rather by becoming cognisant of the possibility that there may be something within that may be preventing the clarity necessary to allow for an evolutionary change."

"Professor, are you saying that even if I change my programming that I still remain a program?"

"Tia, you certainly have a way of simplifying things. Even with a bump on your head."

"So, let me see if I get the crux of what you're saying." says an invigorated Tia, "I don't really have Free Will, but that I only believe I do?"

Logos nods affirmatively.

"So what makes us believe we have the freedom to choose?"

"Now that's another really good question," says Logos, "And one which you sort of inadvertently touched upon the other day."

"I did?" giggles Tia, "I've got to pay more attention to what I say."

"That is what makes you so remarkable, Tia. It is that you do not know that you are."

Tia shyly smiles.

"In the human race there are those who are completely unaware, and so see everything separately." says Logos, "Then there are those who become aware, but consider their new found self separate from their thoughts. And then there are those within whom a moment of pure clarity allows the observer and that which is being observed to be one. And that's when the background noises that the self makes are silenced."

"I don't know, but that sounds sort of liberating." says Tia, with a precocious smile.

"Imagine if the human race could be free from their irrational beliefs?" adds Logos, gently. "Be they beliefs in a deity or any other appeasing ideology, including a belief in NO belief."

"Wait," intervenes Tia, "are you saying that even atheists are unable to see clearly?"

"One cannot enter an investigation with any preconceived mindset — this would have a corruptive effect."

"I guess that sounds logical."

"There is logic in that which seems abstract." says Logos, "Actually, there is even more so than with that which is considered real."

"What about those who are agnostic?"

"Agnostics are just lazy atheists."

"Now that's funny."

"Was it?" replies Logos, innocently.

Tia squints back, "Hmm?"

"I hope I have satisfactorily answered your questions."

"I hate to tell you this, but I'm not sure I got half of what you said." says Tia, eyelashes fluttering. "You do realize that I'm only 16, right?"

"Yes, I know." replies Logos, smiling.

"Professor Logos, to tell you the truth," adds Tia, "I think that I lost you somewhere after you said that I was remarkable."

Logos chortles out loud. "My dear Tia, you do not need to get it in order to BE IT."

Tia giggles quaintly.

"As for enlightenment itself, it is like becoming aware of an inside joke and then finding out that you may be the only one in on it."

"That doesn't sound like much fun."

"It can be," replies Logos, "if everyone else manages to get in on it."

Tia squishes her lips together. "By the way, if I'm like IT and all that, why did someone try to kill me?" she accidentally blurts out. Her face immediately pales with the incubus of her returning memory. Her crest suddenly flashes Yellow.

Logos gets up from his chair and kneels next to her. He places his consoling hand on her arm.

A big tear rolls down Tia's cheek. "Logos, I'm sorry for my outburst."

"There is no need to apologize, sweetie. You have suffered a huge shock."

Tia probes the back of her sore head as if trying to access further memories. "Ramsey! Where is he?! He saved my life!"

"He's gone, sweetie."

Tia's crest changes briefly from Yellow to Black before disappearing back into the white prism of her dress.

Chapter Eight

The commander stands patiently at attention in front of the king's desk.

The king scornfully scrolls through a holographic report. The descriptions within the hologram end. The king shuts it down and gazes up at the commander. "How disappointing, Commander, as it appears that you still have no idea where she's hiding?"

The commander holds steadfastly his ground. "Sire, she seems to have vanished from the collective. Someone must be helping her. I would guess that it's probably a Monochrome."

"Why do you say that?"

"Sire, neither the guards nor the T-Ports have been able to pick up a trace of the girl. And since it's highly doubtful that a Holy White would harbour a fugitive, I surmise that it must be a Monochrome who may still feel bound by his, or her, sense of duty."

"Commander, do I need to remind you that the hour of Ascension is fast approaching?"

"No, Sire — I will find her."

"Good!" replies the king, "By the way, Commander, I didn't see much more said in your report about the appearance of the bizarrely dark T-Crests."

"Sire, our D-Scientists are still at a loss to explain how an operational InsignAnima, which is specifically designed to hold the soul of its host, can possibly lose the soul within. It's as if those afflicted are somehow managing to skip out on their own consciousness."

"Skipping out to where?" says the king, grasping firmly the data chip.

"I don't know, Sire."

"Lazarus, I really don't like this black hole of information."

"Sire, a 'black hole' may be an appropriate analogy to what appears to be happening."

"Oh?"

"May I explain, Sire?"

The king moves forward on his seat. "Go on, Commander."

"The D-Scientists have speculated that the phenomenon of a T-Crest becoming devoid of all colours before the physical death of its bearer is like a person's mind entering the singularity of a black hole, where its own psychological clock momentarily stops. Sire, it was described to me as like being briefly dead without physically dying."

"That's ridiculous! How can one die without being dead?"

"They speculate that..." says Lazarus, momentarily transfixed by the inescapable carmine stains of his own suit.

The king crosses his arms and leans back on his chair. "Yes, Lazarus, I'm listening."

"That is, Sire, if one could escape all the colours of one's InsignAnima, all that would remain would be a black void."

The king leans forward again. "Are you saying that this girl may have no soul?"

"I'm not sure, Sire. But it does appear that when her T-Crest turns dark that that would be the case."

"Could this have something to do with her having an inert God Gene?"

"That is a logical conjecture, Sire."

"And she's infecting other Holy Whites with her mutation?"

"It would appear so, Sire."

"Then she may be even more dangerous then I had originally thought. She must be found and captured at any cost, for she must be the Demon that the Old Age Scriptures warned us all about!"

TÄNKAPODS (T-PODS) — ... they continue to be a marvel of inventions. T-Pods allow thy Holy White soul to momentarily transcend and provide a true glimpse of life in the Thereafter.

2. T-Pods override thy personal T-Vision and melt the soul within it directly into its T-Matches.

3. T-Pods provide thy personal consciousness the ability to fabricate thy Avatars for the T-Matches.

4. The T-Pod shall activate once the combatant's hands and feet are set in place within it. This shall allow the T-Pod's host to effectively manoeuvre the gyroscope within.

5. The T-Pods use an encrypted calculation to randomly select the T-Planets for the T-Matches.

6. The T-Pods shall allow for the collective consciousness of thy Holy White Order to connect during the compulsory Conclaves (see NAT Tech Manual no.2: sec.6 — TänkaMatch). The Conclaves are...

THE NEW AGE TESTAMENT

PART III

THE BLACK BOX

Chapter One

Logos parts the curtain of his low rise residence. He stares at a faint white cloud smoothly gliding beneath the full moon.

His concentration is unlocked by a whimpering sigh behind him. "Oh my concussed thoughts." bemoans Tia.

Tia sits at the dining table with her hands gently covering her face. She lightly opens her hands like the doors of a vestibule and slants a look at Logos. She gets up from her chair and walks over to his side. "Look at the Monochromes working so hard down there." she says, her crest glows briefly Green. "They all seem to know exactly what to do. I wish I was one of them."

"Why?"

"Why?" replies Tia, "I'll tell you why, because no one is trying to kill any of them."

"Tia, have you notice something?"

"What?"

"The moonlight and the way it falls so beautifully on the school grounds?"

"Yeah, it all looks very nice."

"It's easy sometimes to lose sight of the simple things in life?" says Logos.

"Right now all I see from here is a school that is uncomfortably close to the Imperial Palace." replies Tia, "It's as if they wanted to keep an eye on the students or something. Though, if they ever watched me in class they'd see me asleep most of the time."

"Oh?"

"Yeah, I've always thought school quite boring—" Tia stops herself, "I-I didn't mean your class, Professor. Actually right now I'd love to be back in your class — clueless and safe."

"I understand."

Tia returns to her seat and soothingly sits back down. "You know, I'm still confused about what Ramsey did. I really don't understand why he did what he did. I thought he was like an evil guy. And I was convinced that he hated me."

Logos backs away from the window and sits down next to Tia. He pours a hot beverage in her cup and then in his own. "In the human condition love and hate are two sides of the same conditional coin." he says, "The psychology of why people hate is similar to why people conditionally love. It is a matter of how they see themselves in the other."

"What are you saying?" says Tia, "Ramsey first hated what he saw in me and then suddenly his feelings reversed?"

"Whatever he felt, it is obvious that he could not have sacrificed himself to save you for hateful reasons. And definitely not for any belief either."

"So why did he do it?"

Logos leans back on his chair. "Human beings believe themselves so different from one another. But each human holds within them the story of every other human being. If one can read one's own profound story, then one would see that all stories are fundamentally the same."

"Huh?" mumbles Tia.

"All human being are programmed by the same measurable colours of human consciousness — Blue of pride and ambition — Orange of greed and gluttony — the Green of envy and jealousy — Red of pleasure and desire — Yellow of fear and anxiety — Purple of anger and hate."

"Like our T-Crests?"

"Yes. But whether visible or not, all human beings continue to be slaves to the powerful programming prism of their colours."

"But aren't our colours who we are? Who would we be without them? I mean we're told as Greys that we should follow our colourful passions."

"Tia, passion is just an ambitious desire. And a personal ambition is itself is a breeder of violence."

"I don't know about that." replies Tia, "What if I feel ambitious about helping others — that must surely be a good thing, no?"

"If you want to help someone, do you need to be ambitious to do so, or do you just do it?"

"I've never thought about it that way."

"It's hard to see ambition for what it is when it continues to be perceived as a positive motivator."

"Huh, so you're saying that if I were ambitious about doing a good deed then that would be like sort of a selfish thing?"

"Would it not be?" replies Logos, "Ambition originates from the self. And where the self is, there is NO true love."

"I've lost you, again."

Logos merges his fingertips into a steeple. "All colours are the stems of the self that make up the tree of knowledge. But the tree of knowledge itself cannot see beyond its colourful stems."

"Oh? That's much clearer — thanks a lot."

"Tia, can something which is limited see that which may be infinite?"

"I guess not."

"The self, our consciousness, is a limited entity, and it is unable to see beyond its limitations."

"But didn't you say that it may be possible to find out what lies beyond our consciousness?"

"Yes."

"And how then can I do so without my mind? Do you know what I'm getting at?"

"I think so."

"I mean, isn't that like that thing about the thinker trying to stop itself from thinking?"

"That is a very good observation. But yet there is a very distinctive difference."

"Oh?"

"The difference is that unlike meditative techniques which try to suppress thought — the thinker in this case is carefully investigating thoughts without prejudice."

"Without prejudice?" says Tia.

"That means using the brain's enormous capacities to place thoughts in their proper order without the usual interference of the judgemental self."

"Huh?"

"Tia, have you ever studied hard on something?"

"Yeah, and?"

"Have you ever felt a sudden breakthrough?"

"I think so."

"That type of insight occurs when the mind has suddenly put all its thoughts on the matter in their rightful place."

"You mean like a jigsaw puzzle?"

"Sort of, except in the case of spiritual enlightenment when the pieces of the puzzle are placed in their proper places the puzzle itself no longer exists. And all that remains is an infinite moment."

"Infinite moment?" replies Tia.

"Yes, I know that that sounds like an oxymoron. But it nevertheless expresses well a moment that is without the limits of time and hence space."

"Huh?"

"And what is the Universe made of?"

"My head hurts." says Tia, "I feel like I'd actually need infinity to understand what you're talking about."

"Tia, the jigsaw is difficult to see from its pieces."

"I guess it's not an easy puzzle."

"No, it is not."

"Great."

"But it is available for anyone that investigates the Truth."

"What Truth?"

"The Truth of what it means to die."

"Excuse me?"

"Tia, there are different paths that lead to the death of the self. The first and most obvious is a physical death. Hopefully not applicable here."

"That's not funny."

Logos smiles and continues, "But what if one were able to deconstruct all their irrational beliefs?"

"But didn't you say that we are what we believe?"

"Exactly," replies Logos, "And what do you think would happen then?"

"Logos, are you saying that without irrational beliefs the self would die?"

"Would that not be like dying without literally dying?"

"Oh."

"Tia, do you remember when your T-Crest lost its colours?"

"Uh-huh."

"Do you remember what you felt at that very moment?"

"Sort of." replies Tia.

"And what was that?"

"Umm..." mumbles Tia, blushing.

"No need to be shy."

"But it sounds so corny."

"That is fine — I like corn."

"Huh." replies Tia, her face glowing. "Are you are making a joke?"

"Tia, can you answer my question, please?"

"Umm... how did I feel?" replies Tia, "Nothing."

"You felt nothing?"

"It's more like part of nothingness."

"Is that all?"

"And I felt that all my colours were gone."

"And how did that make you feel?"

"Umm..." replies Tia, "I felt whole."

"You felt whole?"

"Yeah, like being connected with everyone and everything. A sort of a wacky all encompassing feeling of being made out of pure affection." adds Tia, "I know, I must sound so weird."

"Being insightful usually does." replies Logos, smiling.

"Insightful — me?" replies Tia, sipping from her cup. "I don't know about that."

"What if Ramsey was the one that needed to be saved. Would you have saved him?"

"I don't know."

"But Ramsey did just that."

"I do remember seeing his T-Crest turning profoundly dark."

"Like yours did when you felt — insightful?"

"Wait. Are you saying that he felt like me?"

"He was free from choice."

"Eh?"

"He had no choice but to do what was right."

"Really?" says Tia, "Why him of all people?"

"Something fundamentally changed in him." replies Logos, leaving his words meandering up in the air.

"What do you mean, 'something changed in him'?" says Tia, wrinkling her face.

Logos removes the dishes from the table. He walks over to the kitchen sink and sets them down. He leans on the counter with his back to Tia.

"I think you should get some much needed rest." says Logos, "I've entered into subject matters that are not always easy to digest."

"No freaking way!" says Tia, abruptly rising to her feet. "Why is it that every time I have a crucial question, you send me to bed?"

Logos chuckles as he picks up a plate of freshly baked cookies. He rejoins Tia at the table. "Sit, please." he says.

"No cookies for me, thanks." she says, crossing her arms firmly together. "But I would like an answer."

"Alright then, I will try to satisfy your inquisitive mind."

"Good!"

"Lord Ramsey sensed a moment without the hindrance of his selfish colours — like you did."

"Oh?"

"Lord Ramsey's mind was able to move past the block that kept it from seeing the Truth."

"What are you talking about? What block?"

"Tia, the human brain is blocked."

"Blocked? Blocked by what?"

"It's blocked by its inability to see beyond its colours."

"But without colours we wouldn't be human."

"It is not possible for human beings to live without colours, or even preferable to do so. But it is possible to live with colours without them colouring the mind."

"And you're saying that Ramsey managed to do that?"

"The wired brain, the self that it represents, or that which the Holy White Order considers its soul, needs to feel complete in order to have meaning." explains Logos, "So the self convinces itself that it can know that which is immeasurable, despite being itself part of a measured existence. And it tries to patch up this incongruent hole with all sorts of irrational beliefs. All of which end up masking that which is true with that which is false."

Tia picks up a cookie and fiercely munches on it. "But you're not answering my question. How did Ramsey manage to see through this supposed block?"

"The block that he had inside him was diffused."

"Oh? How did he manage to do that?"

"Umm...my dear Tia, Lord Ramsey did not remove his block — you did!"

Chapter Two

-1-

It is night and the streets around the palace are quiet. Nearby is a dimly lit gazebo.

"Senex, what are you doing? Stop that!" a woman whispers loudly, "Somebody might see us."

Senex looks around him. "Oh babe." he says.

"Get off of me!" she replies, pulling at his iris outfit.

"Oh, c'mon babe." he insists, "It's been so long."

"Are you crazy? Do you know what would happen to you if we got caught?"

"I don't care, babe."

"You're so wild."

"Admit it, babe." says Senex, "That's what you like about me."

"But what if they blame me instead?"

"Don't worry, babe, I'll protect you."

"I don't like it here."

"But babe, I can't wait any longer."

"You'll have to Senex."

"Please Merenda, there's no one around." says Senex, fondling her bosom.

"I don't care." she says, shrugging him off. "You'll have to wait till we're back in Monochromia."

"But Babe, I just want to feel your lips."

"That's not all you're trying to feel — you dirty old man."

Senex suddenly pulls away from Merenda. "Do I really look old?" he says.

"Aww," mutters Merenda, with pressed lips. "Come here you big hunk." She kisses Senex on the cheek.

"You're driving me crazy, woman."

"Am I?" she says, innocently.

"Merenda, you're so cruel."

Merenda pulls Senex close and kisses him passionately.

34

-2-

"Will you look at that." says the king, his crest glows Red. "Don't they know that I see everything from my lair?!"

"What's this, Sire?" replies the commander.

"Look down there at those two Monochromes."

The commander edges near the king and peers down the window.

"I see what you mean, Sire."

"You'd think they'd be more careful, considering."

"Sire, do you want me to take care of that?"

"Never mind," says the king, his eyes turn inattentively empty. "I've changed my mind."

"As you wish, Sire?" says the commander.

"Let them have their last hours of fun."

The commander slants a look at the king. "What do you mean, Sire?"

The fringe of the king's brow lifts sharply. He backs away from the scene below. "What? What did I say?"

"Sire, you were saying something about their last—"

"Never mind, Commander." interrupts the king, his crest turns Purple. "There are more important things to deal with then those two perverts down there."

"Yes, Sire."

"Commander, you haven't mentioned the girl." says the king with a livid gaze, "I presume that she's still out there?"

"Yes, Sire."

"May I remind you, Commander, that this young woman has spawned rumours about malfunctioning InsignAnimas?"

"Sire, I'm aware of the trouble she's causing."

"And what are you doing about it?"

"Sire, now that we've declared her a fugitive, it's just a matter of time before she's handed over. We know she's still in Doma, but the T-Ports have been unable to locate her InsignAnima."

"I see." says the king, shaking his head. "Have you sent out an Imperial Holocast?"

"No, Sire."

"Why haven't you?"

"I thought we would have found her by now."

"Commander, how does it feel to be outwitted by a young woman?"

"Sire?" says the commander.

"But then again it wouldn't be the first time, would it?"

The commander remains still and unresponsive.

"Commander, I suggest that you send out an Imperial Holocast immediately."

"Yes Sire."

"That should do it."

"Is there anything else, Sire?"

"No." says the king, turning away from the commander.

The commander leaves the chamber.

In his quieted chamber the king returns to gaze down at the active gazebo. His crest fluctuates back and forth between Red and Green.

Chapter Three

Tia coughs out crumbs of her ingested cookie. "What?!" she says, as she covers the spillage from her mouth. "Me?!" she exclaims. "How did I end up in the middle of all of this? I don't get it. How in Nirvia could I have possibly removed this supposed 'block' in Ramsey when I don't even know what it is?"

Logos offers Tia a napkin. "I understand your confusion. But the explanation is quite simple."

Tia peers at Logos with a certain glare of uncertainty. "Oh yeah, Professor, I don't think anything you say is simple."

Logos smiles and offers Tia another cookie. She holds up her hand in a stop motion.

"Human beings have a gene which blocks them from pursuing the Truth." says Logos.

"That's it?"

"I told you it was simple."

"Why do I have the creeping suspicion that there's more to this?" says Tia, leaning back on her chair. "OK, let's have it."

"Smart girl." says Logos, smiling.

"Go on then." says Tia, tapping her fingers nervously on the table. "Tell me quickly before my sugar rush wears off."

"It is ironically named the God Gene." Logos stops for a second to watch Tia's eyes squinting in the information. "This God Gene inhibits the capacity of the human brain to confront the Truth."

"Huh?"

"The Truth that death is the end of one's consciousness." says Logos, "The God Gene acts like a denial gene."

"Umm?" groans Tia.

"What the God Gene does is provoke such despair and loneliness when its host tries to stare into the proverbial abyss of Death that it sends the host's mind running under the covers of delusion."

"Huh?"

"The God Gene inhibits a person's ability to have a clear mind. So instead of dealing with the profound Truth of what Death is, the God Gene contaminates the direct perception of it with a myriad of divisive fundamental dogmatic ideologies."

"Oh?"

"The God Gene works like a spell." adds Logos, "It uses irrational beliefs, or irrational non-beliefs alike, to obscure the mind. And thus creates inescapable internal confusions and conflicts which then materialize externally."

"This is too much," says Tia, grunting. "I just can't believe that all human beings would fall under this spell."

"There are some who did overcome the spell, but they were few and far between. Sure these few beings tried to explain or impart their understanding to others, but their words ended up being expropriated and then manipulated by those who knowingly or unknowingly remained bewitched by the spell."

"But maybe the spell is there for self-preservation. I mean who in their right mind wants to find think about dying and stuff like that. I certainly don't."

"Tia, wanting is one thing, but being unable to is quite another."

"Are you saying that those afflicted by the God Gene are incapable of confronting the true meaning of Death?"

"That is pretty much it."

"But maybe if everyone would know this we'd all be able to come out of this bewitching spell, no?"

"The God Gene is not just a spell." says Logos, seriously. "It is much more ingrained and highly fatal than that."

"Fatal?" says Tia with a puckered brow.
"Yes — Fatal!"

The loft suddenly dims as a cloud smothers the moon.

Tia picks up another cookie and nervously gobbles it down. "OK," she says, "now you're scaring me."

"I am sorry about that, but Truths have a tendency to be disturbing." continues Logos, "People have always felt something fundamentally misguided with their societies, and as they moved from one society to another they would wax poetically about the next society as being the change that they want to see. But in fact the change they have always wanted to see never truly transcended their own personal interests. That is why societies repeat over and over again the same mistakes. Societies are after all but an abstraction of personal relationships. And for the human race to evolve there must be a revolution in personal relationships that is based not on the self, but on what looking into the Death of the self brings."

"Oh."

"And the reason that this revolution cannot occur is because of the God Gene."

"Alrighty then," says Tia with a sardonic face, "so this is what you call a simple explanation."

"Tia, the simple Truth is that the God Gene ultimately covers up the fact that ALL the colours of the self are those of the ego. And now the Holy White Order is about to make these colours virtually immortal."

Tia nervously picks up another cookie.

"I know how all this must sound." adds Logos, "It is a complex and abstract sounding subject matter, but it is nevertheless as real as the cookie you hold in your hand."

Tia dejectedly puts the cookie back down.

"I know that all this is not an easy thing to swallow." says Logos, "But this one gene has done tremendous damage to humanity. It has promoted all sorts of illusions and delusions, which in turn bring about a disconnected view of an interconnected existence. This dislocation from one another is the fatal division that the God Gene carries within it."

"This is really sad."

"And the reason your mind is not defensive about these revelation, Tia, is because you are not blocked by the God Gene."

"I'm not?"

"No, you are not afflicted by the God Gene. That is because your God Gene is inert."

"But what does me being unblocked have to do with unblocking Ramsey from his God Gene?"

"As you know, you had been at the center of Lord Ramsey's attention for quite awhile."

"It sure felt that way." replies Tia, "Sort of like an Imperial Guard has with his punching bag."

"This connection with Lord Ramsey, as well as the more direct connection you had with your T-Match combatant, Lord Narmer, allowed your consciousness to touch both of theirs."

"Huh?"

"During the T-Matches all those in the Holy White Order are collectively connected through their consciousness. But your specific connection to Lord Ramsey and Lord Narmer allowed your consciousness to be amplified within theirs. They felt what you felt."

"I don't remember that?"

"Wasn't there a point when you felt a strong connection with both men?"

Tia takes a sip from her cup. "Umm... I did feel something for Lord Narmer's Avatar."

"And what about Ramsey?" says Logos.

"Oh, I think you're right. I remember hearing Ramsey yelling stuff during the T-Match." says Tia, "I always recognize his voice. And for some reason he grabbed me on my way out too. I remember looking into his eyes and for a moment there I felt a surprisingly warmth within him."

"I know what you mean." says Logos, "And so, this is how it finally begins."

"What does?"

"The revolution of the human consciousness." says Logos.

"Are you saying that I have something to do with that?"

"Tia, you have everything to do with that. And the king has probably figured this out by now."

"Oh, I don't like the sound of that. Is that why someone tried to kill me?"

"Yes, sweetie." says Logos, gently holding her hand.

"But what I still don't understand is why my T-Crest is changing those of others."

"I will try to explain."

"Good. But please keep it simple."

"I will try." says Logos, "Your T-Crests reflect the colours of your InsignAnimas. The colours allow the InsignAnimas to record the synaptic patterns of its hosts which are then set to be reconstituted in their Soulful Avatar in Nirvia."

"I'm aware of that." says Tia, eyes rolling.

"But the dark T-Crest is devoid of all colours." continues Logos, "This can only occur when a being has gone beyond the parameters of their own consciousness. It is this that you helped both Narmer and Ramsey experience. This experience transforms a person's consciousness forever."

"Oh."

"But sadly, they are both gone now."

Tia's crest turns briefly Black. "Narmer is dead too?" she says.

"I am sorry to say, but yes."

"Oh, I don't feel very well."

Logos places his hand over Tia's head.

"But Logos, how do you know about the God Gene?"

"I have a certain insight into its origin."

"I didn't know Sapphires had such knowledge."

"They do not have."

"But you do?"

"Yes sweetie, I do."

"How come?" says Tia.

"Umm," says Logos, hesitantly. "It is because I am not a Sapphire."

Chapter Four

The king sways his head side to side in front of a glassed artefact. He checks his reflection till the encased bust fits his own. He places a mitre on his head and smiles.

"Caesar, how do you like my regal hat?" he says, taking pains to straighten the mitre over his forehead's protruding vein. He glares at himself with an endearing distaste before taking the flamboyant hat off. "I agree," he continues, "it does look silly on me."

The king moves over to the sarcophagus and taps its side. A compartment suddenly pops open. Inside is a book with gold bindings and an empty mould. He unceremoniously places the hat in its cast and taps the sarcophagus once again. The compartment slowly closes and seamlessly disappears.

"Sire?" says the commander.

The king snaps his body around. "How dare you enter my lair without being announced?!" he cries.

"I apologize, Sire. The guards told me that you were expecting me."

"Oh, right." replies the king, "But this is my lair and I'm the only one who gives permission to enter."

"Yes Sire."

"I'll have to have a word with my guards."

"Sire, it was my fault. I did not think—"

"That's right! You didn't think!"

"Yes Sire."

"Now, what is it that you felt it so urgent to forego my formal protocol?"

"Sire..."

"Well? I'm waiting, Commander. I'm guessing that your permissiveness means you've found the girl?"

"No, Sire."

"No?"

"Sire, we haven't yet succeeded in apprehending the fugitive."

"How's that possible?!" the king replies, coughing. "My Holocast didn't bring her out from her hiding place?"

"No, Sire."

"Well then, she must be getting help from an insider."

"I agree, Sire."

"Commander, I want you to add to the Imperial Holocast that anyone found aiding and abetting this girl will be punished to the fullest extent of their most horrid of thoughts."

"Yes Sire, I will include the warning of the Black Box." The commander turns to leave.

"Lazarus!"

"Yes, Sire?"

"The last T-Match is soon to begin. I don't want to be bothered again till you have her, is that clear?"

"Yes, Sire."

"Are we clear, Commander?" reiterates the king with a more forceful tone.

"Dome clear, Sire."

"Now leave me and tell the guards that I do not want to be disturbed."

"Yes Sire."

The king watches the commander leave before returning to the side of his sarcophagus. The sarcophagus opens with a cacophonous whisper. "Now then, let's prepare something that the Holy White Order has never seen before. We will create an Avatar that they will never forget. They shall all carry the memory of my dominance to Nirvia. They shall praise me above all others who came before me."

Chapter Five

Tia snaps back on her chair. "What do you mean you're not a Sapphire? What are you then?"

"Right, I guess this is as good a time as any." replies Logos, biting his lower lip. He takes a sip from his cup. "My dear Tia...I am humanoid, but I am not human."

"What do you mean you're not human?!" she says, pulling away. "Logos, please tell me you're just attempting another of your quirky jokes, or I may be forced to reassess all that you've ever said."

Logos gets up and shuts the lights off. He spreads the curtains wide and allows the moonlight to enter. "I understand how I must sound," he says, glaring out the window. "You are correct to feel cynical, but the fact is that I am not from this planet. Actually, I am from a planet that is quite far from here."

Tia sits incredulously motionless. Her eyes are wide and her face is weirdly docile.

"There are Billions and Billions of stars out there, and that is just in what you call the Milky Way." he explains, glaring up at the night sky. "But beyond your galaxy there are hundreds of Billions of other galaxies. All of which are contained within an expanding universe whose size is so vast that it is measured by the speed of light. It takes approximately 14 billion years for light to travel here from the ends of the Universe. Some planetary systems have been around for billions of years before your own was even born. So, why is it so strange to think that life exists elsewhere?"

"I remember some of the information on space travel from our Virtual Library." replies a subdued Tia, "The distances were deemed to be insurmountable. So, how could you be here?"

"Tia, imagine how far a species could travel working together as opposed to apart."

"I think our collective backs would really have to be against the wall to imagine that type of collaboration."

"Our own beginnings were not so dissimilar to those of the human race. And as we learned about our genealogy we investigated why a small pocket of peace loving people within our midst were so much more evolved than the rest of us. With time we were able to isolate the problem. That is when the genetic block to enlightenment was discovered. It then took many centuries of internal growth within our collective consciousness to render it completely inert."

"Are you talking about the God Gene?" asks Tia.

"Yes." replies Logos, "We called it the mortaphantasia gene."

"OK." replies Tia, "Now I think you're just making things up."

"I wish I were. But this mortaphantasia gene is too devastating not to be real. It deprives the brain the ability to fully imagine the void that death brings. In so doing it fools all those it infects to think divisibly. It does not allow the human mind to realize the futility of its divisiveness. And this blocked understanding does not permit the further insight necessary to see that which does not die."

"But I don't understand why you were able to evolve beyond your God Gene and we haven't?"

"That is a sober question." replies Logos, "Albeit highly destructive the God Gene was just part of my species' natural selection path."

"I don't get it."

"The God Gene is not part of the original human genome."

"Uh, what does that mean?"

"Human evolution had nothing to do with the rise of the God Gene." replies Logos with a culpable gaze.

"I still don't get it?" replies Tia, "If the God Gene didn't come from our ancestors, where did it come from?"

Logos returns to the dining table with his head down. He sits uncomfortably down on his chair. "From my species." he discloses.

"Our God Gene is the fault of aliens?" says Tia, "Oh no."

"Yes, it is." admits Logos, "There was a time when we were also a violent colonizing species. And there was a paranoia that came with our expanding ambitions. It was then that certain military factions convinced our people to use the God Gene as a defensive weapon against possible future threats. The God Gene was then weaponized into a delayed doomsday retrovirus that was introduced into life sustaining planets by means of a directed panspermia."

"Say what?" says Tia with a long face.

"The RNA strands of our doomsday retrovirus would infect the brains of quickly evolving species in order to ultimately become hard wired into their DNA. Subsequently when a species developed a certain level of self-awareness the dormant Doomsday Gene would awaken."

"Did you say, Doomsday Gene?"

"I am ashamed to say, but that is what we call your God Gene."

"Doomsday Gene?!" repeats Tia, dumbfounded.

"The reason we named it so is because it has the effect of pushing the infected species unknowingly toward its own extinction."

Tia's eyes gaze firmly at Logos. "I have difficulty imagining one species doing this to another."

"I have difficulty imagining it too." huffs Logos, "Our society was still one with a self-centered system of power at the time of the mortaphantasia gene discovery. During what we call the 'Fog Era' some leaders were unwilling to let go of their control. And so they used the fear of possible extraterrestrial invasions to justify their positions."

"That's terrible."

"The problem is that once we realized the errors of our way, the retrovirus had already taken root in some species, including the human species."

An awkward silence spreads in the loft.

"I am truly sorry, Tia."

"I can't believe all this?"

"You do not need to believe my story. But it does not change the fact that the human consciousness is unable to evolve due to its inability to tackle the Truth."

"But still, that was a horrible thing that your ancestors did."

"I know it was," says Logos, his tone suddenly deepens with the weight of his words. "And that is why our species has been trying to resolve the problems caused by our Original Sin."

"Trying?"

"We have tried to affect change from without, but it just made things repetitively worse."

"Uh?" says Tia, "In what way worse?"

"Our words were used to nail the God Gene even deeper into the wooden crux of the human psyche."

"I don't get what you mean?"

"Tia," says Logos, picking up his cup. "Take the simple word for water, what would it mean to a being that has never seen the effects of combining two hydrogen atoms with one of oxygen?"

"Say what?"

"Imagine how difficult it would be to explain what water is to someone whose consciousness does not hold any awareness of such a thing."

"I realize you're trying to make a point, Professor, but I don't understand what it is."

"In other words, there is only one way to allow human beings to transform and potentially evolve."

"And what way is that?"

"The God Gene must be neutralized."

"And this will save us?"

"It just might."

"Good!" exclaims Tia, "How are you going to do that?"

"I am not the one." replies Logos. He slowly tilts his head and gazes at Tia. "The future of the human species rests solely on the shoulders of your unhindered consciousness, Istina."

Chapter Six

Tia's face wrinkles and her hands begin to quiver. "I think I'm going to be sick." she says, holding her stomach.

"Here sweetie, take a sip of tea."

"Thanks, but no thanks."

"Tia, you are the only one who can try to break through the delusions that the God Gene has created. The advent of TänkaWorld has made it possible to directly transform the Holy White Order. The other group consciousnesses will slowly change as well, till one day the whole of human consciousness will have evolved to see things as they truly are."

"And how do you propose I do this?"

"You need to stop the Ascension."

"Huh?!" she says, pulling away. "How in Nirvia do you expect me to do that?"

"You will need to win the last Key Keeper's Challenge."

Tia's crest momentarily flashes Purple.

"Tia, I did not mean to upset you."

"Well, you have!"

"Why?" replies Logos.

"Why? Why?" she loudly repeats, "Where do I begin?" She stands up and turns around. "You know, it's nice and easy to say all the things you've said about Truth and Love and so on. But how is sending me to my death fit into all of that, eh?"

"I will admit that there are risks, but I will do my best to guard you against any harm."

"So, let me get this straight. Let's say that you manage to first get me in the Imperial Palace safely, which is highly unlikely. After that you somehow manage to convince the king to allow me to join him on stage in the Holy White Arena. And then he graciously allows me to participate in the Golden T-Hour. What then?"

"Then the match will be begin." replies Logos.

"I'm serious here! Do you really think that even if I get into the T-Match that the king will be nice enough to make me win?" Tia plunks herself back down on her chair. "Look. I don't know what you expect of me, Professor, but I think you've got the wrong girl."

"Tia, the T-Ports will only accept the Golden Key if it is inserted by the Key Keeper. In other words, someone in the Holy White Order must win outright the Golden TänkaKey in order to stop the Ascension. And that could only be you!"

"Logos, I don't think you've heard anything I've said. There are too many obstacles standing in the way for even trying this crazy idea."

"If you do not want to take on this extremely difficult task, I will understand." replies Logos, "But I think you need to know something."

"Like what?"

"That when the Golden TänkaHour comes to an end — all shall die and—"

"I know that." interjects Tia, "We're supposed to leave our bodies behind. Though, I don't think I have to worry about that anymore — there's no way they'll let me ascend now. But I'm good with that. There are worse things than living the rest of my natural life like a Monochrome...alongside people I like," she adds, "or used to."

"Tia, if I may finish?"

"Fine, go ahead."

"After the Holy Whites have ascended to Nirvia the dome will automatically seal itself from the outside world."

"What do you mean?"

"A cataclysmic event will take place at the end of the Golden TänkaHour."

"Excuse me?"

"Monochromia and the lands around it will be destroyed."

"Destroyed? What are you talking about?"

"Beneath Doma are large mechanical devices that will permanently rivet the dome into the bedrock beneath the hill. This was originally meant as an entombment ceremony for Zadok and his flock at their preordained End Times. "

"Oh wow?" says Tia.

"But after the Holy White Order took over they rearranged the apocalypse to begin when their reign ended. And now that their reign is reaching its calculated End, the dome is scheduled to entomb itself."

"What for?!" says Tia, angrily. "The Holy Whites will no longer have any use for it after the Ascension."

"But they do need to protect Doma's memory banks. These memory banks hold within them the virtual world of Nirvia and all its inhabitants."

"Are you saying that this is going to happen so that nobody can have access to the memory banks?"

"Yes.'

"Oh."

"And this entombment will not only destroy Monochromia, but the shock waves will also destroy much of the nearby Outer Lands."

"That's horrible! Can't we bring everyone safely in here?"

"My dear Tia," says Logos, caressing her hand. "Once the Ascension is complete the dome will automatically fumigate and cleanse itself of all life herein."

"No freaking way!" exclaims Tia, her face turns drearily pale. "That means that you will die too?"

"All of Doma's inhabitants will perish."

Tia takes a deep breath and gazes into Logos' hazelnut eyes. "Alright, I'll do it. Or at least I'll try."

"I knew you would."

"Oh did you?"

"Without an active God Gene you have no choice but to do the right thing.

"I'm not sure I know what the right thing is anymore." she replies, sulking.

"When one truly knows the Truth the answers are always clear."

"I think doing the 'right thing' is going to get me killed."

"What better way is there to die?" says Logos with a warm wink.

"OK," says Tia, half-heartedly. "Now I don't know anymore if you're actually trying to be funny or what."

"The Truth can sometimes be quite funny."

"Sure." says Tia, squishing her face.

Logos taps his hand on the table. His pacified face grows tense. "But there is one more piece of information that you must be aware of."

"I don't think my head can take anymore stuff." replies Tia, holding her head in her hands.

Logos hesitates to say another word.

Tia forces out a little smirk. "C'mon then — rip away the rest of what's left of my sanity."

"Tia, you will need to be extremely weary of that which lurks within the T-Match. King Osiris is not only an ominous adversary, but it appears that he has also become the purest embodiment of the self. His pursuit of absolute power has produced the mind of a sociopath. He is a man whose distorted conscience has detached him from almost any sense of right and wrong."

"That's so sad." she says, tearfully. Her crest momentarily flickers Black.

"It is sad." says Logos, gently nodding. "But such a man will show little empathy or none at all."

"No empathy?"

"His God Gene has taken complete hold of his mind. He is no longer able to see himself in another. Any empathy he may once have had has turned itself inward into pure selfishness. There is little that can distract him from his ambitions now."

"How in Nirvia is a plain girl like me supposed to stop such a man?"

"Tia, there is nothing about you that is plain."

"If you don't mind I think I will finally take that nap now." says Tia, slowly getting up from the table. "My head hasn't stop spinning since it hit the floor."

Chapter Seven

Inside the arena are rose and iris coloured workers diligently adding last minute touches to the extravagant scene.

The king observes the work being executed below from the translucent pane at his feet. "It won't be long now" he says, glancing back at the sarcophagus. "The end of this mundane life is finally in sight."

A knock on the door forms a ridge over his brow. "Come in, Commander." he says, nonchalantly.

The commander walks in and stands at attention. His eyes are dark and distended. "You asked for me, Sire?"

"I've been thinking," says the king, "maybe we can add some real fireworks before the Golden T-Hour, what do you think?"

"I don't understand, Sire."

"I would ask you to help with that, but I believe you're busy chasing a young woman." he adds, glowering. "How does it feel to have a young woman continue to ridicule your command like this?"

The commander's face turns dark and broody.

"Commander, she's still out there somewhere — free like a bird of prey. Do I need to take control of this matter myself?"

"No, Sire."

The king forces himself to look at the commander. "Have you sent out my Imperial Holocast?"

The commander nods affirmatively.

The king moves over to his desk and rummages through its top drawer. He pulls out Lazarus' translucent sphere. He flips it up in the air and catches it. Then suddenly slams his hand on his desk.

The commander's eyes widen.

The king opens his hand and the sphere has remained intact. "Lazarus, my old friend, I'm glad to see that you still care for your past soul. I would like to see the old you join me in Nirvia, but you're making it difficult for that to happen."

"Sire?" says Lazarus, apprehensively.

The king lifts Lazarus' translucent sphere and stares through it. "How frail our souls are. Don't you think?"

The commander remains solidly still.

"Commander, I suggest you don't fail me again — do you get my meaning?"

"I understand, Sire."

The king drops the sphere back in his desk drawer. "The Golden T-Hour is near and I don't want to worry about that mutant. So I strongly suggest that you find the little wench."

"I will, Sire." the commander replies, "I've already taken all the appropriate actions."

"I would hope so, Lazarus. My faith in your abilities is quickly thinning." The king's crest turns Blue as he waves the commander away.

A ray of sunlight appears to distract the commander. His eyes lock on the granules of dried blood in the marbled floor.

"Why are you still standing there?" says the king.

The commander takes a step away from his spot and glares at the king. The glitter of sunlight sheers his crestless white suit and exposes his broad muscular body.

The king's crest flickers Yellow. He turns his body away from the commander. "Commander," he says with a splintered tone, "you can leave now."

The commander exits slowly and quietly.

Alone in the chamber the king shakes his head. His crest glows Orange. "If that bonehead thinks I'll allow his past soul to rise up with mine, then he's dumber than I thought."

Chapter Eight

The sunshine has penetrated the bedroom. Tia suddenly awakens with the sheets tightly wound around her. "Again?" she says, "How do I get myself in these traps!?"

She twists and turns her way out. "Ugh," she says, shielding her yes from the penetrating sunlight. "It's really hot in here." She puts on her dress and accidentally knocks over the bedside cabinet. A small metallic chip rolls out of its bottom drawer. She picks up the chip and a holographic image pops out of it. She stares at it for a moment and shuffles over to the kitchenette. She sits down at the dining table and sleepily watches Logos cooking.

She picks up the cup next to her and takes a sip. "Ouch!" she mutters. She peeks inside the cup. "What's in here?"

"It is herbal tea." replies Logos.

"Hmm, smells good. Is it for me?"

"Of course, but be careful as it is probably still hot."

"Oh really," she replies, blowing into the cup. "Thanks for the warning."

"How was your nap?"

"Sweaty." she says, "I dreamt that there was a big snake wrapped around me asking me questions. And I couldn't help myself but to answer it."

Logos serves Tia a platter of mixed vegetables and rice. "I hope you like this."

"I'm not really hungry, but thank-you."

"Have some." insists Logos, pushing the platter closer to Tia. "You need to replenish your energy."

"You know, I don't even remember falling asleep."

"There is little doubt that the events of the past few days have taken their toll on you. How are you feeling?"

"Much better, thanks."

Tia fidgets with the chip in her hand. The hologram pops up once again. "Logos, do you know this woman?"

Logos grabs the metallic chip from her hand. "Where did you find this?"

"The holographic module fell out of your bedside drawer."

"And you think that gave you permission to take it?"

"No, I just picked it up and—"

"I am sorry." says Logos, shaking his head. "I should not have been so curt with you."

"I've never seen you react like that." says Tia, softly. "This young woman must have been very important to you."

"She was — very much so."

"Oh?"

"She is unfortunately no longer with us."

"Oh, that's so sad. You must miss her."

"I do."

"She seemed like an absolutely stunning woman."

"She was much more than that."

Tia's crest briefly flashes Green. "What was her name?"

"Her name was Sistina." replies Logos, while reopening the holographic module.

"I can see by her dress she was a Fuchsia?"

"Umm..."

"What happened to her?"

"She was murdered."

"Murdered — why?"

"That's a good question." replies Logos, "She supposedly died in the Key Keeper's Chamber trying to protect the king from an assassin."

"Oh? That sounds weird."

"I agree." replies Logos, "Especially when one considers that the king was strangely obsessed with her."

"Obsessed with her?"

"I think he had some deep carnal feelings for her."

"But we're not allowed..."

"Tia, those who Rule do not always feel like rules apply to them."

"I don't think I'm grown-up enough to understand that."

"I wouldn't worry about it." says Logos, "The idea of growing up tends to suggest that one should become more understanding in life, but the idiom is used more as a euphemism for the loss of one's idealism."

"Okay..." says Tia with wondering eyes, "What made you think the king was obsessed with your friend?"

"The king lost his grown up head when she showed interest in another and concluded that she was a provocateur. She managed to escape before he declared her a fugitive.""

"She was a fugitive — like me?" Tia's crest flashes Yellow. "And she was murdered?!"

"There, there..." says Logos, tapping Tia's hand.

"I need to get out of this apartment." says Tia, "I need to clear my head."

"I do not think it a good idea right now."

"Maybe they've stopped looking for me. What do you think?" she says, beseechingly.

Logos walks over to the loft's supporting column. He fiddles with a small aperture embedded within it. Suddenly a holographic image of Tia beams out of the column. Tia jumps up out of her chair. "Hey! That's me!"

Beneath her holographic image is written:

'THIS IS AN IMPERIAL HOLOCAST: Anyone found harbouring this fugitive shall be subjected to the Black Box.'

"Logos, are you crazy?! That's a T-Port — they're going to find us!"

"No need to worry." he replies, calmly. "For the time being we are safe here."

"You keep saying that. How do you know we're safe?" says Tia, breathing rapidly. "The Imperial Holocast means that the Ultramarines are going door to door in search of me. So how can I possibly be safe here or anywhere else for that matter?"

"There is no need to panic." says Logos, "The hallway door to this apartment is partially cloaked. There are six floors to this building and it will take them some time before they figure out that they missed one of the apartments."

"You know what, I think I'm really fucked!" says Tia, covering her mouth. "Oops! Sorry Professor, I meant—"

"That's alright," interrupts Logos, "the vulgar term fits the circumstances."

"How do I get out of this mess?" says Tia, "I can't hide here forever. Can I?"

"We will not be staying here much longer."

"We're leaving?" says Tia, scratching her head. "But you just said that it's not a good idea, because—"

"I need to get you into the final T-Match."

"Right," says Tia, "but don't we need a T-Pod to do that?"

"Yes we do."

Tia curiously tilts her head. "But aren't all the T-Pods in the Holy White Arena inside the Imperial Palace?"

"Yes, they are." replies Logos, "And that is why the plan is to go there."

"Go where?"

"To the Imperial Palace." replies Logos.

"Huh?"

"That is the only way to the T-Pods."

"I can't believe this! Your plan is to bring me to where the people who are looking for me are?"

"We have no other choice."

"I feel sick again." says Tia, holding her hand over her stomach.

"It will be alright, sweetie."

"I sure hope so, because I don't feel alright."

"If things go according to plan we should be relatively safe."

Tia's head sinks heavily into her arms. "Oh great." she whimpers, "That makes me feel so relatively better."

Chapter Nine

The king stands opposite to one of his encased relics. The encapsulated relic is the marbled torso of a man. The king combs back his long greying hair till it falls evenly straight. His crest glows Orange. "Unlike you, Alexander," he says, "I will not shed a tear for I DO have another world to conquer."

There is a knock on the chamber's door.

"Again?" he says, "Now what?"

A voice loudly rings back, "Your Majesty, the commander requests an audience."

"Guards," hollers the king, glaring at the door. "I said I did NOT want to be disturbed."

"Your Majesty," interjects the commander, "we have captured the fugitive."

The king's posture perks up. "What are you waiting for, Lazarus, come right in."

The commander walks in as the king's crest changes from Orange to Green. "I wish I had been there with you, Commander. How did you finally manage to get her? It must have been because of my Imperial Holocast. Was she shocked?"

"Sire, we found her trying to sneak into the Holy White Arena."

"Wow! This girl is obviously deranged — poor girl."

"That may be the case, Sire, but—"

"I must admit, Lazarus," interrupts the king, "that I didn't foresee this girl making such a crazy move. I guess girls are not so different from the older ones after all." he says, sniggering. His crest changes to a solid Red. "By the way, what does she look like in person? Does she appear as sweet as her holographic image?"

The commander's stoic face remains coldly indifferent. "Sire, there's one other aspect to our capture."

"What is it, Commander? What else was this girl up to?"

"Sire, she wasn't alone."

"You mean you found the culprit who had been aiding her?" says the king, his crest quickly changes to a livid Purple.

"Yes, Sire."

"Well who was it?"

"He's a Sapphire, Sire."

"That's what I figured." says the king, his crest glows Blue.

"His name is Logos, Sire."

The king places his hand to the side of his copious waist. "Did you say Logos?"

"Yes, Sire."

"I know this Sapphire," replies the king, "he used to be one of my top D-Scientists."

"Oh?" replies the commander, fingering his unresponsive temple implants. "Sire, I don't like the sound of this, I don't think it's a coincidence that this girl and your former D-Scientist happen to end up here together at this crucial time."

"What are you suggesting, Commander?"

"Sire, what I'm saying is that he's not only helping her, but that they're working together."

The king glowers back at his relics. "For once, Lazarus, I agree with you." he says, "I will need to see for myself what to make out of this."

"Yes, Sire"

"Take me to them."

Chapter Ten

Tia walks impatiently in a small circle around Logos. She tries to wipe away the dirt on her white dress.

"This is a quaint little holding cell. Wouldn't you say so, Professor?"

"Hmm?" murmurs Logos.

"Why — look! We can see all the Imperial Guards around us, but sadly they can see us as well in our little glass cage." Tia screens her eyes from the bright lights of the barred enclosure. "Logos are you just going to sit there, or are you going to say something?"

"What would you like me to say, my lady?"

"Oh, I don't know. What about explaining to me how we're going to get out of this glass cubicle? I feel like one of those specimens on display in the Virtual Library."

"You need not to worry about this enclosure." replies Logos, "I do not think we shall be here very long."

"Not to worry, you say?! Well you know what?" she says, "It's you that's worrying me right now."

"Am I?" says Logos with a congenial smile.

"Your apparent lack of concern makes me feel highly uncomfortable."

"What do you mean, my lady?"

"I'm beginning to think that I've been manipulated into this mess?"

"To be human is to be manipulated."

"Great! Thanks for that, Professor."

"All human beings are continuously manipulated. First by their genetic make up, and then by their biochemical induced urges, and so on."

"Yeah-yeah." says Tia.

"I assure you that I am not trying to manipulate you."

Tia continues walking in a small captive circle around Logos. "Fine!" she says, "But what I'm really interested in right now is how we're going to get out of here?"

"There is old proverb that says that patience is a virtue."

"Well then, you're certainly testing my virtue, Professor. And by the way, what's with all the proverbs anyway?"

Logos eyes the top corner of the cell. "My lady, we are not alone."

Tia stops her nervous pacing and follows Logos' gaze. She instinctively shuts her lips tight at the sight of a porthole peeking overhead. "Oh that's just great." she says, moping.

One of the guards outside the cell door suddenly clacks his heels together. Other guards follow his lead.

"Your Majesty!" says the guard.

The king approaches the guard followed closely by the commander. The king makes a small gesture with his hand. The guard immediately turns and swipes his badge over the cell door. The door automatically opens.

"Logos!" the king exclaims as he enters the cell, "How nice it is to see you again."

Logos does not respond.

"What do I owe the honour of your visit, my friend?" adds the king, giving Tia a prolonged look.

Again Logos does not respond.

"Professor," jumps in Tia, dumbstruck. "You know the king?!"

"He sure does, little girl." injects the king, "Before moving to his teaching duties, Logos used to be one of my top science advisors. Did he not mention that to you?"

"Logos is that true?" says Tia, bewildered.

"That was another time and place." replies Logos.

The king glares over Tia's face. His crest turns Red as his brow peaks.

Logos gets up and pulls a stubbornly resistant Tia away from the king.

"Don't touch me!" she says. She turns and sees the commander's carmine stained suit staring back at her.

"My lady, have I seen you before?" says the king.

A transfixed Tia tepidly edges herself to Logos' side.

"Osiris, you need to stop!" says Logos.

"Stop what, my friend?"

"Stop whatever your thinking."

"And what do you think I'm thinking?"

"I do not wish to venture there."

"Sapphire, do not address the king with such familiarity." interjects the commander.

"Why should I not? I know the king well."

The commander takes an antagonistic step towards Logos. The king sticks out his arm and stops him. "That's alright, Commander. This man and I go way back. He's never been much for formality, and I don't expect he's gotten any better with age."

"I guess you can say that about us both." says Logos.

"Wow! Logos, was that an insult?" replies the king, "That doesn't sound like you at all. What's happened to the man of love and peace?"

"He is still here, Sire. The question is more about what has happened to you?"

"I warn you, Sapphire." says the commander, ardently.

"Commander," says the king, "there's no need to be rude to our guest. He's a Sapphire who couldn't hurt a cockroach even if he wanted to. Isn't that right, Logos?"

"Sire," interjects the commander, "maybe he's not the man you once knew."

The king's crest turns Blue. "Commander, you should know by now that men don't ever really change, especially those with ECCD implants."

"That is an undetermined fact." replies Logos.

"There's the Logos I knew," replies the king, "forever the analytical optimist."

"I'm neither an optimist nor a pessimist."

"I've warned you already, Sapphire." says the commander, "Your tone is disrespectful and—"

"That's alright, Commander." interrupts the king. The king examines the cell with an air of satisfaction. He glances back at Lazarus. "Commander, would you be kind enough to take our guests to the dungeon."

"It would be my pleasure, Sire."

"Since my friend here is neither and optimist nor a pessimist can you introduce him to some realism?" says the king, unconsciously licking his lips. His crest turns gaudily Red. "But leave me the girl untouched."

"Sire?" says Lazarus.

"You heard me." replies the king.

Tia's crest flashes momentarily Yellow as she grabs tightly Logos' arm.

"Yes, Sire." replies the commander with a slanted sneer.

GOLDEN KEY — ... thy Golden Key was forged by Zarak Zadok in the archaic ovens of Mountdome with the retrieved morsels of gold from Tutankhamen's mask (see EBOLAD Tech Manual no.1: sec.2).

2. Thy Golden Key is the one and only emergency vehicle that can trigger the fail-safe system to thy Ascension. When inserted at any of Doma's T-Ports the Golden Key shall halt the T-Clock countdown (see NAT Tech Manual no.3: Book of Revelations — System Corruption).

3. Thy Golden Key shall be awarded to the Winner of the yearly Key Keeper's Challenge. The deemed Ruler of thy Realm shall protect thy Golden Key at all times till the End of Time wherein all shall...

....

BEWARE: Thy Golden Key must at all times be secure. Thy Golden Key may only be utilized as a last resort. The misuse of the Golden Key may forever destroy the future of human consciousness and...

NEW AGE TESTAMENT

PART IV

THE ASCENSION

Chapter One

A current of dour air slowly bleeds through a hard wooden door. Inside the dungeon a daunting metallic box rests quietly. A dimming light bulb hangs near the dark life sized box.

Clicking noises distract Tia from the cocoon of her virtual glasses. "Logos, where are you?" she says, looking around.

"I am right here." says Logos, stepping out of the shadows. The tinkering sounds suddenly cease.

"What are you doing near?"

"Have you slept well, my lady?"

Tia lifts herself to her feet. "Slept?! Who could sleep in here — it's cold and smells. Anyway, didn't you notice that I was using my T-Vision." says Tia with a puckered brow, "I wanted to try it out before, but I was too busy being unconscious and all that."

"And do you like it?"

"Nirvia is really something else. It's weird how it seems to know what I like and stuff — it's pretty inviting."

"Oh?"

"You bet." replies Tia, "It's definitely better than this miserable dungeon."

"Does this mean that you have changed your mind about the Ascension?"

"I don't know." says Tia, biting her nails. "I mean Nirvia seems to be a great place to visit, but I'm not sure that I'd want to stay there forever."

"I guess you would miss hanging out with me here, right?"

"Don't you think you've got me in enough trouble?" says Tia, scowling. "Is it really necessary to joke about it?"

"What better time for comedy then at the worse of times." says Logos, "I think humour at times can be a poignant reminder of how truly insignificant we all are, don't you think?"

"Okay. Now I believe you're an alien."

Logos lets out a lively chuckle.

"I wasn't trying to be funny." interjects Tia, "And would you please stop messing about — you're going to get us killed, or worse!"

Logos moves over to the large gloomy box. "Shadows are the children of light." he replies, looking satisfied.

"What's that supposed to mean? And what are you doing over there anyway?"

"I'm just looking over the box."

"That scary looking thing?!" grumbles Tia, "What for?"

"Shush... there are bugs in the room."

"What are you talking about? You know very well that there are no bugs in Doma." pouts Tia, "Well, maybe with the exception of the one that's bugging me right now."

"There are other types of bugs."

"Huh?" groans Tia.

Logos nods toward a small mounted object on the wall.

Tia carefully surveys the shadowed wall opposite her. Her head suddenly stiffens at the sight of a camouflaged porthole. She slowly turns to Logos. "Oh that's just great!" she says, "As if this place wasn't creepy enough."

"Things appear darkest before the light."

"This proverb thing must be like a nervous tick of yours or something." she says, demonstratively.

"Settle down." says Logos with a forced grin, "I have muffled their reception, but they can still see us."

"Logos, will you please tell me what we're doing here?"

"It was the only way in, sweetie."

Tia's crest momentarily flames Purple. "Sweetie?!" reiterates Tia, "OK, now I know we must be in big trouble."

"I understand that you are anxious, but—"

"But what?" she interrupts, "I just can't believe that I allowed myself to follow your stupid plan."

"I told you that this was the only guaranteed way into the Imperial Palace."

"Yeah, but I thought we would end up near the Holy White Arena, not in the freaking dungeon!"

"Please calm down and let me explain."

"You calm down!" she heatedly replies, crossing her arms.

"Alright, I understand that you are upset."

"Did you see the way King Osiris leered at me? I don't know, but it made my skin crawl."

"Yes, I noticed." replies Logos, "It appears that his dissociated behaviour has pushed him even further down the well of self-indulgence than I thought. He displays signs of all that the self incarnates. I fear that he no longer knows right from wrong anymore."

"He looks evil."

"Oh?"

"He scares me." says Tia, "I can't believe that he's our king."

"Tia," says Logos, softly. "Just remember that he is the product of a society who relishes in its perceived superiority. The First Whites wanted dominant Rulers just like him. The problem that they failed to realize is that the more dominant a Ruler is the more dominant his ambitions are."

"Oh."

"Ambition can make a person do almost anything to reach the benben of the self."

"Excuse me, did you say benben?" says Tia with a puckered brow.

"Yes, the benben of the self, or that which sits atop of the pyramid of the self."

"Yes, of course, the benben." says Tia, rolling her eyes. "So, why would the First Whites want such a benben Ruler in the first place?"

"The First Whites wanted to make sure that future Rulers would only want to stop the Ascension if an unforeseen existential threat to their dormant souls developed. And a persona with a strong sense of attachment to their own White soul would be the least likely to use the Golden Key."

"But if they were so concerned about anyone stopping the Ascension why have the Golden Key at all?"

"The Golden Key is a safeguard. The First Whites wanted to make sure that in the highly improbable case that something unforeseen happened that would endanger their souls then the countdown to the Ascension could be halted. And if and when the unforeseen problem was resolved the T-Clock would begin its countdown once again."

"I guess that makes sense."

"In addition, they established the Key Keeper's Challenges for the purpose of making sure that no future Rulers would be in a position to abuse this power."

"What do you mean?"

"The First Whites knew very well that absolute power ultimately corrupts and—"

"And the Key Keeper's Challenges were supposed to prevent that?" injects Tia.

"The Key Keeper's Challenges are meant to evaluate any combatant seeking the high office. The combatant's mental acuities are ascertained and evaluated as per his or her performance in the T-Matches. In other words, the more stable and efficient the mind of the combatant, the better that mind should perform."

"I don't know about that." whispers Tia, "How then do you explain this cookoo King?"

"Shush!" says Logos, "Or look away from the T-Port when you speak."

"Sorry," says Tia, without moving her lips. "But it just doesn't make sense."

"The First Whites did not predict the ultimate outcome of an increasingly ambitious mind. They did not foresee that this would ultimately produce a mind that would alter the rules of their game."

"Alter the rules?"

"King Osiris has managed to find a way to cheat."

"What? How?" says Tia, leaning closer.

"You will need to get that out of him in the T-Match."

"Me? Why is it always me?"

"The rest of the Holy White Order must witness the king's confession. This way if you do win the T-Match they will support your retrieval of the Golden Key from the king. The Holy White Order may not like King Osiris, but they greatly fear and respect his Rule."

"So, first you want me to capture the virtual Golden T-Key in the T-Match and then the real one from the king?"

"That is about it."

"Why don't you just ask me to save the whole planet while you're at it?"

"That's exactly what you will be doing if you succeed."

"Oh." says Tia, "And what do I do with the Golden Key if I manage to get it from the king?"

"You will need to insert it into a T-Port and twist it till it locks."

"Oh, is that all?"

"Yes."

"And so all I have to do is beat the king at a game in which he has ruled as if it were his own Hell?"

"Yes."

"Huh!" whimpers Tia, "I just have to beat the Devil in his own home."

"Tia, do you really think the king is the Devil?"

"Umm," sulks Tia, "he does seem like a really evil man."

Logos places his hand on her shoulder. "You mean like Ramsey?"

Tia flinches as if struck by the thought.

"Tia, the king is a victim of the God Gene, maybe even more so. This was a man with a brilliant mind who became absorbed by the thoughts of power. He rose to the highest levels of the self and with that fell to its deepest depths of obscurity."

"Logos, I really don't know if I can do this."

Logos places his arms around Tia. Tia smothers herself in his chest.

"Do not worry, my dear girl." whispers Logos, gently.

Tia suddenly brushes herself off of Logos' captivating embrace. "I've had enough!" she says, crying. "I don't want to be in here anymore. And I would like to leave now."

"I understand, sweetie."

"Why did you bring me here? I want to leave this horrid place."

"But Tia, this is the right place to be."

"We're in a freaking dungeon!" replies Tia, with open arms.

"Tia look at me." whispers Logos. He pulls Tia closer to him. "That was the objective."

"What are you talking about?" says Tia, wiping away her sniffle. "Without a T-Pod how am I supposed to do all the freaking things you talked about?"

"I am sure it looks bad."

"You think?"

"But it is when the skies are at their darkest that the stars shine at their brightest."

"Logos, I think you've lost your mind." she whispers with a sardonic face.

Logos lets out a small gurgle.

"Why are you laughing?" says Tia, "Did you not hear me? How am I supposed to get my sorry bum in the arena?"

"You do not have to be upstairs in the Holy White Arena in order to get into the T-Match."

"What are you saying?" quietly grouses Tia, "You told me that we needed to find our way to the T-Pods. How do we get to them from here?"

"Not all T-Pods are in the Holy White Arena." replies Logos, suggestively eyeing the arresting box beside him.

Chapter Two

A long ringing sound spreads throughout the dome. Hundreds of people in white suits and dresses begin to line up around the coliseum. The doors of the palace's pillars crank open. The people start shuffling their way in.

The large crowd makes their way past the heavily guarded elevators and up the stairs. The people are stopped before accessing the arena. Men and women in sapphire dresses carefully screen the new arrivals before letting them through.

The arena is lavishly decorated. Holographic images of pristine beaches, green mountains and ancient cities are depicted throughout. Draped over the center of the stage is a holographic banner that reads:

'NIRVIA AWAITS THE HOLY WHITE ORDER'

A low background hum of drumming music slowly begins.

"This is it!" says the first to enter, "The End of Time has finally arrived." she says.

"Take a last look Whites," says a man just behind her, "this is the last time we will need our bodies."

"Nirvia awaits the Chosen." adds another man in a white suit, "Our seating arrangements are ready for our departure."

"I can't wait to see what King Osiris has in store for us on this Faithful night." says yet another man.

"Me too." injects Titi, "I love King Osiris." She brushes back her long golden hair. Her crest glows vividly Red. "I find it just amazing how his incredible mind always finds a way to win."

"It just goes to show that he's the right Key Keeper to lead us to our Promised Lands." another young woman behind her. Her crest glows a bright Blue.

The chattering continues down the line as others make their way up to the arena.

GOLDEN T-HOUR — ... and in the final hour of thy Ascension the last Conclave shall be held and the last T-Match shall be performed.

2. The Final Conclave of the Holy White Order shall take place at this time in order to permit the permanent interfacing of thy soul to thy Avatar upon thy physical Death and thy virtual Resurrection.

3. Thy preordained Ascension shall be ready and waiting as the T-Clock performs its final ticks and Nirvia receives its final updated souls. And as the T-Clock strikes the End Time Nirvia's memory banks shall be complete (see NAT Tech Manual no.2: sec.5: TänkaClock — Spatial Ascription)

4. Thy souls shall then be Reborn and live forever after in a world...

NEW AGE TESTAMENT

Chapter Three

The commander steps out of the elevator. The elevator faces the entrance to the Key Keeper's Chamber. The king's guards immediately clack their feet at attention.

One of the guards knocks on the chamber's door. "Sire," he announces, "Commander Lazarus is—"

"Sire, I'd like a word." interrupts the commander.

The king sits at his desk with his eyes shut. His head sways up and down to the faint rhythmic beat rising from the arena.

"Sire!" hollers the commander.

The king shudders out of his trance. "Commander," says the king, clinching his teeth. "Did I not say that I no longer wanted to be disturbed?!"

"Sire, this is of an urgent matter. I need to discuss the prisoners with you without delay."

"Fine, come in." says the king, "Commander, what in Nirvia could be so important that you deemed it necessary to neglect my standing order?"

"Sire, I think she should be immediately eliminated."

"Who are you babbling about?"

"Sire, I speak of the girl prisoner."

"Lazarus, what's the hurry? Soon it will matter little."

"But Sire, it's my sworn duty to protect the Key Keeper."

The king abruptly stands up. "Protect me from that little girl?! You must be joking, Commander." the king titters, "I had thought to see a succubus in the holding cell, but instead what I saw was just a pretty little vixen."

"But Sire—"

"But what?" interrupts the king, "Commander, are you telling me that you're afraid of that scared little girl? She's as much of a threat to me as you are."

"Sire, there's a high probability that they may be plotting against you."

"How?" replies the king, "By getting idiotically captured?"

"Sire, there's something peculiar about the circumstances of their capture."

"What circumstances are you talking about?"

"The fact that this apparently harmless fugitive arrives here on this all important of days with the conspicuous help of what used to be your top D-Scientist?"

"What in Nirvia are you getting at?"

"I'm not sure, Sire. But I just cannot accept that someone with the aptitude of a Sapphire could logically think that they could enter the palace without being caught."

"It's happened before, Commander."

"Yes, Sire. And I apologize for not finding out the truth of that night. But when that occurred I was not in command."

"Alright Commander, what is it that you have in mind?"

"I suggest that the intruders be immediately eliminated."

"Wow! That sounds pretty extreme, even for you."

"Sire, I just don't trust them."

"Very well..."

"Sire, I'm just thinking of the Ascension and—"

"Alright Commander, I get your point. Please stop talking."

"Yes Sire."

"Commander, you have my permission to kill Logos. But keep the girl under your personal surveillance." the king adds, biting his bottom lip. "If time permits I'd like to deal with her myself." the king flippantly adds, "In the meantime, I'm sure that even you, Commander, can't seriously think that a girl alone in a fortified dungeon can still be a threat."

"But—"

"But nothing!" interjects the king, leaning firmly on his desk. "It may be your task to protect the Realm, but it's mine to rule it!"

"Yes Sire."

"Now leave me in peace." says the king, "I must begin my final preparations. There's nothing more important than the fulfillment of my destiny."

The commander storms out of the chamber.

Chapter Four

Tia paces nervously around the dark metallic box. "Do I understand you correctly?" she says, "You want me to use this scary looking thing for the T-Match?"

"You should know by now not to judge a box by its colours."

"Say what?"

"This sombre looking box is basically the same design as the official T-Pods."

"What do you mean 'basically'?"

"After a few more minor adjustments it will be ready to go."

"Go where?"

"To do what we came here to do."

"I'm getting that sick feeling again."

"Not to worry—"

"You keep saying not to worry." interrupts Tia, "And hearing that makes me worry."

"I apologize, my lady." replies Logos, "Can you please get in the box without being seen by the T-Port. I would like to check something out."

"No freaking way!" snorts Tia, "Why don't you get in it?"

Logos continues to tinker around the machine. "I would," he replies, "but it would not work for me."

"Oh, I get it, because you're not human, right?" she quickly adds, "How convenient."

Logos seems to disappear into thought. Gone is his conciliatory smile. "No, Tia, it's not convenient at all."

"I'm sorry." says Tia, "I really didn't mean anything by it."

"It is not your fault. There is so much weight we have placed on your shoulders that I cannot help but to be grateful by your resilience."

Tia's crest briefly flashes Blue. "Wait, what?" she suddenly says, straightening her shoulders. "What do you mean 'we' placed on my shoulders?"

Logos stops tinkering with the life size box. "Well..."

"Well what?" says Tia, "I really don't like it when you hesitate like that. It's never a good sign."

The heavy dungeon door suddenly creaks open. A morbid scent blows inside and sends the hanging light fixture swerving. The light shines momentarily on the torturous depictions of the box.

"Ugh!" says Tia, "Logos — the box!?"

"Shush!" replies Logos, pulling Tia close to him.

The commander stands at the open door. Two burly guards stand at attention behind him. The commander steps inside the dungeon. He glances back at the guards and the guards stop following him. The Commander nods at them and the guards shut the door behind him.

The commander walks over to the light fixture and steadies it. "We certainly don't need more people in here, do we?" he says, pointing the light at the prisoners.

Tia edges closer to Logos with an uneasy smile.

"I can see why King Osiris was so touched by your charm, my lady," says the commander, his tone is heavily ominous. "But my eyes remain untouched, and what I see in front of me is an ever present danger." He takes a step toward Tia. Tia quickly moves in behind Logos. The commander moves closer.

Logos suddenly thrusts his arms out. "Commander, you cannot harm this girl."

The commander stops and glares at Logos. "Now those are bold words coming from a Sapphire." he says, "Nevertheless, if you really care for this girl let her die by my hand rather than that of the king."

Tia grips tightly Logos' arm.

"It is not solely her fate that you are determining," says Logos, staring down the commander. "It is that of humanity's as well."

"That's an odd statement coming from a cyborg." replies the commander, coldly. "As for the girl, she's a threat to the Ascension. And I cannot allow her to—"

"Commander," interrupts Logos, "you are a rational and fair man. So, I ask you, how is this girl a threat to Nirvia — just another world of the same self-centered dreams as this one?"

"I'm not here to listen to your jargon." replies the commander, "Now move aside."

"Commander, are you so entrenched in your stained uniform that hate has forever clouded your vision of the facts?"

The commander straightens his back and moves threateningly closer to Logos. "How dare you speak to me that way?" he says, menacingly. "Do you know who I am?!"

"I know that you were not always a prisoner of your uniform. There was a time that you cared about life." says Logos, "Especially the life of a young woman not so dissimilar to this one."

Tia questioningly peeks over at Logos' face.

With surprising speed the commander grabs Logos' neck. "How do you know this of me?"

Logos carefully dislodges the commander's hand from his throat. "I knew Sistina." says Logos, massaging his neck.

The commander steps back with eyes cocked. "You knew Sistina?"

"Yes, I knew her well."

"What do you mean you knew her well?" says the commander, fisting his hands. "In what way did you know her?"

"She was one of my own kind." replies Logos.

"What are you talking about? She was not a Sapphire — she was a Fuchsia!" grumbles the commander.

"She was not of any colour. She was not of this planet — she was of mine."

The commander's heavy scowl slowly dissipates. He steps back and let's out a hearty laugh.

The guards open the dungeon door. The commander waves them away. The guards shut the door once again.

"Oh, now I understand why you've been at this fugitive's side all this time." says the commander, "You're insane!"

"I would suggest that insanity is in the eye of the beholder, and your species has shown no inclination of being able to see its own insanity let alone that of another's." says Logos, "This young woman holds the real key to humanity's sanity. I know that people rather escape death than deal with its void, but she can help them see the Truth of that void."

"This young girl's fate was sealed the day she entered your crazy world, Professor."

"Lazarus, are you interested in helping this girl try to save the human race, or do you want to remain the blood thirsty uniformed animal you have become?"

The commander's smile vanishes and a blade suddenly slices a cut over Logos' face.

Tia instantaneously jumps in the way. The commander pulls back in surprise. He glares at Tia before taking hold of her. Tia tries to squirm out of his powerful grip, but to no avail. The commander picks Tia up by her neck with one hand and points the dagger at Logos with the other.

Logos lets go of his bloodied cheek and cries out, "No Lazarus!"

The commander's grip tightens.

"Please Lazarus — she is Sistina's daughter!"

Chapter Five

The king paces alone in his chamber immersed in a conversation. He is addressing a glassed artefact of a mummified body. The mummy is wrapped in roles of reconstituted strips of white linen.

"Power is such a huge responsibility." he says, "Few men have known its burden, and even fewer women have understood it. Though, if there was one woman who could understand what I feel, it would be you, Cleopatra." The king smiles at the encased mummy. "You Pharaohs were way ahead of your time. You had the right idea with the book of the dead, but your technology held you back from capturing the essence of your Ka. But as you can see," he adds, pointing to the thousands of spheres embedded in his chamber, "we instead have succeeded in doing just that. There are many souls here waiting for me to open for them the Pearly Gates."

There are rumbling sounds rising from the arena.

The king freezes still. "Do you hear that?" he whispers, tilting his head down. "The excitement builds for the final countdown to the Ascension. Your manuscripts in the EBOLAD were so right — death is truly only the beginning. It's just too bad your Ka is long gone."

He excitedly edges closer to the translucent floor pane. "Look at my children down there," he continues, "It won't be long now before they begin to chant my name."

The arena below slowly continues to fill.

"One Empire falls and another is born." he continues, as he returns to the side of the mummified figure. "It will be with great pride that I will lift our collective consciousness to our new home." His crest glows Blue. "All Holy Whites of the Order will soon be Reborn in our heavenly Nirvia."

The rhythmic drumming from the arena grows louder.

The king edges over to the sarcophagus. He taps it three times and then two more. The sarcophagus opens and he steps inside.

"This will be the last time I will need your old resting place, my dear Cleopatra."

Celebratory fireworks sparkle outside the chamber.

"You will need to excuse me now." he continues, "I need to prepare my last minute touches to my Avatar. I'm sure everyone is expecting something truly special. And I shall not disappoint." He stares around his chamber with a sour smile. "My only regret is that I didn't have enough time for that young lady waiting for me downstairs." He pinches his chin. "Hmm, I imagine that you must have been just as captivating at one point. But sadly, like you, she will not be joining the rest of us in Nirvia." He lets out an awkward giggle. "I assure you that I would have certainly used my large voting rights to push myself inside of either of your spatial allocations."

The noises continue to reverberate from the arena.

"Oh well, the Soulless Avatars shall have to do. That is till I find other Soulful Avatars that will peak my interests." He gives a broad smile. "I wonder which will pleasure me more. I think the Soulless women will remain my favourites. I think women are at their best when they do a man's bidding, don't you think?" He chuckles out loud. "I'm sure you understand what I mean, Cleopatra, since I imagine that you must have been just as irresistible to women as men. After all, young women cannot help but flock towards power and fame. I wonder how empty they must feel inside to be so easily tempted." The king slides himself inside the sarcophagus. "Which reminds me," he adds, "I'll need to control their conniving Soulful Avatars." he adds, "Especially those women who will try to wiggle their cute little asses into my vast personal space."

The sarcophagus lets out a whispering creak as it begins to close on the king.

The king's face lights up. "Nice! I can already see that it'll be the uninhabitable poisonous grey planet of solar system 2112. I've been working a long time on an Avatar that will be unbeatable in such a planet."

The lid of the sarcophagus seals shut.

Chapter Six

Tia dangles in the air gasping. The commander's grip holds tight against her jugular.

"Please, Lazarus!" cries Logos, "Just look at her!"

The commander tilts Tia's face. His eyes gaze deeply into her suffocating tears. "Hmm?" he says, dropping Tia to the floor. "My lady, I wanted to spare you a long drawn out death, but it appears that your co-conspirator wants to delay it. So I will oblige him and have you first taste death's eternal void." He throws Tia inside the dark metallic box.

"Help me!" cries Tia.

Logos tries to reach for her but the commander stops him cold. The point of the commander's blade is pressed against Logos' throat.

"He can't help you, my lady." responds the commander, "No one can."

The dungeon door opens. "Commander," says the heftier of the two guards, "Is everything alright?"

"Did I call you?"

"No sir."

"Then stay outside till I do."

"Yes sir!"

Tia's outstretched arms and legs are automatically locked in place by the malleable gyroscope. She struggles to detach herself from her diagonal cross position without success.

The commander seals the box and pushes down on a lever. "Show her what awaits her." he says.

The shady box eerily begins to flicker. Its internal gyroscope starts a slow spin.

Tia suddenly finds herself in a playground in the middle of the day. The sun shines brightly and the many people around her appear joyful in their play. Tia sits on a swing moving slowly back and forth. The swing suddenly begins to accelerate. Those around her start to rapidly age. Tia slows down her creaking swing but time continues to accelerate.

"Huh?" she groans.

One by one the people around her inexplicably begin to vanish. The sun dwindles and the colourful playground fades away. Tia is slowly rendered completely and utterly alone. All that is left are the twinkling stars of the cosmos. The stars themselves are then slowly swallowed up by a deep black hole. Tia's body starts to stretch towards the empty void.

Inside the box Tia is trying to escape the grasp of the box's vision. "What's happening to me?" she cries, wriggling.

"It won't be long now." says the Commander, sheathing his knife. "There will be a scream and then it'll all be over. Her mutation will no longer be a threat, and neither will she."

Logos glares at the commander with steely eyes.

"Don't look at me that way," says the commander, "it was you who brought her here."

The stars have disappeared. All that remains is Tia in the fast moving darkness of space and time.

"Logos!" screams Tia.

"There goes her mind, Professor." says the Commander, "Just moments have past here, but in there it must feel like years." he adds, "All that time alone with your own thoughts. Can you imagine that?"

Alone in the solitary darkness Tia's body begins to stretch apart. Her body finally disperses into subatomic molecular bubbles which then explode into the empty void.

The box's lights slowly turn themselves off as it returns to its gloomily dark and silent state.

The commander narrows his brow at a surprisingly temperate Logos. He opens the dark box and pulls Tia out. He looks into her eyes and instantly backs away. "What is this?!" he exclaims, stunned.

Tia's black pupils gleam from the reflection of her shiny Black crest.

"What's going on here?" says Lazarus, peering at Logos. "I want an explanation! Why is she looking at me like that? Her mind appears to still be functioning. How's this possible?!"

Tia appears strangely peaceful. Logos opens his arms towards her but she remains maturely distant.

"Tia, are you alright?" says Logos.

"I'm fine, Professor." she replies, gently.

"I want answers!" interjects the commander. He grasps at Tia but Logos immediately pulls Tia way.

"I will give you your answers, Lazarus." says logos, sternly. "But first you must back off."

The commander gives Logos an unwavering stare before gradually taking a step back.

"Tia, are you sure that you are alright?" reiterates Logos.

Tia nods softly back.

Logos gazes over at the commander. "The scariest combat of all is the one fought in our own minds. To be left alone with one's own thoughts for an indeterminate amount of time is detrimental for any human." he says, "This is the primary function of this unconventional box. It may be camouflaged as just a torturous box, but for all intents and purposes it is a T-Pod."

"Don't lecture me on the functions of the Black Box." replies the commander, hard. "I know very well what it is and what it does, but what I want you to tell me is why this girl appears immune to its effects."

"The reason why others who have entered the Black Box have lost their minds is because they were unable to let go of their colours. But a mind that has retained its plasticity is able to do just that. And such a mind may be forced to bend, but it will not break."

"What are you saying?"

"I am saying that Lady Istina's mind is such a mind."

"You're not making any sense, Sapphire." says the commander, pointing his blade at Logos. "I warn you to answer concisely my questions without your nonsensical words."

"I will try, Commander." replies Logos, "As you know this T-Pod can bring forth the ultimate sense of what it feels like to die. That utter fear of the empty void has mired human thought since its birth."

"And so what?" says the commander, wielding his blade.

"This machine is able to compress time." continues Logos, "It can condense the feelings of pure loneliness to the point of driving people insane. It can bypass all the illusions that protect the human mind from entering such profound feelings of utter despair and emptiness associated with the realization of one's own insignificance. And the outcome can be quite disturbing for any human mind. The utter feeling of being inescapably abandoned provokes the most terrifying and disturbing of feelings to a mind which has lost its elasticity. That is why everyone that has experienced the Black Box has eventually lost their minds."

"Yes, yes, so?" the commander says, his hand twitching.

"Lazarus, this girl has a mind that has not been corrupted by the God Gene. Her mind has not been atrophied by self delusions. Unlike others whose emotions turn into memories that become part of a putrid lake of conditioning, her emotions run through her like water in a river that never lingers long enough to become stale." Logos gives a glancing smile to Tia. "You see, Lazarus, this girl has the ability to go past the time parameters of the Black Box."

"Past the Black Box's parameters?" says the commander, "That's not possible."

"There is a question that lingers in the depths of all our minds, Lazarus."

"What question?"

"The question that arises when consciousness itself is terminally threatened." replies Logos.

"You mean death?"

"That is correct, Lazarus. Death is, as you know, something extremely difficult for a human mind to confront. No one wants to sit alone at night trying to lull themselves asleep with the company of their little internal voice and wonder what will happen when their body dies and that voice is forever gone."

"That's probably the only thing that you've said so far that makes any sense." replies the commander.

"Do you not see what I am getting at, Lazarus?" cuts in Logos, "Without this existential question there would be no way to find the Truth of what is."

"What is what?"

"That which may be eternal."

"And what would that be?"

"It is neither that nor this. It is just that which is."

"Girl!" says the commander, "Has this man been filling your mind with this gibberish all along?"

Tia remains attentively still.

"Sapphire, I'm not a gullible little girl. And I warn you that you're quickly running out of what's left of my patience."

Tia moves slowly away from both men.

"Lazarus, this girl can stop the Holy White Order in making a terrible mistake."

"What mistake?"

"If they ascend they will be locking themselves up in purgatory."

"What are you talking about?"

"Prolonging life is one thing." replies Logos, "But eliminating its end is altogether quite another."

"What?"

"Life is just one side of the duality of existence. And you need both sides to see that which may lie beyond."

"You keep using the conditional. Are you not confident in your premise, Sapphire?"

"It is not up to me to preach the Truth to others."

"Why not?" says the commander.

"All preaching does is give a way out for those who do not, or want not, pursue the Truth themselves. To find out whether there is, or there is not, something beyond our limited consciousnesses, it is up to each and every being capable of investigating the Truth to do so."

"Are you finished, Professor?"

"No." replies Logos, firmly. "You have to understand that the future existence of the human race is in jeopardy, and only this girl can do something about it."

The commander glances over at a self-controlled Tia. "Guards!" he calls forth.

The two guards open the door and enter the dungeon. They eye Logos as he continues to speak.

"Unlike the mythical Phoenix, when all irrational beliefs turn into ashes something totally unprecedented is born. To be free of one's irrational beliefs is to be free of all conditioning. And in that freedom there is no choice, no fear of staring into the abyss of death, because that which fears its death has already died."

"And what makes this girl so dam special?" scoffs the commander.

"Tia is not fully human."

"Sapphire, you really have lost your mind." says the commander, "What in Doma has happened to your brain?!"

Logos looks over at Tia. "Tia, what happened in there?"

"Umm," mutters Tia, "I can't really say."

The commander sneers at Tia. "You can't say, or you won't say?"

Tia jerks away from the commander's intense gape. "I don't really remember, I—"

"Of course you do not remember," interrupts Logos, "That which is, is not part of our consciousness, and hence cannot possibly be part of memory."

"The mind can play all sorts of tricks on a person," interjects the commander, "and that's all you experienced, young girl — a trick of the mind."

"I-I don't know." replies Tia, looking sombrely at her feet. "Though, I did feel something."

"Spit it out girl." says the commander.

"I just don't know how to describe it."

"Lazarus, imagine trying to explain what romantic love is to a five year old. In this case you are the five year old."

"Quiet Sapphire!" replies Lazarus, staring at Tia. "So, what was it that you felt?"

Tia takes a long deep breath. "I guess what I can say is that it was like a warm feeling that had neither beginning nor an end."

"Oh really?" replies the commander, icily.

Tia scowls at the commander's cold facial expression. "Yes," she says, "it was as if the smallest building blocks that make up our existence are made of..."

The commander fixes his gaze at the dark box. "Go on, I'm still listening little girl."

"Lazarus," cuts in Logos, "the only way real change can occur in human consciousness is if the God Gene is neutralized by this girl's unobstructed insight of what lies beyond death — she is the true key to humanity's salvation."

"I said to be quiet, Sapphire." replies the commander, grimly. "I'm waiting girl."

Tia sadly holds her hands over her ears. "Love — OK?!" she blurts out, "I felt a sense of compassion that seemed to have no limits."

The cold dungeon turns very quiet. The guards look at one another.

"I've heard enough! This is all nonsense!" says Lazarus, signalling to his guards. "Place the two prisoners on their knees."

Tia and a pacified Logos are suddenly pressed to their knees.

"Hold him firmly down." says Lazarus to the guard behind Logos, "Let's find out if this D-Scientist's ECCD still works."

"Yes, sir." replies the guard.

"Place your blasters at the lowest setting and increase the setting after each discharge." directs the commander.

"Commander," says Logos, "this girl can find out what happened to Sistina."

The commander halts the guards. And then with one swift movement plunges his dagger into Logos' thigh. Logos' face cringes as his body remains firmly restrained by his attending guard.

Tia scratches herself lose from her guard and kicks the commander on his sturdy jaw. Tia's guard stands in astonishment with a deep scratch on his face. He wraps his arms around her and tries to smother Tia's erratic movements. He accidentally rips the back of her dress as she wriggles away from him. Tia slowly backs away from her guard until she accidentally bumps into the rigid arms of the commander.

"My apologies, Commander." says her guard.

Tia tries to twist her way out of the commander's powerful arms. The commander smiles at her spunky efforts. Suddenly his smile turns into a sullen stare. "Stop!" he says, gazing at her torn dress.

"No!" she replies, trying hard to twist her way lose.

"She certainly is a pesky one. Isn't she, Commander?" says her guard.

The commander reflectively hands Tia back over to her guard. The guard forces Tia back down to her knees.

The commander rubs his sturdy chin. "Hold her down firm this time."

"Yes sir."

Tia stops struggling and closes her eyes.

"Tia?" says Logos, palely.

"I've had enough with these two." says the commander.

The two guards draw their weapons and point them at the prisoners.

"Stop!" says the commander, "Give me your weapons."

"Sir?" replies Tia's guard.

"I want the satisfaction of ending this myself."

Lazarus stretches out both his hands. He waits as the two guards look conspicuously uneasy at one another.

"Now!" shouts the commander.

The guards concede their weapons over to the commander. Lazarus sets the blasters to high. He points the two blasters simultaneously at the heads of Tia and Logos. He lifts the nozzle of the weapons and convincingly discharges them with deadly accuracy.

Chapter Seven

The elevator from the south pillar of the palace opens. The king steps out with four of his guards. Two more guards join his entourage as he begins his descent towards the stage.

The arena is a blanket of white costumes with a tapestry of colourful crests. A chorus of applause accompanies the king to stage.

Titi jumps from her seat and tries to caress the gold key on the king's crippled arm. The guards quickly repel her efforts.

A bald man in a cerulean outfit bows as the king takes center stage. The king's guards immediately form a protective hexagonal box around him. The king nods to his eager audience and then to his guards. The guards slowly retreat to the corners of the stage.

"Ladies and Lords," says the bald man, "My name is John, and I am honoured to continue my duties as your Announcer."

John invites a middle aged woman up to the stage. The woman leaves her seat and goes up to the stage.

"Thank-you, my lady," says the announcer.

One of the guards comes in from his corner and pats the woman down. The king's crest glows Red. The guard finishes his frisk and gives the king a thumps up. The woman's crest glows proudly Blue as the guard returns to his corner.

The announcer takes hold of a virtual microphone and says into it, "Honourable combatants, your colours are now set for the last T-Match. Now please choose your T-Pods."

The king slips off his suit and enters his pod. The pod quickly forms a Red hue around it. Inside the pod the king helps his crippled arm up to the circular frame. The soft frame sucks his hand in place. Then he spreads his other limbs and they too are quickly immobilized by the gyroscope. His opponent follows a similar procedure as she enters her pod.

The announcer loudly declares: "Holy White Order — Thy Golden T-Hour has arrived!"

Screams of excitement invade the arena.

"Guards, please seal the palace doors!"

Four loud cracks are heard from the pillars of the palace.

"Considering the large spatial pool available for this last T-Match, we shall soon discover which of these two combatants will have the right to become the head of the Council of Rulers in thy new home." adds the announcer.

Shouts of expectations ring out from the conclave:

'OSIRIS, OSIRIS, OSIRIS...'

The announcer lifts his arms in a quieting motion. "Settle down, please. First, there's one special instruction that I need to reiterate." says the announcer, "During the Golden T-Hour the final T-Match shall not stop the T-Clock countdown to thy Ascension. Is that clear for everyone?"

"YES!" replies the audience, simultaneously.

"Good!" says the announcer, "And now the final combat shall begin."

There is a loud roar of applause from the crowd.

"Please give a warm welcome to the second runner up in total winnings this year, the Challenger and Ninth of her name, Lady Isis — The Warrior Queen!"

Lady Isis nods from inside her Blue glowing pod. The applause from the audience is widely sporadic.

"And she will be facing the reigning Key Keeper and the most decorated Holy White of all time..."

The announcer's hesitation allows the applause to amplify.

He continues, "The Rex Regis — the Pharaoh of Pharaohs — the Thirteenth of his name — Lord Osiris — The Annihilator!"

The shouts and cries quickly overwhelm those of the king's adversary.

"Guards," says the announcer, "close the T-Pod doors."

The announcer watches as the guards follow his instructions. He then turns to the audience and loudly says: "Is everyone at their assigned seats?"

There is a simultaneous applause.

"Good!" says the announcer, "But before the last TänkaPlanet appears, I would just like to say that I'm personally grateful for the dispensation you have bestowed upon me on this holiest of days. I'm extremely honoured to be a witness to thy Holy White Ascension."

The announcer bows his head and with a last glance at the crowd he shouts: "Holy White Order — Please Insignify!"

The audience members take hold of their armrests and their seats immediately recline. The arena goes dark as rays of light explode from their crests. The rays converge as they beam up through the translucent floor pane of the Key Keeper's Chamber. The chamber lights up before a vortex forms underneath it.

The vortex is quickly replaced by a hologram which envelopes the arena. Inside the panoramic hologram a beacon flashes in the southern hemisphere of a greyish planet. The hologram zooms out and shows the grey planet as being the fifteenth of a twenty planet solar system.

Two stationary spaceships suddenly appear at the edge of the system. They abruptly begin to race toward the grey planet. They swing critically close to one another till the Blue craft ably takes the lead. The Red spaceship fires its Red lasers. The Blue craft sidesteps the blasts and hurtles itself in the lead.

All of a sudden the signal from the grey planet disappears. The two spaceships come to a full stop.

Suddenly they are both transported to another planetary system. A beacon begins to flicker on the third planet from its sun.

There is a collective gasp from the audience.

The Blue spaceship is first to react. It darts toward the blue planet. A few seconds later the Red spaceship takes pursuit.

A resounding sound of incredulity echoes through the white conclave as a flickering Black spaceship inexplicably appears in the galactic hologram.

Chapter Eight

A Black hue has formed around the dreary box in the dungeon. Tia is locked in place inside the gyroscope. The tear on the upper part of her dress exposes her birthmark.

The commander stands assiduously next to the Black pod. "The girl wears a mark that has baffled me for a full cycle. I cannot logically dismiss this sign as a coincidence," he says, glancing over at the wounded Logos. "You've stated that this girl is Sistina's daughter?"

"Yes Commander, I did." replies Logos, clamping down on his wounded leg. "Tia has in her the ability to change humanity's dismal fate."

"I don't care about humanity's fate." replies Lazarus, "I just want to know what happened to Sistina."

"I understand." replies Logos, "I am sure that Tia will do her best to find the truth you seek, but she will first need to defeat the king."

"I admire the confidence you show in this girl, but there's a reason why Osiris is still King. His consciousness has never failed to format the most efficient and effective of combat Avatars. The king has an uncanny sense of preparation." adds Lazarus, "It's as if he knows what's coming."

"I do not doubt King Osiris' skill in doing whatever is takes to maintain his addiction to power." says Logos, "Tia has none of that, but what she now has is an incorruptible clarity of thought. And that is something the TänkaMatches were originally designed to ascertain and reward."

"Nevertheless," interjects Lazarus, "I still give this girl a very small chance, if any at all."

"But yet you have given her this chance — why?"

"I need to know the truth before it's too late."

"So you do suspect the king of something untoward?"

"I've had my suspicions, but have given my word to protect the Realm. And the Key Keeper is its Ruler."

"I see, Commander."

The commander stares at the flickering lights emanating from the Black pod. "But I fear that my emotions may have corrupted my mind." he says, shaking his head. "It has just dawned on me that I've just placed my fate in the hands of a young girl."

"Maybe your instincts tell you that she is her mother's daughter."

"That's the problem that I've just surmised." says the commander, solemnly. "Sistina was a heartfelt pacifist. And if this girl is truly her daughter then she may have absolutely no chance to defeat the formidable combat tested king."

Logos bends his wounded leg to the ground and mutters under his breath, "But she is also her father's daughter."

Chapter Nine

The Black spaceship trails the other two as they all precipitously accelerate toward the planet. The planetary beacon flickers on the northwest area of the blue planet.

The arena begins to shake with a thunderous applause as the Red spaceship is the first to gain orbit.

A holographic panel forms inside the spaceships. The following information scrolls across it:

'PLANET NOMENCLATURE:
Hydrogen/Oxygen/Varied Elemental Contaminants
3 Parts Water, 1 Part Land/ Oceanic Desalination/
Extreme Weather Patterns/ Pockets of high radiation
High Lead and Bacterial Levels/
Principle Inhabitants – Humanoid Species/
Self Destructive in Nature...'

"Hey! That's our planet!" yells out a male voice.

"Quiet!" yells another.

A harmony of disaccording murmurs erupts in the arena.

The planetary beacon is visibly flickering high atop a hill. Inside the Red pod the king's eyes grow large. He quickly plunges his ship towards the beacon. He lands at the bottom of the hill just outside two high parallel running walls.

The audience quiets down as the Red spacecraft opens its doors. A devilish zombie like creature emerges. Its gruesome face is scarred with lodged pieces of barbed wire. Its Red glowing eyes bulge out of their sockets and peer in the direction of the hill.

A synchronized murmur of disgust emerges from the spectators.

The greyish creature moves with incredible speed towards the first wall. Its partially open flesh flaps in the wind. The zombie coldly bites through factions of desolated humans standing outside of the walls.

Light murmurs emanate from the audience.

Long searing claws abruptly spring out of the creature's limbs as it climbs the first wall. It reaches the top and quickly hurtles over it. It speedily crawls through a bone dry area to a second high wall. It scurries its way up the next wall and flings itself down to the other side.

The beast glares up the hill. The beacon is flashing inside a translucent hilltop dome. The scales on the creature's body turn prickly rigid as it gallops up the high hill. The gruesome zombie methodically shreds the monochromatically dressed people in its way.

There are gasps of displeasure from the audience.

The zombie enters the dome and suddenly stops. It gawks at the beacon flickering in a dwelling high above a coliseum. It lets out a loud growl: "Grrrno!"

There are growing murmurs from the spectators.

The creature picks up speed and quickly reaches one of the dwelling's supporting pillars. It latches on to the pillar and begins its climb toward the chamber.

The virtual clock of the hologram ticks:

'000:000:00:51:39, 000:000:00:51:38...'

Suddenly a knight in Blue flying armour appears inside the dome. It veers left and right around the arena till it spots the zombie voraciously climbing. The flying knight unsheathes its Blue sword from its scabbard and fires a Blue ray at the zombie. The zombie dodges the shot as it swings its body under the arching pillar. The knight dips down and at its lower altitude discharges another Blue laser from its sword. The ray ineffectively bounces off of the zombie's scaly back. Long claws pop out of the zombies fingers as it reaches towards the flying knight. The knight swerves away from the zombie arm and fires another shot. The laser manages to penetrate beneath the exposed underarm of the zombie. The zombie wavers and loses its balance. It quickly latches one of its piercing claws on a small ridge on the pillar. But as it precariously sways back and forth the knight whizzes by and slashes the zombie's hinged claw off. The zombie falls and crashes to the deck below.

The Blue armoured knight flies down to the motionless body of the zombie. The knight raises its sword high above the zombie's skull. The knight thrusts its sword down but the zombie rolls with lightning speed out of its way. The fast moving zombie jumps up at the knight and with its sharp claws and serrated teeth tears away at the knight's armour.

A chorus of the king's name begins to invade the arena. But the chant abruptly stops.

The zombie is poking through the knight's helmet with its elongated claws. It manages to pick at the face of the shielded knight.

There is a squirming cry that suddenly emanates from the Blue pod.

The zombie holds the knights detached eyeball in its claw. It puts it in its mouth and munches on it.

Squeamish cries follow in the audience.

The knight blindly lashes out with its sword and manages to find its target. The sword is plunged deep inside the zombie's chest. The zombie appears momentarily surprised and weakened. But it fights back and gnaws the hand of the knight off of the sword. The zombie pulls the inserted sword soullessly out of its chest.

The virtual clock continues to tick:

'000:000:00:27:12, 000:000:00:27:11…'

A dark figure slowly makes its way past the two tussling combatants.

"Look out!" screams out a voice from the audience.

The zombie turns and sees the silhouette of the obscured figure entering an open shaft. The zombie turns its attention back to the imprisoned knight and with its protruding teeth bites through the knight's protective neck mail.

The knight tries to push the zombie off of it, but with one strong thrust the zombie's elongated teeth plunge deeper. The knight's Blue blood squirts out of its shiny Blue armour until it moves no more.

"Shit! Shit! Shit!" says Isis, as the gyroscope inside her Blue pod comes to a stop. She steps out of her pod and waves apologetically to the audience. Then her eyes tilt as she notices another player inside the hologram. She returns to her assigned seat and watches in dismay.

The cloaked figure is quietly travelling in a subterranean passageway. It slows as crunching sounds radiate from beneath its feet. A 'HSB' sign can be clearly seen over its head as a stream of bloodied skeletal remains flow past.

"That's from our Hydroponics Sub Center!?" yells out a spectator. A cacophony of grumbles rises in the arena.

The cloaked figure wobbles its way out of the area. It runs inside an open elevator. The elevator quickly begins its upward trajectory.

The unhindered zombie has reached the top of the pillar. It jumps from it and crashes through the chamber's window. It hurriedly makes its way through the chamber's relics and right to the sarcophagus. It taps the sarcophagus three times and then two more. The sarcophagus opens and a mitre lies there flashing. The zombie grabs the hat and throws it to the floor. A gold key rests in the mitre's mould.

The zombie places its back against the sarcophagus and protectively snarls. It glances at the holographic clock. "Come and get it before it's too late." it invitingly says with a guttural sound.

Suddenly a long thin strip smacks the zombie in the face. The thin strap wraps itself around the zombie. The zombie tugs and pulls at the tough skin, but it is unable to release itself from it. The zombie's Red eyes gaze over at the gold key. It tries to grab the key but a strong pull stops it.

"What's going on? What are you?!" cries out the king from his pod.

The zombie mouths out similarly sounding words. The zombie finally manages to unhinge one of its arms. It turns all around itself tugging at the thin strap. The zombie manages to weave itself out its entanglement. It turns and snarls at the intruder. "I'm free!" it howls, raising its scaly back. "No one can stop me now. Get ready to die — whatever you are!"

The cloaked figure steps out of the shadows.

The zombie licks its fangs and claws. "I'm too fast for any combatant!" it snarls, loading its legs for a forward spring.

The cloaked figure drops its cloak.

The zombie does not thrust forward. Its inflamed Red eyes fixate on the haunting vision opposite it.

Confronting the zombie is the voluptuous figure of Sistina. She wears a short leather skirt with an even shorter tank top. Her dark hair is straight and long. Her pupils have a deep Black glow.

The zombie gawks at the ghostly image as she sensually unwinds a thin Black belt from her petite waist.

The zombie's eyes suddenly pop as Sistina unexpectedly flogs her Black leather belt at it. The zombie tries to duck out of the way but the leathery twine catches its neck. The thin belt quickly tangles itself around the rest of the zombie's encrusted body.

"Grrrno!" howls the zombie, squirming.

Sistina approaches her restrained predator and slowly scrapes her sharp fingernails along its underbelly. The zombie lets out a faint whimper as Sistina's nails find an opening in its prickly scales.

"There, there," she says, softly.

The sound of her voice appears to momentarily diffuse the zombie's Red burning eyes. Sistina gently pulls the zombie away from the sarcophagus.

"How did you open this thing?"

"Grrr." replies the creature.

"What is this sarcophagus?" asks Sistina.

"It's my secret."

"What kind of secret?"

"Grrrno!" resists the zombie.

"We want to know." says Sistina, "Tell us!"

A concurring murmur rises in the audience.

The king is mouthing words inside his Red glowing pod.

"I don't want the Holy White Order to know." grunts the zombie.

"Know what?" says Sistina.

The zombie struggles hard to unwrap itself. "I-I don't want..." The thin Black belt counters its efforts by tightening further. "It's a T-Pod." the zombie finally blurts out.

The audience lets out a concerted accusatory sneer.

"Sire, this sarcophagus is a T-Pod?"

"Grrryes."

"What are you doing with an unregistered T-Pod?" asks Sistina, pulling hard at her belt.

"I need — I deserve to Rule in Nirvia."

"You deserve?"

"Yes! I deserve to Rule the next Realm just as I Rule this one."

"And what does this have to do with this secret T-Pod?"

"I needed to make sure I'd win my T-Matches."

"How?" says Sistina.

"I needed to have prior knowledge of what T-Planet would be selected for the T-Matches."

"And this T-Pod allowed you to do that?"

"Yes...and..." it replies, trying hard to resist.

"Yes continue."

"And it also helped me to see what the rest of Holy White Order was thinking."

"Crista!?" screams out a man from the audience.

"Go on, Sire."

"I am the king."

"Yes, we all know that. What else?"

The zombie's ineffective efforts to get away turn into impotent droplets of sweat on the king's forehead. The king tries to unfasten himself from his Red pod's grip. But unable to escape he capitulates.

"I'm also the Avatar known as Crista." groans the zombie.

"Sire, do you mean that all this time you've been spying on your own people?"

"Yes!"

Disgruntled moans from the spectators litter the arena.

"Why, Sire?"

"It's my duty to make sure that everyone is ready and willing to ascend." growls the zombie, struggling hard in the twined belt.

"Why?"

"I'm the keeper of the Book of Revelations. And only I can handle the truths that lay therein."

"What truths?" Sistina commands, "Tell us!"

The audience sits quietly listening.

"The law prohibiting physical fornication was solely made to protect us from ourselves."

"In what way do you mean, Sire?"

"The Holy White Order is as a testament to the purity of human thought. It's meant to allow humanity to rise beyond its physical body and to ascend to the promised new world." replies the zombie.

"We all know that. What else?"

"The First Whites understood as did their forefathers that generations of the same families inside of a gated area would end up compromising the quality of their original genes. Unlike the First Citizen's of Doma they could not allow their future to be corrupted by an eventual distortion of their own DNA?

"Sire, what are you getting at?"

"And in order to do so, no more babies could be reproduced naturally. But knowing the frailties of human beings they realized that the only effective means to stop our carnal urges was to make it an unquestioningly religious ideology. It was then that the law against procreation became the principle doctrine in the New Age Testament. But Lady Crista knew that even this could not hold forever. That's when she decided to create the automated T-Clock countdown to the Ascension."

"Sire, what else are you hiding?"

The zombie fights back hard. "I do...not...want to...answer."

"It matters little what you want now, Sire. You shall answer me, for I have scratched you with the only power a woman needs — the serum of truth!"

The zombie's suppressed mouth opens brazenly wide. "Nirvia is our saving grace." it says, "We must escape this life before it's too late."

"Too late?" repeats Sistina.

"The lifespan of the original DNA has past its limits as predicted. And the DNA of the Outers has also deteriorated much faster than expected. There's no future here on Earth for the best of human thought. The T-Clock countdown has already taken too long."

Sistina glances over her shoulder at the virtual clock. "You call your mind the best of human thought?" she rebukes.

"I did whatever was necessary to bring about the wishes of the First Whites." groans the zombie.

"And what is it that you found 'necessary' to do, Sire?"

"I had to devise a means to survive the quickly diminishing return of Monochromia's top soil. So, I used Doma's underground irrigation system to fertilize the hydroponics lab and..." the zombie forces itself to shut its mouth.

"Sire, why do you hesitate? We want to hear the truth — we need to hear it!"

"Some truths are better left buried." it replies.

"That won't free you, Sire." replies Sistina, "Tell us!"

Agreeing murmurs echo in the arena.

The zombie inescapably opens its forked tongue. "There was less and less edible food available. If we didn't harvest the Outer babies we wouldn't have made it to our glorious Ascension. The body is temporary, but Nirvia is forever."

The zombie's cold disclosure silences the spectators. Inside the Black pod Tia lets out a disheartened breath.

"Sire," says Sistina, "do you mean the Outer children that we trade for food are they themselves converted to grow food?!"

The zombie nods.

"That's the most despicable and disgusting thing that I've ever heard. The Outer children are meant to become Monochromes — such has always been our exchange promise."

The zombie voluntarily adds, "More and more Outer babies carry the madness gene. The Outers cannibalistic behaviours have rendered most of their offspring unsuitable to be our servants."

"Sire, you made them part of our food source. Don't you realize that you've made us unknowingly cannibals as well?"

A loud grumble rises in the audience.

"I did what was necessary to get us to the Ascension."

"Do you fear death so, Sire?"

"Grrryes!" it replies.

"I find you irreprehensible, Sire. Minds like yours are forever doomed to remain lost. Is that what you want for us all?"

"Better to live forever than forever die." replies the zombie.

Sistina gazes deep inside the zombie's Red eyes. At that very moment the zombie appears to lower its guard.

"Why didn't you love me?" it says.

"Whom are you speaking to, Sire?" says Sistina, gently.

The zombie stares deeply at Tia's avatar. "Sistina," it says, "no one has ever looked at me that way. It was the only time that the voice in my head ever stopped." A tear drops from the zombie's scaly face. "You should have been mine. I'm sorry for what happened to you, but I couldn't stand the idea of you being in the arms of another."

"And what happened to me?" inquires Sistina, diligently.

The zombie's Red eyes puff up. "I killed you!" it hisses out.

"But why?" asks Sistina, sadly.

The door of the dungeon slams open.

"You didn't want me," replies the zombie, "and I could never accept to see you happy with anyone else — I loved you!"

"I feel for you, Sire." states Sistina, "Because you believe that all your jealousies, your envies, your pleasures, and your desires have something to do with the love? But no Sire, that's not love. You've just made it abundantly clear what it would mean to send our souls to Nirvia."

The zombie scoffs at Sistina's words.

"Don't you get it, Sire? If we can't leave our colours behind, we're not going to back to Eden — we're just prolonging our eviction from it."

Sistina sympathetically watches as the zombie tries to struggle away from her.

"Sire, the Black Box has recently forced me to confront the Truth of what it means to die. I cannot explain it, but what I can say is that the answer to our existence does not reside in our colours."

The zombie twists its neck unwilling to hear.

Tia tightens her words further. "Sire, without the ability to confront Death we shall forever block ourselves from having access to that which is eternal. And we would be condemning ourselves to this perpetual life of meaningless colours."

The zombie finally stops struggling. It quietly gazes at Sistina.

"Sire, Heaven does not come in the form of a virtual Paradise, it comes from a moment of pure unconditional feeling of love."

The audience is rendered silent.

"Don't you get it yet, Sire?" she continues, while caressing the zombie's ghastly face. "Whenever you're conscious of your self — there is No Love. See the Truth of this and you will know Death. And then the love that knows No Colours, No Self, No Soul, No Avatar and No Beliefs shall manifest itself."

Suddenly an elevator door opens in the arena. Stepping out is the darkened figure of the commander. The mystified looking audience watches as Lazarus races down to the stage.

The king's guards unite to confront him.

"Commander, what are you going?!" cries Lieutenant Noa.

The commander hastens his pace.

The lieutenant glances at his cohort of guards. "What are you waiting for — stop him!" he cries, "Stop the Commander! Protect the king!"

The guards unsteadily place themselves between the commander and the king's pod. The lieutenant draws out his weapon first, but before he can raise it a projectile has pierced his neck.

The other guards fire at the oncoming commander. The commander eloquently closes in on bent lieutenant and in one effortless movement withdraws his knife from the lieutenant's throat and slashes his way through the other guards.

The commander stops wielding his bloodied blade as no guards remain standing. He edges closer to the Red pod with his blood dripping dagger ready.

Suddenly his dagger drops out of his hand. He turns around disoriented at the perturbed audience and falls to his knees. There is blood gushing out of his legs and chest. He forcibly picks up his dagger and drudges over to the Red pod. He opens its door and plunges himself inside it.

To the shocking consternating sounds of the audience the pod's Red glow is replaced by blotches of red blood.

The king wobbles out of the pod with his chest exuding blood. He struggles to stand straight as he faces the crowd. Blood spurts out from his mouth as he says, "I plead Ascension." And with a sly smile he falls backward with a loud thump. His crest becomes translucent as his blood curdles around it.

The commander crawls out of the bloodied pod and drags himself to the side of the king. He plunges his knife in the king's chest and extricates the king's embedded sphere. Then with the bud end of his knife bangs at it till it cracks open and turns Black. The commander drops his knife and his body follows it down.

-3-

Inside the hologram the eyes of the zombie have lost their Red glow. Sistina gapes puzzlingly at the unresponsive zombie. "Sire?" she says. She lets go of her belt. The thin belt unwinds from the zombie and rewinds around her waist.

The body of the zombie slowly disappears. Sistina picks up the gold key from the sarcophagus.

The holographic clock continues to countdown:

'000:000:00:06:18, 000:000:00:06:17...'

She steps out of the Black pod and wipes away her perspiration. Her crest is profoundly Black.

Logos stands nearby with an endearing smile. She races over to him and gives him a big hug. "What's happened?" she asks, "Is it over?"

"You were just brilliant, sweetie."

Tia buries her head in his chest.

"But you need to hurry and retrieve the Golden Key," says Logos, "Quickly! You need to stop the T-Clock." He grabs her hand and rushes her out of the dungeon.

"Hey," she notes, "the door's open. How—" she interrupts herself, "Where's the commander?"

Logos stumbles and falls.

"Logos!" cries Tia.

"I am alright." he says, "The elevator is open — Go now!"

"Are you sure you're OK?"

"Yes, I will be right behind you — Go!"

"Right." says Tia, "The king has the key."

-4-

The crowd looks in dismay as Tia runs out of the elevator and down the isle. Her crest is still Black. Many in the reawakened audience surprisingly notice their colourful crests temporarily flickering Black.

Tia races up to the stage. Her eyes grow big at the sight of the bloodbath.

The commander staggers back up to his feet. Tia rushes over to his side. She uses her body like a crutch to help him up.

"You'll be fine, Commander." she says.

The commander crumbles back down. Tia tries hard to raise him up again, but he stops her.

He gazes deeply into her eyes. "Yes, I think I finally will be." he says, his mangled hand tries to reach Tia's tear. "Go on now, child. Put an end to it — use the key." Tia's tear drops on his hand.

"Tia!" yells Logos, just emerging from the elevator.

Tia looks up at the virtual clock which continues to tick:

'000:000:00:01:16, 000:000:00:01:15...'

"I've gotta hurry!" she mutters, as she runs over to the king's body. She turns away from his bloodied face and grabs the gold key from his sleeve. With the gold key in hand she swerves through the other dead bodies and jumps off the stage. She checks around and spots a porthole embedded on the supporting base of the stage. She tries to insert the key but the porthole is too high up. She checks around and finds a small wooden box. She places the box beneath the porthole. She takes a desperate leap from it and manages to insert the gold key inside the porthole. She drops back down and glances back at the clock which is still counting down. She gazes up at the injured Logos who is signalling to her a turning motion with his hands.

She jumps back up and twists the key. She suddenly falls back to the ground with a piece of the gold key in her hand. The rest of the key remains lodged inside the porthole. The clock comes to a full stop:

'000:000:00:00:08.'

She quickly makes her way back up to Logos' side. She helps him toward the seats. A seated man in a white suit quickly offers Tia his seat. The audience gawks at Tia as she allows Logos to sit in her place.

"I'm sorry, Logos," she says, "but I think I broke everything."

"You did what should have been done long ago." replies Logos, holding his wounded thigh. He gently wipes away the tears from Tia's cheeks. "How did you think of Sistina as your T-Match Avatar?"

"I don't know," she replies, softly. "I had a feeling that King Osiris would hesitate before harming her again."

"You are really something else." says Logos with a gentle smile.

"But I broke the Golden Key?!"

"Yes, but you have given the human race something much more valuable — the true key to salvation."

"I did?"

"Yes, you did." replies Logos, "You have shared with the Holy White Order an insight into that which is eternal. That insightful flicker shall slowly diffuse the effects of the mortaphantasia gene."

"You mean that the God Gene will no longer harm us?"

"The God Gene has already become dormant in many of those you have touched here tonight."

"What about everyone else?"

"You have begun the necessary transformation. With time the human race may finally come to understand the limits of its consciousness. And that in it of itself will change it. And it is that will change the human condition from one based on the self to one based on unconditional love."

"I sure hope so." replies Tia, "I'd love to see that."

"But that road still remains a tricky one." says Logos, "There will be resistance along the way from those who remain afraid to run through the residual gauntlets of the delusions and illusions that remain of the self."

"I have a feeling that this will take some doing. Will you help me?"

"I am sorry to say, Your Highness, but my time here is finished."

"What did you call me?"

"You have won the T-Match. And that makes the Queen of the Realm."

Tia suddenly notices the audience waiting for her next course of action. "But I don't want to be the Ruler."

"That is a good sign." says Logos, smiling.

"But I don't know what to do."

"Your Highness, you are not blocked by the God Gene — you will know what to do because your mind is clear."

"How can you be so sure?"

"Because you are aware of what it means to truly love."

"But can that be enough?"

"That will depend on whether the collective consciousness of the Holy White Order completes its transformation."

"How will I know when or if that's happened?"

"You will notice their colours suddenly turning on and off at a much faster pace. Just like yours have always done."

"They have?"

"Yes."

"How come?" replies Tia.

"Without the God Gene your colours were never able to fuse their conditioning into your brain's synapses." replies Logos, "You have always remained innocent to their influences."

"I don't know what that means?"

"My dear sweet Tia, you are what the human race was meant to be. You neither suppress nor reward the colours you feel. Your mind remains untainted by your colourful emotions. And your view is unobstructed to that which is forever innocent."

"Huh?"

"Tia, you have provided the Holy White Order a taste of what it means to be free from a life ruled by colours. And with this unobstructed view the evolutionary line for the entire human race can eventually be crossed."

"Do you really think we can all be free from the influences of our colours one day?"

"The future is never a sure thing, but the Rule of the divisive self has begun its descent and that which is...eternal has begun its ascent."

Chapter Ten

Logos stands alone in the spotlight of the indistinct chamber. The heavy mist beneath its translucent floor slowly clears.

"It is done." he says.

The congregated group of elders around him let out a coordinated solemn sigh. One of them steps out of the circle. He drops his hood and his long grey hair falls on his fragile shoulders. He prays his hands together. "The price we have paid has been extremely high." he says, sadly.

"I agree, sir," replies Logos, "Sistina was a heavy loss for us all. She was our most enlightened of beings."

"She sacrificed so much, and yet I remain concerned," adds the elder man, "As we all know, their so called God Gene will remain dormant within them for quite some time to come."

"I understand, sir. But the collective group consciousness of the Holy White Order has shared a moment of complete and utter clarity. They have collectively witnessed something that their current mindset will not be able to reconcile. This will lead them to investigate further. And this time the mortaphantasia gene will not be able to obstruct the vision of their mind's eye."

"It would be something truly special to finally witness the evolution of their consciousness." says an elder woman, "But yet I too continue to have my worries."

"Ma'am?" replies Logos.

"The mortaphantasia gene may no longer hinder their profound pursuit of the Truth, but it does not guarantee the pursuit itself."

"Nevertheless, ma'am, they will no longer lose sight of the profound question."

"But for many it will still be too difficult to accept the Truth." she adds, "I'm afraid that many will once again retreat to the dark trenches of their self denials."

"Maybe at first that may be their conditioned response."

"That's what we are afraid of."

"I understand, ma'am. But without the mortaphantasia gene distracting them from the Truth there is no reason why they cannot finally be the change that they've always aspired to be."

"My dear Logos, you may be overestimating their ability to change. The little voice in that is in all our heads will fight hard to maintain its relevance within them. It will not be easily for them to accept that its existence is finite. It will be a depressing time for them once they realize the insignificance of what they have for so long identified as being real."

"I understand your concern, ma'am, but at least now they have a real chance to be the change that they have always aspired to be."

The elder gentleman edges closer to Logos. He places his hand on Logos' shoulder. "Logos, you must see now why we were reticent from the start."

"I do sir." replies Logos, "I understand that despite our efforts the outcome is still unclear."

"But nevertheless it was your right to try." says the elder gentleman, "On behalf of the Council, we thank-you."

Clicking sounds of agreement animate the chamber.

"Your acknowledgement is greatly appreciated, Honourable Council." says Logos with a catch in his throat, "But it is all the doings of a humble mom and her Truth that have reset the human species on the right path."

Voices of approval sift through the star filled chamber.

The mist beneath the spotlight has completely cleared. Logos takes a step back and pensively gazes down.

An incandescent dome atop a hill quickly diminishes in size to become but a flickering beacon on its planet. The blue planet quickly shrinks in size and appears as the third planet revolving around its star.

Ω

End of Book II

Printed in Great Britain
by Amazon

62450213R00180